D0435002

THE JOE LEAPHORN MYSTERIES

THREE COMPLETE NOVELS

TONY HILLERMAN

THE JOE LEAPHORN MYSTERIES

THE BLESSING WAY

DANCE HALL OF THE DEAD

LISTENING WOMAN

WINGS BOOKS
New York / Avenel, New Jersey

This 1992 edition is published by Wings Books,
distributed by Outlet Book Company, Inc., a Random House Company,
40 Engelhard Avenue, Avenel, New Jersey, 07001, by arrangement
with HarperCollins Publishers.

Printed and bound in the United States of America

Library of Congress Cataloging-in-Publication Data
Hillerman, Tony.
The Joe Leaphorn mysteries : three classic Hillerman mysteries featuring Lt. Joe Leaphorn / Tony Hillerman.
p. cm.
Contents: The blessing way -- Dance hall of the dead -- Listening woman.
ISBN 0-517-07771-X
1. Leaphorn, Joe, Lt. (Fictitious character) --Fiction.
2. Detective and mystery stories, American. 3. Navajo Indians --Fiction. I. Title.
PS3558.I45J6 1992
813'.54--dc20 91-38809
CIP

8 7 6 5 4 3 2 1

CONTENTS

THE BLESSING WAY

ACKNOWLEDGMENT

While ethnological material as used in this book is not intended to meet scholarly and scientific standards, the author wishes to acknowledge information derived from publications of Willard W. Hill, Leland C. Wyman, Mary C. Wheelwright, Father Berard Haile, Clyde Kluckhohn, and Washington Matthews; and the advice and information provided by his own friends among the Navajo people.

LUIS HORSEMAN LEANED the flat stone very carefully against the piñon twig, adjusted its balance exactly, and then cautiously withdrew his hand. The twig bent, but held. Horseman rocked back on his heels and surveyed the deadfall. He should have put a little more blood on the twig, he thought, but it might be enough. He had placed this one just right, with the twig at the edge of the kangaroo rat's trail. The least nibble and the stone would fall. He reached into his shirt front, pulled out a leather pouch, extracted an odd-shaped lump of turquoise, and placed it on the ground in front of him. Then he started to sing:

"The Sky it talks about it.
The Talking God One he tells about it.
The Darkness to Be One knows about it.

The Talking God is with me.
With the Talking God I kill the game.
With the Talking God I kill the male game."

There was another part of the song, but Horseman couldn't remember it. He sat very still, thinking. Something about the Black God, but he couldn't think how it went. The Black God didn't have anything to do with game, but his uncle had said you have to put it in about him to make the chant come out right. He stared at the turquoise bear. It said nothing. He glanced at his watch. It was almost six. By the time he got back to the rimrock it would be late enough to make a little fire, dark enough to hide the smoke. Now he must finish this.

"The dark horn of the bica,
No matter who would do evil to me,
The evil shall not harm me.
The dark horn is a shield of beaten buckskin."

Horseman chanted in a barely audible voice, just loud enough to be heard in the minds of the animals.

"That evil which the Ye-i turned toward me
cannot reach me through the dark horn,
through the shield the bica carries.
It brings me harmony with the male game.
It makes the male game hear my heartbeat.
From four directions they trot toward me.
They step and turn their sides toward me.

So my arrow misses bone when I shoot.
The death of male game comes toward me.
The blood of male game will wash my body.
The male game will obey my thoughts."

He replaced the turquoise bear in the medicine pouch and rose stiffly to his feet. He was pretty sure that wasn't the right song. It was for deer, he thought. To make the deer come out where you could shoot them. But maybe the kangaroo rats would hear it, too. He looked carefully across the plateau, searching the foreground first, then the mid-distance, finally the great green slopes of the Lukachukai Mountains, which rose to the east. Then he moved away from the shelter of the stunted juniper and walked rapidly northwestward, moving silently and keeping to the bottom of the shallow arroyos when he could. He walked gracefully and silently. Suddenly he stopped. The corner of his eye had caught motion on the floor of the Kam Bimghi Valley. Far below him and a dozen miles to the west, a puff of dust was suddenly visible against a formation of weathered red rocks. It might be a dust devil, kicked up by one of the Hard Flint Boys playing their tricks on the Wind Children. But it was windless now. The stillness of late afternoon had settled over the eroded waste below him.

Must have been a truck, Horseman thought, and the feeling of dread returned. He moved cautiously out of the wash behind a screen of piñons and stood motionless, examining the landscape below him. Far to the west, Bearer of the Sun had moved down the sky and was outlining in brilliant white the form of a thunderhead over Hoskininie Mesa. The plateau where Horseman stood was in its shadow but the slanting sunlight still lit the expanse of the Kam Bimghi. There was no dust by the red rocks now, and Horseman wondered if his eyes had tricked him. Then he saw it again. A puff of dust moving slowly across the valley floor. A truck, Horseman thought, or a car. It would be on that track that came across the slick rocks and branched out toward Horse Fell and Many Ruins Canyon, and now to Tall Poles Butte where the radar station was. It must be a truck, or a jeep. That track wasn't much even in good weather. Horseman watched intently. In a minute he could tell. And if it turned toward Many Ruins Canyon, he would move east across the plateau and up into the Lukachukais. And that would mean being hungry.

The dust disappeared as the vehicle dropped into one of the mazes of arroyos which cut the valley into a crazy quilt of erosion. Then he saw it again and promptly lost it where the track wound to the west of Natani Tso, the great flattopped lava butte which dominated the north end of the valley. Almost five minutes passed before he saw the dust again.

"Ho," Horseman said, and relaxed. The truck had turned toward Tall Poles. It would be the Army people who watched the radar place. He moved away from the tree, trotting now. He was hungry and there was a porcupine to singe, clean, and roast before he would eat.

Luis Horseman had chosen this camp with care. Here the plateau was cut by one of the hundred nameless canyons which drained into the depth of Many Ruins Canyon. Along the rim, the plateau's granite cap, its sandstone support eroded away, had fractured under its own weight. Some of these great blocks of stone had crashed into the canyon bottom, leaving behind room-sized gaps in the rimrock. Others had merely tilted and slid. Behind one of these, Horseman knelt over his fire. It was a small fire, built in the extreme corner of the natural enclosure. With nothing overhead to reflect its light, it would have been visible only to one standing on the parapet, looking down. Now its flickering light gave the face of Luis Horseman a reddish cast. It was a young face, thin and sensitive, with large black eyes and a sullen mouth. The forehead was high, partly hidden by a red cloth band knotted at the back, and the nose was curved and thin. Hawklike. He sat crosslegged on the hump of sand drifted into the enclosure from the plateau floor above. The only sound was the hissing of grease cooking from the strip of porcupine flesh he held over the flame. The animal had been a yearling, and small, and he ate about two-thirds of it. He sprinkled sand on the fire and put the remainder of the meat on the embers to be eaten in the morning. Then he lay back in the darkness. The moon would rise sometime after midnight, but now there were only the stars overhead. For the first time in three days, Luis Horseman felt entirely safe. As he relaxed, he felt an aching weariness. He would sleep in a little while, but first he had to think.

Tomorrow, if he could, he would build a sweat house and take a bath. He would have to get a Singer somehow when it was safe and have a Blessing Way held for him, but that would have to wait. A sweat bath would have to do for now. It would take time, but tomorrow he would have time. He had what was left of the porcupine and he would have kangaroo rats. He was sure of that. He put out twelve or thirteen deadfalls baited with blood and porcupine fat and he thought the chant had been about right. Not exactly, but probably close enough. He would not think beyond tomorrow. Not now. By then they would know he had not gone back down to the Tsay-Begi country, to the clan of his in-laws, and they would be looking for him here.

Horseman felt the dread again, and wished suddenly that he had his boots and something that would hold water. It was a long climb down into the canyon to the seep. They would be looking anywhere there was water and even if he covered his tracks, there would be a sign—broken grass at least. The porcupine stomach would hold a little water, enough for a day. He would use that until he could find something or kill something bigger. But there was nothing he could do about his feet. They hurt now, from all day walking in town shoes, and the shoes wouldn't last if he had to cover much country.

Then Horseman became aware of the sound, faint at first and then gradually louder. It was unmistakable. A truck. No. Two trucks. Driving in low gear. A long way off to the west. The light night breeze shifted slightly and the sound was gone. And when it blew faintly again from the west, he could barely hear the motors. Finally he could hear nothing. Only the call of the nighthawk hunting across the plateau and the crickets chirping down by the seep. Must have been in Many Ruins Canyon, Horseman thought. It sounded like they were going down the canyon, away from him. But why? And who would it be? None of his clan would be in the canyon. His Red Forehead people stayed away from it, stayed clear of the Anasazi Houses. The Ye-i and the Horned Monster had eaten the Anasazi long ago—before the Monster Slayer came. But the ghosts of the Old People were there in the great rock hogans under the cliffs and his people stayed away. That was one of the reasons he had come here. Not too close to the Houses of the Enemy Dead, but close enough so the Blue Policeman wouldn't think to look.

Horseman felt his knife in his pocket pressing painfully against his hip. He shifted his weight, took it out, opened the long blade, and laid it across his chest. Soon the moon rose over the plateau, and lit the figure of a thin young man sleeping, barefoot, on a hump of drifted sand.

Horseman was at the seep a little after daylight. He drank thirstily from the pool under the rock and then cleaned the porcupine stomach sac thoroughly with sand, rinsed it, knotted the tube to the intestine and filled it with water. It held about two cups. The sweat bath would have to wait. He couldn't risk building the sweat house here. And, if he built it in the protection of his camp, he had nothing large enough to carry water to pour on the rocks after he had heated them. He erased his tracks thoroughly with a brush of rabbit brush, and kept to the rocks on the long climb back to the canyon rim.

Four of his deadfalls had been sprung but he found dead

kangaroo rats under only two of the stones. Another yielded a wood mouse, which he threw away in disgust, and the other was empty. He glumly reset the traps. Two rats were not enough. There were frogs around the seep, but killing frogs would make you a cripple. He would try for the prairie dogs. A grown one would make a meal.

The place Horseman had seen the prairie-dog colony was about a mile to the east. He used thirty minutes covering the distance, remembering the sound of the truck motors and moving cautiously. Maybe another of those rockets had fallen. He remembered the first time that had happened. It was the year he was initiated and there had been Army all over. Trucks and jeeps and helicopters flying around the valley, and they had come around to all the hogans and said there would be $10,000 paid to anyone who found it. But nobody ever did. Then they cut that road up Tall Poles and built the radar place and when the next rocket fell a year ago they had found it in two or three days.

He stopped by a dead juniper, broke off a crooked limb, and started whittling a throwing stick. He could sometimes hit a rabbit with one, but usually not prairie dogs. They were too careful. While he shaped the stick he stared out across the Kam Bimghi. Nothing at all was moving now, and that probably meant it wasn't a rocket down. There would be a lot going on now if it was that. Besides, they wouldn't have been hunting a rocket at night.

He didn't have a chance to use the throwing stick. The burrows of the colony were bunched below a hummock of piñon and one of the rodents saw him long before he was in range. There was a chittering outburst of warning calls, and in a second the dogs were in their holes.

Horseman put the throwing stick in his hip pocket and broke a smaller limb from a piñon. He sharpened one end, split the other. Back at the prairie-dog colony, Horseman selected a hole which faced the west. He stuck the stick in the ground in front of it, pulled a thin sheet of mica from his medicine pouch, and slipped it into the split. He adjusted the mica carefully so that it reflected the light from the rising sun down the hole.

Now he could only wait. In time the light would attract one

of the curious prairie dogs. It would come out of its hole blinded by the reflected sun. And he would be close enough to use the stick. He glanced around for a place to stand. And then he saw the Navajo Wolf.

He had heard nothing. But the man was standing not fifty feet away, watching him silently. He was a big man with his wolf skin draped across his shoulders. The forepaws hung limply down the front of his black shirt and the empty skull of the beast was pushed back on his forehead, its snout pointing upward.

The Wolf looked at Horseman. And then he smiled.

"I won't tell," Horseman said. His voice was loud, rising almost to a scream. And then he turned and ran, ran frantically down the dry wash which drained away from the prairie-dog colony. And behind him he heard the Wolf laughing.

THAT NIGHT THE WIND PEOPLE moved across the Reservation. On the Navajo calendar it was eight days from the end of the Season When the Thunder Sleeps, the 25th of May, a night of a late sliver of moon. The wind pushed out of a high-pressure system centered over the Nevada plateau and carved shapes in the winter snowpack on San Francisco peaks, the Sacred Mountain of Blue Flint Woman. Below, at Flagstaff airport, it registered gusts up to thirty-two knots—the dry, chilled wind of high-country spring.

On the west slope of the Lukachukai Mountains, the Wind People whined past the boulder where Luis Horseman was huddled, his body darkened by ashes to blind the ghosts. Horseman was calm now. He had thought and he had made his decision. The witch had not followed him. The man in the dog skin didn't know him, had no reason to destroy him. And there was no place else to hide. Soon Billy Nez would know he was on this plateau and would bring him food, and then it would be better. Here the Blue Policeman could never find him. Here he must stay despite the Navajo Wolf.

Horseman opened his medicine pouch and inspected the contents. Enough pollen but only a small pinch of the gall medicine which was the best proof against the Navajo Wolves. He removed the turquoise bear and set it on his knee.

"Horn of the bica, protect me," he chanted. "From the Darkness to Be One, protect me." He wished, as he wished many times now that he was older, that he had listened when his uncle had taught him how to talk to the Holy People.

A hundred miles south at Window Rock, the Wind People rattled at the windows of the Law and Order Building, where Joe Leaphorn was working his way through a week's stack of unfinished case files. The file folder bearing the name of Luis Horseman was third from the bottom and it was almost ten o'clock when Leaphorn reached it. He read through it, leaned back in his chair, lit the last cigarette in his pack, tapped his finger against the edge of his desk, and thought. *I know where Horseman is. I'm sure I know. But there is no hurry about it. Horseman will keep.* And then he listened to the voices in the wind, and thought of witches, and of Bergen McKee, his friend who studied them. He smiled, remembering, but the smile faded. Bergen, himself, was the victim of a witch—the woman who had married him, and damaged him, and left him to heal if he could. And apparently he couldn't.

He considered the letter he had received that week from McKee—talking of coming back to the Reservation to continue his witchcraft research. There had been such letters before, but McKee hadn't come. And he won't come this time, Leaphorn thought. Each year he waits to pick up his old life it will be harder for him. And maybe now it's already too hard. And, thinking that, Leaphorn snapped off his desk lamp and sat a moment in the dark listening to the wind.

At Albuquerque, four hundred miles to the east, the wind showed itself briefly in the apartment of Bergen McKee, as it shook the television transmission tower atop Sandia Crest and sent a brief flicker across the face of the TV screen he wasn't watching. He had turned off the sound an hour ago, intending to grade final-examination papers. But the wind made him nervous. He had mixed a shaker of martinis instead, and drank slowly, making them last until, finally, he could sleep.

Tomorrow, perhaps, there would be the answer to his letter, and Joe Leaphorn would tell him that it was a good season for witchcraft gossip, or a poor season, or a fair season. And maybe, if prospects were good, he would go to the Reservation next week and spend the summer completing the case studies he needed to finish the book that no longer mattered to him. Or maybe he wouldn't go.

He snapped on the radio and stood by the glass door opening on his apartment balcony. The wind had raveled away the cloud cover over Sandia Mountain and its dark outline bulked against the stars on the eastern horizon.

Ten stories below, the lights of the city spread toward the foothills, a lake of phosphorescence in an infinity of night. Behind him the radio announced that tomorrow would be cooler with diminishing winds. It then produced a guitar and a young man singing of trouble.

"But," the singer promised, "life goes on.

"And years roll by,
And time heals all,
And soon we're dead,
We're peaceful dead."

The sentiment parodied McKee's mood so perfectly that he laughed. He walked back to his desk—a bulky, big-boned, tired-faced man who looked at once powerful and clumsy. He shuffled the ungraded exam papers together, dumped them into his briefcase, poured a final martini from the shaker, and took it into the bedroom. He looked at the certificate framed on the wall. It needed dusting. McKee brushed the glass with his handkerchief.

"Whereas," the proclamation began, "it is commonly and universally known by all students of Anthropology that Bergen Leroy McKee, B.A., M.A., Ph.D., is in truth and in fact none other than MONSTER SLAYER, otherwise identified as the Hero Twin in the Navajo Origin Myth;

"And Whereas this fact is attested and demonstrated by unhealthy obsession and preoccupation of said Professor McKee, hereafter known as MONSTER SLAYER, with belaboring his students with aforesaid Origin Myth;

"And Whereas MONSTER SLAYER is known to have been born of Changing Woman and sired by the Sun;

"And Whereas the aforesaid sexual union was without benefit of Holy Matrimony, and is commonly known to have been illicit, illegal, unsanctified, and otherwise improper fornication;

"Therefore be it known to all men that the aforesaid MONSTER SLAYER meets the popular and legal definition of Bastard, and demonstrates his claim to this title each semester by the manner in which he grades the papers of his Graduate Seminar in Primitive Superstition."

The proclamation had been laboriously hand-lettered in Gothic script, embossed with a notary public's seal, and signed by all seven members of McKee's seminar. Signed six years ago, the year he had won tenure on the University of New Mexico anthropology faculty—full membership in the elite of the students of man with W. W. Hill, and Hibben, Ellis and Gonzales, Schwerin, Canfield, Campbell, Bock and Stan Newman, Spuhler, and the others. The year he became part of a team unmatched between Harvard and Berkeley. The last good year. The year before coming home to this apartment and finding Sara's closets empty and Sara's note. Fourteen words in blue ink on blue paper. The last year of excitement, and enthusiasm, and plans for research which would tie all Navajo superstitions into a tidy, orderly bundle. The last year before reality.

McKee drained the martini, switched off the lights, and lay in the darkness, hearing the wind and remembering how it had been to be Monster Slayer.

BERGEN MCKEE APPROACHED his faculty mailbox on the morning of May 26 as he habitually approached it—with a faint tickle of expectation. Years of experience, of pulling out notices to the faculty, lecture handbills, and book advertisements, had submerged this quirk without totally extinguishing it. Sometimes when he had other things on his mind, McKee reached into the box without this brief flash of optimism, the thought that today it might offer some unimaginable surprise. But today as he walked through the doorway into the department secretary's outer office, said good morning to Mrs. Kreutzer, and made the right turn to reach the mail slots, he had no such distraction. If the delivery was as barren as usual, he would be required to turn his thoughts immediately to the problem of grading eighty-four final-examination papers by noon tomorrow. It was a dreary prospect.

"Did Dr. Canfield find you?" Mrs. Kreutzer was holding her head down slightly, looking at him through the top half of her bifocals.

"No ma'am. I haven't seen Jeremy for two or three days."

The top envelope was from *Ethnology Abstracts.* The form inside notified him that his subscription had expired.

"He wanted you to talk to a woman," Mrs. Kreutzer said. "I think you just missed her."

"O.K.," McKee said. "What about?" The second envelope contained a mimeographed form from Dr. Green officially reminding all faculty members of what they already knew—that final semester grades must be registered by noon, May 27.

"Something about the Navajo Reservation," Mrs. Kreutzer said. "She's trying to locate someone working out there. Dr. Canfield thought you might know where she could look."

McKee grinned. It was more likely that Mrs. Kreutzer had decided the woman was unattached and of marriageable age, and might—in some mysterious way—find McKee attractive. Mrs. Kreutzer worried about people. He remembered then that he had met a woman leaving as he came into the Anthropology Building, a young woman with dark hair and dark eyes.

"Was she my type?" he asked. The third and last letter was postmarked Window Rock, Arizona, with the return address of the Division of Law and Order, Navajo Tribal Council. It would be from Joe Leaphorn. McKee put it into his pocket.

Mrs. Kreutzer was looking at him reproachfully, knowing what he was thinking, and not liking his tone. McKee felt a twinge of remorse.

"She seemed nice," Mrs. Kreutzer said. "I'd think you'd want to help her."

"I'll do what I can," he said.

"Jeremy told me you were going to the reservation with him this summer," Mrs. Kreutzer said. "I think that's nice."

"It's not definite," McKee said. "I may have to take a summer-session course."

"Let somebody else teach this summer," Mrs. Kreutzer said. She looked at him over her glasses. "You're getting pale."

McKee knew he was not getting pale. His face, at the moment, was peeling from sunburn. But he also knew that Mrs. Kreutzer was speaking allegorically. He had once heard her give a Nigerian graduate student the same warning, and when the student had asked him what Mrs. Kreutzer could possibly have meant by it, McKee had explained that it meant she was worrying about him.

"You ought to tell them to go to hell," Mrs. Kreutzer said, and the vehemence surprised McKee as much as the language. "Everybody imposes on you."

"Not really," McKee said. "Anyway, I don't mind."

But as he walked down the hall toward his office he did mind, at least a little. George Everett had asked him to take his classes this summer, because Everett had an offer to handle an excavation in Guatemala, and it irritated McKee now to remember how sure Everett had been that good old Bergen would do him the favor. And he minded a little being the continuing object of Mrs. Kreutzer's pity. The cuckold needs no reminder of his horns and the reject no reminder of his failure.

He took the Law and Order envelope from his pocket and looked at it, neglecting his habitual glance through the hallway window at the chipping plaster on the rear of the Alumni Chapel. Instead he thought of how it had been to be twenty-seven years old in search of truth on the Navajo Reservation, still excited and innocent, still optimistic, not yet taught that he was less than a man. He couldn't quite recapture the feeling.

It wasn't until he had opened the blinds, turned on the air conditioner, and registered the familiar creak of his swivel chair as he lowered his weight into it that he opened the letter.

Dear Berg:

I asked around some in re your inquiry about witchcraft cases and it looks only moderately promising. There's been some gossip down around the No Agua Wash country, and an incident or two over in the Lukachukais east of Chinle, and some talk of trouble west of the Colorado River gorge up on the Utah border. None of it sounds very threatening or unusual—if that's what you're looking for. I gather the No Agua business involves trouble between two outfits in the Salt Cedar Clan over some grazing land. The business up in Utah seems to center on an old Singer with a bad reputation, and our people in the Chinle subagency tell me that they don't know what's going on yet in the Lukachukai area. The story they get (about fourth-hand) is that there's a cave of Navajo Wolves somewhere back in that west slope canyon country. The witches are supposed to be coming around the summer hogans up there, abusing the animals and the usual. And, as usual, the stories vary depending on which rumor you hear.

The first two look like they fit the theories expressed in *Social and Psychotherapeutic Utility of Navajo Wolf and Frenzy Superstitions,* but you should know, since you wrote it. I'm not sure about the Lukachukai business. It might have something to do with a man we're looking for up there. Or maybe it's a real genuine Witch, who really turns himself into a werewolf and wouldn't that knock hell out of you scientific types?

There were two more paragraphs, one reporting on Leaphorn's wife and family and a mutual friend of their undergraduate days at Arizona State, and the other offering help if McKee decided to "go witch-hunting this summer."

McKee smiled. Leaphorn had been of immense help in his original research, arranging to open the Law and Order Division files to him and helping him find the sort of people he had to see, the unacculturized Indians who knew about witchcraft. He had always regretted that Leaphorn wouldn't completely buy his thesis—that the Wolf superstition was a simple scapegoat procedure, giving a primitive people a necessary outlet for blame in times of trouble and frustration.

He leaned back in the chair, rereading the letter and recalling their arguments—Leaphorn insisting that there was a basis of truth in the Navajo Origin Myth, that some people did deliberately turn antisocial, away from the golden mean of nature, deliberately choose the unnatural, and therefore, in Navajo belief, the evil way. McKee remembered with pleasure those long evenings in Leaphorn's home, Leaphorn lapsing into Navajo in his vehemence and Emma—a bride then—laughing at both of them and bringing them beer. It would be good to see them both again, but the letter didn't sound promising. He needed a dozen case studies for the new book—enough to demonstrate all facets of his theory.

Jeremy Canfield walked in without knocking. "I've got a question for you," he said. "Where do you look on the Navajo Reservation for an electrical engineer testing his gadgets?"

He extracted a pipe from his coat pocket and began cleaning debris from the bowl into McKee's ashtray. "Just one more helpful hint. We know he has a light-green van truck. We don't know what kind of equipment it is, but this research needs to be away from such things as electrical transmission lines, telephone wires, and stuff like that."

"That helps a lot," McKee said. "That still leaves about ninety percent of the Reservation—ninety percent of twenty-five thousand square miles. Find one green truck in a landscape bigger than all New England."

"It's this daughter of a friend of mine. Girl named Ellen Leon," Canfield said. "She's trying to find this bird from U.C.L.A." He was a very small man, bent slightly by a spinal deformity, with a round, cheerful face made rounder by utter baldness.

"Goddamn flatlanders never know geography," Canfield said. "Think the Reservation's about the size of Central Park."

"Why's she looking for him?" McKee asked.

Canfield looked pained.

"You don't ask a woman something like that, Berg. Just imagine it's something romantic. Imagine she's hot for his body." Canfield lit the pipe. "Imagine she has spurned him, he has gone away to mend a broken heart, and now she has repented."

Or, McKee thought, imagine she's a fool like me. Imagine she's been left and is still too young to know it's hopeless.

"Anyway, I told her maybe in the Chuska Range, or the Lukachukais if he liked the mountains, or the Kam Bimghi Valley if he liked the desert, or up there north of the Hopi Villages, or a couple of other places. I marked a map for her and showed her where the trading posts were where he'd be likely to buy his supplies."

"Maybe they're married," McKee said. He was interested, which surprised him.

"Her name's Ellen Leon," Canfield said with emphatic

patience. "His is Jimmie W. Hall, Ph.D. Besides, no wedding ring. From which I deduce they're not married."

"O.K., Sherlock," McKee said. "I deduce from your attitude that this woman was about five feet five, slim, with long blackish hair and wearing . . ." McKee paused for thought, ". . . a sort of funny-colored suit."

"I deduce from that that you saw her in the hall," Canfield said. "Anyway, I told her we'd keep our eyes open for this bird and let her know where we'd be camping so she could check." He looked at McKee. "Where do you want to start hunting your witches?"

McKee started to mention Leaphorn's letter and say he hadn't decided yet whether to go. Instead he thought of the girl at the front entrance of the Anthropology Building, who had looked tired and disappointed and somehow very sad.

"I don't know," McKee said. "Maybe down around No Agua, or way over west of the Colorado gorge, or on the west slope of the Lukies." He thought a moment. Canfield's current project involved poking into the burial sites of the Anasazis, the pre-Navajo cliff dwellers. There were no known sites around No Agua and only a few in the Colorado River country. "How about starting over in those west slope canyons in the Lukachukais?"

"That's good for me," Canfield said. "If you've got some witches in there to scrutinize, there's plenty of ruins to keep me busy. And I'll take my guitar and try to teach you how to sing harmony."

At the door, Canfield paused, his face suddenly serious.

"I'm glad you decided to go, Bergen. I think you need . . ." He stopped, catching himself on the verge of invading a zone of private grief. "I think maybe I should ask a guarantee that your witches won't get me." It came out a little lamely, not hiding the embarrassment.

"My Navajo Wolves, being strictly psychotherapeutic, are certified harmless," McKee said. He pulled open a desk drawer, rummaged through an assortment of paper clips, carved bones, arrow heads, and potsherds, and extracted an egg-sized turquoise stone, formed roughly in the shape of a crouching frog. He tossed it to Canfield.

"Reed Clan totem," McKee said. "One of the Holy People. Good for fending off corpse powder. No self-respecting Navajo Wolf will bother you. I guarantee it."

"I'll keep it with me always," Canfield said.

The words would come back to McKee later, come back to haunt him.

BERGEN MCKEE HAD SPENT most of the afternoon in the canvas chair beside the front door in Shoemaker's. It was a slow day for trading and only a few of The People had come in. But McKee had collected witchcraft rumors from three of them, and had managed to extract the names of two Navajos who might know more about it. It was, he felt, a good beginning.

He glanced at Leaphorn. Joe was leaning against the counter, listening patiently to another of the endless stories of Old Man Shoemaker, and McKee felt guilty. Leaphorn had insisted that he needed to go to the trading post—that he had, in fact, delayed the call to take McKee along—but more likely it was a convenient piece of made-work to do a friend a graceful favor.

"There is a young man back in there we want to pick up," Leaphorn had said. He pushed a file folder across the desk. "He cut a Mexican in Gallup last month."

The file concerned someone named Luis Horseman, aged twenty-two, son of Annie Horseman of the Red Forehead Clan. Married to Elsie Tso, daughter of Lilly Tso of the Many Goats Clan. Residence, Sabito Wash, twenty-seven miles south of Klagetoh. The file included three arrest reports, for drunk and disorderly, assault and battery, and driving while under the influence of narcotics. The last entry was an account of the knifing in a Gallup bar and of a car stolen and abandoned after the knifing.

"What makes you think he's over in the Lukachukai country?" McKee had asked. "Why not back around Klagetoh with his wife?"

"It isn't very complicated," Leaphorn had said. Horseman probably thought he had killed the Mexican and was scared. His in-laws detested him. Horseman would know that and know they would turn him in, so he had run for the country of his mother's clan, where he could stay hidden.

"How the devil can you find him, then?" McKee had asked. "It would take the Marine Corps to search those canyons."

And Leaphorn had explained again—that the knife victim was now off the critical list and that if the good news was gotten to Horseman one of two things would happen. He would either turn himself in to face an assault charge, or, being less frightened, would get careless and show up in Chinle, or at Shoemaker's, or some other trading post. Either way, he'd be picked up and the file closed.

"And so I go to Shoemaker's today and spread the word to whatever Red Foreheads come in, and one of them will be a cousin, or a nephew, or something, and the news gets to Horseman. And if you don't want a free ride you can stay and help Emma with the housework."

And now Leaphorn was spreading the word again, talking to the big bareheaded Navajo who had been collecting canned goods off the shelves. "He's sort of skinny," Leaphorn was saying, "about twenty-two years old and wears his hair the old way."

"I don't know him," the Big Navajo said. He inspected Leaphorn carefully, then moved to the racks where the clothing was hung. He tried on a black felt hat. It was several sizes too small, but he left it sitting ludicrously atop his head as he sorted through the stock.

"My head got big since the last time I bought a hat," the Navajo said. He spoke in English, glancing at McKee to see if the white man appreciated Navajo clowning. "Have to have a seven-and-a-half now."

"Get that hair cut off and you could wear your old hat," Shoemaker said.

The Big Navajo wore braids, in the conservative fashion,

but very short braids. Maybe, McKee thought, he had had a white man's haircut and was letting it grow out.

"Some son of a bitch stole the old one," the Big Navajo said. He tried on another hat.

McKee yawned and looked out the open door of the trading post. Heat waves were rising from the bare earth in front. To the northeast a thunderhead was building up in the sky over Carrizo Mountain. It was early in the season for that. Tomorrow was Wednesday. McKee decided he would accept Leaphorn's invitation to spend another day with him. And then he would take his own pickup and try to find the summer hogan of Old Lady Gray Rocks. He would start with her, since she was supposed to be the source of one of the better rumors. And by Thursday when Canfield arrived they would move into Many Ruins Canyon, set up camp, and work out of the canyon.

The Big Navajo had found a hat that fitted him, another black one with a broad brim and a high crown—the high fashion of old-generation Navajos. He looked like a Tuba City Navajo, McKee decided, long-faced and raw-boned with heavy eyebrows and a wide mouth.

"O.K.," the man said. "How much do I owe you now?"

The Big Navajo had taken a silver concho band from his hip pocket. He let it hang over his wrist while he handed Shoemaker the bills and waited for his change. The metal glowed softly—hammered discs bigger than silver dollars. McKee guessed the conchos would bring $200 in pawn. He looked at the big man with new interest. The Navajo was slipping the silver band down over the crown of his hat.

"This Horseman," Leaphorn was saying, "cut up a Mexican over in Gallup. Got drunk and did it, but the Nakai didn't die. He's getting better now. They want to talk to Horseman about it over at Window Rock."

"I don't know anything about him," the big man said.

"He's the son of Annie Horseman," Leaphorn said. "Used to live back over there across the Kam Bimghi, over on the west slope of the Lukachukais." He indicated the direction, Navajo fashion, with a twitch of his lips.

The Big Navajo had been picking up his box of groceries. He put it down and looked at Leaphorn a moment and then ran his tongue over his teeth, thoughtfully.

"Whereabouts on the west slope?" he asked. "Law and Order know where he is?"

"General idea," Leaphorn said. "But it would be better if he came on in himself. You know. Otherwise we'll go in there and get him. Make it worse for everybody."

"Horseman," the Big Navajo said. "Is he . . ."

Leaphorn was waiting for the rest of the question.

"What'd you say this kid looks like?"

"Slender fellow. Had on denims and a red shirt. Wears his hair the old way and ties it back in a red sweatband."

"I don't know him," the big man said. "But it would be good if he came in." He hoisted the box under his arm and walked toward the door.

"This man's a college professor," Leaphorn said, pointing to McKee. "He's looking for some information out here about witches."

The Navajo shook hands. He looked amused.

"They say there's a Wolf over toward the Lukachukais," McKee said. "Maybe it's just gossip."

"I heard some of that talk." He looked at McKee and smiled. "It's old-woman talk. A man out there's supposed to had a dream about the Gum-Tooth Woman and about a three-legged dog coming into his hogan and he woke up and he saw this dog in his brush arbor, and when he yelled at it, it turned into a man and threw corpse powder on him."

The Navajo laughed and slapped McKee on the shoulder.

"Horse manure," he said. "Maybe the Wolf is this boy the policeman is hunting for." He looked at Leaphorn. "I guess you'll be after that boy if he don't come in. Are you hunting for him now?"

"I don't think we're looking very hard yet," Leaphorn said. "I think he'll come in to see us."

The Big Navajo went through the door.

"Be better if he came in," he said.

△ △ △

It was almost sundown when Leaphorn pulled the Law and Order carryall onto the pavement of Navajo Route 8 at Round Rock. Two hours' drive back to Window Rock.

"Pretty fair day's work for me," McKee said. "But I think you wasted your time."

"No. I got done about what I wanted."

McKee was surprised.

"You still think Horseman's back in there? Nobody had seen him."

Leaphorn smiled. "Nobody admitted they'd seen him. There wasn't any reason for them to admit it. They know how the system works. But that old man who came in the wagon . . ." Leaphorn picked his clipboard of notes off the dashboard and inspected it. "Nagani Lum, it was. He damned sure knew something about it. Did you notice how interested he was?"

"Lum was one who was telling me about a witching case," McKee recalled. "Pretty standard stuff." A two-headed colt had been born. Lum hadn't seen it but a relative had. The brother-in-law of an uncle, as McKee remembered it. And then the boy who herded sheep for his uncle's brother-in-law had actually seen the Navajo Wolf. Thought it was a dog bothering the sheep, but when he shot at it with his .22, he saw it had turned into a man. But it was getting dark and he didn't think he'd hit it. As usual, McKee thought, it was a little too dark to really see and, as usual, the source was a boy.

"I think that joker who was buying himself the new hat knew something about Horseman, too," Leaphorn was saying. "The one who was kidding you about your witch stories."

"He said he didn't."

"He also said somebody stole his hat."

"What do you mean?" McKee asked.

"Did you see that concho hatband? Why would anybody steal an old felt hat and leave behind all that fancy silver?"

They had passed Chinle now, Leaphorn driving the white carryall at a steady seventy. The highway skirted the immense, lifeless depression which falls away into the Biz-E-Ahi and Nazlini washes. It was lit now by the sunset, a fantastic jumble of eroded geological formations. The white man sees the desolation and calls it a desert, McKee thought, but the Navajo name for it means "Beautiful Valley."

"Can you tell me why that man would lie about somebody stealing his hat?" Leaphorn asked. His face was intent with the puzzle. "Or, if he wasn't lying, who would steal an old felt hat and leave that silver band behind?"

JOSEPH BEGAY AWAKENED earlier than usual. He lay still a moment, allowing consciousness to seep through him, noticing first the pre-dawn chill and that his wife had captured most of the blankets they shared. Then he registered the rain smells, dampened dust, wet sage, piñon resin, and buffalo grass. Now fully awake, he remembered the sudden midnight shower which had awakened them in the brush arbor and driven the family to shelter in the hogan. Through the open hogan door, he saw the eastern horizon was not yet brightening behind the familiar upthrusting shape of Mount Taylor, seventy miles away in New Mexico. Reaches for the Sky was one of the four sacred mountains which marked the four corners of the Land of the People, and Joseph Begay thought, as he had thought many mornings, that he had chosen this site well. The old hogan which he and his brothers-in-law had built near his mother-in-law's place had been located on low ground, near water but closed in with the hills. He had never liked the site. When the son they had called Long Fingers had died of the choking sickness in the night—died so suddenly that they had not had time to move him out of the hogan so that the ghost could go free—he had not been sorry that they had to leave the site. He had boarded up the door himself and covered the smoke hole so the ghost of Long Fingers would not bother his in-law people and had decided right away that this place on the mesa would be the place for the new hogan.

And, when he had built it, he had not faced the door exactly east as the Old People had said it must be faced, but very slightly north of east so that when he awoke in the morning he would see Reaches for the Sky outlined by the dawn, and remember that it was a place of beauty where Changing Woman had borne the Hero Twins. It would be a good thought to awaken with, and because he had not made the door exactly east he had been very careful to follow the Navajo Way with the remainder of the construction. He had driven a peg and used a rope to mark off the circle to assure that the hogan wall would be round and of the prescribed circumference. He had put the smoke hole in exactly the proper place and, when he had plastered the stones with adobe, he had sprinkled a pinch of corn pollen on the mud and sung the song from the Blessing Way.

Joseph Begay slipped off the pallet and pulled on his pants and shirt, moving silently in the darkness to avoid awakening his wife and two sons, who slept across the hogan. He moved around their feet, with the Navajo's unconscious care not to step over another human being, and ducked through the door. His boots, forgotten in the brush arbor, were only slightly damp. He put them on as he heated water for a cup of coffee.

He was a short, round-faced man with the barrel chest characteristic of a Navajo-Pueblo blood mixture, from a clan which had captured Pueblo brides and with them the heavier, shorter bone structure of the Keresan Indians. He poured the coffee into a mug and sipped it while he ate a strip of dried mutton. The rain had been light, a brief shower, but it was a good omen.

He knew the Callers of the Clouds had been at work on the Hopi and Zuñi reservations and that along the Rio Grande, far to the east, the Pueblo Indians were holding their rain dances. The magic of these pueblo dwellers had always been strong, older than the medicine of the Navajos and more potent. It was a little early for this first shower and Begay knew that was promising.

Begay finished his coffee before he allowed his thoughts to turn to his reasons for rising early. In a very few hours he would see his daughter, his daughter whom he hadn't seen since last summer. He would drive to the bus stop at Ganado, and the bus would come and he would put her suitcases and her boxes in the pickup truck and drive with her back to the hogan. She would be with them all summer. Begay had deliberately postponed thinking about this, because the Navajo Way was the Middle Way, which avoided all excesses—even of happiness. The shower at midnight and the smell of the earth and the beauty of the morning had been enough. But now Begay thought of it as he started the pickup truck and drove in second gear down the bumpy track across the mesa. And, as he drove, he sang a song his great uncle had taught him:

"I usually walk where the rains fall.
Below the east I walk.
I being Born of Water,
I usually walk where the rains fall.
Within the dawn I walk.

I usually walk where the rains fall.
Among the white corn I walk.
Among the soft goods I walk.
Among the collected waters I walk.
Among the pollen I walk.
I usually walk where the rain falls."

It was brightening on the eastern horizon as he shifted into low gear to wind down the switchback down the long slope toward the highway. The descent took almost fifteen minutes, and at the bottom, skirting the base of the mesa, was Teastah Wash. If it had rained harder elsewhere on the mesa, he might not be able to drive through the wash until the runoff water cleared. He stopped just as his truck tilted down the steep incline, put on the emergency brake, and stepped out. The headlights, illuminating the bottom of the wash, showed only a slight trickle of water across the sandy expanse. What little runoff there had been was mostly gone now.

It was when he was turning to climb back into the pickup that he saw the owl. It flew almost directly at the truck, startling him, flitted through the headlight beams, and disappeared abruptly in the dawn half-light up the wash. He sat behind the wheel a moment, feeling shaken. The owl had acted strangely, he thought, and it was known that ghosts sometimes took on that form when they moved in the darkness. It looked like a burrowing owl, Begay thought, but maybe it was a ghost returning with the dawn to a grave or a death hogan.

He was still thinking of the owl as he let the pickup ease slowly down the steep bank and then raced it across the soft bottom. And he was thinking of it as the truck climbed out of the arroyo, its motor laboring in low gear. But by now the mood of the morning had recaptured him and he thought that it was just a burrowing owl, going home from the night's hunting and confused by his headlights. It was just beyond the rim of the shallow canyon, just after the pickup had regained level ground and he had shifted into second gear, that he saw that he was wrong.

The body lay just beside the track and his headlights first reflected from the soles of its shoes. Before he could stop, the pickup was almost beside it. Joseph Begay shifted into neutral and left the motor running. He unbuttoned his shirt and extracted a small leather pouch hung from his neck by a thong. The pouch contained a small bit of jet flint in the crude shape of a bear, and about an ounce of yellow pollen. Begay put his thumb in the pollen and rubbed it against his chest. He chanted:

"Everywhere I go, myself
May I have luck,
Everywhere my close relatives go
May they have their good luck."

The ghost was gone—at least for the moment. He had seen it flying up Teastah Wash. He got out of the truck and stood beside the body. It was a young man dressed in jeans and a red shirt and with town shoes on. The body lay on its back, the legs slightly parted, right arm outflung and left arm across the chest with the wrist and hand extending, oddly rigid. There was no visible blood but the clothing was damp from the rain.

As Begay drove the last mile down the bumpy track toward

the highway, driving faster than he should have, he thought that he would have to report this body to Law and Order before he went to the bus station. He tried not to think of the expression frozen on the face of the young man, the dead eyes bulging and the lips drawn back in naked terror.

IT WAS MIDMORNING when the news of Horseman reached Leaphorn's office. In the two hours since breakfast, McKee had sorted through two filing cabinets, extracted Manila folders marked "Witchcraft" and segregated those identified as "Wolf" from those labeled "Frenzy" and "Datura." The datura cases involved narcotics users, and most frenzy incidents, McKee knew, centered on mental illness. If he had time, he'd look through those later. He was marking Wolf incident locations on a Bureau of Indian Affairs reservation map, coding them with numbers, and then making notes of names of witnesses, when the radio dispatcher stopped at the door and told Leaphorn that Luis Horseman had been found.

"When did he come in?"

"Found his body," the dispatcher said.

Leaphorn stared at the dispatcher, waiting for more.

"The captain wants to know if you can pick up the coroner and clear the body?"

"Why don't they handle it out of the Chinle subagency?" Leaphorn asked. "They're a hundred miles closer."

"They found him down near Ganado. You're supposed to pick up the coroner there."

"Ganado?" Leaphorn looked incredulous. "What killed him? Suicide?"

"Apparently natural," the dispatcher said. "Too much booze. But nobody's looked at him yet."

"Ganado," Leaphorn said. "How the devil did he get down there?"

It was forty-five minutes to Ganado and Leaphorn spent most of them worrying to McKee about being wrong.

"Congratulations," McKee said. "You're forty years old and you just made your first mistake."

"It's not that. It just doesn't make sense." And then, for the third time, Leaphorn reviewed his reasoning—looking for a flaw. The Gallup police had reported the car Horseman had taken after the knifing was last seen heading north on U.S. 666, the right direction. It had been found later, abandoned near Greasewood. The right place, if he was returning to the west-slope canyon country of his mother's clan. And there was every reason to think he would. Horseman was scared. The territory was empty, and a fugitive's dream for hiding out. His kinsmen would feed him and keep their mouths shut. And at Shoemaker's Leaphorn was certain that at least two of those he had talked to had known about Horseman. There was the old man with the witch story and it was even more obvious with the boy who had come in late. He had clearly been relieved to hear the Mexican hadn't died and clearly was in a hurry to end the conversation and go tell someone about it. And then there was the Big Navajo. "He was interested," Leaphorn said. "Remember he asked me to describe Horseman. And Shoemaker said he was new around there. Why would he be interested if he hadn't seen him?"

"You're hung up on the hat thing," McKee said.

"All right," Leaphorn said. "You explain the hat."

"Sure. He took the hatband off and while it was off, somebody stole the hat."

"When's the last time you took off your hatband?"

"I don't wear silver conchos on my hat," McKee said.

They picked up the coroner-justice of the peace at a Conoco station in Ganado, a man named Rudolph Bitsi. Bitsi told them to drive south.

The late morning sun was hot by the time they arrived at the edge of Teastah Wash and the Navajo policeman who had been left with the body had retreated into the shade of the arroyo wall. He climbed into the sunlight, blinking, as the carryall stopped. He looked very young, and a little nervous. Leaphorn said the policeman was Dick Roanhorse, just out of recruit school.

"Find anything interesting?" Leaphorn asked.

"No, sir. Just this bottle. The only tracks are the ones made by Begay's pickup. Rain washed everything else out."

"The body was here before the rain, then," Leaphorn said. It was more a statement than a question, and the policeman only nodded.

Leaphorn pulled the blanket off the body. They looked at what had been Luis Horseman.

"Well," Bitsi said, "looks like he might have had some sort of seizure."

"Looks like it," Leaphorn said.

Bitsi squatted, examining the face. He was a short, middle-aged man, tending to fat, and he grunted as he lowered himself. He sniffed at Horseman's nose and lips.

"Alcohol. You can just barely get a whiff of it."

Leaphorn was looking at Horseman's legs. McKee noticed they were rigidly straight—as if he had died erect and tumbled backward, which wasn't likely.

Bitsi was still examining the face. "I saw one that looked like that two, three years ago. Crazy bastard had made him a brew out of jimson weed to get more potent and it poisoned him."

Leaphorn was looking at Horseman's left arm. The watch on his wrist was running, which would mean he had wound it the previous day—probably less than twenty-four hours earlier. It was a cheap watch, the kind that cost about $8 or $10, with a stainless-steel expansion band. Leaphorn stared at the left hand. The arm lay across Horseman's chest with the wrist and hand extended, unsupported.

"Pretty fair booze," Bitsi said, holding up the bottle. The label was red and proclaimed the contents to be sour-mash whiskey. About a half ounce of amber liquid remained in the bottle.

"Looks like he overdid it," Bitsi said. "Looks like he strangled. Fell down while he was throwing up, and passed out and strangled."

"That's what it looks like," Leaphorn said.

"Might as well haul him in," Bitsi said. He rose from his squat, grunting again.

"No tracks at all?" Leaphorn asked the policeman.

"Just Begay's. Where he got out of his pickup and came over to look at the body. Nothing but that."

There were plenty of tracks now. Mostly Roanhorse's, Leaphorn guessed.

"Where was the bottle?"

"Four or five feet from the body," Roanhorse said. "Like he dropped it."

"O.K.," Leaphorn said. He was looking across the flat through which Teastah Wash had eroded, an expanse of scrubby creosote bush with a scattering of sage. At the lip of the wash bank, a few yards upstream from the road, two small junipers had managed to get roots deep enough to live. Leaphorn walked suddenly to the nearest bush and examined it. He motioned to Roanhorse, and McKee followed.

"You pull a limb off this for anything?"

Roanhorse shook his head.

There was a raw wound on the lower trunk where a limb had been broken away. Leaphorn put his thumb against the exposed cambium layer and showed it to McKee. It was sticky with fresh sap.

"What do you think of that?"

"Nothing," McKee said. "How about you?"

"I don't know. Probably nothing."

He started walking back toward the body, through the creosote bush, searching. Bitsi, McKee noticed, had climbed back into the carryall.

"Look around across the road there," Leaphorn said, "and see if you can find that juniper branch."

But he found it himself. The frail needles were dirty and broken. McKee guessed it had been used as a broom even before Leaphorn told him.

"That looked pretty smart, Joe," McKee said. "Where does it take you?"

"I don't know." Leaphorn was looking intently at the body. "Notice how his legs are stretched out straight. He could have pushed 'em out that way after he fell down, but if you do that laying on the ground, looks like it would push your pants cuffs away from your ankles." He stood silently, surveying the body. "Maybe that's all right though. It could happen." He looked at McKee. "That wrist couldn't happen, though."

He squatted beside the body, looking up.

"Ever try to pick up an unconscious man? He's limp. Absolutely limp. After he's dead two-three hours, he starts getting stiff."

That's why I noticed the arm, McKee thought. It doesn't look natural.

"You think he was dead, and somebody put him here?"

"Maybe," Leaphorn said. "And whoever did it didn't know it was going to rain so they brushed out their tracks."

"But why?" McKee asked. He looked around. Here the body was sure to be found and down in the wash it could have been buried, probably forever.

"I've got better questions than that," Leaphorn said. "Like how did he die? We can find that out. And then maybe it will be who did it, and why. Why would anyone want to kill the poor bastard?"

OLD WOMAN GRAY ROCKS leaned back against the cedar pole supporting one corner of the brush hogan and took a long pull on the cigarette McKee had lit for her. She blew the smoke out her nostrils. Behind her, the foothills of the Lukachukais shimmered under the blinding sun—gray mesquite and creosote bush, gray-green scrub cedar, and the paler gray of the eroded gullies, and above the grayness the blue-green of the higher slopes shaded now by an embryo early-afternoon thundercloud. By sundown, McKee thought, the cloud would be producing lightning and those frail curtains of rain which would, in arid-country fashion, evaporate high above the ground. He wondered idly if Leaphorn had been right—if Horseman had been hiding back in that broken canyon country.

He refocused his eyes to the dimmer light under the brush and saw that Old Woman Gray Rocks was smiling at him.

"The way they do it," she said, "is catch the Wolf and tie him down. Not give him anything to eat or any water and not let him take his pants down for anything until he tells that he's the one that's doing the witching. Once they tell it, it's all right after that. Then the witching turns around and the man he did it to gets all right and the witch gets sick and dies."

Old Woman Gray Rocks removed the cigarette and held it between thumb and first finger. It occurred to McKee that every Navajo he had ever seen smoking—including children—used the same unorthodox grip.

"I don't think they're going to catch this one," she said.

"Why do you say that?" McKee was feeling good that his command of Navajo had returned. Two days ago he would only have said "Why?" which required a single monosyllabic guttural. He had only had time for one afternoon in the language lab listening to tapes and his pronunciation had been rough at first. Now he was almost as fluent as he had been at twenty-seven. "Kintahgoo' bil i noolhtah?" he said, repeating the question and relishing the sound.

"They don't think he lives around here. He's a stranger."

McKee was suddenly mildly interested. He had been feeling drowsy, the effect of an unusually heavy meal (lamb stew, floating in fat, boiled corn, fried cornbread, and canned peaches) and of a certainty, established not long after Canfield had dropped him off at the hogan, that the woman would tell him nothing useful. He had hoped he would learn something of the motivation behind the witchcraft gossip, detect the sickness, or the intra-family tensions, or the jealousies, or whatever trouble had produced a need for a scapegoat witch. This hope had grown when Old Woman Gray Rocks had proved friendly and welcomed him warmly. All morning long it had faded. But there was nothing to do now but wait for Canfield to stop on his way back from buying supplies to pick him up. If there was serious trouble in the clan, natural or human, Old Woman Gray Rocks seemed genuinely unaware of it. She gossiped cheerfully about minor affairs. The nephew of an uncle by marriage had left his wife and taken up with a woman in the Peach Tree Clan at Moenkopi. He had stolen one of his wife's horses. One of the sons of Hosteen Tom had gone to Farmington to join the Marine Corps but they said now that he was working at the place where they mined the coal near Four Corners. They said the Marines didn't take him because he didn't do right on the papers.

There had been much other information. The winter had been wet and early grazing was pretty good. The price of wool was down a little but the price of mutton was up. Some of the nephews had found jobs at the new sawmill the Tribal Council had opened. George Charley had seen trucks way over by Los Gigantes Buttes and the men told him they belonged to an oil company and that Hosteen Charley had better move his sheep out of there because they would be shooting off dynamite. Old

Woman Gray Rocks thought this was strange and McKee had not felt his Navajo good enough to undertake an explanation of how seismograph crews record shock waves in searching for petroleum deposits.

Until now, only two of her remarks had been worth remembering. She had mentioned that a man driving a truck had stopped her sister's husband and asked him about a road. McKee had asked her about that, thinking of Miss Leon's misplaced electrical engineer. The road had been the one which leads into Many Ruins Canyon. Old Woman Gray Rocks said the driver had been a Belacani like McKee and the truck had been pulling a little two-wheel trailer, and it was like those they haul bread in, with a door in the back—which meant it might be a van, like Dr. Hall's van. She didn't know what color it was but her grandson had seen it parked in Hard Goods Canyon three or four weeks ago when he was trapping rabbits. Hard Goods was the wash that runs into Many Ruins Canyon about nine miles up from the mouth, she said.

And then Old Woman Gray Rocks had returned to the subject of the decline of the younger generation, and mentioned a cousin of her nephews had cut up a Nakai in Gallup and stolen a car and run away.

"I heard about that at Window Rock," McKee said. "I heard his name was Luis Horseman." He checked an impulse to tell her that Horseman was dead and to ask her if the cousin of her nephews had come home to hide. It was better to let her talk.

"That's his name," Old Woman Gray Rocks said. She spit on the ground. "He always acted like he didn't have any relatives. Got drunk all the time and fought people. His mother wasn't any good either. Run off from her children." She lit another cigarette.

McKee wondered how far Leaphorn's news had spread. "Did he kill that man in Gallup?"

"They say he got well," she said. "A policeman came to Shoemaker's and said that, and said he should come in to talk to Law and Order. It would be better if he did that."

"How's he going to know?"

Old Woman Gray Rocks looked toward the Lukachukais.

"They said somebody went back in there and told him about it," she said. "I think it was one of those boys in the Nez outfit went to tell him."

And that, McKee thought, will tell Joe Leaphorn that he guessed right about Horseman coming home to hide. And maybe it will tell him somebody named Nez saw Horseman the evening before his body turned up. That gave him a chance to return one of Leaphorn's many favors.

And now it seemed that this gossipy woman knew more about the witching incidents than she had been willing to admit. He thought about her statement that the Wolf was a stranger. A few hours earlier he would have rejected such an idea as incongruous. The witch should be one of the clan, a known irritant or target of envy. But now he was faced with a new set of facts. There seemed to be, if Old Woman Gray Rocks was well informed, none of the usual causes to produce a scapegoat witch. The cause, when he found it, now would likely be something isolated and outside the usual social pattern. He decided to pursue this point very gingerly.

"Who is the Navajo who says this Wolf is a stranger?" McKee asked.

"I heard that from my husband. He said they told him that one of the Tsosie boys found the place in an arroyo over that way"—Old Woman Gray Rocks made a vague gesture with her lips toward the Lukachukai slopes—"where the Wolf had camped. It was a dry camp and there was a spring just a mile up the arroyo. If he lived around here he would have known where the water was."

"How did they know it was the Wolf's camp?" McKee asked.

"They said to my husband that the boot tracks were the same tracks that Tsosie Begay found around his sheep pen after the Wolf came there."

So, thought McKee.

"Is this boy of the family of Charley Tsosie?" he asked.

"It is the son of Charley," Old Woman Gray Rocks said. "He didn't get married so he is still with the clan."

"And the Tsosie place is the one the Wolf came to?"

"That's what is said. Charley Tsosie was one of them he bothered."

"Do you know the name of the other ones?" McKee asked. Before their meal she had assured him that she didn't know the identity of anyone who claimed to be troubled by a Wolf. McKee considered this small lie, now gracefully retracted, not as an indication of Navajo secrecy but as a further demonstration of the mystery of womanhood. He had no theory concerning why Old Woman Gray Rocks had withheld this information earlier, and no theory concerning why she had decided to confide it to him now, and no idea whether she would tell him more. McKee had concluded years ago that the intricacies of feminine logic were beyond his comprehension.

Old Woman Gray Rocks seemed not to have heard the question. She was looking down the slope toward the pole corral, where two young grandsons were putting a saddle on a scrubby-looking horse.

"I heard at the trading post that the other one the Wolf came after was a man they called Afraid of His Horse," McKee said. "But someone else said that wasn't right. And someone else told it was a fellow named Shelton Nakai, but they didn't know where he lived now."

"Who told you it was Afraid of His Horse?" Old Woman Gray Rocks asked.

"I don't remember who it was now," McKee said. It had been Mr. Shoemaker at the trading post, and Shoemaker had also told him that Afraid of His Horse was the son-in-law of Old Woman Gray Rocks.

"Maybe it was Ben Yazzie the witch was after," the woman said slowly. "I don't know where he lives now. He used to graze some sheep way up on the high slopes over there by Horse Fell and Many Ruins Canyons. That's where he used to have his summer hogan."

McKee thought she looked nervous, and he thought he knew why. She didn't want her son-in-law connected, even in gossip, with witching, so she was turning his attention to Yazzie. He would find Charley Tsosie, Ben Yazzie, and Afraid of His Horse later, and talk to them, but now he would change the subject. He wanted to learn more, if Old Woman Gray Rocks would tell him, about why this witch was thought to be a stranger.

"I don't know why they think this Wolf doesn't live around here," McKee said. "Maybe he made that dry camp in the arroyo because he thought somebody would come to the spring and he didn't want them to find him."

"Somebody saw him one night," the old woman said. She spoke very slowly, weighing what she would say, and how much she would say. "Witches come out mostly when there is a moon and there was a moon that night. This man he woke up in the night and heard a coyote singing and he went out to see about some lambs he had penned up out there and he saw the witch there in the moonlight. It wasn't anyone who has his hogan around here."

McKee started to ask the name of this man, and thought better of it. This "someone" would be Afraid of His Horse, the old woman's son-in-law.

"But how did this man know he was seeing a witch?" McKee asked. "Maybe it was just somebody walking through there."

McKee thought, for a long moment, that Old Woman Gray Rocks would ignore the question. He let it hang in the heavy silence. Behind the winter hogan, the dogs began to bark and McKee heard the sound of the pickup truck—Canfield coming back from Shoemaker's with the groceries.

"The way I heard it," Old Woman Gray Rocks said, still slowly, "this witch had a wolf skin over his back and he was down where those rams were penned, killing them with a knife."

Canfield arrived from Shoemaker's with $43 worth of groceries in the camper, a case of beer, and a letter from Ellen Leon, postmarked Page, Arizona. She planned to spend a day or two checking the trading posts around Mormon Ridge and the Kaibab Plateau in the northwest section of the Reservation. And then she would come to Chinle on Thursday and drive over to Shoemaker's trading post and find out where she could meet them. Canfield had left a note and a penciled map telling her they would be camped about five miles up the main branch of

Many Ruins Canyon and showing her how to get there.

"Works out good for everybody," Canfield said. "You've got your witchery business going on in the neighborhood, and if we have time, we can look around up in there and see if we can find that green van." He grinned. "Let's hope we don't find it. We'll get out my guitar and serenade her and spend bacchanal evenings under the Navajo moon."

"I don't know if I've got any witchery business yet," McKee said. "I've got to find this Tsosie family and find out what their trouble is, if anything. According to the old lady, Charley usually has his summer hogan just a few miles south of where we'll be camping, so that should be easy. Then maybe the Tsosies can tell me where to find Afraid of His Horse. The old lady didn't want to talk about him. They don't like witch trouble in the family."

"What are you going to do about Horseman?"

McKee thought about it. "I think I ought to go on back to Chinle tomorrow and call Leaphorn about it," he said.

"Your cop really think it wasn't a natural death?"

"I don't think he knows," McKee said. "But he guessed right about Horseman coming back in here to hide."

Canfield let the pickup idle along the hard-packed sand of the canyon floor, turning occasionally to side canyons to check his map and his memory of where cliff ruins he would inspect were located. The sun was low as they penetrated the upper canyon. Here the cliffs closed in, rising in sheer, almost smooth walls nearly four hundred feet to a narrow slit of sky above. Here in this slot of eroded stone darkness came early. Canfield had switched on his headlights before he found a likely camp—a hillock of rocky debris which had collected enough soil to support an expanse of grass and even a growth of young cottonwoods and willows.

By the time they had Canfield's working tent pitched and supper cooked, the first stars were visible over the canyon walls. A nighthawk flashed past them, hunting. Up canyon a rasping hoot touched off a dull pattern of echoes.

"Saw-whet owl," Canfield said. He grinned at McKee. "If Leaphorn was right, maybe that's Horseman's ghost enjoying the night out."

They ate and then sat in the silent darkness, watching the light of the early moon light the top of the canyon walls. From some infinite distance came the faint sound of barking.

"Take your pick," McKee said. "A coyote, some sheepherder's lost dog, or one of my witches turned into a wolf for the evening."

Canfield took the turquoise frog from his pocket and rubbed it, chuckling.

"I'll say it's a witch," he said, "because this keeps me safe from witches."

Actually, McKee remembered, the turquoise shape wasn't a Navajo charm. It was a much older Anasazi fertility totem with nothing at all to do with witches.

Of course it didn't really matter.

MCKEE LEFT THE CAMPSITE before dawn, called Leaphorn's office from the Gulf station on the highway at Chinle, and then ate a leisurely breakfast at Bishbito's Diner while he waited for the policeman to make the sixty-mile drive from Window Rock. Leaphorn arrived while he was finishing his third cup of coffee. He handed McKee a sheet of paper and sat down.

"Take a look at that," he said. "And then let's go and find that boy who went to warn Horseman."

The paper was a carbon of an autopsy report form:

SUBJECT: Luis Horseman (war name unknown).
AGE: 23.
ADDRESS: 27 miles southwest of Klagetoh.
NEXT OF KIN: Wife, Agnes (Tso) Horseman, Many Goats Clan.
TIME OF DEATH: Between 6 P.M. and 12 midnight, June 11 (estimated).
CAUSE OF DEATH: Suffocation. Substantial accumulation of fine granular material in lung tissue, windpipe, throat, and nostrils.

There was more information, negative reports on blood alcohol and on abrasions and concussions, and an analysis indicating the "fine granular material" was common silica-based sand.

"The medical examiner said it looked like he got caught

in a cave-in," Leaphorn said. "Like he had been buried in sand."

"You think so?"

"And somebody dug him out? And laid him out there at Teastah Wash with the bottle of whiskey he hadn't drunk?" Leaphorn thought about his own questions. "I don't know. Maybe. But there wasn't any sand in his cuffs, or in his pockets, or anywhere else."

"It wouldn't make any sense anyway," McKee said.

Leaphorn was looking out the window. "I think I know a lot about witches," he said. "You think you know a lot about witches. How do you kill a witch?"

The question surprised McKee. He thought about it. "You mean do you smother them?"

"Remember that case over at Fruitland?" Leaphorn asked. "That guy whose daughter died of t.b.? He shot four of them. And then there was that old Singer up near Teec Nos Pas a couple of years ago. He was beaten to death."

"There's no special way that I know of," McKee said. "There was supposed to be a hanging back in the 1930s but there wasn't any proof and they think it was just gossip. Usually, though, it's heat-of-passion stuff—beating, shooting, or knifing. Something like that. Why? You think somebody thought Horseman was a witch?"

"Makes a certain amount of sense," Leaphorn said. "But I don't know." He was still staring out the window. "Why kill somebody like Horseman? Just another poor soul who didn't quite know how to be a Navajo and couldn't learn to act like a white. No good for anything."

McKee could think of nothing to say. Out the window there was the highway, the asphalt strip of Navajo Route 9, and across it to the east, the blue-gray mass of the Lukachukai Range. He wondered what Leaphorn was seeing out there.

"I was in charge of the Shiprock subagency when that Fruitland thing happened," Leaphorn said. "That one was mine. I heard that Navajo Wolf talk and I didn't pay much attention to it and so we had five bodies to bury."

"Four," McKee said.

"No. It was five." Leaphorn turned, smiling grimly. "This

isn't Salem," he said. "We don't recognize witchcraft legally and the guy shot an old Hand Trembler and his wife, and a schoolteacher and her husband, and then he shot himself. Didn't want to stand trial for murder."

"What are you trying to do?" McKee asked. "Figure out a way to blame yourself for Horseman?"

"I could have gone in and looked for him."

"But not found him," McKee said. "Besides, Horseman wasn't a stranger. The old woman said the Wolf is a stranger."

"Yeah," Leaphorn said. "That's what she said. Maybe she had a reason to lie. Let's go find that boy who went out to warn Horseman." He looked at his notes. "Billy Nez. Let's go find Billy and see what he knows."

But finding Billy Nez was not possible.

They found his family's hogans east of Chinle, not far from Shoemaker's, but not Billy. His uncle was sore about it.

"Kid took a horse and took off after breakfast," he said. "He's gone all the time. Screwing around back up in the mountains somewhere, when he's supposed to be helping out."

Would he be back tonight? The uncle couldn't guess. Sometimes he was gone for days. He and Leaphorn talked a moment and then the lieutenant returned to the carryall, and turned it back toward Chinle.

"Found out a little," Leaphorn said. "The boy knew where Horseman was hiding—somewhere back up in those canyons. But when he went to tell him he hadn't killed anybody, Horseman was gone." Leaphorn paused. "Or at least the kid said he was gone."

"You don't think he was?"

"Probably," Leaphorn said. "The uncle also told me something else. Billy Nez is Horseman's younger brother."

"His brother?" McKee said. "How about the different name?"

"Family broke up," Leaphorn said. "Billy was living with his uncle so he used Nez instead of Horseman. You know how it is with the Dinee. The only name that really counts is the war name you get when you're little. And that one's a secret inside your family and it's only used in your Blessing Way ceremonial or if you get somebody to sing you a cure."

It was noon when they reached the Chinle subagency office and the man Leaphorn wanted to see was at lunch. They found him at the diner, and Leaphorn introduced him as Sam George Takes. He was a round-faced, barrel-chested young man, wearing the uniform of a Law and Order sergeant. McKee ordered chicken-fried steak, more lunch than he usually allowed himself.

"Hell, you know how it is, Joe," Takes was saying. "It's summer, school's out. He's probably chasing some girl and no telling when he gets back."

"That's right," Leaphorn said. "That's what you do when you're sixteen or so. Hanging around some girl's hogan. Or, if your brother is missing, maybe looking for your brother."

Takes put down his fork. "And he don't find him and he comes home and his uncle sends him in here like he said he would and we find out whatever he knows, which is probably nothing, and that's the end of it. Why are you worrying?"

"It could work out like that," Leaphorn said. "But you know how news travels on this reservation. It could be by now he knows his brother is dead. So maybe he connects it to this witching gossip. Then he collects some cousins and uncles and goes looking for the Wolf."

McKee's lunch arrived, with the gravy poured over the French fries.

"Al's cook quit again," Takes said. "Son of a bitch is trying to do his own cooking."

"The problem is where to start looking," Leaphorn said. "It's your territory, Sam. Where do you think?"

Takes looked glum. "Son of a bitch could be anywhere. You remember when we had that bootlegger in there working a still right after the Korean War. We never did find him." Takes looked as though the thought still irritated him. "We knew he had to be close to water and at least have a horse to haul the grain in, but booze came out of there for four years and we never found nothing."

"It wouldn't take that Nez outfit four years to find itself a witch," Leaphorn said.

Takes laughed. "If you're worrying about that," he said,

"they're going to have an Enemy Way. That ought to take care of the witch."

"Who's having it?" Leaphorn asked. "Somebody in the Nez family?"

"I heard it was Charley Tsosie," Takes said. "But they're Nez kinfolks—part of the same outfit."

McKee was interested. Old Lady Gray Rocks had mentioned Tsosie being bothered by the witch. But the Prostitution Way was the curing ceremonial held for those exposed to witchcraft—to turn the evil around and direct it back against the Wolf who started it. Why an Enemy Way? McKee thought about the rite. It had grown out of the fighting between the Dinee and the Utes, and the only times he had heard of its being used was when members of The People came home after being off the Reservation, people like discharged servicemen, people who had been in contact with foreign influences—white men, or Pueblo Indians, or Mexicans. He remembered again what the old woman had said about the witch being a stranger. Leaphorn was looking at him.

"If they're having an Enemy Way, that old woman must have told you right," Leaphorn said. "They think it's an outsider, and if they think that, they didn't think it was Horseman and that wasn't why he was killed."

"Wonder why he was," Takes said. "Usually there's a feud, or fighting over a woman, or somebody bad-mouthing somebody."

"Maybe he found that whiskey still you were looking for," McKee said.

"Hasn't been any bootleg whiskey turning up in years," Takes said.

"How about that rocket the military lost three, four years ago?" Leaphorn said. "Is that ten-thousand-dollar reward still out for anyone finding that thing?"

"I don't know," Takes said. "I don't think they ever found it."

"I'll call the people up at the Tonepah Range and find out if they're still offering ten thousand dollars," Leaphorn said. He explained to McKee that missiles fired from the Tonepah test site in Utah to the impact area at White Sands Proving Grounds in New Mexico passed over the empty eastern expanse of the Reservation.

"They used to lose one now and then when a second stage misfired, and then they'd have a hell of a time finding it," Leaphorn said. "But now they have a radar station over on Tall Poles Butte and they track 'em all the way to the ground."

"You think maybe Horseman and somebody else both found the old rocket and fought over who'd get the reward?" McKee asked.

Leaphorn shrugged. He asked Bishbito if he could use his office telephone for a long-distance call.

McKee finished his meal, eating dutifully, feeling simultaneously disappointed and ashamed of that disappointment. He had once again, as he had for years, fallen victim to his optimism. Expecting something when there was always nothing. Anticipating some romantic mystery in what Takes and Leaphorn must already see as a sordid, routine little homicide. It was this flaw, he knew, that had cost him these last eight years of anguish, turned to misery, turned to what now was simply numbness. He could still see the note, blue ink on blue paper in Sara's easy script:

"Berg. I am meeting Scotty in Las Vegas tonight. I won't contest the divorce."

Simply that, and her signature. It was not Sara's style to add the unnecessary explanation, to say that he was a dull, nondescript man in a dull, dead-end job, and that Scotty was exciting, in an exciting world of money and executive jets and Caribbean weekends. He cursed himself as he always did when he thought of it, cursed the flaw that made him ignore the fact that he was a clumsy, unbrilliant, average man, grotesquely misfit in the circle of slim, cool Saras and reckless, witty Scotts.

He turned away from the memory and thought of Horseman, another failure as a man, wondering why he had let himself expect anything exotic in his death. And then he turned away from that thought, too. Horseman was none of his business. He would get back to his research, now. The Charley Tsosie family would be busy, taking ritual sweat baths and preparing for their curing ceremonial. But there was still Ben

Yazzie to be interviewed and Afraid of His Horse to be found.

He flipped through his notebook. Old Lady Gray Rocks had said Ben Yazzie grazed his sheep back on the Lukachukai plateau in the summer. He would go to the subagency office and find out where Yazzie and Afraid of His Horse had their hogans. And then he would get on with his interviewing. He reread the notes he had accumulated at Shoemaker's and from talking to the old woman. Nothing much on Afraid of His Horse, but the Yazzie gossip followed the usual pattern. A man at the trading post had said Yazzie had noticed a coyote following him, and since the coyote was the messenger of the Holy People, Yazzie had accepted this as a sign of danger. And then there had been the usual sounds in the night, interpreted as the witch trying to put corpse powder down the smoke hole in the hogan roof, and the usual dead lambs, and the usual third-hand account in which Yazzie had seen a dog hanging around the flock and, when the dog ran away, it turned into a man.

Leaphorn was returning from his telephone call; McKee returned the notebook to his pocket. He would start with Yazzie this afternoon.

"Well," Leaphorn said, "there went our motive." He sat down. "The colonel said the reward expired two years ago. Their lost bird is obsolete now." He laughed. "In fact, I think he's hoping it stays lost. Sort of embarrassing to lose one like that and then have it turn up after everybody's forgotten about it."

"So we're right back noplace," Takes said.

"I had an idea," McKee said. "Let's say somebody else was hiding out back in that area and they didn't want the Navajo police coming in with a search party. Let's say they decided the way to keep that from happening was to get Horseman out where he would be found."

As he said it, McKee realized it sounded hopelessly farfetched, but Leaphorn's face was grim.

"I thought of that, too," he said. "The autopsy showed he was killed between six and midnight the day I was at Shoemaker's telling everybody we were going in after him if he didn't come out. If we figure it that way, I'm the one who got him killed."

BERGEN MCKEE HONKED THE HORN of his pickup when he crossed the final eroded ridge and saw the hogan of Ben Yazzie on the slope below. It was an unnecessary gesture—since the engine could have been heard long before the horn—but a courteous one. It gave official notice to the hogan that a visitor was coming and McKee guessed it was a universal custom among rural people. His father, he remembered, would never approach another's farmhouse without pausing at the gate to holler, "Hello," until properly acknowledged. Among people who depended more upon distance from neighbors than window blinds to preserve their privacy it was a practical habit.

The place consisted of two octagonal hogans of unpeeled ponderosa logs, a small plank storage shack, and two brush arbors, all built in a cluster of cedar at the edge of a small arroyo. Just over the lip of the arroyo, two sheep pens had been built of cedar poles, with the arroyo bank furnishing one wall. The pens were empty now, and as McKee coasted his truck slowly past them he saw that the hogans were equally deserted.

No cooking pots hung under the brush shelter, no clothing hung out to air, none of the accumulated odds and ends of Navajo living cluttered the area. He climbed out of the truck and sat in the scanty shade, feeling tired and disappointed.

McKee lit a cigarette and considered his next step. In time, he could relocate the Yazzie family through Shoemaker. They traded there and some of Ben Yazzie's silver concho belts were in pawn there. But it might be weeks before any of the Yazzie family, or anyone who knew where he had moved, showed up at the store. That left just two possible sources in the Many Ruins area; Afraid of His Horse, whose sheep camp was supposed to be somewhere north of the canyon, and Charley Tsosie. Tsosie would be occupied at the Enemy Way for at least two days. Sheep camp tended to move with the grazing and would be hard to find. But he would look for Afraid of His Horse.

It was easy to see why Yazzie had built his hogan here. Behind the habitations, the sandstone cliffs of a butte rose abruptly to the north and west—a hundred centuries of talus at its base, then two hundred feet of sheer, smooth reddish stone, with streaks of dark discoloration from seepage, then a softer gray layer of perlite, pocked and carved with blowholes and caves, and above this the overhanging cap of hard, black igneous rock. It gave the hogans shelter from the southwest winds and shade from the late-afternoon sun. To the north and east, the country was a fantastic jumble of colossal erosion dominated by another towering flat-topped butte. All the colors of the spectrum are there, McKee thought. Everything but pure green. What little grass there was was out of sight, hidden in the pockets where soil could collect to hold roots and where runoff from the immensity of rocks could be held and absorbed. He had passed several such grassy places following the wagon trail here. Some, he had noticed, had been heavily grazed by sheep. Most had not. Yazzie must have been badly frightened to move his flock away from grass.

The clouds were building now above the Lukachukai peaks and McKee thought there might be a thunder shower over Many Ruins Canyon by sundown. He and Canfield had camped well up off the floor of the canyon, safe from flash floods, but he had left most of his gear outside the tent. Canfield might be there to take care of things, or he might be out digging into the burial site at one of the ruins; when he was working, Canfield could not be depended upon to notice it was raining.

McKee butted out his cigarette and pushed himself to his feet, noticing the stiffness of his muscles and thinking ruefully that sitting behind a desk was poor conditioning for a field trip. It was then he noticed the smell.

It was a faint smell, borne on a sudden light breeze which had fanned up the arroyo past the hogans. McKee recognized it instantly. The smell of death and decaying flesh. He stood stock-still beside the truck, studying the silent hogans. If the odor had come from them, he would have noticed it earlier. He walked slowly down the slope. Beyond the brush arbor he stopped and stood silently again, listening. Behind the hogans, the arroyo curved sharply around a high outcropping of rock topped by a growth of juniper and piñon. Something behind this ridge was making a sound, a tuneless symphony of low notes which would not have been audible except for the otherwise eerie silence of the place. He walked slowly toward the trees, listening, feeling the tenseness of irrational nervousness. Then the sound explained itself.

A raven flapped out of one of the piñons with a raucous caw. A second later a cloud of the black scavenger birds erupted from the arroyo in an explosion of flapping. McKee stood a moment feeling simultaneously weak from the sudden start and foolish at his skittishness. He trotted to the top of the ridge to see what had attracted the scavengers.

In the arroyo bend, against the perpendicular wall of eroded sandstone, Ben Yazzie had built a third pole sheep corral. In it were bodies of five rams with the heavy dark wool of Merinos. Looking directly down into the pen, McKee could see its floor was blackened in several places where blood had soaked into the sand. He could also see that the ravens, now raising a noisy clamor from the trees fifty yards down the arroyo, had been at work on the throats of the animals. That meant, McKee thought, they had been killed by a wolf, or coyotes, or perhaps by dogs.

It took almost exactly an hour for McKee to cover the nine miles of wagon road from the Yazzie hogans to the mouth of Many Ruins Canyon. Even before he left the place he had concluded that the dead rams, and the cause of their death, probably explained the origin of at least some of the witchcraft gossip. When he found Yazzie he would learn that Yazzie had lost many sheep to this "witch" and that he had decided to abandon his traditional grazing grounds and his hogan because a witch is, after all, more than a man can be expected to cope with.

Yazzie would not be likely to admit, even to himself, that he could not deal with coyotes, or even with an unusually bold wolf of the natural, four-legged variety. When McKee found Afraid of His Horse, he would learn the coyotes were also active this season north of Many Ruins. Taken together, he thought, the two linked incidents would provide the first of the specific examples he needed to support his scapegoat thesis. He felt suddenly optimistic.

It was not until he had turned the truck up the sandy bottom of Many Ruins Canyon that McKee realized that he wasn't sure exactly how a coyote could have gotten into the rams' pen. The pen was built in a rough half-circle extending from the arroyo wall. McKee remembered he had not been able to look over the pen from the arroyo bed. That meant the pole wall was about six feet high—too high for a coyote, or even a wolf, to jump. It occurred to him then that Yazzie must surely have built the corral with coyotes or wolves much in mind and designed it to keep them out. The poles were wired together, top and bottom, and the bases had been buried in the sandy soil. The gate, a narrow door of poles held together by horizontal braces, had also been wired securely shut. McKee remembered this clearly because of the time it had taken him to unfasten the wires. If Yazzie had carelessly left the gate insecurely fastened the night the wolf got in, why would he have bothered to fasten it so securely after the damage was done?

McKee drove slowly along the hard-packed canyon floor. The cloud he had noticed earlier had built higher now and there had been a shower somewhere. The breeze was cool and smelled of wet pine. In places the going was slow and rocky. Here the canyon walls closed in, sheer smooth cliffs which funneled the water of the occasional flash floods into a narrow torrent. But generally the road was smooth and the canyon bottom broadened to a hundred yards or more. The runoff stream here required only a small portion of the canyon floor. Its bed wandered between tumbled hills of rocky debris and there were grass and even a few cottonwoods. Here the sandstone had been softer and more readily destroyed by wind and water. It was in places like these that the Anasazis had built on the talus slopes and high under the overhanging shelter of the canyon walls the cliff houses which gave the canyon its name. McKee passed three of these stone ruins on his way to the campsite without giving them more than a glance. He was, by then, thoroughly disgusted with himself for his oversight at the sheep pens—carelessness which meant he would have to return to the Yazzie hogans and find out exactly how the coyotes had gotten in. He was so immersed in this problem that it was not until he turned his truck up the slope to the campsite that he noticed Canfield's camper truck was gone.

McKee switched off the ignition and sat silently a moment. The exhaust noise echoed up and down the canyon and then died, leaving an utter stillness. The butane campstove was unlit, McKee noticed, and there was no sign that Canfield had started cooking supper, although it was his turn for the chore.

"Where in the devil could he have gone?" McKee said aloud. He was inside the tent when he saw the note, a sheet of typing paper on the folding table weighted by a turquoise frog—Canfield's proof against witches.

> Bergen—
>
> A Navajo dragged himself up here with a leg all swollen up with snakebite. I'm taking him to Teec Nos Pas. Be back tomorrow morning.
>
> *John*

McKee reread the note and stared at the signature; Dr. J. R. Canfield's first name was Jeremy, not John.

10

SANDOVAL SQUATTED beside the sand painting and told Charley Tsosie to put his knees on the knees of the Corn Beetle. He showed him how to lean forward with one hand on each hand of the figure. When Tsosie was just right, Sandoval began singing the part about how the corn beetles called out to tell the Changing Woman that her Hero Twins, the Monster Slayer and the Water Child, were coming home again safely. His voice rose in pitch on the "lo-lo-loo" cry of the beetle, and then fell as he chanted the part about the Hero Twins visiting the sun, and slaughtering the monster Ye-i. It was stifling in the hogan and Tsosie's bare back was glistening with sweat. Even his loin cloth was discolored with it. That was good. The enemy was coming out. And now Sandoval was ready for the next part. He sprinkled a pinch of corn pollen on Tsosie's shoulders and had him stand up and step off the sand painting—carefully so that the pattern wouldn't be disturbed.

Sandoval felt good about the painting. He hadn't done an Enemy Way since just after the foreign war when the young men had come back from the Marines. He was afraid he might have forgotten how to do it. But it had worked out just right. The arroyo sand he had poured out on the hogan floor for the base was a little darker than he liked but he had known it was going to work all right when he poured out the colored sand to make the Encircling Guardian. He had made it in a square as his father had taught him, with the east side open to keep from trapping in any of the Holy People. The Guardian's head was at the north end, with his two arms inward, and his feet were at the south end. His body was four alternating lines of red and yellow sand, and at the opening Sandoval had drawn the elaborate figure of Thunder, wearing the three crooked arrows in his headdress and carrying the crooked arrows under his wings.

"Put Thunder there when you sing for a witching," his father had told him. "His lightning kills the witches."

Sandoval repaired the Corn Beetle deftly, sifting colored sand through his fingers to re-form the lines where Tsosie's hands and knees had pressed. He added a tiny sprinkle of black sand to the single feather in the headdress of Big Fly.

Sandoval stood up then and looked into the pot where he had brewed the medicine. The water was still steaming and the juniper leaves he had mixed into it had turned the solution milky. It looked about right but Sandoval thought it would have been better if he had had a waterproof basket so it could have been done the old way. The People are losing too many of the old ways, Sandoval thought, and he thought it again when he had to tell Tsosie how to sit on the feet of Big Fly, and even had to remind him to face the east. When Sandoval was a boy learning the ways from his father, his father had not had to tell people how to sit. They knew.

Sandoval sang then the chant of the Big Fly, and how he had come to The People to tell them that Black God and the warriors were returning victorious from their war against the Taos Pueblo and how the two girls had been sent by the people to carry food to the war band. This was the last chant before the vomiting and Sandoval was glad of that. It was the second day of the Enemy Way. His voice was hoarse and he was tired and there was still much to be done, much ritual to be completed before this man was free of the witch trouble. His daughter had been right and he should have listened to her. He was eighty-one (or eighty-two by the white man's way of counting) and loaded with too many years to conduct a three-day Sing like an Enemy Way.

Sandoval dipped the ceremonial gourd into the pot, filling it with the hot, milky fluid, and handed the gourd to Tsosie.

"Drink all of it," he ordered, thinking you shouldn't have to tell a man that. And, while Tsosie drank, he sang the last two chants. He refilled the gourd and handed it to Agnes Tsosie and then to the two sons. Let the others get their own, Sandoval thought, and he ducked past the double curtains hung over the hogan doorway to see if the time was right.

Outside the air was cool, almost cold after the closeness of the hogan. The eastern horizon was turning from red to yellow and Sandoval saw it was about the right time. He pulled back the curtains and called to Tsosie.

"Go out there behind the brush shelter," he ordered, "and remember that to make it right you want to vomit out the witching just as you can see the top rim of the sun coming up." When Tsosie came past the curtain, Sandoval handed him a chicken feather.

"Just when the sun is first coming up," Sandoval reminded him. "If the medicine isn't working, stick that feather down your throat."

Sandoval sat on the ground and leaned back on the wall of the hogan, relishing the coolness. He would have about thirty minutes before the vomiting was finished and then one more chant to sing while Tsosie and his family were rubbing the juniper stew on their bodies. Then it would be time for the people from the Stick Receivers to arrive. Sandoval yawned and stretched and looked out across the brush flats where the visitors were camping. Probably four or five hundred, he thought, and there would be more arriving today, mostly women bringing their girls to look for husbands at the Girl Dance tonight, and young men looking for girls, and gambling, and drinking, and trouble. Sandoval had meant to think about the ceremonial, to think just good thoughts and keep in harmony with the event. But he couldn't help thinking how times were changing. Mostly they came in their pickups and cars now. There were dozens of them parked out there and just a few wagons. And that was part of it. The white man's machines made it easy to travel about and people came just to visit and fool around. In the old days there wouldn't have been any drinking and gambling at a ceremonial like this. Sandoval watched a white carryall with the humped buffalo insignia of Law and Order drive up across the flat, and a man in blue jeans and a checked shirt get out of it and talk to a woman starting a cook fire near one of the pickups. The woman pointed in Sandoval's direction and the man came walking toward him.

He was short, with heavy shoulders and a Roman nose, and when he stopped in front of Sandoval and said, "My grandfather, I hope all is well with you," his voice was very clear and distinct. Sandoval, who had noticed lately that most young people mumbled, liked this. He invited the young man to sit beside him.

"I am called Joe Leaphorn," the young man said, "and I work for Law and Order," but after that he talked about other things—about the rains starting early this year, which was good, and about drinking and gambling at the ceremonials, which was bad. Sandoval approved of this, knowing that the policeman would get around to his business in good time and appreciating that here was a young one who knew the old and patient ways.

"There has not been an Enemy Way in this country in a long time," the policeman said, and from the way he said it, Sandoval thought that the time had come for business.

"I guess," the policeman added, "that they had a Star Gazer, or a Hand Trembler come." It was not a question, exactly, but the tone confirmed Sandoval's guess. The policeman was talking business now.

"Hand Tremble," Sandoval said. "They got Jimmy Hudson to come out here and hold his hand over Charley Tsosie and Hudson found out he had been witched. Hudson said the witch blew something on him."

"There was a man lived out here who they called Luis Horseman," the policeman said. "I wonder if he was a witch?"

"I don't know about him."

"I guess the Enemy Way will work even if you don't know who the witch is. But, my grandfather, I am an ignorant man about many things. There were no Singers in my family and I don't know how the Scalp Shooter gets the scalp if you don't know who the witch is."

"They know something about him," Sandoval said. He was enjoying this. Enjoying the young man's finesse and the sparring with words.

"I knew a Hand Trembler once who was wrong. He said a

ghost had got at my uncle's brother's son and they had a Shooting Way Sing for that. Turned out he had tuberculosis."

"Hand trembling's not much good usually," Sandoval agreed. "But this time he got it right. They said this Navajo Wolf came down and bothered Tsosie's sheep in the night and Tsosie saw him. Looked like a big coyote but it was a man. And then after Hudson came and hand trembled, they got one of the outfit who knew some of the chants and they did a blackening on Tsosie and after that he felt better for a little while." Sandoval hadn't liked the remark about tuberculosis. He wondered sourly if the young man believed in witches. The policeman had a white man's haircut. Not the way the Changing Woman had taught. He was looking out across the sagebrush flat now, thinking. Sandoval guessed the next question would tell him something.

"My grandfather, I am using too much of your time today, but I keep wondering about this. I know you have never listened to gossip but I will tell you something you might need to know for your Sing. This man Horseman is dead now, and if he was the witch, you might need to know about it for the way you hold the Sing."

Sandoval wondered why the policeman thought a man named Horseman was the witch. The question would come now. Maybe it would tell him.

"As I said, I am ignorant about many things. I know it would be easier to cure Tsosie if the witch was already dead. But how would be the best way to kill the witch?"

Sandoval turned the question over carefully. "The best way is with clubs."

The policeman was looking at him closely now.

"Would it be a good thing to smother him? To pour sand over his head?"

"I never heard that. Sometimes with clubs and sometimes they shoot them." Sandoval was puzzled. He had never heard of Horseman and he had never heard of a man being killed like that. He saw Tsosie was coming back now from behind the brush shelter and he got to his feet. His bones felt stiff and he was irritated. He suspected the young man had left the Navajo Way and was on the Jesus Road.

"My grandson, I must go back into the hogan now. But now I have a question for you to answer. Tell me if you believe in witching."

"My father taught me about it," the policeman said. "When the water rose in the Fourth World and the Holy People emerged through the hollow reed, First Man and First Woman came up, too. But they forgot witchcraft and so they sent Diving Heron back for it. They told him to bring out 'the way to get rich' so the Holy People wouldn't know what he was getting. And Heron brought it out and gave it to First Man and First Woman and they gave some of it to Snake. But Snake couldn't swallow it so he had to hold it in his mouth. And that's why it kills you when a snake strikes you."

The words were right, Sandoval thought, but he recited them like a lesson.

"You didn't tell me whether you believe it."

The man named Leaphorn smiled very slightly.

"My grandfather," he said, "I have learned to believe in evil."

Lieutenant Joe Leaphorn had returned to his carryall intending to get some sleep. He had left Window Rock a little after midnight to drive to the Tsosie place. But the track over the slick rock country had been even worse than he remembered and the two hours' rest he had hoped to have when he arrived had been used up in low-gear driving over the great waste of eroded slopes west of the Lukachukais. Now he had time. He had learned nothing positive from Sandoval. He had asked around and learned that Billy Nez was not yet here. There was nothing to do but wait. The sun, now rising, would have to be halfway up the sky before it was time for the Encounter Between the Camps and then there would be the exchange of gifts and other ritual before the scalp shooting could be held. He leaned back against the seat, feeling exhausted but wide awake. He found himself again retracing all he knew of Luis Horseman, again examining each assorted fact for some semblance of pattern.

The file on Luis Horseman at Window Rock had been typical of those for the relatively few young men who gave Law and

Order the bulk of its business. A few scattered years of schooling on the Reservation, arrests at Gallup and Farmington and Tuba City for drunk and disorderly, beginning when he was seventeen. Short-term jobs on the Santa Fe railroad maintenance crews and at the strip mine. A marriage into the Minnie Tso family, a fight, a six-month term in the tribal jail for aggravated assault, and then the knifing at Gallup and the stolen car. All that was familiar enough. Too familiar.

"He acted like he had no relatives," Leaphorn thought and grinned wryly at the old-fashioned expression. When he was a boy, it was the worst thing his mother could say about anyone. But then the Navajo Way made the relatives totally responsible for anything one of the family did. Now that was changing and there were more young men like Horseman. Souls lost somewhere between the values of The People and the values of the whites. No good even at crime.

"Not worth killing," Leaphorn thought. But someone had killed him, and gone to considerable trouble in doing it. Why so much trouble? Why had Horseman's body been moved? Why had it been left beside the road when it could so easily have been lost forever, buried under the bank of a thousand arroyos or left for the ravens anywhere in twenty-five thousand empty square miles? And *why* had Horseman been killed? Above all, why had he been killed in that peculiar manner?

The question always brought him back to witchcraft. But all of yesterday afternoon and evening, hours of driving from place to place and hours of frustrating questioning of Hand Tremblers, Listeners, and Singers—all the practitioners who knew the most about magic—had told him nothing. Only that the Hand Trembler who examined Tsosie had learned in his trance that the witch was a stranger and that the cure must be an Enemy Way. It was not, Leaphorn knew, a ceremonial lightly undertaken. It required two Singers, one for the patient and one at the Stick Receiver's camp, and the Scalp Shooter. In some cases there would also be a team of Tail Singers for the Coyote songs, and the seven Black Dancers. Even without the special performers, the Singers and the Scalp Shooter would cost the Tsosie family at least $200 in fees. Dozens of sheep would have to be killed to feed the crowds at both camps, and several hundred dollars more would go for the gift exchanges. Leaphorn thought the Tsosie uncles and cousins who would have to help bear this heavy cost would approve the Sing only if they were sure there had been a witching. And how the devil could they be sure if they hadn't identified the witch?

Leaphorn saw smoke rising from the smoke hole of the ceremonial hogan. Sandoval, who had been burning pine and willow bark by the brush shelter, had collected his ashes and gone into the log building. The fire inside would be to burn sweetgrass, dodgeweed, rock sage, and grama mixed with crow and buzzard feathers, producing a sooty substance to be mixed with the bark ashes and used to blacken the patient for his attack on the enemy scalp. Over the fire, Sandoval would be singing the old chants, the old songs to the Holy People—not prayers of humility or supplication, and not pleas for forgiveness, but songs which sought nothing but to restore man's harmony with all that was elemental.

The sagebrush flats were stirring with activity now. A horse race was being organized behind an array of parked pickups. There will be gambling on that, Leaphorn thought, and maybe a fight. Cook fires were burning everywhere. By the hogans, the women of the family were preparing the ceremonial food which two girls would soon take out to provide the ritual meal for those coming from the other camp. Leaphorn felt a sudden fierce pride in The People. He remembered the Blessing Way held when he and his cousins had left after their last furlough for Camp Pendleton and then for Saigon and Okinawa.

He remembered the sweat bath and the Singer, even older than Sandoval, sprinkling his shoulders with the sacred pollen, and the old, cracked voice rising over the rhythm of the pot drum.

"In the house made of dawn,
in the house made of the evening twilight,
in the house made of dark cloud,
happily may he walk.

In beauty may he walk,
with beauty above him, he walks
with beauty all around him, he walks
with beauty it is finished,
with beauty it is finished."

Leaphorn was sleepy now. The horse race had been run and won by a boy on a pinto, amid much loud laughter. A small bare-bottomed boy had walked by the carryall, smiled shyly at Leaphorn, and relieved himself in the sage nearby. A dozen or more women, with their families fed for the morning, were gossiping raucously around an old and rusty sedan. Three teen-aged girls had led a string of wagon horses down to the spring, watered them, and put them back on the picket rope. The sky was cloudless now but light blue and hazy on the horizons. Later the thunderclouds would be building up and there would be showers—at least over the mountains. Leaphorn saw the two messenger girls lope away carrying the ritual food baskets tied to their saddles. A moment later to the north he heard a flurry of rifle shots and a swarm of horsemen appeared over the rim of the flat, whooping and trailing plumes of dust. Leaphorn climbed stiffly out of the carryall to watch the Encounter Between the Camps. He glanced at his watch. It was 10:12 A.M.

It was late afternoon before the second serenade had been finished and the gifts exchanged. They had been thrown out to the crowd of visitors—first the sacrificial sack of tobacco thrown through the smoke hole of the hogan and caught by a little girl so skinny that it seemed to Leaphorn that she might blow away if the now-gusty breeze caught in her voluminous skirts. The child had run to her mother and been rewarded with a hug, and then three men of Tsosie's family began tossing out the gifts stacked under the brush shelter. There were much scrambling and laughing and some sort of practical joke played on a tall man with a mustache and two long braids hanging down his back. The joke caused an uproar of laughter and knee slapping and even the victim was grinning.

Leaphorn had been talking to a young woman from over near Toadlena and had missed the point of the fun, but he gathered from the shouted remarks that it was bawdy. He had, by now, been talking for almost six hours and had lost all count of the number of people he had questioned. Most of them, like this young Salt Water woman from Toadlena, seemed to know nothing at all about subjects which interested Leaphorn. But he had been able to confirm again beyond any shade of doubt that Horseman had returned to this country after the affair in Gallup and to learn that Billy Nez was at the Stick Carrier's camp. The plump young man with the horn-rimmed glasses had told him that. And Horn Rims had been out looking for a stray mule and had seen Horseman walking along a sheep trail back toward the Lukachukais. Horseman was his second cousin and he had stopped to talk and had given Horseman some tobacco.

"I think his wife had gone off with somebody and he was coming back to his mother's family," Horn Rims had said. He then explained that Luis was a "worthless son of a bitch." In Navajo, the insult came out literally to the effect that Horn Rim's second cousin was a stunted male member of a litter produced by a collie bitch. Navajo is a very precise and unambiguous language and the statement left no question that Horn Rims strongly disapproved of his second cousin. But almost two weeks had passed since Horn Rims had seen Horseman and he had no other information to offer, except that Billy Nez was with the Stick Carrier.

The long afternoon of chatting on the subject of the witch had been even less productive. Leaphorn felt he had fairly well confirmed what Sandoval had implied—that the identity of the witch was not exactly known. Not known, at least, by name, and family, and clan. Leaphorn's instinct told him that several of the Red Forehead clan he had talked to, mostly kinsmen of Tsosies, or members of their extended "outfit," thought of this witch as a specific person, with a specific face, and shape, and habits. It was nothing he could confirm. Leaphorn was a stranger to this clan and he faced the traditional caution of The People where witchcraft was concerned. He had noticed one man slip his hand into his overalls to finger a sacred shape in the medicine bag tied to his loin cloth. The gesture was typical of what he knew others had felt. How did they know that Leaphorn himself was not a witch? And perhaps seeking those who knew of him to make them his future victims? And yet among the garrulous ones, the gossips, there had been some specific details. Several had said the witch was a man, had indicated he was a tall man; all references to him were on foot, none had him riding a horse. The accounts Leaphorn had collected of the witching incidents were conflicting and overlapping and some were obviously wildly imaginative. But he concluded there probably had been at least two or three persons bothered in addition to Tsosie. He had jotted some names in his notebook, but even as he did it he wondered why. The laws he enforced had been taken by the Tribal Council from the white man's laws and the white man did not recognize witchcraft as an offense.

It would become an offense only if some specified crime was involved. There had been a case of extortion once, nothing they had ever proved, but enough circumstantial evidence to indicate a conspiracy between a Star Gazer and a Singer to diagnose witchings and split fees for the curing ceremonial.

Agnes Tsosie came out of the ceremonial hogan now and went to the brush shelter with a crowd of women relatives and the Singer from the Stick Carrier's camp. Leaphorn saw that one of the women was rubbing tallow on her chin and juniper sap on her forehead. Inside the hogan the same thing would be happening to Tsosie and the other male kinfolks who would be taking part in the attack on the scalp. They would be blackened more thoroughly with the ceremonial ashes, as Monster Slayer had been to make himself invisible before his attack on the Ye-i. If Leaphorn's memory of the ceremonial was correct, Agnes Tsosie would only watch the attack, with a male relative serving as her stand-in during the ritual. The Singer wasn't needed during the blackening and Leaphorn saw Old Man Sandoval talking to the Scalp Shooter, who had been sitting all afternoon beside the hogan entrance, guarding a pile of ashes.

Scalp shooting required a professional, although his role in the ceremonial was simply to shoot the scalp with an arrow and sprinkle it with symbolic ashes to signify its death. Leaphorn thought he had seen this man before, helping Singers at other ceremonials. He wondered idly what Sandoval was using for the symbolic scalp. Ideally, it would be something from the witch's person, a clipping of hair if that could be had, something with his blood on it, or some article of clothing which had absorbed his sweat. Since this witch was unidentified, the symbolic scalp would have to be something else. Leaphorn guessed they might use a pouch of sand from a footprint or something else they thought the witch had touched.

If it's hair, Leaphorn thought, it's going to mean that Sandoval and some others have been lying. If it was hair or something bloody he would have to confiscate it after the ceremonial ended. He would have the lab check it with Horseman's and, if it matched, have a messy murder investigation on his hands. But he was fairly sure Sandoval hadn't been lying. Linking Horseman to the witching case had never really made sense, never really been more than a faint possibility where no other possibilities were offered. As far as Leaphorn could pin down the witching gossip, Horseman had hardly returned to the Lukachukais when the incidents started, and at least one had happened before the knifing in Gallup. Besides, the types suspected of witchcraft were always older, usually with a lot of material possessions and a lot of enemies.

There was the sound of chanting from the ceremonial hogan now, and the thudding of the pot drum. Sandoval came through the curtain, followed by Tsosie, two cousins, and the uncle who was representing Agnes Tsosie. Even their loin cloths had been blackened with ashes, and each held in his right hand a raven beak, secured to a juniper stick with yucca and buckskin thongs. The Scalp Shooter picked up his basket of ashes and was walking north-northeast. It was the direction, Leaphorn noted, of the higher central peaks of the Lukachukais. Over the peaks, a tremendous thunderhead was rising, its top boiling in relentless slow motion into the stratosphere, its bottom black with shadow and trailing the first thin curtains of rain.

Sandoval will know his medicine is working, Leaphorn thought. He has called for Thunder to kill the Wolf and Thunder has come to the appointed place. It was interesting that the

Singer from the Stick Carrier's camp had placed the scalp so carefully north-by-northeast of the hogan. That meant they believed the Wolf was now somewhere in that direction.

Leaphorn trailed along with the crowd. The Scalp Shooter had stopped at a dead creosote bush about two hundred yards from the hogan and was sprinkling something under the bush with ash. He stepped aside and Tsosie and his kinsmen poked at the object with their raven bills, killing it with this symbol of contempt. Leaphorn pushed through the crowd. The spectators were silent now and he could hear the attackers muttering, "It is dead. It is dead," each time they struck the symbolic scalp.

The object the crowbills were striking was a high-crowned black hat.

Instantly, Leaphorn correlated this new fact with other information, with the bulky stranger trying on hats in Shoemaker's, with the question of why a worthless hat would be stolen and a valuable silver concho band left behind.

The hat was thoroughly coated with ashes now, but there was still a dark outline against the faded felt, the outline of linked circles where heavy silver conchos had once protected the dye from the sun.

When I look in the hatband, Leaphorn thought, it will be size seven and three-eighths. The Big Navajo was the Navajo Wolf. But why was he the witch? This was why the Hand Trembler and Sandoval had decided to prescribe an Enemy Way. The Navajo Wolf was a man nobody knew. A stranger to the clan and to the entire linked-clan society of the Lukachukai slopes. But what had he done to be singled out for this terrible proscription of The People? Death within the year by his own witchcraft—turned against him by the medicine of the Enemy Way. Or, Leaphorn thought grimly, death much sooner if the Tsosies or the Nez family happen to catch him.

The high slopes of the Lukachukais were obscured now by the darkness of the cloud. Light from the setting sun glittered from the strata of ice crystals forming in the thin, frigid air at its upper levels. Deep within it, the structure of the cloud was lit by a sudden flare of sheet lightning. And then there was a single lightning bolt, an abrupt vivid streak of white light pulsing an electric moment against the black of the rain, connecting cloud and mountain slope.

If the witch was there, he's dead enough, Leaphorn thought. And he couldn't blame himself for that. Not the way he would blame himself if The People found the Wolf before he did and executed this sentence of death.

THERE HAD BEEN intermittent thunder for several minutes. But, even so prepared, McKee had been startled by the sudden brighter-than-day flash of the lightning bolt. The explosion of thunder had followed it almost instantly, setting off a racketing barrage of echoes cannonading from the canyon cliffs. The light breeze, shifting suddenly down canyon, carried the faintly acrid smell of ozone released by the electrical charge and the perfume of dampened dust and rain-struck grass.

It filled McKee's nostrils with nostalgia. There was none of the odor of steaming asphalt, dissolving dirt, and exhaust fumes trapped in humidity which marked an urban rain. It was the smell of a country childhood, all the more evocative because it had been forgotten. And for the moment McKee dismissed the irritation of J. R. Canfield and reveled mentally in happy recollections of Nebraska, of cornfields, and of days when dreams still seemed real and plausible. Then a splatter of rain hit; big, cold, high-velocity drops sent him running to the tent for his raincoat and back out into the sudden shower to rescue the eggs frying on the butane stove and the bedrolls spread out on the sand beside a jumble of boulders.

When he reached them the rain stopped as abruptly as it had begun. McKee dropped Canfield's blankets and cautiously inspected the slice of sky visible above the canyon. Up canyon it was blue-black, with a continuing intermittent rumble of thunder. Directly overhead, the clouds were a mixture of gray and white. Down canyon to the south and east there was the dark blue of open sky and, nearer the horizon, the violent reds and yellows of the setting sun. The breeze had shifted back to the southwest now and he saw the rain was drifting across the canyon higher in the mountains. Only the trailing edge of it had touched here.

McKee decided it would be safe to leave the bedrolls out. He walked back to the butane cooker, forked an egg onto a piece of bread and folded it into a sandwich. The sunset now was flooding the canyon with eerie rose light, which made the eroded sandstone and granite of the cliff seem to glow. McKee heard the water then, a small sound, moving down the canyon floor below him. The rain had been little more than a heavy sprinkle here but northwestward on the mesa it had been heavy enough to send runoff down the network of washes which fed Many Ruins Canyon. It would have to rise into a torrent eight or ten feet deep before it topped the high mound of talus where the camp was and McKee estimated the stream, now spreading across the flat sand on the canyon bed below him, was no more than six inches deep. It was muddy, carrying a burden of sticks, pine needles, and assorted debris, but it wouldn't get much deeper unless the rain upstream turned into something like a cloudburst. If that happened, it might be a little tough driving on the canyon bottom tomorrow. That turned McKee's thoughts again to Canfield.

Ever since his return to the camp he had alternated between uneasy worry that some inconceivable something had led Canfield to sign a false name to his note, irritation at himself for such foolishness, and then irritation at Canfield for causing this uneasiness. He was all the more irked by the thought that, when Canfield returned and explained the signature had been inspired by some ridiculous Canfieldian whim, the whole affair would seem too asinine and trivial for complaint.

"Silly bastard," McKee muttered. He folded the third egg into a sandwich, poured himself a mug of coffee, and scrubbed out the frying pan with sand. By now the light in the canyon had faded from rose to dusky red and McKee's mood had shifted with it, back to irritation with himself for being nervous.

It was about ten when he finished going through his accumulation of notes in the tent and planning his activities for the next day. He would have to stay in camp at least until Canfield returned because tomorrow Miss Leon was supposed to arrive. If Canfield was finding anything interesting in his digging, he wouldn't want to stop—and someone should take the girl up into the labyrinth of canyons to try to locate the van truck. It might, or might not, belong to her electrical engineer, but it shouldn't be too hard to find. Not if it was still parked in Hard Goods Canyon, and not if, as Old Woman Gray Rocks had said, the canyon ran into Many Ruins nine miles up from the mouth. That would make it only about four miles up from their camp.

He turned off the butane lantern and stood at the tent flap a moment, letting his eyes adjust to the night before walking back to the bedrolls. He felt tired now, ready for sleep. He left his boots beside the bedding, rolled his shirt in his trousers for a pillow and slid into the blankets. The storm cloud had drifted away and he heard, far to the northeast, the faint suggestion of thunder. His side of the canyon was in total darkness but the top of the sheer cliff on the west side was tinged now by the dim yellow light of the rising moon. It would be about three-quarters full tonight, McKee thought, and he felt a sudden inexpressible loneliness, a loneliness almost as intense as in a dream he sometimes had. In the dream he floated in a great airy blackness, wanting to shout, but remembering—dream fashion—that he had shouted before and his voice had been lost in an infinite echoless distance. Remembering this would sadden him because it told him there was no one anywhere but him. When he had this dream, sometimes when he was overtired and depressed, it would awaken him and he would sit on the side of his bed and smoke a cigarette, and sometimes two or three.

A whippoorwill sounded its whistling call far down the canyon and was answered by an echo. And then it was eerily silent.

Directly overhead McKee picked out the stars of the Pleiades—six in two parallel rows and the seventh trailing to close the double line. From these, McKee remembered, the seven

Hard Flint Boys of the Navajo myth had descended to follow Monster Slayer on his heroic odyssey among the evil things. And to spread their own mischief among the Dinee. And to receive ceremonial offerings of cornmeal every spring from a thousand sheepherders in a thousand little sacred shrines on a thousand mesas and mountains across the Reservation. McKee located two stars, each surrounded by the hazy light of a nebula, which represented the Hard Flint Woman and a contestant in the Bounding Stick Game. He couldn't dredge up the name of the other Holy Person but he vaguely remembered that in the myth there was an argument over the outcome and a solution based on the trickery so inevitable in both Greek and Navajo myth. Far up the west rim of the canyon, a coyote yipped twice, and then poured out its soul in a full-throated bay. The sound seemed to float down from the stars, the voice of some primeval hound drifting infinite sorrow across the sky.

It might be my coyote, McKee thought, the one that got into Yazzie's ram pen. He would go back tomorrow to find out how, if his guide duties with Miss Leon allowed. He shifted his weight on the packed sand and felt suddenly less sure that he would find any way a coyote could have invaded that tight little enclosure. In this silent darkness mystery seemed suddenly natural, almost rational. Down the canyon the whippoorwill called again and then there was the odd, rasping cry of a saw-whet owl, sounding, McKee thought, like an ogre filing off his chains. He reached for his cigarette pack, decided against it, and thought again of the note Canfield had left, and why Jeremy Robert Canfield, whose first name was part of a private anthropology faculty joke, would sign "John" to this note. He drifted uneasily on the margin of sleep.

The sound jerked him abruptly up from the blankets, wide awake, staring across the canyon. It had been the clatter of a falling pebble, bouncing down the eroded cliff and dislodging a small shower of other pebbles. The residue of faint echoes lingered a second in the stillness and then faded. McKee sat stock-still, listening, feeling the tenseness of muscle fiber flooded with adrenalin and the taste of primitive fear in his mouth. He slid his legs out of the bedroll and slipped them into his trousers, put on his boots, picked up his shirt, and stood. The moon had risen halfway up the sky and the west wall of the canyon was flooded now with pale light. McKee stood in a rigid crouch, listening, studying the worn outcroppings of sandstone from which the sound had come. There was nothing but the silence. A sinister shape half hidden by juniper at the foot of the outcrop became, as McKee's eyes better adjusted to the half light, an oddly eroded boulder. McKee relaxed slightly, feeling the panic leaving him. It could have been an animal. And, as he thought this, it seemed ridiculous to think it could be anything but an animal—perhaps a night-prowling porcupine. He stood there, feeling suddenly slightly weak and very foolish. But still there was something primitive within his mind signaling danger and urging caution. Five black rams with bloody throats and the wrong name signed to a simple note. A burrowing owl glided slowly down the moonlit side of the canyon floor, scouting for night-feeding kangaroo rats. It swerved suddenly away from the outcrop, flapped its wings wildly, and disappeared in the darkness down canyon from McKee. And, as it disappeared, his fear returned. Something had startled the owl. It would not have been frightened by anything small.

He moved cautiously away from the bedroll, farther back into the darkness up the talus slope toward the east cliff, taking each step carefully, climbing slowly over the smaller boulders, carefully skirting the larger ones. In a pocket of water-cut rock directly under the overhanging cliff he stopped and turned back to look behind him, surprised that he was panting from the brief exertion and fighting to keep his breathing silent.

The light of the climbing moon had moved halfway across the canyon floor. Nothing stirred. The canyon was a crevice of immense, motionless, brooding quiet. McKee studied the outcropping carefully, shifted his eyes slowly down canyon, examining every shape under the flat, yellow light, and then examining every shadow. He felt the rough surface of the rock cutting into his knees and started to shift his weight, but again there was the primal urging to caution. It was then he caught the motion.

Something in the black shadow behind the outcrop had moved slightly. McKee stared until his eyes burned, rubbed them, and then stared again. And he saw the dog's head. It inched slowly out of the shadow into the moonlight. First a muzzle and then the head, its ears upright and—McKee strained his eyes until he was sure—its mouth hanging unnaturally open. The head remained there, motionless. McKee stared, every muscle rigid. The dog's head seemed unnaturally high—unless, McKee thought, it was standing on some sort of ledge behind the outcropping. And then there was motion again.

The dog became a man. A large man with the skin of a wolf over his shoulders, its empty skull atop his own head. He moved across a patch of moonlight and disappeared behind a growth of bushes at a foot of the west cliff talus. When the shape reappeared a moment later, McKee thought for a split second that his eyes had been deceiving him—that it actually was a wolf. But it was a man, running in a crouch across the damp sand of the canyon bottom, running with silent swiftness directly toward McKee's tent. The man held something in his right hand, something perhaps a foot long, metal which reflected the moonlight. It was a long-barreled pistol, with an ammunition clip jutting down in front of the trigger. A machine pistol.

The shape disappeared again, out of sight behind the talus slope on McKee's side of the canyon. McKee bent and felt around his feet for a rock, selected one about the size of a softball. When he raised his head, the figure was back in view—in the shadow but silhouetted now against the moonlit cliff. McKee gripped the stone and watched. The panic was gone now, replaced by a kind of grim anger. The figure was at the tent, standing motionless. Listening, McKee thought. Listening and not hearing a damned thing and wondering about it. Then the shape was gone, out of sight behind the tent. McKee had almost decided the man had somehow slipped away when he saw him again, by the bedrolls now, but brush and boulders obscured the area and he couldn't see what the man was doing. He studied the cliff wall on both sides of his pocket. He could climb out of this sheltered place by working his way past a huge block of sandstone just beside him. He could probably make his way down canyon without being in view from the camp.

But if he comes this way, McKee thought, this might be the best place to face him. I could probably knock him down with my rock before he saw me. Unless he has a flashlight as well as the gun. Then there wouldn't be much chance.

And, while he thought this, the utter irrationality of it all occurred to him. It was unreal. Like some crazy childhood nightmare.

But the man was there, real enough, back by the tent now and no longer seeming to make any effort at concealment. He raised the hood of McKee's truck and McKee had a sudden wild hope that he would start it, climb in, and race away, nothing more than a thief. Instead, he closed the hood and walked back and into the tent. A moment later a spot of light showed through the canvas. The flashlight beam shifted, held steady, shifted again, and then stopped. He's looking through my papers, McKee thought. He wondered what the man would make of his notes on the witchcraft interviews. And he had a sudden impulse to walk into the tent, confront the man, and demand to know what the devil he was doing. Then the light snapped off and the man appeared again in front of the tent, staring almost directly toward McKee's hiding place. McKee felt the impulse die.

"Doctor McKee?"

The man called in an even, sonorous voice, not much above a conversational tone. But in the stillness the sound seemed obscenely loud. And the canyon walls said "Kee-Kee-Kee" in a receding echo of his name.

"Bergen McKee," the voice repeated. "I need to . . ." The echoes drowned the rest of it. "I need to talk to you about Doctor Canfield," the voice said. And the man stood silent until the echoes died again. Who is he? McKee wondered. The Navajo bitten by the snake? Or was this man a Navajo? He couldn't tell anything from the voice. There was no trace of accent. But then educated Navajos rarely had accents, except for sometimes dropping the "th" sound.

The man stood silent a long moment, staring up, and then down, the canyon. Listening. And he won't hear a damn thing, McKee thought. Not from me.

"John's hurt," the voice said. The voice was louder now

and the cliffs bounced the "hurt" between them until it blended into a single note. "He needs help."

John. John, not Jeremy. The man standing down there in the darkness, the man with the wolf skin, the man who had stalked him like an animal, had some connection with Canfield's note, with Canfield's peculiar signature.

"I should go down there," McKee thought, but he remembered the thing that had reflected the moonlight in this man's hand as he had crossed the canyon floor. Why the pistol? Why the dog skin? And he leaned motionless against the boulder, feeling the rough coldness of the rock against his legs and the cold sweat on his palms, knowing he would go nowhere near this man. Not alone in this dark canyon. Not without a weapon.

And then the man was gone. Suddenly he was no longer beside the tent. And then McKee saw him, trotting diagonally across the canyon bottom, the wolf skin dangling from one hand.

McKee relaxed against the boulder, suddenly aware that he was cold and that his shirt was wet with sweat. Far down canyon the saw-whet owl made its strange, rasping cry. Signaling a kill, McKee thought.

IT WAS WELL AFTER MIDNIGHT when Leaphorn finally learned who had collected the scalp for the ceremonial. He had talked until he was tired of talking—tired and frustrated and irritated at his close-mouthed people. And then a girl had told him, proudly and without prompting, that Billy Nez—whom he still hadn't located—had stolen the hat. Billy Nez had tracked the truck of the witch and had watched from hiding until he finally had the opportunity. Leaphorn had been captured by the girl, a plump and pretty youngster wearing a T-shirt with "Chinle High School" printed across it, during the Girl Dance. She had grabbed his arm while he was talking to an old man.

"Come on, Blue Policeman," she had said. "I've got you and you've got to dance." And Leaphorn had let her tow him to the great fire, because he had already decided the old man would tell him nothing, and because it was the tradition at this ceremonial. He would dance with the girl a little, and after a while he would pay her the proper ransom for his release, and then he would continue wandering through the crowd asking for Billy Nez but no longer really expecting to find him here.

Blue Policeman, he thought. A hell of a lot of good it does to leave your uniform at home. There's not an adult at this Sing by now who doesn't know I'm the law.

The chant rose in the firelight. Ya Ha He Ya Na He. Rising and falling with the rhythm of the pot drums. And then the words. "Lie closer to me," the singers chanted. "Bring your sheepskin and we will go into the darkness. What are you going to do out there?" Leaphorn glanced at his partner, curious whether the ribald suggestion of the song would embarrass a boarding-school girl. She danced gracefully, gripping his left arm with her right.

"I wonder why Hosteen Policeman looks at me," she said. "Are you going to arrest me?"

Leaphorn returned the smile. "I would if I thought you could tell me anything."

"Who are you after? What do you want to know?"

"I'd like to know all about a witch," Leaphorn said.

"I'll bet you don't even believe in witches."

"I believe in a witch who used to wear a big black Stetson hat until somebody got it away from him."

"That was Billy Nez," the girl had said. There it was, as simple as that. Billy Nez was around here somewhere (the girl glanced over her shoulder into the darkness, frowning).

"I'd like to talk to Hosteen Nez," Leaphorn said.

"So would I. I caught him and made him dance and he just paid me twenty-five cents. And he said he'd let me catch him again." The girl frowned into the darkness again and then looked up at Leaphorn. "But he's no Hosteen yet. He's just a boy."

"How old is just a boy?"

"He's just sixteen."

And you're about fifteen, Leaphorn thought, and if Billy Nez isn't careful his clan is going to lose itself a boy, and a bride's price to boot.

"Just a boy," Leaphorn said.

"But he's the one who got the hat. Billy was the Scalp Carrier. He followed that man's pickup, and he watched from where the witch couldn't see him, and when he went away Billy was the one who got the scalp."

And that seemed to be exactly all the girl knew about it. She knew Nez was Red Forehead, and that he raised sheep with his uncle over on Cottonwood Flats near Chinle, and that he was wearing a red-checked shirt and a red baseball cap, and some of the other things that fifteen-year-old girls learn about sixteen-year-old boys. And then suddenly the pot drums and the chanting stopped, and there were much haggling and laughing and banter as the women collected their ransom fees. Leaphorn gave the girl a dollar.

"That's the most I got all night," she said. But she wouldn't come with him to point out Nez.

Leaphorn spotted the Carrier of the Scalp a half hour later. The Sway Dancing had started then and he saw Nez in his ball cap among the line of dancers from the Stick Receiver's camp. The rhythm was faster now and the rising, falling sound of the voices was as old as the earth. But the words were about a rocket.

"Belacani's rocket fell on the mesa," the singers chanted.

And then the line of men from the patient's camp began the rhythmic swaying and the words changed.

"Belacani's rocket start the brush burning."

Track down the man who started that one, Leaphorn thought, and you'd find the missile the Army spent half the winter looking for four years ago. Trouble was it would be easier to find the missile than the song writer.

But he had, at least, found Billy Nez, and now the dancing was over for a time and Nez was walking toward him, talking to a younger boy who, Leaphorn guessed, would be his cousin.

"My nephew," Leaphorn said, "I would like to talk for a moment with the man who carried the scalp."

Billy Nez looked surprised and pleased. But, Leaphorn noticed, he also moved his hand toward his shirt front to touch his medicine pouch with its gallstone proof against witches. One was careful of strangers at an Enemy Way.

"I myself am a policeman," Leaphorn said. "It is sometimes my business to track people and it would be good for me to hear how you tracked this Wolf."

The boy looked down. "It was nothing very much," he said. And then, remembering his manners, added, "My uncle." For the first time in a long day, Leaphorn felt he was handling someone exactly right.

"And yet nobody else got the scalp for this Sing. It was you, Hosteen Nez."

"Billy tracked him three days," the younger boy said. He grinned at Leaphorn. "I'm Billy's uncle's son."

"We might sit here by this pickup and smoke," Leaphorn

said. He took a cigarette and handed the pack to the younger boy. And when the pack came to Billy Nez he took a cigarette, and lit it, and told Joe Leaphorn everything he knew. And he started, as Leaphorn knew he would start, from the beginning.

The witch had first come around the summer hogans of his uncle at mid-spring not long after his uncle's family had driven the sheep up from the winter grazing in the Chinle Valley to the summer range in the Lukachukais.

Two days after they had settled down, he and the two boys were driving the sheep up there on the plateau. His uncle was driving his own sheep and the boys were driving his uncle's wife's sheep. And they saw this truck coming across this arroyo there. It wasn't really a truck. More like a jeep, only bigger and with a cloth top on it.

"Was it a Land-Rover?" Leaphorn said.

"I don't know," Billy Nez said. "I never saw another one like it. It was gray."

The Big Navajo had left Shoemaker's store in a Land-Rover, Leaphorn thought. Gray and hard to see and I wonder if that's a coincidence.

The truck had stopped at first and his uncle had seen the driver looking at them. And then it drove up and the man asked my uncle where he was taking those sheep and how long he was going to keep them in that high country. His uncle had said all summer and the man had asked if he didn't know there was a witch cave up in that country and a bunch of wolves up there that got after people that came into their territory.

Billy Nez took a long drag on his cigarette, inhaled, and then blew out the smoke.

"What'd your uncle say?" Leaphorn asked, and was instantly irked with himself for his impatience.

"He thought it was kind of funny this Nakai knowing so much about Navajo Wolves."

Leaphorn looked at Billy Nez sharply.

"Why Nakai? Did your uncle think this man was a Mexican?"

"Nakai, or Belacana, or something," Billy Nez said. "Anyhow my uncle said he didn't talk much good Navajo. Wanted to talk in English and my uncle don't talk that much, so he tried to talk in Spanish and this man didn't know that good." Billy Nez paused. "So I guess he wasn't a Nakai, come to think of it. Maybe a Ute or something."

So, Leaphorn thought. No doubt now why the Hand Tremble had prescribed the Enemy Way instead of the Prostitution Way. Here's why they thought the witch was a foreigner—an enemy ghost to be exorcised. But the man in the Land-Rover, the man with the black hat, had been a Navajo. Leaphorn was certain of it.

Anyway, Billy Nez was saying, his uncle had said he didn't pay much attention to witches when he needed grass for his sheep and the sheep of his wife, and the man had driven away. But after that his uncle had known something was going to be wrong.

The first week they were back in the high country a young coyote had trailed his uncle, followed his horse all the way across the mesa one morning. That was the Coyote People telling him to watch out. The Coyote People caused a lot of trouble, Billy Nez said, but they were good about warning people.

A little bit after that, at night, his uncle heard the Wolf on top of his hogan. Some dirt had fallen down from the roof on the east side of the hogan (and now, Leaphorn thought, the other three compass points), and then on the south side, and then on the west side and then some dirt fell down on the north side. And then his uncle had known the Wolf would be looking down the smoke hole to see where they were and to blow some corpse powder down on them. But the uncle of Billy Nez was not afraid of a Wolf. He ran outside the hogan to chase him away but he didn't see anything for sure. Maybe he saw a dog running away but he wasn't sure.

"That would have been about the first part of May?" Leaphorn asked.

"A little bit before that," Billy Nez said. "The moon was in its last quarter two cycles so it would have been in the last part of April."

Almost two weeks before Luis Horseman came home to die.

But the second time his uncle had seen the Wolf. It was daylight then, sundown but still daylight, and his uncle was bringing some of the sheep in for watering and he had thought something was watching him maybe. He looked up to the rim of the mesa and there was this witch standing there, looking at him. He was up on the mesa rim on the rocks with this wolf skin on him, but his uncle could tell it was a man. His uncle had said this witch had stood there looking at him and then made some medicine with his hands. His uncle had thought he might be calling to the other witches to come out of their cave and help. His uncle drove the sheep down to the hogan then and they sprinkled pollen and sang the songs from the Night Way. The songs against witches.

"What day was that?"

"That was three or four days after the first time on the roof," Billy Nez said. "I think it was three days."

After that, his uncle had taken his .30-30 with him when he herded the sheep and he had left one of the boys at the hogan with his wife, in case the witch would come there while he was gone. And he thought he had better track this Wolf and kill it. He went up on the mesa where he had seen the Wolf, and he found tracks there. Some of them were big boot tracks and some were like a big dog. It was still the Season When the Thunder Sleeps and the ground was damp from the snow thaw and tracking was easy.

"My father is a brave man," said the cousin of Billy Nez, and was instantly embarrassed by his rudeness. They smoked a moment in silence to let the incident pass. Then Billy Nez resumed his story.

Under the other slope of the mesa, his uncle had found tire tracks. The Wolf had driven up there and left his truck and then come back to it and driven away. After that the Wolf had started bothering the livestock. That first night, his uncle had heard the horses whinnying like they were scared and then he heard one of them screaming, and when he ran out there to where he had them penned, two of them had their tendons cut and his uncle had to kill them.

Leaphorn raised a hand in interruption. This surprised him. He had expected nothing so concrete.

"My nephew, did you see these horses?"

"I saw them. The Wolf must have done it with a hand ax.

He cut both of the rear tendons on the mare and he hit the colt so hard that it broke his legbone."

Good enough, thought Leaphorn. I've got another reason for finding this son of a bitch. The Tribal Council had a law against cruelty to animals. Besides, Leaphorn didn't like a man who would do that to a horse.

After that, Billy Nez continued, it was the sheep. His uncle lay out all night with his .30-30 but the Wolf didn't come back any more for a while. And then the moon came and one white night he heard some rifle shots and he ran out there and the witch had been shooting into where the flock was sleeping. Three of them were dead and he had to butcher some of the others that were hurt.

"After that my uncle talked about it with my aunt and they decided to bring those sheep out of there. They didn't think they could catch that witch and he might get them. So they came on down here."

Leaphorn passed around his cigarette pack again.

"When was it he shot those sheep?"

"Night just like this," Billy Nez said. He looked at the moon, which was two nights short of full phase.

"Be about twenty-six, twenty-seven days ago. One moon back."

"And when did you go after the witch?" Leaphorn asked.

"Well, my uncle's father came over to our place with some of the other men of the outfit and they talked it over. And then they got that Hand Trembler in and he sang the hand-trembling songs and held his arm out over my uncle and it shook and shook. He said the reasons he'd been having these dreams was this foreign witch was bothering him."

Billy Nez took another deep drag on the cigarette.

"Or maybe it was the ghost of the witch. Anyway, after that they tried it out by having a blackening. My uncle slept that night with the ashes on him and he didn't have any dreams, so they decided the Hand Trembler was right. The ghost couldn't find him with those ashes on him. So the next night they got together again there in our hogan and decided they ought to find a Singer who knew the Enemy Way."

Billy Nez paused again.

"And my cousin told them he would find the Wolf and carry the scalp," the younger boy said.

"My grandfather didn't want me to do it. He said it was supposed to be an older man who got the scalp. Somebody who'd had an Enemy Way sung over him. But finally they said I could do it."

"You know the Tracking Bear Song?" Leaphorn asked.

"My grandfather taught me that," Billy Nez said. He laid his cigarette on the ground and chanted softly:

"In shoes of dark flint I track the Ute warrior,
In armor of flint I slay the Ute enemy.
With Big Snake Man I go, tracking the warrior.
I usually slay the Ute men and slay the Ute women.
Tracking Bear I go, taking Ute scalps."

Billy Nez stopped, suddenly embarrassed, and recovered his cigarette.

The three sat in silence a long moment. The chanting had started at the fire again, another sway dance. This time the song was old, a pattern of rhythmic monosyllables which had lost coherent meaning somewhere in time.

"How did you know where to look for the scalp?" Leaphorn asked.

That had taken time, Billy Nez said. His uncle had drawn for him the way the tracks of that truck had looked.

"Like this," Billy Nez said. He smoothed the bare earth with his palm and opened his pocket knife.

"The front tires had a track like this." He drew the tread pattern in the earth. "And the outside of the track, it wasn't as deep. Like he needed a front end job on his truck. Tires wearing on the outside. And the back tires were like this." He drew the pattern of high-traction mud treads. "Cut real deep. I thought I could find them."

"And I guess you did," Leaphorn said.

It had taken Billy Nez almost a week. Three hard days on a horse before he had picked up the first of the tracks—old ones, already almost erased by the wind. On the fourth day, he had caught a glimpse of the Land-Rover. He had been on Talking

Rock Mesa and had seen it moving down a wash into the Kam Bimghi Valley. After sunrise the next day he found where the witch was working—clearing a track for his truck up the sloping backside of Ceniza Mesa. And, later that day, he had made his scalp coup.

"I left my horse hobbled up there on top," Billy Nez said, "and I hid out there in the rocks, down near where he was working. He was rolling those rocks out of the way and cutting brush to clear the track. Finally he stopped a while and sat down under a piñon there and ate some stuff and some canned peaches and threw away the can. I thought maybe I'd get that can he'd ate out of for the scalp but that wouldn't be very good and so later on I got the hat."

"Tell how you got it," the younger cousin urged.

"Well, along later in the afternoon the clouds built up the way they do and it got shady and the wind got up. He was wrestling with those rocks and his hat kept blowing off. So the next time he moved that truck farther up the slope, he left that hat there on the seat of the truck. When he was working again, I slipped up there and got it."

"And took off the hatband and left it behind," Leaphorn said.

Billy Nez looked surprised. "Yeh. It was silver conchos."

"There was a rifle there in the truck," younger cousin said.

"Think it was a Remington," Billy Nez said. "Had a long barrel and a telescopic sight. Looked like a .30-06 deer rifle."

"Anything else in there?" Leaphorn asked.

"There was a map folded up there over the dashboard. I think it was a map. And a paper sack on the seat. Maybe part of his lunch. And there was a set of pulleys in the back." The boy paused, thinking.

"A block-and-tackle?" Leaphorn suggested.

"Yes," Nez said.

"Anything else?"

"No. I didn't look much. Just got that hat and then I thought I didn't want to steal that concho band so I took it off. Tied a yucca thong to that hat and tied it on the scalp stick like my grandfather said to do with the scalp—that's so you aren't handling it with your hands so much. And then when I got back up on the mesa away from there, I sang the Tracking Bear Song and used pollen and rode on back to the hogan."

Leaphorn gave the boys each a third cigarette.

"And now," he said, "I want you to tell me about your brother. I want you to tell about Luis Horseman." He tried to read Billy Nez's face. Was it surprise, or fear, or anger? The boy looked at the tip of the cigarette, and then took a long drag and blew out the smoke.

"I heard Law and Order already found him," Billy Nez said. "I heard Luis Horseman is dead."

"We found his body," Leaphorn said. "He was way down by Ganado when we found him, a hundred miles south of here. We don't know how he got there."

"I don't know," Billy Nez said. "He was staying up there on the plateau between Many Ruins and Horse Fell canyons."

"And you went up there to tell him that he didn't kill that Nakai at Gallup—that the man got well and he should come in and talk to us about it," Leaphorn said. "You did that, didn't you?" His voice was gentle.

"I heard you telling that at Shoemaker's," Billy Nez said. "And I thought you were right. It would be better if Luis Horseman went in to Window Rock and didn't try to run and hide any more. But when I went up there to tell him and take him some food he was gone."

"That was four days ago," Leaphorn said. "Tuesday. The day I was at Shoemaker's?"

Nez nodded.

"What time did you go? What time did you get there?"

"I waited until it got dark," Billy Nez said. "Luis Horseman told me to do that so nobody would see. But he wasn't there. I got there maybe two hours after midnight and he was gone."

"Blue Policeman," the smaller boy said, "my cousin found something strange there."

"I looked around where he was camping in some rocks and I thought he had taken everything he had with him," Billy Nez said. "And then I looked around some more and I found that the food he had left was buried there—just covered up with sand."

"Were the ashes covered up, too?" Leaphorn asked.

"Covered up with sand and smoothed over."

"Did you see anything else?"

"It was dark. I rode on down into the Chinle Valley and slept until it was light and then I went back up again. Then I found those tracks again."

"The tracks like the Land-Rover left?"

"Same tracks," Billy Nez said. "Up there on the mesa, maybe a half mile from where Luis Horseman was." He paused. "My brother would have taken that food with him. He wouldn't have spoiled it like that."

They sat, smoking in silence.

"I told Luis Horseman that wasn't a good place to stay. Too many houses of the Old People down in those canyons," Billy Nez said. "Too many ghosts. Nobody likes that country but witches."

The boy was silent again, staring at the fire where the sway dancers were again being moved by the drums in two rhythmic lines.

"I think that Wolf killed my brother," Billy Nez said. His tone was flat, emotionless.

"Listen, my nephew," Leaphorn said. "Listen to me. I think you might be right. But you might be wrong." Leaphorn paused. It would do no good at all to warn this boy against any danger. "This is our business now—Law and Order business. If you hunt this man you would hunt him to kill him and that would be wrong. That man might not be the one who did it. Don't hunt him."

Billy Nez got up and dusted off his jeans.

"I must go now, my uncle, and dance with Chinle High School Girl. Go in beauty."

"Go in beauty," Leaphorn said.

He sat against the truck, thinking about it, sorting out what he knew.

The Dinee, at least the Dinee who lived in the district east of Chinle, thought the Big Navajo was their witch. Billy Nez had found his Land-Rover tracks near Horseman's camp. But they might be old tracks, and they would be gone now. It had rained tonight on the Lukachukai slopes. And the witch, whoever he was, was a violent witch, or a cruel one—a man who would cripple horses with an ax. That was all he knew. That, and the certainty that Billy Nez would be hunting the man who drove the Land-Rover, a danger to the man if he was innocent and a danger to the boy if he was not.

The first sign of paleness was showing at the eastern edge of the night. Soon Charley Tsosie and his wife and sons would come out of the ceremonial hogan. Sandoval would sing the four First Songs and the Coyote Song, and the Tsosies would inhale the required four deep breaths of the air of the Dawn People. Then Charley Tsosie and his people would be cured and the witch who drove the gray Land-Rover and who might, or might not, have maimed two horses with an ax would have his witchcraft turned against him. The Origin Myth gave him one year to live. One year, if the Tsosies or Billy Nez didn't find him first.

IT WAS A LITTLE MORE than an hour after daylight when McKee heard the car puttering up the canyon, its exhaust leaving a faint wake of echoes from the cliffs. Canfield had said Miss Leon would be driving a Volkswagen and this sounded like one. It certainly didn't have the throaty roar of whatever it was the man who had stalked him had driven away in the night before.

McKee moved out of the thicket of willows where he had been lying, and prepared himself for a moment he had been dreading. If the car which would soon round the corner ahead was a Volkswagen he would wave it to a stop. If the driver was Miss Leon, she would be confronted with the startling spectacle of a large man with a badly torn shirt, a bruised and swollen face, and an injured hand, who would tell her a wild, irrational story of being spooked out of his bed by a werewolf, and who would order her to turn around and flee with him out of the canyon. McKee had thought of this impending confrontation for hours, ever since it had occurred to him that he couldn't simply escape from this canyon—and whatever crazy danger it held—and go for help to find Canfield. To do so would be to leave Miss Leon to face whatever he was running from.

The car which came around the cliff into view was a baby-blue Volkswagen sedan, driven by a young woman with dark hair. McKee trotted down the slope onto the hard-packed sand, signaling it to stop.

The Volkswagen slowed. McKee saw the woman staring at

him, her eyes very large. And then, suddenly, she spun the wheel, the rear wheels spurted sand, and the car roared past him.

"Miss Leon," McKee screamed. "Stop."

The Volkswagen stopped.

McKee ran to it and pulled at the door. It was locked. He looked through the window. The girl sat huddled against the door on the driver's side, frightened eyes in a pale face.

McKee cursed inwardly, tried to pull his gaping shirt together, and tapped on the window.

"Miss Leon," he said. "I'm Bergen McKee. I was supposed to meet you here. Dr. Canfield and I."

The girl, obviously, couldn't understand him. McKee repeated it all, shouting this time, conscious that the man with the machine pistol must have heard the Volkswagen and might now be taking aim.

The girl leaned across the front seat and pulled up the lock button; McKee was inside in an instant.

"Start turning the car around," McKee ordered. "Head it out of here."

"What's wrong?" Miss Leon said. "Where's Dr. Canfield?"

"Drive," McKee ordered. "Turn it around and drive and I'll explain."

Miss Leon backed the car across the sand, cut the wheel sharply, and pulled the Volks back on the track. McKee opened his door and leaned out, staring back up the canyon. Nothing moved. He looked at Miss Leon, trying to decide how to start.

"What's wrong?" she asked again. "What are we doing?"

She looked less frightened, but now as he turned toward her she saw the bruised side of his face, with the dried blood. Her expression became a mixture of shock and pity.

"I'm Bergen McKee," McKee repeated. He felt immensely foolish. "I'm not sure exactly what's wrong, but I want you to get out of this canyon until I can find out."

Miss Leon looked at him wordlessly, and McKee felt himself flushing.

"I'm sorry I had to give you a scare like that," he said.

"But what in the world is happening? Where's Dr. Canfield? And what happened to your face?"

"I don't know," McKee said. "I mean I don't know where Dr. Canfield is. It's going to be hard to explain it."

He had spent much of his time since daylight planning how he would explain it all, and thinking how ridiculous he must inevitably seem while he tried.

During the night he had worked his way steadily down the canyon, keeping to the rocks close to the canyon wall. When the moon rose directly overhead, flooding the north side of the cliffs with light, he had lain under a growth of brush, resting and listening. And in this silence he had heard the sound of something moving on the rimrock, across the canyon and high above him. Whatever it was—and McKee had no doubt at all that it was the man with the wolf skin—its movements were stealthy. There was not the steady sound of unguarded footsteps on the rock. Only an occasional and very slight noise, with long pauses when there was no sound at all. In those pauses, McKee sensed the man was looking down from the rim, searching the canyon floor and listening for the sound of movement. The feeling was familiar, and less frightening because he had felt it before. Years before, when his company of the First Cavalry had been rearguard in the long, leap-frog retreat down the Korean Peninsula from Seoul toward the Pusan beachhead, he had learned how it felt to be hunted. And, he thought grimly, he had learned how to survive.

The sound had finally moved away from the rim. McKee allowed thirty minutes of silence, and then sprinted across the sand to the south wall. Here the moon's shadow would now fall and here he would be less visible from the rim. He had kept as high on the talus as he could, trading the easier going along the bottom for the invisibility offered by the rocks and brush. He moved steadily, but with infinite caution. His plan was simple. He would travel as far as he could until daylight and then he would find a place from which he could watch the bottom. There he would wait to intercept the car of Miss Leon. He would warn her, get her out of the canyon, send her back to Shoemaker's to get help, and then he would come back to look for Canfield. He no longer had even the faintest hope that the morning would bring Canfield driving up the canyon, safely back from a mercy trip with a snake-bitten Navajo. The sounds on the rimrock had killed that hope. If the motives of the man hunting him were less than sinister he would have been calling for him, not stalking him in silence. And that man, the man with the wolf skin and the pistol, must have stood beside Jeremy as he wrote the note and signed it "John."

He knew my name, McKee had thought. He must have read it in my papers in the tent. He could have learned Canfield's name the same way, but only his initials. And Canfield must have told him the J. was for John and tried, thus, to leave a warning. It occurred to McKee that if the Wolf had taken this trouble to learn who was living in the tent, he would also know of Ellen Leon. Her letter announcing her arrival time was on the table. The Wolf would only have to wait for her.

It had all seemed very obvious in darkness. The man who had stalked him must be insane. There seemed to be no other rational explanation. And this, too, might explain the puzzle of Horseman's murder.

An hour before dawn, when the moon was down and the canyon was almost totally dark, McKee had fallen. A stone shifted under his weight and he had plunged, off balance, eight feet against a slab of rock below. The impact had stunned him for a moment but he was back on his feet before he realized that the little finger on his right hand was pulled from its socket. He noticed its odd immobility before he felt the pain, saw that it was bent grotesquely backward and, when he tried to straighten it, felt the agony of the injured joint. He had sat on the stone then, frightened, trying to listen, to determine if his clumsy fall had alerted the man, but there was a roaring in his ears from the pain. Finally he had gone on, carrying his injured hand inside his shirt. It was then he heard the sound of the motor starting. There was the quick whine of the starter, the sound of a heavy motor, and gears shifting, and then the noise of wheels crunching over a stony surface. The sound came from above, and some distance down canyon. It moved away from him and in a few minutes there was silence again. The man who had stalked him had driven away. He had no way of guessing how far.

McKee had climbed down to the canyon bottom then. Walking was easy on the sand and soon it was dawn. He stopped at a pool where runoff had been trapped in a pocket of rocks. He drank thirstily of the sandy water and then used his left hand to wash as much blood as he could from his face. The skin had been scraped from the right side of his cheek and the bone felt bruised. He rested on a rock and gingerly examined his finger. It seemed to be broken in the knuckle and the tendon pulled loose in his palm. The sky overhead was lightening now and the rocks and trees across the canyon were clearly visible. Night had given way to dawn.

McKee pulled off his left boot and shook out the gravel it had picked up somehow during the night. And then he examined his left hand again. It was a broad hand with strong blunt fingers, two of them crooked. He wiggled the bent knuckle of his first finger and tried to remember how it had felt when he stuck it into that line drive when he was seventeen. He could only remember that it had been swollen for days and that the error had let in two unearned runs.

The distorted knuckle on the second finger was the souvenir of a less serious mishap. He had picked it up in practice where the errors didn't go into the record books. Funny thing about his fielding, McKee thought. Never could learn it. He could hit anybody who ever pitched to him. Bunt and hit to either field, and he had had the power for a kid his age, but finally the coach had used him as a pinch hitter. "Damnit, Berg," the coach had said, "if I leave you out there, you're going to get hit on the head and killed." That had ended his ambitions to be a baseball player, but it still seemed odd to him that the simple skill of timing a grounder and sensing the trajectory of a fly ball had been beyond him. McKee carefully replaced the injured hand in his shirt front. It was throbbing now, but the pain was tolerable. He stood up, surprised at how quickly his leg muscles had stiffened. A mockingbird flew out of a young cottonwood tree, whistling raucously. It was then McKee was suddenly struck with the dismaying thought of Miss Ellen Leon.

Almost certainly in a very few hours he would meet her and, when he did, he would have to make her believe an absolutely incredible story. He walked slowly down the canyon, thinking of how he would tell it. As he thought, the incident seemed first wildly ridiculous and then entirely unreal. The canyon was filled with the cool, gray light of full dawn now. All that had happened under the moonlight was utterly absurd, like something out of a bad melodrama, and his own role in it had been thoroughly unheroic. Yet Miss Leon had to be told—to get her out of the canyon. There simply was no way to explain it all without sounding like a complete fool. McKee wished fervently that the visitor were a man.

He trudged steadily down the canyon, turning in his mind the problem of confronting the woman. He had skipped shaving yesterday in his haste to get to Chinle and call Leaphorn. Now the face which confronted him each morning in his bathroom mirror would be worse by two days' growth of bristles. And the torn and dirty shirt and the scraped cheekbone certainly wouldn't inspire confidence in a female. Neither, he thought glumly, would the improbable tale he had to tell.

When he heard the sound of the motor again, it came almost as a relief. He was crossing the point where a large tributary canyon drained into Many Ruins and where centuries of turbulent runoff had carved the cliffs into a series of horseshoe bends. The motor sound and its confusion of echoes seemed first to come from upstream, and then from downstream. Before it died abruptly away he decided the vehicle might be somewhere up the tributary. Talking Rock Canyon, he thought it was, but he wasn't sure. In the morning sunlight the sound of the truck seemed natural and sane, reassuring him that all that had happened in the darkness had not been merely nightmare.

And now he was sitting beside Miss Leon and she was saying that she wanted very badly to see Dr. Canfield this morning.

McKee converted his embarrassment to irritation.

"Listen," he said. "There's a man somewhere up this canyon who isn't acting rationally. I think he may have done something to Dr. Canfield. I don't know where the hell Canfield is and I can't start looking for him until I get you out of here."

Miss Leon said, "Oh," in a small voice and looked at McKee. He noticed again that she was a very pretty woman.

She thinks I'm a nut, he thought.

"Canfield was gone when I got back to the camp yesterday," McKee went on. "Left me a note and signed it 'John.' His name's Jeremy." Even as he said it, the explanation sounded ridiculous. Miss Leon glanced at him.

"What did the note say?"

"It said a Navajo had come by with a snakebite and he was taking him to Teec Nos Pas." The text of the note now seemed completely reasonable. "But why would he sign it with a phony name?"

"Maybe it was a joke," Miss Leon said.

Maybe it *was* a joke, McKee thought. If it is, I'll kill the smirking bastard.

"I thought of that, too," McKee said. "But last night, sometime after midnight, I saw a man sneaking up on our tent. Had a wolf skin over his head." He had planned not to mention the wolf skin, thinking it might frighten her, or merely make the entire episode seem more ludicrous. But he blurted it out.

"Is that how you got that awful bruise? Did he hit you?"

The sympathy in her voice made McKee feel about seven years old.

"No. No," he said, impatiently. "I fell on a rock."

Miss Leon slowed the Volks and shifted into low gear to make her way across a bed of rocks.

"Your hand's hurt, too," Miss Leon said.

"I'd like you to drive back to Shoemaker's," McKee said. "When you get there, tell Shoemaker that something happened to Canfield and ask him to call Chinle and get the Law and Order boys to send someone in here to help look."

McKee made a wry face.

"Or, if you meet Canfield on your way to Shoemaker's, just forget the whole thing." He laughed. "Tell Canfield you met some kind of nut up the canyon named Bergen McKee."

"All right," Miss Leon said. She glanced at the right hand held rigidly inside his shirt front. "How badly . . ."

Immediately ahead of them around an abrupt bend of the canyon, there was the whining sound of a motor running at a high speed.

"Stop a minute," McKee said, but Miss Leon was already braking the car.

As he reached across with his left hand for the door handle, he brushed the injured finger and felt suddenly sick and weak as a fresh wave of pain engulfed his brain. He swung his legs out of the Volks and sat for a moment, head down, while the dizziness passed. He heard Miss Leon opening her door.

"I'll go see what's going on," he said. "You wait here." He realized, with self-disgust, that the words came slowly and his voice was thick. When he got to his feet she was already out of the car. Let it go, he thought. He didn't feel like arguing.

It was less than fifty yards to the canyon bend but McKee had identified the sound before they reached it. He was almost certain it was a winch working. His first glance around the rocky point confirmed this guess. Some five hundred yards downstream the canyon bent sharply to the north through a narrow defile. Here a section of the undercut cliff had collapsed, tumbling huge blocks of rimrock to the canyon floor. Just beyond this pile of talus, McKee saw a gray Land-Rover parked. A cable from the winch reel on its front bumper was attached to a ponderosa pine carried into the canyon by the landslide. The massive trunk of the long-dead tree was being swung slowly across the canyon.

"Looks like we walk out," McKee said softly.

"What in the world is he doing?"

"He's blocking us in with that tree."

"He is, isn't he?" She said it in a very small voice.

McKee couldn't see the man in the Land-Rover very well. He was wearing a black hat and there was something which might be a rifle barrel jutting at an angle out of the side window. The high whining noise of the winching operation had apparently covered the sound of their approach.

"Let's go," McKee said. "We'll drive back up the canyon and find one of those run-in washes, and climb out of here."

The sound of the winch stopped just as they reached the car. There was a long moment of silence as they climbed into the Volkswagen, and then the sound began again. McKee motioned for Miss Leon to start the motor.

"Quietly as you can," he said. "Don't race the motor and get it into second quick as possible."

She said nothing, driving competently and, McKee noticed

out of the side of his eye, occasionally biting her lower lip.

"But why would that man want to block the road?" she asked suddenly. "Do you think we should just drive down there and ask him to let us through?"

"I don't think so," McKee said. He felt very, very tired.

"Was that the man you saw last night? The man with the wolf skin?"

"I don't know. I guess it is."

A half mile up the canyon he had her turn off the ignition. From far behind them there still came the high whine of the winch, a faint sound now.

"Anyway, he can't follow us," Miss Leon said. She smiled at McKee. "He's on the wrong side of his roadblock."

"That's right," McKee said. But he knew it wasn't right. He had to work the winch from the down side because the tree top was pointing upstream. He'll simply swing the trunk downstream far enough so he can drive past it and then re-attach his winch line from the upstream side and pull it back in place across the canyon. He'll drive in and close the gate behind him. McKee wondered if Land-Rovers had four-wheel drive. He was almost certain they did. The Land-Rover could go anyplace the Volks could go, and lots of places it couldn't. The sense of urgency returned, and his hand and cheekbone began throbbing in harmony.

"Is your hand broken?"

"No," McKee said. "Sprained my little finger."

She looked at him. The sympathy in her eyes embarrassed him and he looked away. "But it hurts a lot," she said. "It would feel better if you let me bandage it."

"I think we better keep going," McKee said. "We'll drive up to our camp and get some water and stuff and find us a place we can climb out of here."

"Maybe Dr. Canfield will be back now," she said. "That is, if he didn't go out to Shoemaker's."

"Maybe so."

She still thinks I'm imagining a lot of this, McKee thought. That was good, in a way. No reason to frighten her more than he already had as long as she would cooperate. And yet it would be easier, somehow, if she shared his knowledge of danger.

Canfield was not at the camp. Nor was there any sign he had been there since McKee had left it. McKee hurriedly filled his canteen. He couldn't find Canfield's. It was probably in the camper truck. His papers were still on the folding table in the tent. If the man had examined them he had taken some care not to disarrange them. He pushed two cans of meat into his pocket, pushed the canteen into the front of his shirt, and picked up a box of crackers. What else would they need? He thought of the can opener on his pocket knife, found it beside his typewriter, and dropped it into his shirt pocket. His pickup, it occurred to him suddenly, would be better than the Volks. They could run it much farther up a side canyon—maybe even get it to the top. He trotted to the truck, switched on the ignition and kicked the starter. Nothing happened. He kicked the starter again and then he remembered seeing the man raising the hood. He raised the hood himself and looked down at the motor. The spark-plug wires were missing. He may be crazy, McKee thought as he trotted back to the Volks, but he's sure efficient.

"O.K.," he told Miss Leon. "We'll drive up the canyon about a mile. There's a place up there we can turn up a side canyon. We'll drive up it as far as this Volks will go and then we'll climb out."

Miss Leon was driving very slowly. McKee looked at her impatiently.

"Better speed it up."

Miss Leon was biting her lip again.

"Dr. McKee. Really. Don't you think we should wait there at camp?" She looked at him, her face determined. "I'm sure Dr. Canfield will be coming back soon, and if he doesn't . . . that man we saw down the canyon, I'm sure that man would help us."

Oh, God, McKee thought. Now I've got trouble with her.

"You can't possibly climb out of this canyon and walk all the way back to Shoemaker's with your head hurt like that. We're going back."

"Do you know why that pickup of mine wouldn't start?"

Miss Leon looked at him again.

"Why not?"

"Our friend had pulled the wires off the spark plugs."

She doesn't believe it, McKee thought. He felt suddenly dizzy with fatigue and pain.

"Look," he said. "If we had time, I'd take you back there and show you. But we don't have time." His voice was fierce. "Now drive and keep driving until I tell you to turn right."

Miss Leon drove, looking straight ahead. McKee looked at her profile. Her face was angry, but there was no sign of fear. It would be better if she was a little afraid, he thought, and he tried to think of what he might say. The pain in his hand had become suddenly like a knife through his knuckles, making concentration impossible. He inched it carefully out of his shirt front. The finger was rigid now, turning a bluish color, and the swelling had spread up the palm to the heel of his hand. He heard her sudden, sharp intake of breath.

"You need a doctor," Miss Leon said. "That hand's broken."

McKee put the hand carefully back inside his shirt, irritated at himself for giving her a chance to see it.

"It's just a dislocated knuckle. The swelling makes it look worse than it is."

"This is absolutely insane. I'm going to turn around and we're going back where you're camped and soak that hand." She started slowing the Volks.

McKee put his boot on top of her foot on the accelerator and pressed. The little car jerked forward and she pulled at the wheel to control it.

"Now get this straight," McKee said. His voice was angry and he spaced the words for emphasis. "I had a hard day yesterday. I was up all night. I'm tired and my hand hurts. I'm worried about Jeremy. You're going to behave and do what you're told. And I'm telling you again that we're going to climb out of this canyon."

"All right, then," Miss Leon said. "Have it your way."

There was a long, strained silence.

"If I'm wrong about that guy, I'll apologize," McKee said. "But really I can't take a chance on being wrong. Not if he's as crazy as I think he is."

Miss Leon was silent. He glanced at her. She looked away.

McKee suddenly realized she was crying and the thought dismayed him. He slumped down in the seat, baffled.

"Is this where we turn?"

"Right, up that side canyon."

The tributary seemed narrower now than it had when he and Canfield had poked into it earlier. Just day before yesterday. It seemed like a week.

McKee wondered what he could say. What did you say when you made a woman cry? "Getting pretty narrow," he said.

"Yes."

The canyon bent abruptly and the stream bed here was too narrow for all four wheels. The Volks tilted sharply as the right wheels rolled over a slab of exposed sandstone. It jolted down, slamming the rear bumper against the stone.

McKee suddenly noticed tire tracks on the bank ahead of them. A truck had been in here recently, but before yesterday's rain. Runoff had wiped out the tracks on the sandy bottom but the rain had only softened the imprint where the stream hadn't reached.

McKee was suddenly alert and nervous.

Miss Leon slowed the Volkswagen.

"Do you want me to try to drive over that?" she asked. Just ahead the canyon walls pinched together and water-worn rocks upthrust through the sand.

"I'll take a look," McKee said. He climbed stiffly from the Volks. The rocks were partly obscured by brush and didn't look too formidable. A few yards upstream they gave way to another stretch of sand. Beyond, the canyon rose sharply and was crowded with boulders from a rock slide. It was probably impassable for a vehicle.

"Put it in low and angle to the left," McKee directed. "We can get it past that brush and leave it there out of sight."

The Volks jolted over the rocks more easily than McKee had expected. He showed Miss Leon where to park it out of the water course behind the brush and then collected the canteen and cracker box.

"We can lock the car," he said. "You can take anything you think you'll need, but I'd keep it light."

"I have a box of things I was taking to Dr. Hall," Miss Leon said. "I couldn't replace those."

"We can take it," McKee said. It was then he noticed she was wearing an engagement ring—a ring with an impressive diamond. Why be surprised? he thought. Why be disappointed? Of course she was engaged. Not that it could possibly matter.

Walking was easy for the first fifty yards across the hard-packed sand, but then it became a matter of climbing carefully over the rocks. McKee noticed with surprise that the truck had apparently made it across this barrier. Its path was marked by broken brush. He glanced back. Miss Leon was sitting on a rock, holding her ankle. He noticed she hadn't brought the box.

"What happened?"

"I twisted it." She looked frightened.

He looked at her wordlessly, feeling for the first time in his life absolutely helpless. He walked back down the rocks toward her.

"How bad is it?" He squatted beside her, looking at the ankle. It was a very trim ankle, with no sign yet of swelling.

"I don't know. It hurts."

"Can you put your weight on it?"

"I don't think so."

McKee sat down and rubbed the back of his hand across his forehead. His head ached.

"We'll wait awhile," he said finally. "When it feels better, we'll go on."

He tried to think. If her ankle was sprained, it would swell soon. And if it was sprained it would be almost impossible for her to make the climb out. The long walk across rough country to Shoemaker's would be even more impossible. At least twenty-five miles, he calculated. Perhaps farther from here. What if they simply waited here? Would the man in the Land-Rover follow them? And what if he did? McKee tried to retrace all that had happened since yesterday. The rams with their throats slashed. The note from Canfield. The man who came in the darkness. What had that been in his hand there in the moonlight? Had it really been a pistol? The feeling of being hunted down the canyon. That seemed unreal now. Incredible.

But the tree being winched across the canyon had been real. He tried to think of an explanation for it. There was none. It must have been intended to close the canyon behind Miss Leon's Volkswagen. To pen them in. He rubbed his forehead again, and pulled out his cigarettes. Miss Leon was sitting motionless just below him, resting her head on her hand.

She's not very big, he thought. Maybe 110 pounds. If it wasn't for this damned hand he could carry her. Miss Leon's short-cut hair had fallen around her face. Her neck was very slender and very smooth. He felt a sharp, poignant sadness.

"Would you like a cigarette?"

"No thank you," Miss Leon said. She didn't look up.

"I can't tell you how sorry I am," McKee said slowly. "I know you must think I'm out of my mind. But that man . . ." He stopped. There was nothing to be gained by going over it again.

She looked at him then.

"There's no reason for you to be sorry," she said. "I know you're just trying to protect me."

McKee had thought her eyes were black or brown. They were dark blue. He looked away. If he was wrong about this she would forever think of him as the ultimate in idiots. And even if he was right, and she knew he was right, there was her fiancé, the man she was trying so hard to find. And, he realized bleakly, it wouldn't matter anyway.

"But I think we should go back now. We have to go back."

"Maybe so," he said. If she couldn't walk there were no happy alternatives. He would simply have to gamble that he had been insanely wrong about it all. It occurred to him then that Miss Leon might be faking the injured ankle. He didn't think that would be like her. And then he thought about the tire tracks. There had only been one set, which meant the truck had either come out of this canyon before yesterday's rain, or had driven in and parked. A round trip would have left two sets of tracks. He walked up the canyon a few yards to where the brush closed in over the rocks. The branches had obviously been broken by something tearing its way upward. And unless the canyon bottom widened suddenly, and flattened—which looked impossible from here—it couldn't have gone much farther. "I'll be right back," McKee said. "I'm going to see where that truck went."

It proved easy enough to follow. Beyond the barrier of brush, its wheels had straddled the now-narrow stream bed, leaving two deep tracks in the loamy soil—tracks which disappeared behind a brush-covered outcropping of rock a hundred feet upstream. McKee walked slowly toward this screen, feeling a growing tenseness. Behind it he would find some sort of vehicle. It couldn't possibly be the Land-Rover. It might be, he realized, Canfield's camper. Or the pickup of some Navajo sheepherder. If it was Canfield's truck, where was Jeremy?

Canfield's camper was parked just behind the outcropping, its front wheels pulled up on a rock slope, tilting it at a sharp angle. McKee stood a moment looking at it. Then he looked up the canyon and stared up at the rimrock above. Nothing was in sight.

"Jeremy?" He kept his voice low.

There was no answer.

The truck was locked. He looked through the side window. No keys in the ignition. But Canfield's hat was on the floorboards. It was a plaid canvas fishing hat, with an oversized feather. A ridiculous hat, but why had Canfield left it behind?

McKee walked to the back of the pickup and peered through the small back window of the camper compartment. Canfield had stripped the interior and used it primarily for weather-proof storage. It was dark inside and McKee could see nothing at first. He pressed his face against the glass and used his left hand as a shield against the reflecting sunlight. He saw, first, a khaki shirt front and then the legs of a man. One was bent sharply at the knee and the other, extended, crossed it at the ankle. The man's head was out of sight, against the tailgate of the camper and directly below the window, outside McKee's line of vision.

He knew instantly that the form was that of Jeremy Canfield and the civilized instincts of his consciousness proclaimed that Canfield was asleep. But some infinitesimal fraction of a second later his reason told him that Jeremy was not asleep. Men did not sleep, head down, on such a steep slope.

McKee tried the handle on the camper again. It was locked. He looked around him for a rock, wrapped his left hand in his handkerchief, and smashed at the glass. It took five blows to force his way through the laminated safety window. He picked out the shards of glass still in the way and reached through, unsnapped the catchlock on the inside, raised the top panel on its hinges and dropped the tailgate. There was an outflow of warmer air escaping from the camper compartment and what had been Dr. J.R. Canfield slid a few inches toward him.

McKee took a short step backward and stared. Canfield's mouth was stretched open in some frozen, soundless shout. McKee swallowed and then sat on the tailgate. With his thumb he gently closed Canfield's eyes. The eyelids felt sandy under his touch and he noticed then that there was also sand around the mouth and in his friend's thinning hair. He rubbed his hand absently against his pant leg and stared blindly out across the canyon. He found himself wondering where Canfield had left his guitar. Back in the tent, he thought. Canfield had been working on one of his "ethnics" to celebrate the arrival of Miss Leon. McKee tried to remember the words. They were witty, he recalled, and unusually unprofane for one of Jeremy's productions. Then he could think only of Miss Leon, a slight, slender, weary figure sitting on the rock with her head resting on her arm.

McKee got up, pushed Canfield's body a few inches back up the steep incline of the pickup bed and closed the tailgate. He moved rapidly down the canyon.

There was no alternative now. No question of turning back. But was there a way to get Miss Leon out of this trap without bringing her past this truck? He looked again at the canyon walls. With two good hands he might be able to make it to the top here, but he was sure she couldn't. And he didn't have two good hands. He cursed vehemently as his jogging trot started the throbbing again. If only he hadn't been so clumsy. He would have to bring her past the truck. There was no other way. But he would keep her from looking in.

She was still on the rock when he pushed his way through the bushes, and she looked up and smiled at him.

"We have to go now," he said. "How's the ankle?"

"I don't think I can do more than hobble on it," she said. "We'll have to go back."

"We're not going back. I found Canfield's truck up there. Someone broke in the back window and he's gone."

"But we can't possibly . . ."

"Get up," McKee ordered. His voice was hoarse. "Get on your feet. I'll help you."

"I'm not going," Miss Leon said.

"You're going, and right now." McKee's voice was grim. He gripped her arm and lifted her to her feet, surprised at how light she seemed. The box of crackers was on the rock where he had left it. How could he have been silly enough to bring crackers?

She tried to jerk away from his grip, and then faced him. McKee noticed there were tears in her eyes.

"You've got a concussion. We just can't go stumbling around like this. We've got to get you to a doctor. Please," she said. "Please, Dr. McKee. Please come back to the camp and Dr. Canfield will help you."

McKee looked at her. There was dust on her face and a tear had streaked it. He looked away, feeling baffled and helpless. Maybe he would have to tell her about Canfield.

"Come on," he said. "I'll help you."

"You're hurting my arm."

McKee was suddenly conscious of the feel of her arm under his fingers, of the softness under the shirt sleeve. He jerked his hand away.

Miss Leon ran. She spun away from him and ran lightly down the rocks toward the Volkswagen. McKee stood, too surprised to move, thinking: There's nothing wrong with her ankle. Then he swore, and ran after her, clumsily because of his injured hand. Before he reached the Volkswagen, she had rolled up the windows and locked herself in. For a wild moment, McKee thought she would start the car and drive off and he had a vision of himself trying to keep himself in front of the Volkswagen—performing an idiotic game of dodgem in reverse. But she simply sat behind the wheel, looking at him.

He tapped on the window, and tried to keep his voice sounding normal.

"Really, Miss Leon. I'm not crazy. And we really do have to get out of here."

Miss Leon looked at him. He saw no fear in her expression, nor anger. She simply looked worried.

"Roll down the window."

"Not until you give me your word of honor you'll go back to the camp."

Her voice was faint through the glass.

My day for breaking windows, McKee thought. He picked up a rock, and wrapped the handkerchief around his left hand again. He saw Miss Leon looked frightened now.

"Roll it down."

"No."

McKee hesitated. He thought of Jeremy's body, and of the sand on his face. Breaking his word would be quicker than the window.

"I promise," he said. "Let me in and we'll go back to camp."

"I don't know now," Miss Leon said. "I'm not sure I can trust you."

Good lord, McKee thought. Women left him utterly baffled.

He held up the rock.

"Open up, or I break in."

Miss Leon unlocked the door and he pulled it open.

"Get out now. No more of this horsing around. Get out of there or I'll have to drag you out."

Miss Leon got out. He gripped her arm and walked with her rapidly up the canyon. And then he stopped.

A tall man wearing a new black hat emerged from the screen of bushes just in front of them. He was the Big Navajo who had been shopping in Shoemaker's. In his right hand he held a machine pistol, pointed approximately at McKee's stomach. It was of shiny, gunmetal blue—something which would have reflected in the moonlight.

"That's right," the man said. "Just stand still."

He walked across the rocks toward them, keeping his eyes on McKee.

The pistol, McKee saw, had a wire stock, now folded down, and a long cartridge magazine extending downward from the chamber.

"You're Bergen McKee," the man said. "And the young lady would be Ellen Leon."

McKee pulled Miss Leon's arm, moving her behind him. "What do you want?"

The man smiled at McKee. It was a pleasant smile. And the face was pleasant. A long, rawboned Navajo face, with heavy eyebrows and a generous mouth. McKee saw he wore short braids, tied with red cord.

"Just the pleasure of your company for a while," the big man said. "But right now I want you to take that hand out of your shirt front, very, very slowly."

McKee pulled out the hand.

"Well," the man said. "I see I've been too suspicious." He smiled again. "That's quite a finger."

McKee said nothing.

"Now, I'll have you put your hands against that tree." He flicked the long barrel of the pistol toward the trunk of a piñon. "Lean against it while I see what you have in those pockets. And, Ellen, you stand over here where I can watch you."

The man stood behind McKee and searched him deftly. He pulled out the cans of meat and dropped them, took the pickup keys and his billfold, ran his hand quickly around McKee's belt line and patted his shirt. Then the hand was gone, but the voice came from directly behind him.

"You will hold that position until I finish checking Miss Leon's possessions. I don't want any movement at all. I don't have to tell you that I will use this pistol."

"No," Bergen said glumly. "You don't."

He heard the voice telling Miss Leon to hold her arms out. McKee looked back over his shoulder.

The blow was so sudden and vicious that he dropped to his knees and huddled against the pain of it. The man had jabbed him, full strength, above the kidney with the muzzle of the pistol.

"You didn't pay attention to what I said," he heard the man saying. "I said not to move. But now you can get up."

McKee pulled himself to his feet. He had hurt his finger again and his hand throbbed violently. He saw Miss Leon looking at him, her face very white. The man was looking at him too, still smiling slightly. He wore a black shirt and denims tucked into the tops of his boots.

"You know, I almost missed you again," the man said. He stopped smiling. "You've been a hell of a lot of trouble. When we have a little time I want you to tell me how you got away from me last night at your camp. That's been puzzling me." The man stopped a moment, staring at McKee.

"I think I know why I didn't catch you at my tree. You were farther down the canyon than I thought you could be and you heard the winch. Didn't you?"

"That's right," McKee said.

"I almost waited there too long," the man said. "You were smart enough to run, but then you gave away your advantage. I wonder why you waited for me here." He looked at McKee thoughtfully. "You could have made me hunt you another day," he said. "Why did you stop? Did you give up?"

McKee didn't look at Miss Leon.

"We didn't think anyone would know where we were."

The Navajo laughed. He seemed genuinely amused. "If you didn't know this was the only way out, I had some luck with you."

"Who the hell are you?" McKee asked. "And what do you want with us?"

"Let's go now. You will walk a little ahead and do as you're told."

He turned the machine pistol sideways, and tapped the safety button beside the trigger guard.

"I carry it cocked, with the safety off. It's a .38 caliber and I'm good with it."

"I'll bet you are," McKee said.

The man kept well behind them as they walked past the brush and over the rocks. McKee walked silently, trying to think.

Miss Leon touched his arm. "I'm sorry." Her voice was very small.

"Nothing to be sorry for."

"If I hadn't been so stupid," she whispered. "I thought it was because you had hurt your head."

"What else could you think? It still seems crazy."

"I'm sorry. You could have gotten away."

"I should have been able to manage it anyway," McKee said. His voice was bitter.

"How did he know our names?"

"He looked through the papers in our tent," McKee said. "I guess he saw them there."

"No talking," the Navajo said. "Save your breath."

They walked in silence up the sand and around the outcropping where Canfield's camper was parked.

"We'll stop here a moment," the man said.

McKee saw Miss Leon looking at the truck. He was glad he had had sense enough to close the tailgate.

"I noticed you looked in it," the man said. "I wish you hadn't broken that window. What did you think that would accomplish? It's going to look funny."

The Navajo moved toward the pickup, watching them as he did. He glanced inside and then briefly inspected the broken window.

"This Canfield seemed like a nice fella," he said. "Full of jokes."

"Then why did you kill him?" McKee asked fiercely. He spoke in Navajo.

The big man looked at him, as if trying to understand the question. He answered in English. "Just bad luck. There wasn't any other way to handle it." He looked at McKee solemnly and pursed his lips. The expression was rueful. "Have to go on now," he said. "It's more than a mile to my car and a lot of climbing."

Within a few hundred yards, the going became increasingly difficult. The canyon floor rose sharply now and was choked by brush and tumbled boulders. McKee climbed stolidly, helping Miss Leon when he could and trying to think. What kind of a monster was this? He seemed perfectly sane, as if this crazy episode were simply business. He had apparently killed Jeremy as unemotionally as he would swat a fly. McKee was absolutely certain he would kill Miss Leon and him with the same coolness. And, as usual, he could do nothing about it. He had thought about turning suddenly and trying to hit the man with a rock. But his right hand was almost useless and the Navajo kept a cautious distance behind them.

It didn't seem likely the man would leave them alive, not with the knowledge that he was a murderer. But why hadn't he simply shot them by the camper? McKee had sensed that the man had considered this, at least for a moment, after he had confirmed that Canfield's body was still in the truck. But he had dropped the idea. He must have some use for us alive, McKee thought. Either that, or he wants our bodies somewhere else, and it's easier to have us walk. But why? The man seemed sane but there was no conceivable sanity in any of this.

"We'll climb out here," the Navajo said. He indicated a gap in a rockslide which had broken out of the south wall of the canyon. "You go first, Dr. McKee. When you reach the top you will lie down with your feet sticking out over the rim where I can see them. Ellen will be just ahead of me and if you try anything foolish I will have to shoot her so I can come after you. Do you understand how it will work?"

He studied McKee's face.

"You may think I'm bluffing. I'm not. I don't really think I'll need Miss Leon."

McKee looked at her. She stood just below him, breathing heavily from the exertion, her face damp with perspiration. She attempted a smile.

Somehow, McKee thought, I'm going to get her out of this. Even if it kills me.

He began climbing. It was slow because of his right hand, and by the time he reached the top he was drained with exhaustion. He lowered himself onto the rimrock, with his feet jutting out.

"Stay on your stomach," the voice from below ordered.

The position left him completely helpless. He couldn't move without the Navajo seeing him and he had no doubt at all that the man would kill Miss Leon the moment he did. He wondered what the man had meant about probably not needing her. Why would he need her? And why did he need him?

The Navajo reached the top before Miss Leon and stood well aside while she finished the climb.

"Walk right over there to the truck," he said. McKee saw the Land-Rover almost hidden behind a growth of juniper. "But first hold that hand out so I can see it."

McKee held out his left hand, palm open.

"Are you left-handed, Dr. McKee?"

"No. I'm right-handed."

"I was afraid you would be. Let me see it."

McKee slowly raised his injured hand. He suppressed a wince as motion renewed the pain. The sun was directly south now and that might explain some of the weakness in his legs. It was noon and he hadn't eaten anything since yesterday afternoon.

"That looks bad," the Navajo said. "We may have to soak it to get that swelling down."

McKee saw that Miss Leon was also staring at his hand. He dropped it, flinched again, and the blood drained into it.

"I'm touched by your sympathy," McKee said.

The Navajo chuckled. "It's not really that," he said, grinning at McKee. "It's just that I have to have you write a letter for us."

THERE IS NO COMFORTABLE WAY, McKee found, to lie face down on the backseat of a moving vehicle with his wrists tied together and roped to his ankles. The best he could arrange involved staring directly at the back of the front seat. By looking out of the right corner of his eye, he could see the back of the Big Navajo's neck. The man had his hat pushed forward on his forehead. That would be because they were driving west and the sun was low through the windshield. By looking down his cheek, he could see Miss Leon, sitting stiffly against the right door of the Land-Rover, as far as she could get from the Indian.

The Land-Rover lurched over something and McKee spread his knees to keep from shifting on the seat. Making the move started the throbbing again in his right hand. The Navajo was saying something but it was lost in dizziness.

"I don't know," Miss Leon said.

"How about you? How long were you planning to stay?"

The question sounded so ordinary and social that McKee had an impulse to laugh. But when Miss Leon had answered two or three days, the Navajo had turned his head toward her. There was a long silence then, and when the Navajo spoke again, McKee realized the question had not been casual at all.

"Did anyone know where you were going?"

"Everyone knew."

"This Dr. Green at Albuquerque knew," the Navajo said.

"Who else? What about your husband? Did he know you were coming to this canyon?"

"I don't have a husband."

There was another silence then.

"Who else knew then?" the Navajo asked.

"Some other friends of mine, of course, and my family. Why? What difference does it make?"

"Another thing. Why did McKee sit around in the canyon and let me cut him off?"

"Ask him," Miss Leon said.

"You tell me," the Navajo said.

"Because I was a fool," Miss Leon said.

"You slow him down?" The Navajo chuckled. "Didn't you believe there was a Navajo Wolf?"

"He had that horrible bruise on his forehead," Miss Leon said, "I thought it was that."

"Well, I would have got him anyway."

"No," she said. "If it hadn't been for me, Dr. McKee would have gotten away."

"Maybe you don't know about us Navajo Wolves. We turn ourselves into coyotes, and dogs, bears, foxes, owls, and crows."

McKee stared at the back of the Navajo's head. He had ticked off the litany of were-animals in a voice heavy with sarcasm. And he listed bears, and owls, and crows. There had been a scholarly argument about that when Greersen first published his book about witchcraft beliefs in the 1920s. Greersen had listed only one account of each. The bear story had come out of the Navajo Mountain district and the owl and crow incidents were both far to the east—over on the Checkerboard Reservation in New Mexico. McKee had never found a source who knew of more than were-dogs, were-wolves, and were-coyotes. The big man must have read Greersen, and that had to mean he had researched somewhere with an anthropological library. But why, and where?

"And we fly through the air when it's dark and we need to," the Navajo was saying. "McKee wouldn't have got away."

"He'd already gotten away once." Miss Leon's voice was angry and insistent. "He outsmarted you last night. And today he outsmarted you again. He . . ."

"Lady. Drop it. You don't know who I am. Nobody gets away."

That had ended the conversation. The Land-Rover had turned sharply and tilted downward—moving mostly in first gear down the narrow bottom of a dry wash. And after what McKee guessed must have been three or four miles there was the feel of smooth flat sand under the wheels and the Navajo drove much faster. There was no sun on the Land-Rover now and McKee was sure they were back on the floor of Many Ruins but he wasn't sure of directions.

A dull pain from the bruise on his forehead and the throbbing of his hand made it difficult to concentrate. Who was the Navajo? In this part of the Reservation, The People linked owls with ghosts, but not with witches, and gave crows and ravens no supernatural significance at all. Obviously, the man's tone was heavily ironic when he listed the birds and animals. McKee could think of no source for such a list except Greersen's *Case Studies in Navajo Ethnographic Aberrations.* It was a notoriously ponderous and difficult volume intended for cultural anthropologists. Why would the Navajo read such a book? When McKee tried to make sense of this, his mind kept turning to the sound of Ellen Leon's voice defending him. "He outsmarted you," she had said.

The Land-Rover stopped and McKee heard the hand brake go on.

"You stay here," the Indian said. "Don't try to untie McKee and don't try anything funny."

And then the door opened, the big man was gone, and Miss Leon was leaning over the back of the seat. She looked dusty, disheveled, very tired, and very sympathetic. "Are you all right?" she asked.

"Where are we? Where did he go?"

"At the tree," Miss Leon said. "The one he pulled across the canyon. Are you all right?"

"What's he doing? Putting on the winch?"

"Yes. Dr. McKee, I'm sorry I was such a silly fool. I didn't . . ."

"I couldn't hear part of the conversation. Did he tell you anything useful? Who he was, or anything like that?"

"No. I don't think so. He said nobody ever got away from him."

"I heard that," McKee said. "Did he say anything else?"

"I can't think of anything." She paused. "He asked me why we waited in the canyon so he could catch us."

"I heard that, too. Don't worry about it."

And then he heard the big man climbing back into the Land-Rover. There was the sound of shifting gears, the whine of the winch, and the cracking noise of limbs breaking. Then the winch stopped and the man climbed out again.

"I want you to be very, very careful," McKee said. "Do exactly what he tells you to do. And keep your eyes open. Watch for a chance to get away. If you can get out of his sight, hide. Hide and don't move until it's pitch dark and then get out of the canyon. Go to Shoemaker's. That's south by southwest of here. You know how to tell your directions at night?"

"Yes," Ellen said.

She probably doesn't, McKee thought, but it seemed entirely academic.

"Find the Big Dipper," McKee said. "The two stars in the line at the end of the cup point to the Pole Star. That's due north."

"He's coming back," she said.

"Remember. Watch for a chance."

And then the big man was leaning over the seat, looking at him. "I hope you were giving Miss Leon good advice."

"I told her to follow orders."

"That's good advice," the Navajo said.

They drove about ten minutes by McKee's estimate before the Land-Rover stopped again.

"This time you better come along, Miss Leon," the man said. "Slide out on my side."

"Where are you taking her?" McKee's voice was loud.

"I won't hurt her," the man said. "We're just going to get some of your papers."

McKee twisted his shoulders and neck, straining to see out the rear window. Only the top of the cliff was in his line of sight, but it was enough to confirm that they were at their camping place.

They were gone only a moment. And then the Land-Rover was moving again, smoothly at first up the sandy floor of Many Ruins and then a jolting, twisting ride. Suddenly they weren't moving. McKee heard the hand brake pulled on.

"I see you got a woman, George. Where's the man you were after?"

The voice was soft. A Virginia accent, McKee thought, or maybe Carolina or Maryland.

"In the backseat," the Navajo said. "Get out, Miss Leon."

The door by McKee's head opened and he saw a man looking down at him. On his stomach, with his head turned to one side, McKee could see only out of the corner of his right eye. He could see a belt buckle, and a navy-blue vest with black buttons, and the bottom of the man's chin and up his nostrils.

"He's tied up," the voice above him said. It seemed to McKee a remarkably stupid thing to say.

"Move a little bit out of the way," the Navajo said. Then McKee felt the Indian's hands, deftly untying the knots.

"Get any calls while you were gone?" the soft voice asked. "Do they know when we can haul out of this hole?"

"No calls," the Big Navajo said. "You see anything?"

"No," the soft voice said. "Just that kid on the horse again. Up on the top. Way off across the mesa."

"You can get up now, Dr. McKee."

McKee sat up and examined the man with the blue vest. He was a tall young man with a pale face shaded by a light-blue straw hat. He looked back at McKee and nodded politely—blue eyes under blond eyebrows—and then turned toward Miss Leon.

"How do you do," he said. Ellen Leon ignored him.

The young man wore a harness over his vest supporting a shoulder holster with a semi-automatic pistol in it. McKee didn't recognize the type, but it seemed to be about .38 caliber. Miss Leon stood stiffly in front of the truck. She looked frightened.

"Come on," the Big Navajo said. "Get out now. I'm in a hurry."

McKee climbed out of the Land-Rover, his muscles stiff. His head ached, but the ache was lost in the violent throbbing of his injured hand. He held it stiffly at his side and glanced around.

They were up a narrow side canyon. Below, not more than two hundred yards, McKee could see the broad sandy bed of Many Ruins bright in the afternoon sun. Here there was shadow and it was a moment before he noticed the cliff dwelling high on the sandstone wall behind the blond man. It was large for an Anasazi ruin—built in a long horizontal fault cleft some forty feet above the talus slope and protected from above by the sloping overhang of the cliff. He wondered, fleetingly, if it was one of those excavated by the Harvard-Smithsonian teams. It would be hard to reach, but that made it all the more attractive to the archaeologists. Less chance it had been disturbed.

"Dr. McKee is going to write that letter for us, Eddie," the Navajo said. "It may take some time, and while I'm thinking about the letter, you want to be thinking about McKee. He's tricky."

"He hasn't written it yet?" the blond man asked. He sounded surprised.

"I could have had him write it back at his camp," the Indian said. "I think I could handle him. Ninety-nine chances out of a hundred. But why take chances with one this slippery?"

"Too much money involved," Eddie said. "Way too much money for taking chances."

He slipped the pistol deftly from the holster, handling it, McKee noticed glumly, as naturally as a pipe smoker handles a pipe.

"Don't talk so much," the Big Navajo said. "We're going to leave these two behind and the less they hear the better."

Eddie said, "Oh?" The word came out as another question.

The Navajo reached into the Land-Rover, pulled out a pile of papers, stacked them on the hood, sorted swiftly through them, extracted a letter, and skimmed it.

"How about this Dr. Green? Looks like he's your boss. He'd probably be the one to write."

"Green's chairman of the department," McKee said. "We usually try to keep in touch when we're in the field."

How long, McKee wondered, had Canfield lived after he

wrote his note for this man? Just long enough for the Navajo to kill him without marks of violence. Only one thing was clear in this incredible situation—the Navajo's need for this letter was all that kept Miss Leon and himself alive. He wouldn't write it, but it had to be handled exactly right.

The Big Navajo handed him Dr. Canfield's ballpoint pen. It was a slim silver pen, and as McKee accepted it with his left hand he felt his resolution harden. He would never, under any circumstances, write this letter.

"I didn't find any stationery so I guess you use your notebook?"

"That's right," McKee said.

"We'll make it to Dr. Green," the Navajo said. "What do you call him? Dr. Green? Or his first name?"

"Dr. Green," McKee lied. "He's pretty stuffy."

The Navajo looked at him thoughtfully. "What was Dr. Canfield's first name? Was it John?"

"John Robert Canfield," McKee said.

The Big Navajo studied him.

"Dr. McKee," he said finally, "what happened to Dr. Canfield was too bad. It couldn't be helped because Dr. Canfield tried to get away and he didn't leave me any alternative. But there is no reason at all for you and Miss Leon to die. If this letter is written properly it will give us time to finish what we are doing here. And then we will leave and we can afford to leave you behind." He said all this very slowly, watching McKee intently. McKee kept his expression studiously noncommittal.

"You may doubt that, but it's true. When we are finished here, there will be no way at all to trace us. If you cooperate, we can leave you up in that cliff dwelling with food and water. In time, perhaps you could find a way to get down. If not, someone will come in here sooner or later and find you."

"What happens if I don't write the letter?"

The Navajo's expression remained perfectly pleasant.

"Then I'll have to kill you both. Without the letter we'd have to hurry. You would slow us down some, because someone will have to watch you. Nothing personal about it, Dr. McKee.

It's simply a matter of money." He smiled. "You know our Origin Myth. That's what witchcraft is all about—the way to make money."

"What do you want me to write?" McKee asked.

"That's part of the problem. We want a letter to Dr. Green telling him that you're leaving this canyon and going somewhere else—somewhere it would be natural for you to go. You and Dr. Canfield and Miss Leon. And it has to be written so that Dr. Green won't suspect anything."

The Big Navajo paused, staring at McKee.

"You can see that, can't you? If someone gets worried and comes in here looking for you, we would simply have to kill you."

I have to do this exactly right, McKee thought.

"I don't think I can believe you," he said. "You killed John after he wrote the letter."

"Your Dr. Canfield was very foolish. He wrote you the note, and then he tried to escape. He jumped me."

"I see," McKee said.

"And I think that Dr. Canfield warned you somehow in that note of his. What was it? Why were you expecting me?"

McKee grinned. "You're right, of course. It was the name. His name's Jeremy. When I saw that signature I knew something was wrong. I'd been over to the Yazzie hogan and found those rams you killed and I was nervous about that anyway."

McKee was satisfied that his voice had sounded natural. He hoped desperately that his timing had been right. Maybe he should have waited longer, but he saw a slight relaxation in the Navajo's face. It's like poker, he thought, and this man's weakness, if he has one, is his vanity.

"You shouldn't try anything like that."

"I don't have any reason to trust you," McKee said. "Just one thing. You kill one man and they hunt for you awhile but it is not so very unusual. You kill two men and a woman and it's something nobody forgets and they keep looking for you."

He was watching the Navajo's face. It relaxed a little more.

"You've been thinking of that, haven't you?" McKee asked.

"This is just business with me, Dr. McKee," the Navajo said. "A way to make a lot of money. You're right. The more people who get hurt, the harder they hunt."

With an effort, McKee avoided looking at the blond man. From the corner of his eye, he had seen a faint smile on Eddie's face.

"All right," McKee said. "What do you think we should say?"

"Well. You'll have to say you're leaving here. All of you." He paused. "Say you are leaving day after tomorrow. A day after we mail this at Shoemaker's."

McKee tried to seem thoughtful. "Canfield was looking for Folsom Man artifacts in the Anasazi ruins," he said, aware that the Navajo must already know that. "We'll say he wasn't finding any around here and that I haven't had much luck finding anyone willing to talk about witchcraft incidents."

He glanced up at the Navajo's face.

"If you don't believe that's true, you can send somebody back to get my notes. That really is what I'm working on."

"I believe you," the Navajo said. "Write it here on the hood of the truck."

The son of a bitch read my notes, McKee thought. He felt elated. Then he saw Ellen Leon watching him, her face without expression. The elation died. She thinks I'm a coward or a fool, he thought. Maybe that was best.

"I'll tell Green that we're moving on up into the Monument Valley country in Utah—where the Navajos are less exposed to outside influences and less accultured. That would make sense for both of us. Canfield is . . ." He hesitated a second, sickened at this play-acting. "Canfield was trying to establish some pattern of Folsom Man hunting camps in this area. The early pueblo builders collected Folsom lance points and kept them as totems. That would be a good place for him to be looking."

He was fairly confident that the big man knew all about what both of them were doing, and he tried to make his voice sound persuasive. He doubted if the man knew about Ellen Leon. There was nothing mentioning her in the tent. Just her brief note.

"And it would be a natural place for me to work. In the

back country is where you find people still believing in the Navajo Wolves."

"How about Miss Leon?"

"I told him I was just your graduate assistant," Miss Leon interrupted, "but I don't think he believes me."

"Green would naturally expect her to go along with us," McKee said. "That's what she gets paid for. To help."

He paused again, thinking of the sand on Canfield's lips and that something might go wrong with this plan.

"That sound all right?" he asked.

The Big Navajo moved his thumb absently back and forth over his fingertips, studying McKee's face.

"Does Green have any schedule of where you're supposed to go next?"

"We didn't have any definite plans."

"Would Green be writing you anywhere? Anywhere set up to pick up letters?"

"Just Shoemaker's while we were here." He noticed Miss Leon was still looking at him and he felt himself flush. "We tell him where to forward to if we move. He'd get this letter from me saying where we were going and telling him to send our mail to the store at Mexican Water. It seems natural. You think he'd check on it?"

"Let's see how it looks on paper," the Navajo said.

McKee had been holding his right hand straight down. It had hurt, but the increased blood pressure should, he thought, build up the swelling. He raised it now, intending to feign pain. No pretense was necessary. The hurt was so far beyond what he had expected that his gasp was involuntary. He felt sweat on his face and nausea in his throat. When he finally rested his right forearm on the hood, he slumped against the truck, breathing hard, too dizzy to notice whether the Navajo had registered all this. I can't spoil this now, he thought. He has to believe I'm really trying.

"I'll start it, 'Dear Dr. Green,' " he said. His voice was thick.

He moved his right hand slowly and took the pen between his thumb and forefinger. In a moment he had one more gamble to make. He would suggest that he try to write the letter with his left hand, explaining to Dr. Green that he had injured his right one. He didn't think the big man would call this bluff. If the man was as smart as he seemed to be, he would see the objections. Green would wonder why Canfield hadn't written instead. And he would wonder why McKee wasn't coming in for medical attention. And the handwriting would be unidentifiable anyway—and that obviously was important. But, if he didn't see the objections, this whole desperate play for time might collapse.

He shifted the pen into the proper position, lowered the point and started the "D." The Navajo was watching him intently.

Again, a fresh wave of pain helped his performance. The flinch was completely involuntary, the spasm of a tortured nerve.

"Don't write it," Miss Leon said suddenly. "I don't trust him."

The Navajo turned toward her.

"Ellen," McKee said hurriedly, "if you had shown a little sense earlier we wouldn't be here. If you'd use what little brains you have, you'd see that this letter is our only way out of this mess. Now shut up."

He hoped, as he said it, that the anger would sound sincere to the Navajo and insincere to Miss Leon and thought bitterly that the reverse would probably be true. The hurt in Miss Leon's face looked genuine and the Navajo's expression was unreadable.

He tried again with the pen, finishing the "Dear" this time, and inspected the wavering scrawl with satisfaction.

"That's fairly close," he said. It looked nothing at all like his handwriting and the Navajo had plenty of samples in his field notes to make the comparison.

"It's not close enough," the Navajo said.

"How about writing it with my left hand?" McKee said suddenly. "We could say I'd hurt my right one." He tried to make his glance at the Indian seem natural, and held his breath.

"Dr. McKee. Think about it. That wouldn't look like your handwriting. If it doesn't look like your handwriting, it won't work no matter what you say." The Navajo was looking at

McKee curiously. "Why would you write Dr. Green a left-handed letter with Dr. Canfield around to write letters?"

"Just a thought," McKee mumbled.

The Navajo looked at his watch and then, for a long moment, at the man called Eddie. Eddie shrugged. "Whatever you think," he said. "I don't know the odds."

McKee was suddenly chillingly aware that his life was being decided. The Navajo looked at him, his face bland, with no trace of malice or anger. McKee was conscious of the ragged line rimming the iris of the Indian's eyes, of the blackness of the pupils; conscious that behind that blackness an intelligence was balancing whatever considerations it gave weight and deciding whether he would die.

"The hell of it is," the Big Navajo said, "we don't know how long we're stuck here."

"Whatever you think," Eddie said again. "Lot of money involved."

"Let's see that hand again," the Indian ordered.

McKee raised it slowly, palm upward, toward the Navajo.

He leaned slightly forward, scrutinizing the twisted finger. Like, McKee thought, a housewife inspecting a slightly off-color roast.

"Maybe soaking it will get that swelling down," the Indian said. "Soak it in hot water and get the swelling out. We'll take 'em up to the cliff place, Eddie."

From behind him, McKee heard a faint click. Eddie had slipped the safety catch on his automatic back into place.

"It's almost four o'clock," the Navajo said. "The hell of it is with this job we never know how much time we have."

AT APPROXIMATELY FOUR O'CLOCK Joe Leaphorn, sweating profusely, led his borrowed horse the last steep yards to the top of the ridge behind Ceniza Mesa. Almost immediately he found exactly what he had hoped to find. And when he found it the pieces of the puzzle locked neatly into place—confirming his meticulously logical conclusions. He knew why Luis Horseman had been killed. He knew, with equal certainty, that the Big Navajo had done the killing. The fact that he had no idea how he could prove it was not, for the moment, important.

At about ten minutes after four o'clock, Lieutenant Leaphorn found something he had not expected to find on the Ceniza ridge. And suddenly he was no longer sure of anything. This unexpected fact visible at his feet fell like a stone in a reflecting pool, turning the mirrored image into shattered confusion. The answer he had found converted itself into another question. Leaphorn no longer had any idea why Horseman had died. He was, in fact, more baffled than ever.

Leaphorn had left the Chinle subagency at noon, towing Sam George Takes's horse and trailer, determined to learn what the Big Navajo had been doing at Ceniza Mesa. At first he drove faster than he should because he was worried. Billy Nez had come home from the Enemy Way, picked up his rifle, and left again on his pony. Charley Nez, as usual, didn't know where he had gone. But Leaphorn could guess. And he didn't like the conclusion. He was sure Billy Nez would ride to the place where Luis Horseman had hidden. Nez would pick up the tracks of the Big Navajo's Land-Rover there, and he would follow it. Because Leaphorn couldn't think his way through the puzzle of Luis Horseman's death, he had no idea what Nez would find—if anything. And because Leaphorn didn't know he worried.

Leaphorn began driving more slowly and worrying less as the carryall climbed the long slope past Many Farms. He had been working his way methodically around the crucial question, the question which held the key to this entire affair, the question of motive. By the time the carryall reached the summit of the grade and began the gradual drop to Agua Sal Wash the answer was taking shape. He pulled off the asphalt, parked on the shoulder and sat, examining his potential solution for flaws. He could find no serious ones, and that eliminated his worry about young Nez. Nez almost certainly wouldn't find the Big Navajo on the Lukachukai plateau. The man would be long gone. And, if he did find him, it wouldn't matter much unless Nez did something remarkably foolish.

Leaphorn went through his solution again, looking for a hole. The Big Navajo must have found the Army's missing rocket on Ciniza Mesa.

Why, Leaphorn asked himself angrily, had he been so quick to reject this idea when he learned the reward was canceled? The Big Navajo had been clearing a track to the top when Billy Nez found him and stole the hat. He would have needed such a road to haul the remains down. And then he had cached the rocket somewhere until he could find out how to collect the reward. Horseman had found the rocket and claimed it. A Navajo would not kill for money, but he would kill in anger. The two had fought—fought in some sandy arroyo bottom. Horseman had been smothered. And the Big Navajo had moved his body down to Teastah Wash. Why? "To avoid having the area where his rocket was hidden searched by Law and Order people looking for Horseman." Now the Big Navajo was waiting, with the inbred patience of the Dinee, for the moment when sun, wind, and birdsong made the time seem right to claim the Army's $10,000. Or perhaps he had learned by now that the reward had been canceled. It seemed to make little difference. Leaphorn could think of no possible way to connect the missile with the murder.

He looked out across the expanse of the Agua Sal Valley, past Los Gigantes Buttes. There was Ceniza Mesa—twenty miles away, a table-topped mass of stone rising out of an ocean of ragged erosion like an immense aircraft carrier. Eons ago the mesa had been part of the Lukachukai plateau. It was still moored to the mountain ramparts by a swaybacked saddle ridge. It was on that saddle ridge that Billy Nez had seen the Big Navajo working and it was there Leaphorn would prove his theory. Perhaps Billy Nez had lied. Leaphorn thought about it. Billy Nez hadn't lied.

He pulled the carryall back on the pavement and drove down the slope toward Round Rock, enjoying the beauty of the view. For the first time since the body of Luis Horseman had been found he felt at peace with himself. He switched on the radio. "Ha at isshq nilj?" the broadcast voice demanded. "What clan are you? Are you in the Jesus clan?" Navajo with a Texas accent. A radio preacher from Gallup. Leaphorn pushed the button. Country music from Cortez. He snapped off the radio.

"He stirs, he stirs, he stirs, he stirs," Leaphorn sang.

"Among the lands of dawning, he stirs, he stirs.
The pollen of dawning, he stirs, he stirs.
Now in old age wandering, he stirs, he stirs.
Now on the trail of beauty, he stirs,
Talking God, he stirs. . . ."

The mood lasted past Round Rock, past the turnoff at Seklagaidesi, down eleven jolting miles of ungraded wagon track. Leaphorn still sang the endless ritual verses from the Night Way as he unloaded the horse where the track dead-ended at an abandoned death hogan. He trotted the animal across the broken, empty landscape, skirting Toh-Chin-Lini Butte, moving southeastward toward the Ceniza saddle. He saw the bones of a sheep, the empty burrows of a prairie-dog town, and the moving shadow of a Cooper's hawk swinging in the sky above him. He saw no tire tracks and he expected to see none. That would have been luck. Leaphorn never counted on luck. Instead he expected order—the natural sequence of behavior, the cause producing the natural effect, the human behaving in the way it was natural for him to behave. He counted on that and upon his own ability to sort out the chaos of observed facts and find in them this natural order. Leaphorn knew from experience that he was unusually adept at this. As a policeman, he found it to be talent which saved him a great deal of labor. It was a talent which, when it worked unusually well, caused him a faint subconscious uneasiness, grating on his ingrained Navajo conviction that any emergence from the human norm was unnatural and—therefore—unhealthy. And it was a talent which caused him, when the facts refused to fall into the pattern demanded by nature and the Navajo Way, acute mental discomfort.

He had felt that discomfort ever since Horseman had turned up dead—contrary to nature and Leaphorn's logic—far from the place where nature and logic insisted he should be. But as he led his borrowed horse the last steep yards to the crest of the Ceniza saddle the discomfort was gone. The top of the ridge was narrow. In a very few moments he would find tire tracks and the tracks would match the tread pattern drawn for him by Billy Nez. Of that Leaphorn was certain. When he examined these tracks he would find the Land-Rover had driven up the saddle to the mesa top empty and had come down with a heavy weight on its rear tires. And then the irritatingly chaotic affair of Luis Horseman would be basically orderly, with only a few minor puzzles to solve.

The narrow ridge offered few choices of paths, even for a four-wheel-drive vehicle, and Leaphorn found the tire tracks quickly. There were four sets instead of the two he had expected to find, indicating two trips up and two trips down. He made no attempt to find meaning in that. He concentrated on the fresher tracks, establishing by the traction direction which of them had been made going up the slope. In an area where the soil was soft he checked the depth of the tire marks. Exactly as he had expected. On the trip down, the rear tires had cut almost a half-inch deeper.

Behind him the horse snorted and stamped, fighting off the flies.

"Horse," Leaphorn said, "it comes out just the way we figured it would."

Leaphorn rose from his squat and brushed a fly from the horse's back. There was no trace left of the nagging sense of wrongness and urgency that had dogged him for days, none of that vague, undefined feeling that something unnatural and evil was afoot in his territory. He understood now. It was a good feeling.

And then Lieutenant Joe Leaphorn took two short steps across the small place of soft, loamy earth and looked down at the older tracks. He recorded the fact that they had been dimmed by at least one rain shower. He noticed that this set, too, varied in the depth the rear tires had cut. It had taken, Leaphorn thought at first, two trips to haul down the remains of the shattered rocket. A split second later his mind processed what his eyes were seeing. On this round trip, the Land-Rover had carried its heavy load on the way up—not on the way down.

The Navajo language is too specific and precise to lend itself to effective profanity. Leaphorn cursed in Spanish and then—at length—in English.

It took Leaphorn almost three hours to piece together as much as he could of what had happened on this ridge and on the mesa to which it led. He worked methodically and carefully, resisting an urge to hurry. And when he put it all together, he had nothing but another enigma which offered no possibility of solution.

To Leaphorn's surprise the Land-Rover had approached the saddle from the southeast, emerging from the Chinle Desert from the direction of the Lukachukai ramparts. On the first trip up—perhaps as long as a month earlier—it had carried a heavy load over its rear axle. At several places the driver had stopped to cut brush out of the way, sometimes using an ax and sometimes a power chain saw. To traverse the steepest slope, where the saddle rose sharply to the lip of the mesa rimrock, he had used a winch line in several places to help pull the vehicle up. Once on top, the vehicle had driven fairly directly about a mile across the mesa. There something heavy and metallic had been unloaded on a flat outcropping of sandstone, scoring the soft rock. From this point, the Land-Rover had made a backing turn and driven directly back over the original track.

Even though the other tracks were weeks fresher, he had spent most of the time sorting out the second trip. He finally concluded that on this trip the Land-Rover had driven directly to the sandstone outcropping. Then it had returned to the rim where the saddle joined the mesa. There several small trees had been cut and a score of boulders moved, apparently to clear a better roadway. At the site of this heavy work, Leaphorn found the tracks of Billy Nez's rubber-soled sneakers, marks of the Big Navajo's flat-heeled boots, a bread wrapper, and an empty Vienna sausage can. After Billy Nez had been here—and presumably after he had left with the Big Navajo's stolen hat—the Land-Rover had driven back over the rim and back to the sandstone. There the heavy object had been reloaded and the Land-Rover had driven down off the mesa. This much was clear. Leaphorn had found three ponderosa poles used as a tripod, which must have supported the pulley used to lift whatever it was the Big Navajo had unloaded and then reloaded.

Leaphorn rubbed his fingertips over his forehead, trying to recreate exactly what the Big Navajo had done on that second visit to the Ceniza Mesa.

He had first driven to the heavy object. And what then? Looked at it? Assured himself it was still there? Adjusted it? Fed it? Put fuel in it? Turned it off? Or on? No hope of guessing. And then the Big Navajo had driven back to the rim to improve the steep approach. Why? If he could winch the loaded Land-Rover up the slope he could winch it down, given enough time. Was that it? Time? Did he expect to be in a hurry coming down? Maybe, Leaphorn thought. Maybe that was it. Time. But Navajos didn't hurry. In fact, there was no word in the Navajo language for time.

And then the Big Navajo had discovered his hat had been

stolen, had found the tracks of Billy Nez, and knew someone had watched him. Knowing this, he had driven back over the top, reloaded the heavy object, and hauled it down off the mesa. Why? Maybe because Billy Nez might find it. But where had the big man taken it? And what was it?

Leaphorn stood on the mesa rimrock and stared out across the Chinle at the Lukachukai slopes. The sun was down now. The tops of the evening thunderheads over the mountains were still a dazzling sunlit white, but below the fifteen-thousand-foot level they turned abruptly dark blue with shadow of oncoming night. The desert was streaked with pink, red, and purple now, the reflected afterglow from cloud formations to the west. Normally Leaphorn would have been struck by the immensity of this beauty. Now he hardly noticed it. He stared at the darkening line of the Lukachukai ramparts, searching out the points of blackness, the open mouths of the canyons which drained it. Since the Land-Rover had come from the southeast, across the Chinle, it must have come from one of these. He could backtrack it. Twenty miles, he guessed. Maybe twenty-five, and a lot of it would be over bare slick rock. Even in daylight he wouldn't average a mile an hour. At night it would be impossible.

A burrowing owl, its wings stiff, planed up from the desert below him, banked into the invisible elevator of air rising up the mesa wall. It hung on the current a few feet below him—its yellow eyes examining the rimrock for incautious rodents feeding early. Leaphorn envied its mobility. Since the moment he had seen his orderly, logical explanation of Luis Horseman's death demolished by the hard facts of the Land-Rover's tire tracks, the old sense of urgency had returned. He had resisted it by sheer strength of will, forcing himself to concentrate on deciphering what had happened at this mesa. Now he resisted no longer. Instead, he thought about it—turning this itching impulse to hurry in his mind. What was it that bothered him?

He laughed, and the owl, making a second and slightly higher sweep over the mesa wall, panicked at the sound. It flapped past him, trailing its chittering *quick-quick-quick-quick* call, and vanished in the shadows.

Everything was bothering him, Leaphorn thought. Nothing fit. Everything was irrational. But why this sense of time running out, of something dangerous?

Leaphorn lit a cigarette and smoked it slowly, thinking hard. Luis Horseman had been killed. Billy Nez had found the tracks of the Big Navajo's Land-Rover near where Horseman had hidden. A Navajo had been killed and a Navajo had killed him—that was the presumption. Leaphorn studied this presumption, again seeking an answer to the central question. Why? Why did Navajos kill? Not as lightly as white men, because the Navajo Way made life the ultimate value and death unrelieved terror. Usually the motive for homicide on the Reservation was simple. Anger, or fear, or a mixture of both. Or a mixture of one with alcohol. Navajos did not kill with cold-blooded premeditation. Nor did they kill for profit. To do so violated the scale of values of The People. Beyond meeting simple immediate needs, the Navajo Way placed little worth on property. In fact, being richer than one's clansmen carried with it a social stigma. It was unnatural, and therefore suspicious. From far behind him on the mesa came the voice of the owl. *Ta-whoo,* it said. *Whoo.*

Where, then, was the motive? There was something about all this that seemed strangely un-Navajo. But the big man who drove the Land-Rover was one of The People. Leaphorn was sure of that, remembering the face in Shoemaker's. There had been times at first at Arizona State when Leaphorn had trouble with the faces of white men. He had noticed only the roundness of their eyes and their paleness and all Belacani had looked alike to him. But he had no trouble with the faces of the Dinee. The Big Man had the face and the frame of a Tuba City Navajo—heavy-boned without the delicacy and softness added by the Pueblo blood mixture. And he wore braids. The trademark of the man who held to the Navajo Way. But why were the braids so short?

Leaphorn thought about that for a moment. And abruptly he again had an answer. Not all of it. But enough to make him urge the horse down the ridgeline much faster than the tired animal wanted to move. Enough to tell him that Billy Nez, hunting his witch in the Lukachukai canyons, might actually find one to his mortal danger. Enough to tell him that he must be at the hogan of Charley Nez at dawn. There he would pick up the boy's trail. The unshod horse should be easy to follow.

Mars rose over the black outline of Toh-Chin-Lini Butte as he loped across the Chinle breaks, his mood matching the gathering darkness. He was remembering his words to the Big Navajo at Shoemaker's—the casual words which he now was sure had caused Luis Horseman to die.

BERGEN MCKEE had been dreaming. He stood detached from himself, watching his figure moving slowly across a frozen lake, knowing with the dreamer's omniscience that there was no water under the ice—only emptiness—and dreading the nightmare plunge which would inevitably come. And then the raucous cawing of the ravens mixed with the dream and broke it and suddenly he was awake.

He sat motionless for a second, perplexed by the dim light and the blank wall before him. Then full consciousness flooded back and with it the awareness that he was sitting, cold and stiff, on the dusty floor of a room in the Anasazi cliff dwelling.

McKee pushed his back up against the wall and looked at Ellen Leon, lying limply opposite him, face to the wall, breathing evenly in her sleep. He looked at his watch. It was almost five, which meant he had slept about six hours and that it would soon be full dawn on the mesa above the canyon. With that thought came a quick sense of urgency.

He looked at his hand, tightly wrapped now in bandage, and then glanced quickly around the room. The enclosure was much too large for living quarters. It had been built either as a communal meeting place for one of the pueblo's warrior secret societies or as a storeroom for grain—three stone walls built out from the face of the cliff and, like the cliff, sloping slightly inward at the top. The only way out was the way they had come in—through a crawl hole in the roof where the wall joined the cliff. And there was no way to reach the hole without the ladder—the ladder which the Big Navajo had carefully withdrawn after leaving them here.

Outside, a raven cawed again and then there was silence. McKee leaned against the wall and tried to sort it out.

Whatever was happening here was the product of meticulous planning. That was clear. Behind the brush at the foot of the cliff there had been four sections of aluminum-alloy ladder. The man called Eddie had fit them quickly together, fastened them with bolts and wing nuts, and they reached exactly from a massive sandstone block at the top of the talus slope to this shelf. If the ladder was not custom-built for the purpose, at least the bolt holes had been drilled with this cliff dwelling in mind.

And, when they had reached the top, Eddie had pulled up the ladder, and laid it carefully out of sight. The action obviously had long since become habit. It would leave anyone passing below no hint that this cleft was occupied. It was equally obvious that the peculiar hide-out had been occupied for weeks. Behind a screen of bushes which grew back from the ledge under the overhanging cliff there was all the equipment for a permanent camp—a two-burner kerosene stove, a half-dozen five-gallon cans and a tarp stretched low to the ground protecting cartons and boxes. And there had been two bedrolls. Whoever else was involved must sleep somewhere else, perhaps directing this operation from somewhere outside. From what Eddie had said, others would tell them when they could leave.

And whoever they were, they had a radio transmitter. After Eddie had fished cans of meat and beans from under the tarp and fed them and started him soaking his hand in a pot of steaming water, the Big Navajo had climbed back down the ladder. He had sat for a long time in the Land-Rover and when he returned he had news.

McKee rubbed his knuckles across his forehead, remembering exactly. The big man had been grinning when he walked up to where Eddie was sitting—grinning broadly.

"Girlie says maybe tomorrow afternoon will do it," the

Navajo had said. Eddie had looked pleased, but he had said something noncommittal. Something like Girlie's been wrong before. No. It was Girlie's been wrong three times, because the Indian had laughed then and said, "Fourth time's the charm for us." It had occurred to McKee then that if these men were leaving tomorrow they would no longer need a letter written by him. Once they had finished what they had come to do and had left this canyon why would it matter if someone came looking for Canfield and Miss Leon and himself? It would only matter that no one be left alive to describe them. Thinking that, he had decided to throw the water pot at the Big Navajo and jump Eddie, trying for Eddie's pistol. He hadn't thought he would get the pistol, but there would be nothing to lose in trying. And then the Navajo had baffled him again.

"Dr. McKee," he had said, "I think we'd better try to get that knuckle of yours back into joint, and tie it up with a splint. I'm going to be busy tomorrow, but by tomorrow night I'll want to get that writing done."

Thinking about it now, McKee was still puzzled. Eddie had carried a section of the ladder to the cliff ruin and they had climbed against the overhang to the top of this wall . . . and then down into the pitch darkness of this room. The Navajo had told him to sit on the floor and hold out his hand. He had argued with the Indian that the joint was broken, not just dislocated.

The Navajo had laughed. "They feel like that when they're pulled out, but we can get it back in the socket."

The big man had squatted beside him, with Eddie holding the flashlight from above, and had taken McKee's swollen right hand in both of his own, and suddenly there had been pain beyond endurance. When he had returned to awareness, Miss Leon was holding his head and his hand was tightly wrapped. He had been sick then, violently sick, and then they had talked.

"Where did they go?" McKee had asked. It was almost totally dark in the windowless room, with only a small spot of moonlight reflecting through the roof hole relieving the blackness.

"I heard them a little while ago," Miss Leon had said. "I think they were both out there where their sleeping rolls are.

And then I heard what sounded like the ladder being moved."

"I guess they climbed down," McKee said.

There was a long silence. McKee felt her shoe against his leg. The touch seemed somehow personal, and intimate, and comforting.

"Dr. McKee." Her voice was very small. "I didn't hear all of what you and that Navajo said when we were at Dr. Canfield's camper. Dr. Canfield's body was in there, wasn't it? He killed Dr. Canfield?"

"Yes," McKee said. There was no use trying to lie to her. "I guess he did."

"Then he'll kill us, too," she said.

"No," McKee said. "We'll find a way out." He could think of no possible way.

"There isn't any way out," Miss Leon said. "It would take a magician to get out of this."

McKee was glad it was dark. Judging from the sound of her voice, she was on the ragged edge of tears.

"I didn't have a chance to tell you," he said. "We think maybe that electrical engineer you were looking for may be working somewhere way up the canyon."

"Jim? Did you find him?"

"Some Indians saw a van truck driving up in here. Do you know if he was pulling a generator?"

"There was a little trailer behind his truck," she said. "Would that be a generator?"

"Probably," McKee said. He searched his mind for some way to keep this conversation going, to keep her from thinking of sudden death.

"I noticed your ring, Miss Leon. Is this Dr. Hall—er, Jim—the one you're engaged to?"

"Why don't you call me Ellen?" she said. There was a pause. "Yes, I was going to marry him."

McKee noticed the past tense instantly. And then it occurred to him why she used it. She thought she would soon be dead.

"What's he like?" McKee asked. "Tell me about him."

"He's tall," she said. "And rather slim. Blond hair, blue eyes. He's very handsome really. And he's—he's, well—sometimes moody. And sometimes very happy. And always very smart."

The voice stopped. I match none of that, McKee thought, except the mood part.

"He graduated magna cum laude." The voice paused, then continued, "And our society doesn't have the proper respect for magna cum laude."

"I guess not," McKee said.

Ellen laughed. "I was quoting Jim," she said. "Jim is—well, Jim is very ambitious. He wants things. He wants a lot of things, and he's very, very smart—and—and so he'll get them."

"I don't know why," McKee said. "But I guess I never was very ambitious." He wished instantly that he hadn't said it. It sounded self-pitying.

"What else about him?" McKee asked. He didn't enjoy hearing her talk about the man. But it was better for her to talk, better than having her sitting silent in the dark—dreading tomorrow. She talked rapidly now, sounding sometimes as if she had waited a long time for someone to listen, and sometimes as if she was talking only to herself, trying to understand the tale she was telling.

She had met Jim at Pennsylvania State on the first day of a Shakespeare's Tragedies class. He had taken the chair to her left and she had hardly noticed him until the professor called the roll. But the professor's voice had risen slightly in a question as he read "Jimmy Willie Hall" off the class card. The professor had intended no rudeness and he made this clear by nodding in acknowledgment to Jim's "Heah," but someone in the back of the room had sniggered and this churlishness to a stranger had embarrassed Ellen, embarrassed her all the more because she, too, had smiled at the ludicrous sound. She had glanced at the young man with the outlandish name and noticed he wore cowboy boots and had a wide-brimmed gray felt hat pushed under his chair. On a campus where styles were set by the casual, careless conformity of young men from Philadelphia one was as out of place as the other. And, when she had looked at him again, she had seen that while his face, neck, and hands were incredibly sunburned his forearms about the wrists were as white as the shirt he was wearing.

"He looked very strange and out of place," Ellen said. And suddenly she laughed. "I thought he would be lonely," she said, sounding incredulous.

She had spoken to this Jimmy Willie Hall in the lecture building hallway. Jim had said, in reply to her comment that he wasn't from the East, that he was from Hall, New Mexico, and when she had asked where that was, he had said he wasn't really from Hall, exactly, because their place was twenty-one miles northwest of there, in the foothills of the Oscura Mountains. It was just that they picked up their mail at Hall. He guessed he should say he was from Corona, which was larger and slightly closer.

The conversation had been inane and pointless, Ellen recalled, as exploratory chats with strangers tend to be. She asked why, if Corona was larger and nearer, they picked up their mail at Hall, and he had explained that there was no road from the Hall ranch to Corona. To get there you had to go through the Oscura Range and Jicarilla Apache Reservation or over the malpais—across seven miles of broken lava country. You can't even get a horse over that, he had explained. The only time he had tried, his horse had broken a leg and he had been bitten by a rattlesnake.

"That sounds like he was trying to impress me," she said. "But he wasn't. A girl can tell about that. He was just telling me about a silly mistake he had made." Ellen's voice stopped. "I guess I knew right then he wasn't lonely," she continued, thoughtfully, "and that I had never seen anyone like him."

He had seemed, she remembered, like someone visiting from the far side of the globe her father kept in the office of his pharmacy—someone completely foreign to all she knew. As different from the men she had dated as his empty Oscura foothills were from her family's elm-shaded residential street in a Philadelphia suburb.

"You remember *Othello?"* Ellen asked suddenly.

"Othello?" McKee said, surprised.

"Yes. The Moor of Venice. We studied it that semester, after *Hamlet.* You remember how Desdemona was fascinated by Othello?"

"I remember," McKee said, trying to remember.

"That was us," Ellen said. "That was our private joke."

"Remember how it goes?" She paused a moment.

"A maiden never bold;
Of spirit so still and quiet that her motion
Blush'd at herself; and she—in spite of nature,
Of years, of country, credit, everything—
To fall in love with what she fear'd to look on!
It is a judgment maim'd and most imperfect . . ."

"Yes," said McKee, "I remember it." He felt immensely sad.

"I would say that," Ellen said, "and Jim would say Othello's lines:

'It was my hint to speak—such was the process;
And of the Cannibals that each other eat,
The Anthropophagi, and men whose heads
Do grow beneath their shoulders. This to hear
Would Desdemona seriously incline. . . .' "

Ellen stopped again. And when she continued the voice was shaky.

"I loved him for the dangers he had passed.
And he loved me that I did pity them."

McKee reached across the darkness and found her hand. "It's going to be all right," he said. "We'll get out of here and find him."

"Can't you understand?" she asked, and her voice sounded angry now. "Why should I pity someone like Jim Hall? Why should anyone pity anybody who has everything?"

McKee couldn't think of an answer.

"Because he doesn't know he has everything?" Ellen suggested. "Because he isn't happy?

"Sometimes he is, but mostly he isn't. He's angry. He says he's caught in a system which keeps you on the treadmill. Forty years on the treadmill, he says. He talks about it a lot, about how it takes a million dollars to beat the system, to pay your own ransom, to buy back your own life."

She laughed again, a bitter sound. "I guess he . . . Well, I guess Jim will make a million dollars," she said.

"Not teaching on an engineering faculty," McKee said.

"Oh, he's not going to do that," she said. "He's going with one of the electronic communications products companies and he's bringing along one of his patents, so it's a very good job."

"Is that what he's working on out here?" McKee asked. "Trying it out."

"Oh, no. This is another one, I think. I—well, I wish I understood it better. Something to do with very narrow-range sound transmission. He explained it to me—quite often—but I don't really understand it."

McKee started to ask her why she was looking for Dr. Hall and bit back the question. The answer was obvious, and none of his business. A woman who loves a man would simply want to see him.

"Dr. Canfield was nice, he was nice, a nice man," Ellen said. "But he was too polite to ask why I was chasing after Jim. And you've been nice, too. But would you like to know?"

"It's your private business," McKee said. "No, I don't want to know."

"I want to tell you. I have to tell someone," she said. "I came because I wanted to tell Jim—to tell him that I think he's wrong, and he's going to have to make a choice. He's got to quit wanting a million dollars. He has to. I've come all the way out here. He has to understand."

It sounded utterly feminine to McKee, the reverse side of Sara's logic, and a simpler assignment. A brilliant, ambitious man could easily enough fail to make a fortune. But how could a Bergen McKee, a natural on the treadmill, make himself rich?

And, thinking that, McKee, after forty hours without rest, was suddenly asleep.

Now he was fully awake again. He pushed himself to his feet and surveyed the room. The floor was covered with a heavy deposit of dust. He could feel it, flourlike, under the soles of his shoes. But the condition of the room was surprising. It was virtually intact. The roof sagged only at one corner, where the ceiling beams had snapped with rot, and plaster still clung to most of the lower portion of the walls.

McKee flaked off a section of plaster with his thumbnail, broke it and examined it. Inside it was almost black—a mixture of animal blood and caliche clay used by the pueblo-building people. It was stone-hard and would last for centuries, and so would the cedar poles in the roof when protected from weather under a cliff. But not for this many centuries. Left alone, the roof would have crumbled long ago and the top of the walls would have fallen inward. This ruin must have been partially rebuilt—restored by one of the later pueblo people who used the canyon before the Navajos arrived and drove them out.

It was then he saw the face. He stood for a moment staring at it, putting together what it meant, feeling a sense of excitement building within him. The face was drawn on the plaster in something yellow—probably ocher. It was faded now and partly missing where chips of plaster had fallen away. A roundish outline with a topknot, long ears, and a collar. The figure was unquestionably a Hopi Kachina—either the Dung Carrier or the Mud Head Clown. And below it to the right were two more stylized outlines.

From the Hopi mythology McKee recognized Chowilawu, the spirit of Terrible Power, with four black-tipped feathers rising vertically from his squarish head and a horizontal band of red blinding his eyes. The third head had been almost erased by flaking. Only the dim outline of a protruding ear and the double vertical cheek stripes signifying a warrior spirit remained. Down the wall there were other markings—the zigzag of lightning, bird tracks, the stair-stepped triangles of clouds, and a row of phallic symbols. Undoubtedly, one of the Hopi clans had used this as a ceremonial kiva.

He stood absolutely silent a moment, thinking, and then squatted beside Miss Leon and put his hand on her shoulder.

"Time to wake up."

She rubbed her arm across her eyes.

"Very domestic," McKee said.

She looked up at him and then pushed herself up against the wall, trying to straighten her tousled hair with her fingers. "Oh. What time is it?"

"About four forty-five," McKee said. "We shouldn't have wasted all that time. We need to get out of here."

"Out of here? But I don't see how we can." Miss Leon looked up at the exit hole in the roof and then at McKee. "What do you mean? How can we?"

"The Hopis lived in this. They rebuilt it. Have you read anything about how the Hopis build their pueblos?" It occurred to McKee as he said it that he was showing off and the thought embarrassed him. Ellen looked puzzled.

"They always built an escape hatch at the bottom of a wall," he explained. "A hole into the next room, and then they would fill it in with rocks that could be easily pulled out. Kept them from being penned up in part of the structure if they were under attack."

"Oh," Ellen said. "You think there's a way out, then."

"I think so. We can find out. It would be in one of the inside corners."

And most likely, McKee thought, in the corner adjoining the cliff. Bracing over the escape hole would have been easier there.

The corner was littered with broken cedar sticks. Above, occasional moisture seeping down the cliff face had accelerated the slow work of decay. The builders had cut holes into the soft stone to support the ends of ceiling beams and here the rot had started first.

McKee selected one of the sticks and began pushing the debris away from the corner. He worked carefully, trying to avoid noise. But the powdery dust rose in a cloud around him. Ellen knelt beside him, pushing the dust back carefully with her hands.

"Don't make any noise."

"Do you have any idea what this is all about?" she whispered. "Why does he want you to write that letter?"

"I don't know what's going on," McKee said. "Maybe they're crazy."

"I think you know about the letter," Miss Leon said. She

stopped digging and looked at him. Her face was chalky with dust. White and strained. McKee looked away.

"He explained why he wanted the letter," McKee said.

"And if you believed him, you would have written it," Ellen said. She sat back on her heels, still looking at him. "Why don't you stop treating me like a child? You know as well as I do that if they were going to turn us loose they wouldn't need the letter."

"O.K.," McKee said. "I think you're right. They want the letter because they know that someday there's going to be a search started for us and they don't want the search to be in here. They don't want the search to be in this canyon ever—or at least not for a long, long time."

"But why not? Do you know why?"

"No," McKee said. "Can't even make a good guess at it. But it has to be right."

He leaned back against the cliff and wiped the dust off his face.

"I didn't think so at first. I thought that, whatever they were doing here, it was making them wait for something, and they didn't know how long the wait would be, so they didn't want interference. But that's not right, because it seems to be happening today. They could just leave us here, and it would be a long time before anyone found us. A lot more time than they would need to get away."

"That's what I thought of, too," Ellen said.

"Did you notice how they camped?" McKee asked. "No garbage hole. Put all the cans and stuff in gunny sacks. And Eddie, when he lit the stove, he put the burned match in his vest pocket."

"I didn't notice. I guess I didn't think of that."

"When they pull out of here there won't be any traces left. Not after the August rainy season, anyway. Unless there was some reason for a search, no one could ever know anyone had been in here."

Beneath the pile of debris in the corner, the plaster looked almost new. He jabbed it with his stick and cursed inwardly when the rotten wood snapped. For this he needed his pocket knife and the Big Navajo had taken it when he had searched him. Or had he?

McKee suddenly was aware of the weight of the knife in his shirt pocket. He had dropped it there with his cigarette pack when he hurried from their tent—hands full of odds and ends—in his futile race to escape. It was a ridiculous place to carry a pocket knife, and the Navajo had overlooked it.

McKee fished it out and pulled open the blade—noticing he could hold it between the thumb and forefinger of his right hand with little pain. With the knuckle back in joint the swelling must be going down. There would be no chance now of persuading the Navajo that he couldn't write.

The plaster chipped away in sections, revealing a rough surface of stone with mud mortar chinking. A moment later a yard-square sheet crumbled and McKee saw he had guessed right. The fitted stonework ended in a crude half-arch in the corner two feet above the floor. The first stone he pulled on was jammed tightly, but the second slipped out easily.

McKee rocked back on his heels, looking at the stone. It was about the size of a grapefruit and felt clumsy in his left hand. He tried to shift it to the right, but it fell into the dust.

Miss Leon looked at the stone and then at him.

"I think we can get out," he said. "We can if the room on the other side hasn't fallen in and buried this crawl hole under a lot of big rocks."

"What do we do if we get out?" Her voice was very small.

"Did you hear them come back during the night?" McKee said.

"No. I didn't hear anything. But we don't even know if they left. Maybe just one climbed down."

"The Big Navajo said he had to leave," McKee said. "And he said he might not be back until tonight. If Eddie didn't stay up here on the ledge, we'll try to find a way off."

Miss Leon looked skeptical.

"Come on," McKee said. "The Hopis lived here long enough to rebuild part of this place and they didn't like being in places where they could be boxed in. There's a good enough chance that they had some sort of escape route off the cliff. They always had a hidden way out if they could."

There was another alternative. If they found no way off the cliff, he could try to keep Eddie and the Indian from climbing back up. He might surprise them, catch them on the ladder—defenseless from a rock dropped from above. With surprise it might work. But there was a rifle in the Land-Rover. They would be good with it—probably very good.

"But what if Eddie stayed up here?" Ellen said. "I'll bet he did."

"I don't know," McKee said. "Just let's hope he didn't."

He tried to make his grin reassuring without much success. He was thinking of the way Eddie handled the pistol. For the first time it occurred to him exactly what his problem might be. He might have to find a way to kill a man. He turned away from the thought.

Outside the hole he stood tensely, listening. The ravens had flown away now and the only sound was the morning wind and the faint whistling of a horned lark on the canyon rim high above him. The Hopis had repaired this room, too. He could tell from the remnants of plaster. But a slab of stone had fallen from the cliff, crashing through the roof and tumbling much of the east wall outward. Denied this support and protection, the roof had collapsed and centuries of wind had drifted a hump of sand and dust against what remained of the wall. Over this hump, McKee surveyed what he could see of the east end of the ruins.

The shelf gradually narrowed to the east. From what he remembered seeing yesterday from the canyon bottom, this entire east end was filled with ruined walls, ending just short of the point where a structural fault split the canyon wall from floor to rim. That would be the place to look for an escape route. That narrow chimney would be the only possible way up. The thought of it made his stomach knot. As a graduate student, he had climbed down such a slot to reach a cliff house at Mesa Verde, and the memory of it was an unpleasant mixture of fear and vertigo.

He climbed cautiously over the rubble of the exterior wall at the edge of the shelf and looked down into the canyon. The Land-Rover was not in sight. That should mean the Navajo had not returned from wherever his business had taken him. Nor was there any sign of Eddie. That meant nothing. Eddie might be sleeping below him in any of a thousand invisible places. Or Eddie might be only a few yards away on the cliff.

Here the Anasazis had crowded their building almost to the edge of the cliff, leaving along the lip of the precipice a narrow walkway, which was now buried under debris. McKee moved along it gingerly, keeping as close as the fallen rocks would allow to the wall of the storeroom. At the corner, behind a water-starved growth of juniper, he stopped.

When he looked around the corner, Eddie would be standing there. Eddie would have the pistol in his hand and would—without any change of expression—shoot him in the head. McKee thought about it for a moment. Eddie might look faintly apologetic, as he had when he had introduced himself at the Land-Rover. But he would pull the trigger.

McKee stood with his back pressed against the stones and looked out across the canyon. It was almost full dawn now. Light from the sun, barely below the horizon, reflected a reddish light from a cloud formation somewhere to the east onto the tops of the opposite cliffs. A piñon jay exploded out of a juniper across the canyon in a flurry of black and white. He heard the ravens again, far up the canyon now. It was a beautiful morning.

McKee leaned forward and looked around the wall.

Eddie was not in sight. The stretched tarp was there, and the stove, and other equipment. Both sleeping bags were gone. So was the ladder. McKee felt himself relaxing. Eddie must have climbed down and left them alone on the shelf.

McKee was suddenly aware that he would be plainly visible from below. He moved back behind the juniper and stood, thinking it through. He glanced at his watch. Five A.M. Then he heard Eddie whistling.

Eddie walked around the jumble of fallen rock at the west end of the shelf, not fifty feet away. He was carrying his bedroll under his right arm and his coat slung over his left shoulder—whistling something that sounded familiar. He dumped the bedroll, folded the coat neatly across an outcrop of sandstone, and squatted beside the stove.

McKee stared numbly through the juniper. Of course the

Big Navajo had left nothing at all to luck. He had taken the ladder but left the guard behind.

Eddie was combing his hair. His shoulder holster, with the pistol in it, was strapped over his vest. About twenty yards away, McKee guessed. He could cover maybe ten yards before Eddie saw him, and another five before Eddie could get the pistol out, and then Eddie would shoot him as many times as were necessary.

The first plan McKee considered as he worked his way slowly back along the cliff edge involved waiting in ambush at the corner of the storeroom until Eddie mounted the ladder to bring them their breakfast. He imagined himself sprinting the fifteen feet before Eddie, encumbered with food, could draw the pistol, knocking the ladder from under him and triumphantly disarming him.

It might work—if Eddie brought them breakfast. There was no reason to believe he would. Much more likely he would first check on his prisoners with pistol in hand.

The second plan, even more fleeting, involved having Miss Leon raise a clamor—perhaps shouting that he was sick. This would probably bring Eddie up the ladder to look in the hole in the storehouse roof. But he would come cautiously and suspiciously. The third plan survived a little longer because—if it worked—it did not involve facing Eddie's pistol. He and Miss Leon would work their way—unmissed and unheard—to the east end of the shelf. There they would find the Hopi escape route in the chimney and would climb to freedom. It was a pleasant idea and utterly impractical. It was far from likely that Ellen could make the climb and impossible for anyone to make it without noise. McKee considered for a moment how it would feel to be hanging on handholds a hundred feet up the chimney with Eddie standing below aiming at him. He hurriedly considered other possibilities.

One involved finding a hiding place back in the ruins and waiting in ambush, rock in hand, for Eddie to come hunting for him. The flaw in this one was easy to see. There would be no reason for Eddie to hunt. He would simply wait for the Navajo to return, believing there was no way off the cliff.

It would be necessary to make Eddie come after him.

McKee dropped on his stomach at the crawl hole.

"I'm right here," Ellen whispered. "I heard him whistling. Did he see you?"

"No," McKee said. "He's cooking breakfast."

"You know what," Ellen said. "I said it would take a magician to get out of this room. You're a magician."

"Um-m. Look—make sure your watch is wound," McKee said. "I want you to wait thirty minutes and then come out here and make some sort of noise. Knock a rock off the wall or something to attract him. But don't run. Don't give him any reason to shoot."

"What are you going to do?" Her whisper was so faint he could hardly hear it.

"Remember. When he comes, give up right away. Put your hands up. And tell him I'm climbing up the escapeway back where the cliff is split at the east end of the ruins. Tell him I'm going for the police."

"Is there really a place you can climb out?"

"I don't know yet," McKee said. "The idea is to get the jump on him."

"There isn't any place. He's going to kill you." She made it a flat statement.

If Ellen said anything else, McKee didn't hear it.

"Ellen," he whispered. "Do you understand what to do?"

"Yes. I guess I do. But is thirty minutes enough?"

McKee thought about it. Every minute that passed might bring Eddie checking. Or it might bring the Big Navajo back. He was suddenly acutely conscious that he was probably setting the time limit on his life.

"I think thirty minutes," he said.

It was eight minutes more than Eddie allowed him.

It had taken very little time to defeat his hopes that the ruins would offer a point of ambush. Along the narrow pathway which followed the lip of the shelf, the walls were too crumbled to provide a place of concealment from which he could attack. Under the cliff itself the ruins were better preserved—some still standing in two stories—but they offered only a hiding place, no place from which to launch an attack. At the end of the shelf, where massive geologic fault had shifted the earth's crust eons ago and split the cliff, there was no effective cover at all. McKee edged his way carefully past the dwelling's final crumbled corner.

Here the path was buried under tumbled stones. A misstep meant a plunge into the crevasse left by the fault.

McKee looked at his watch. He had used thirteen minutes and accomplished nothing. Here at its mouth the crevasse was about fifteen feet across. Beyond it the shelf continued. It was slightly lower and after a few yards tapered away to nothing.

From where he stood it was impossible to see what the crevasse in the cliff offered. The Anasazis had built their structure to the very base of the cliff wall. The exterior wall had fallen outward over the precipice, but the spreading limbs of piñon screened the narrow opening.

He moved carefully over what remained of partition walls, pausing once to look down into the crack. The split was sheer, and although the narrow slot was partly filled with broken slabs of rock flaked off the walls above, it was much too far to jump.

McKee hurt his hand again climbing what remained of the back wall. He had forgotten the finger for a moment in the overpowering need to know if the crevasse held some possibility for him, and had shifted his weight to it. He was still sick with the pain when he lowered himself into the darkness behind the wall. A minute ticked away as he sat in the dust, holding his hand stiffly in front of him, letting the throbbing diminish and his eyes adjust to the darkness. What he saw both disappointed and encouraged him.

There was no natural pathway into the crevasse as he had hoped. The shelf did not extend into it. But the Anasazis had cut foot- and handholds into the sandstone, making it possible for a person to work his way back into the slot. Somewhere back in the darkness where the crack narrowed, where a man could brace himself between the opposing walls, there would be a way to the top. If he could dispose of Eddie, he could make it. But what about Eddie?

McKee studied his position. There were two ways into this dark cul-de-sac where he now sat between wall and crevasse—over the crumbled wall as he had come, or by pushing past the outthrusting branches of the piñon. Eddie would probably come over the wall for exactly the same reason he had done so. The piñon had angled outward toward the sunlight. One could force his way past it, but bending by the heavy branches would require a tightrope walk along the very lip of the crevasse. Not knowing where McKee would be, Eddie wasn't likely to risk that. He would choose the wall.

McKee thought about it. If Eddie came over the wall fast—moving from the bright morning light on the shelf into this darkness—then there would be a chance. But that wasn't likely to happen. Eddie would be taking no risks. He would climb the tumbled rocks of the wall slowly, pistol ready. He would pause at the top, studying the gloom. And, if he did, McKee would be a mouse in a trap.

He tested the extending main branch of the piñon. If he could pull it back enough and tie it to something, the route past the tree would be inviting. He could use his shirt as a rope, and tie one end well out on the branch. By putting his full weight against it, he could bend the tree well back from the lip of the cliff—opening an easy walkway. But where could he tie it?

A second after the ideas came to him, he heard Ellen.

Her voice was high, almost hysterical. He heard Eddie, an angry sound, and Ellen again—shouting now. And then the shot. A single crack of noise which released a rumble of echoes to bounce up and down the canyon.

"And now she is dead," McKee thought. "Canfield is dead and she is dead."

He bit the corner of the khaki shirt collar between his front teeth, pulled it taut with his left hand and split it gingerly with the knife. The pain was there when he held the knife, but he could tolerate it. He ripped the shirt down the back, twisted the two sections, and knotted them to his makeshift rope. Then he pulled out his belt and looped it around an outcrop of stone beside the wall.

Now it would reach. He pulled against the tree, thinking numbly that Eddie had not given him thirty minutes and that Ellen had chosen to shout a warning in the face of Eddie's pistol. He strained against the rope of shirt, pulled it through the looped belt, and wrapped it twice. His right hand was no help with this heavy work and he used his teeth to pull the knot tight. In a moment he would confront Eddie.

He was almost ready. He laid the knife on a rock protruding from the wall, sorted through stones in the dust at his feet and chose one which fit well in his left hand. In a very few minutes it would be over. Eddie would come. If Eddie walked past the tree, he would cut the shirt and the limb would slash at Eddie. And, as he cut the rope, he would come over the wall with the rock. If Eddie had been blinded by the whipping limb, or hurt, or even confused, he would kill Eddie. Either way, it would be over then. McKee thought of that. It was better than thinking of Ellen's voice and the sound of the pistol.

Eddie came almost too soon. McKee settled himself high on the rubble and looked over the top and Eddie was there. He was standing on the pathway at the corner, where the shelf was cut by the crevasse, studying the ruins. McKee shrank back behind the screen of piñon limbs as Eddie turned toward him. The gunman's vest was unbuttoned now and he held the pistol in his right hand, close to his body. The barrel, McKee noticed, always pointed with his eyes, like the flashlight of a man searching in the dark.

McKee felt a pressure in his chest and became aware he was holding his breath. He released it and gripped the rock.

Eddie moved now. He walked directly along the edge of the crevasse, just as McKee had done, stepping carefully over the tumbled partition walls. Twenty feet away he stopped and stood in a half crouch, studying the tree and the wall.

"McKee," he said. "I had to shoot your woman." Eddie's tone was conversational. He stood for a moment listening—no more than the polite pause for reply.

"Killing you is going to cost me thirty thousand dollars," Eddie said. "It's going to cost George twice that much." He paused again. "Are you going to make me do it?"

McKee found he was holding his breath again. Eddie was examining the wall, making his choice.

McKee looked at the rock in his hand. He turned his body, braced himself, and threw it in a high arching toss up the crevasse. There was a sudden echoing clatter as the stone bounced from wall to wall. Eddie took five quick, almost running, steps down the path and then stopped abruptly just short of the piñon.

McKee held the knife blade against the taut cloth. Eddie looked up along the wall and then squatted, peering past the lower branches of the piñon, so close now that McKee could only see his left shoulder and part of his back.

It happened very quickly then.

Eddie moved swiftly into the gap between tree and crevasse and McKee slashed downward with the knife. He knew even as the rope parted that Eddie had stopped again. He had underestimated the gunman's caution.

Coming over the wall, McKee saw only part of what happened. There was the blast of Eddie's pistol, fired into the swinging mass of the limb. Then the blond man, with lightning reflexes, leaped backward in a spinning crouch—swinging the pistol barrel toward him.

Eddie, suddenly, was no longer there. There was a cry—a sound mixed of surprise and anger and fear—and a crashing thump. Eddie's reflexive leap had carried him off the edge of the cliff into the crevasse.

When McKee first looked into the crevasse he presumed Eddie was dead. The man had apparently struck a sloping slab of sandstone about twenty feet below the shelf, bounced from that against a block-shaped mass of black rock, which jammed the center of the crack, and then fallen another ten feet. He was caught in an awkward jackknifed sitting position between rocks about fifteen feet above the sandy floor of the crevasse. Eddie's pistol lay on the sand, about forty-five feet down. McKee stared at it longingly. It was as unreachable as the moon.

And then he saw Eddie's head move. Eddie was looking up at him. His nose was bleeding, McKee noticed, and he was breathing through his mouth. McKee stared at the man, feeling a mixture of embarrassment and pity.

"I fell off," Eddie said.

"Yeh," McKee said. "When you jumped back from that tree."

He started to say he was sorry, but caught himself.

"Can you get down here to me? I got to have help."

"I don't know," McKee said. "George took the ladder down. You know any other way?"

"I was going to draw forty-five thousand dollars," Eddie said. "They had it written up so I'd get fifteen thousand when they were finished and then thirty thousand if nobody knew about it a year from now. That's why we had to have you write that letter."

The blood from Eddie's nose ran across his chin. He coughed. "I can't feel anything in my arms."

"Who are they?" McKee asked. "What are you doing in here?"

"George was getting more because he made the contract and it was up to him," Eddie said. "After this one, if we got it all, I'd of had almost two hundred thousand dollars saved up." He coughed again. "You don't pay taxes on it."

Eddie's head tilted forward. He seemed to be staring at the rock in front of him. McKee knew he was looking at death. If Eddie had been Navajo, soon his ghost would have been escaping to wander eternally, combining all that was weak, and evil, and unnatural in the man, and leaving behind all that was natural and good. Only the Dinee who died before their first cry at birth, or of a natural old age, escaped this fate and enjoyed simple oblivion. Eddie's ghost would be a greedy one, McKee thought, always coveting material possessions—the Navajo ultimate of unnatural wickedness.

Eddie coughed.

"Eddie, where's George now? How long will it be before he comes back?"

It took Eddie a moment to raise his head. "Today's when they were trying to get it finished. George had to go out and uncover the sets and after that . . ." Eddie paused to cough again. "Then we were going to pull out of here. One more day for George to clean up and then we'd be finished."

"But when will George be back?"

"I—I don't know," Eddie said.

"Please," McKee said. "I have to know."

"No. It wouldn't help. He works out of Los Angeles, but I heard about him all the way back East. They say he never broke a contract." Eddie coughed again. "Never screwed up a job.

He'll kill you and your woman and then he'll go on away."

McKee felt a sudden surge of hope. It lasted only a second.

"Didn't you kill her?"

"Oh," Eddie said. His voice was weak. "I forgot for a minute."

He peered up at McKee, frowning. "Told her not to yell," he said. "Maybe it didn't kill her."

McKee left him talking. He ran, hurdling the crumbled walls, back to where Ellen would be.

She was lying almost out of the crawl hole. She had apparently been emerging on hands and knees when Eddie shot her. McKee stood a long moment looking at her, feeling infinitely lonely and terribly tired. It wasn't until he lifted her that he realized she was still alive.

The bullet had cut through her cheek, deflected past her jawbone, struck the top of her shoulder, and torn out through the back of her shirt. McKee brought water, canned food, the first-aid kit, and one of the sleeping bags from the campsite. He laid her on the bed roll and examined the wounds. The slug apparently had hit her right shoulder blade, breaking it. It had deflected out through the back muscle, leaving a hole around which a seep of blood was beginning to clot. He rinsed the wounds, powdered them with disinfectant from the kit, bandaged her face, and applied a pad of gauze to the ragged tear where the bullet had finally emerged.

There was nothing else to do. He trotted back to the crevasse. Maybe Eddie could tell him something useful. Eddie was still staring at the rock in front of him, but now Eddie would answer no more questions.

McKee stared down at the body, thinking of what the blond man had told him. The Big Navajo was from Los Angeles. Probably, McKee thought, a "Relocation Navajo"—a child of one of those unfortunate families moved off the drought-stricken Reservation to urban centers during the 1930s. It had been one of the most disastrous experiments of the Bureau of Indian Affairs, turning hungry sheepherders into hungry city alcoholics. If George had been raised in Los Angeles, it would explain his weak command of the Navajo gutturals, and why what he knew of witches came from books. And maybe it would explain an Indian with the underworld connections which Eddie had seemed to imply. But it didn't explain why George and Eddie had been assigned to scare sheepherders out of this canyon country. Or why it was so important that no one learned they had been here.

The metal of Eddie's pistol reflected the early-morning sun. With that, McKee thought, he could simply wait for the Big Navajo to return, shoot him, carry Ellen down the ladder and take her to the hospital in the Land-Rover. But the pistol was beyond recovery. No way down into the crevasse and no way up if he got down.

He thought about it. Without the pistol he could probably keep the Big Navajo off the cliff. There were food and water at the camp. He could wait the big man out. But Ellen would be dying.

McKee chewed on his lip, trying desperately to think of the best solution. It was then he remembered the truck. Old Woman Gray Rocks had said it was parked in Hard Goods Canyon, nine miles up from the mouth of Many Ruins. That must be close—within two miles at the most. He made his decision.

It took him only a few minutes to hide Ellen Leon where the Big Navajo might not be able to find her. He carried her on the sleeping bag back into the ruins under the cliff. He put her in a room, with food and water beside her, and readjusted the bandage on her face. He saw then that her eyes were open.

"Bergen." She held out her hand and he took it—conscious of how small and fragile it felt.

"Lie very still," he said. "I'm going to climb out and get help."

"Bergen," she said again. "Be careful."

He ran back to the fissure in the cliff. He would climb out and find the truck. Somehow he would find the truck. If he didn't it would take a day and a night to walk to Shoemaker's. Eighteen or twenty hours, he guessed, which was about twelve more than he could spare.

He pushed past the piñon tree into the dark fissure, swallowing his dread of the climb. She had said Hall was smart—brilliant. If he could find Jim Hall, maybe Hall would be smart enough to save the girl he was engaged to marry.

THE SUN WAS ALMOST directly overhead when McKee found the wires. He squatted in the thin shade of a juniper and examined them—a cable about the diameter of his finger paralleled by a lighter wire. Both were heavily insulated with gray rubber, almost invisible on the rocky ground. The heavier one, McKee thought, would carry electrical current. The lighter one might be anything, maybe even a telephone wire. They must be part of the data-collection system for Dr. Hall's sound experiments, McKee knew, and they gave him the second hope he had felt since emerging from the chimney three hours earlier.

The first had come an hour ago when he had seen the boy on the horse. He had stopped to catch his breath and make sure of his directions on the plateau. He had glanced behind him, and the boy had been there—not two hundred yards away—silently staring at him. A boy wearing what looked like a red cap. But, when McKee had waved and shouted, the horse and rider had simply disappeared. They had vanished so suddenly that McKee almost doubted his eyes.

"He knows he's in witch country," McKee thought, "and he's spooky." Trying to follow him would be a foredoomed waste of time.

Following the wires, on the other hand, would be simple. At one end there would be some sort of gadget of the sort which concern electrical engineers. At the other end—with any luck at all—he would find the engineer. And Hall would have a truck and maybe a radio transmitter. The cable ran southeast across the plateau toward the Kam Bimghi Valley and northwest back toward the branch canyon McKee had been skirting. It was an easy choice. McKee trotted toward the canyon, following the cable.

At the rim, the cable looped downward, disappearing under brush and reappearing where it was strung across rocky outcrops. McKee paused at the rim, staring up the canyon after the cable.

This branch canyon was much shallower than Many Ruins and its broken walls offered several fairly easy ways down. From the canyon floor, McKee heard an echoing ping, ping, ping—the sound of metal striking metal. A flood of elation erased his weariness. Hall's truck must be there, and Hall with it. And it wasn't more than a quarter of a mile away.

The pain came with absolutely no warning, just as he took a step down off the rimrock. Behind the pain, perhaps a second, he was conscious of the flat snap of a rifle fired a long way off. Then he was conscious only that he was falling and of suffocation—of a terrible need to draw a breath into lungs that wouldn't work. He was on his back now, on a pile of talus just under the rim. The sky in front of his eyes was dark blue. He could breathe again, although inhaling hurt. And he could think again. He put his hand where the pain was, on his right chest. It came away hot and red. Someone had shot him. Who? The boy on the horse? That made no sense. The Big Navajo. Yes, of course.

McKee pushed himself into a sitting position against the rimrock and gingerly examined the damage. He could feel the bullet hole on his back—a small burning spot. It had come out left of his left nipple, tearing a hole through which blood now welled. Broken ribs, he thought, but the lung must have been missed. It still inflated.

McKee coughed and flinched at the knife in his ribs. He tried to think. The Big Navajo must have returned to the cliff, and had found Ellen. No use thinking about it.

From up canyon he heard the dim, puttering sound of a two-cycle engine. Probably a generator motor. And probably down in the canyon bottom Hall hadn't heard the shot. Or if he had heard it would have no reason to be warned by it. He had to reach Hall in time to tell him.

McKee pulled himself to his feet, took three steps along the talus and stopped, gasping, supporting himself by hanging on to the rubber-clad cable strung across the rocks. It would take him half an hour at this rate to reach the truck. And he didn't think he had that much time.

Over the rim he could see nothing at first. An expanse of plateau, sparse clumps of buffalo grass, a scattering of drought-dwarfed piñon, juniper, and creosote bush, a stony surface on which nothing moved. Then he saw, to his left, the figure of a man. The man walked slowly, a rifle with a telescopic sight held across his chest. He moved unhurriedly, relentlessly, inexorably toward the point of rimrock from which McKee had fallen. Five hundred yards away, walking almost casually toward him under a broad-brimmed black hat, was certain death.

McKee fought down a desperate impulse to run. When he conquered the panic he found it replaced by a hard, cold, overpowering anger. He looked around for a weapon and became abruptly conscious of the soft rubber insulation of the cable gripped in his palm.

You son of a bitch. You bastard. You won't just finish me off like a crippled animal. You'll have to come and get me.

Had the Big Navajo been careless, had he simply walked his slow walk directly to the rimrock, McKee would have run out of time. But the Big Navajo took no chances at all. When McKee finally heard his boots, the sound came from below. The hunter was stalking cautiously, skirting the point on the rim where he must have seen McKee knocked down by his bullet, taking his time.

McKee had worked feverishly. He pulled the slack cable over a boulder and slammed it twice with a rock. The cable severed and the end sprang away in a shower of sparks. He stripped five feet of the thick rubber tubing from the dead end with his pocket knife. While he worked, the plan formed in his mind. Just up the canyon, a huge ponderosa had fallen against the rocky cliff—a dead log half obscured by a thick growth of pine saplings. He would crawl into that darkness, tie the rubber to two sapling trunks to make a catapult, cut himself a lance from another sapling, and hope the Big Navajo made a mistake.

The Big Navajo was making no mistakes. McKee could see him now, moving in a half-crouch ten yards below the rimrock. The big man stared upward at the place where McKee's blood smeared the boulder. McKee could see his profile, shaded under the broad rim of the new black hat. It was a handsome face, hawklike and intent. The Big Navajo moved up to the boulder and knelt beside it. He examined the bloody talus debris and then stood, scanned the slope below, and began walking carefully along the route McKee had taken.

McKee pushed his heels deeper into the pine needles and tested his lance against the tension of the rubber. He had cut a yard-long length of a three-quarter-inch pine stem, given it a crude point, and then hammered the punch tool of his knife into the soft wood six inches from the heavy end. Snapped off, this prong of steel provided the hook on which he had caught the rubber.

He was lying almost flat, his weight pulling against the tough rubber. Down the shaft of the sapling, he saw the Navajo's hat rise into view as he moved slowly up the slope. Then his shoulders, then his belt. The man stopped. He looked at the fallen tree, at the growth of young ponderosa. He stared intently from the sunlight into the deep shadows.

McKee held his breath, fought against the dizziness. Four or five steps closer, he prayed. Keep coming. Keep coming.

The Navajo stood, staring directly at him. His face was thoughtful. Suddenly he smiled.

"Well," he said. "There you are."

It seemed to McKee to take quite a little time. The Big Navajo's right hand brought the rifle butt smoothly up to the right shoulder, the left hand swung the barrel toward him, the Navajo's face moved slightly to the right, behind the telescopic sight. All this while McKee was releasing the lance.

Most likely the telescope made the difference. Over open sights, the Indian would have seen the lance at the moment of its launch, seen it soon enough to simply step aside. Behind the sight, he saw it too late. There was a sound—which McKee would remember—something like a hammer striking a melon. And the clatter of the rifle falling on the rocks. And the sound of the Big Navajo tumbling backward down the slope.

McKee crawled out of the thicket and picked up the rifle. It seemed incredibly heavy. The Big Navajo had slid, head downward, between two boulders. McKee looked at the man and hastily looked away. The pine shaft had struck him low on the chest. There was no chance at all that he was alive. The black hat lay by the boulder, the sun reflecting off the rich silver of its concho band. And up the slope was a furry bundle tied with a leather thong. McKee untied the thong. A wolf skin unrolled itself.

McKee felt a whirling dizziness. *Always wanted a witch's skin. Hang it on my office wall. Maybe give it to Canfield.*

He remembered, then, that Canfield was dead, and was conscious that his side was wet and his pant leg was sticking to his thigh. He put the wolf skin over his arm and started down the slope toward the canyon floor. He fell once. But he remembered Ellen Leon and got back to his feet. And finally he was on the sandy canyon floor, where walking was easy.

"Put down the rifle."

"What?" McKee said. A boy was standing behind a clump of willows. There was a horse by him, the reins dragging.

"Put down the rifle." The boy had on a red baseball cap and he had a short-barreled rifle in his hands. An old .30-30. It was pointed at McKee.

McKee dropped the Big Navajo's rifle. The wolf skin fell with it, dropping in a folded hump on the sand.

"Where's the other witch?"

"What?" McKee said. It was important to think about this. "He's dead," he said, after a moment. "He shot me and I killed him. Back up there under the rimrock." McKee pushed the wolf skin with his toes. "This is his witch skin," he said, speaking now in Navajo. "I am not a witch. I am one who teaches in school."

The boy was looking at him, his face expressionless.

"There is a truck a little ways up here," McKee said. "You must let me get to that truck and the man there will help me."

"All right." The boy hesitated, thinking. "You walk. I will walk behind you."

He was within thirty yards of the truck before he saw it—parked in a thicket of tamarisk and willow just off the canyon floor. Beside it a gasoline generator was running. The back door of the van stood open, a padlock dangling in the hasp. Through the doorway McKee heard the faint sound of someone whistling and then of metal tapping on metal.

McKee stopped.

"Hello," he shouted. It didn't sound like his voice.

McKee took two more steps toward the truck, conscious the whistling had stopped.

A man appeared in the doorway of the van, blond, in a denim jacket, taller than McKee and younger, with a hearing aid behind his left ear. His blue eyes rested for a second on McKee, registering surprise and shock.

"What the hell happened?" he said. And then he was out of the truck, coming toward McKee.

"Got shot," McKee said. "Somebody shot me." His voice sounded thick. "Get the bleeding stopped." He sat down abruptly on the sand.

The blond man was saying something.

"Don't talk," McKee said. "Listen. Are you Jim Hall?"

"How did you know that?"

"Listen," McKee said. "Tell this boy here that I'm not a witch and he will help you." He paused now and started again, trying to pronounce the words.

"Ellen Leon was shot, too. Ellen Leon. She's up at that big cliff dwelling in a canyon. . . ." McKee tried to think. "In that canyon that runs into Many Ruins south and west of here."

The man was squatting beside McKee now, his face close. McKee had trouble focusing on the face. The face was surprised, amazed, excited, maybe frightened.

"You said Ellen?" the man said. "What the devil is she doing out here? What happened to her?"

"Man shot her. Needs help," McKee said. "Go help her."

"Who shot her?" the man asked.

"Man named Eddie," McKee said. He was very tired. Why didn't this fool go? "Don't worry," he said, "Eddie's dead now."

He heard the man asking him something but he couldn't think of an answer. And then the man's hands were on his face, the man was talking right into his face.

"Listen. Tell me. What happened to Eddie? What happened to Eddie? And was there a man with him? Where's the man who was with him?"

McKee couldn't think of how to answer. Something was wrong.

He tried to say, "Dead," but Jim Hall was talking again.

"Answer me, damn you," Hall said, his voice fierce. "Do the police know about this? Has anybody told the police?"

McKee thought he would answer in a moment. Now he was concentrating on not falling over on his side.

Hall stood up. He was talking to the boy with the red baseball cap, and then the boy was talking. McKee could hear part of it.

"Did you see the witch he killed?"

He couldn't hear what the boy answered.

"You were right when you guessed that," Hall was saying. "This man here is a Navajo Wolf. Give me your rifle."

McKee stopped listening. He was asking himself how Jim Hall knew about the man with Eddie, asking himself why Hall was acting the way he was acting. Almost immediately, with sick, despairing clarity, he saw the answer. Hall was the Big Navajo's other man.

The boy hadn't given Hall the rifle. He was standing there, looking doubtful.

"Put the rifle in the truck then," Hall said. "We'll leave the witch here. Tie him up first. And then we'll drive to Chinle and tell the police about him." Hall paused. "Hand me the rifle and I'll put it in the truck."

"Don't," McKee said. "Don't give him the rifle."

Hall turned to look at him. McKee focused on the face. It looked angry. And then it didn't look angry any more. Another voice had said something, something in Navajo.

It said, "That's right, Billy Nez, don't give him your rifle." And the anger left Jim Hall's face as McKee looked at it, and it looked shocked and sick. Then it was gone.

McKee gave up. He fell over on his side. Much better.

The metallic sound of the door in the van slamming and then a voice, the voice of Joe Leaphorn, and a little later a single loud pop.

I can't faint now, McKee told himself, because I have to tell him about Ellen. But he fainted.

18

HE WAS AWARE FIRST of the vague sick smell of ether, of the feel of hospital sheets, of the cast on his chest, and of the splint bandaged tightly on his right hand. The room was dark. There was the shape of a man standing looking out the window into the sunlight. The man was Joe Leaphorn.

"Did you find her?" McKee asked.

"Sure," Leaphorn said. He sat beside the bed. "We found her before we found you, as a matter of fact." He interrupted McKee's question. "She's right down the hall. Broken cheekbone and a broken shoulder and some lost blood."

He looked down at McKee, grinning. "They had to put about ten gallons in you. You were dry."

"She's going to be all right?"

"She's already all right. You've been in here two days."

McKee thought for a while.

"Her boyfriend," he said. "How'd it all come out in the canyon?"

"Son of a bitch shot himself," Leaphorn said. "Walked right away from me into the truck, and slammed the door and locked it and got out a little .22 he had in there and shot himself right through the forehead." Leaphorn's expression was sour. "Walked right in with me just standing there," he added. He didn't sound like he could make himself believe it.

McKee felt sick. Maybe it was the ether.

"You've got more Navajo blood in you now than I do,"

Leaphorn said. "The doc said you had a busted oil pan. Took ten gallons."

"I guess you had to tell her about Hall."

"She knows."

"He must have been crazy," McKee said.

"Crazy to get rich," Leaphorn said. "You call it ambition. Sometimes we call it witchcraft. You remember the Origin Myth, when First Woman sent the Heron diving back into the Fourth World to get the witchcraft bundle. She told him to swim down and bring back 'the way to make money.' "

"Knock off the philosophy," McKee said. "What happened? How did you find her?"

"I've noticed this before," Leaphorn said. "Belacani women are smarter than you Belacani men. Miss Leon got herself over to that camp stove on that cliff. She poured out the kerosene and made herself a smoky little smudge fire. You could see it for miles."

He grinned at McKee.

"Something else she figured out that you might like to know about. She was having her doubts about Hall when I got there. All excited. Said you'd gone to find him and she was afraid something might happen to you. Miss Leon wanted me to climb up that split in the cliff and go chasing across that plateau to rescue you."

McKee felt better. He was, in fact, feeling wonderful.

"Why didn't you think of something simple, like making a big smoke?" Leaphorn asked. "Climbing up that crack in the rock was showing off."

"How was I going to know you'd be wandering around out there?" McKee asked. "It's supposed to be the cavalry that arrives in the nick of time, not the blanket-ass Indians."

McKee had a sobering thought. "I guess you know I killed those two men?"

"Not officially, you didn't," Leaphorn said. "Officially, we've got just two dead people. Officially, Dr. Canfield and Jim Hall were killed in a truck accident. Miss Leon and you were hurt in the crash. And officially Eddie Poher and George Jackson never existed."

"Was that their names? And what was going on in there, anyway? What was Hall doing?"

"It's a secret," Leaphorn said.

"Like hell it's a secret," McKee said. "If you want me to tell some phony story about Canfield getting killed in a truck wreck, you don't have secrets."

"I'm not really supposed to know all of it myself."

"But you do," McKee said.

Leaphorn looked at him a long moment.

"Well," he said. "You cut one of his cables so I guess you know Hall had portable radar sets staked out on that plateau. And you know that plateau is under the route from the Tonepah Range up in Utah down to White Sands Proving Grounds."

"Yeah," McKee said. "I knew that much." He wondered why he hadn't thought of radar.

"Hall was sitting with his radar right under what the military calls its 'Bird Path,' and when the birds flew from Tonepah the radar was feeding information into a computer in the van. Hall was putting it into tapes."

"What were they testing?"

"The military intelligence people don't tell a Navajo cop things like that."

"I'll bet you can guess."

Leaphorn looked at him again. "Maybe the MIRV. The Multiple Intercontinental Re-entry Vehicle. Read about it in *Newsweek.* One missile, but it drops off five or six warheads and some decoys. I'd guess that if I was guessing."

"It still doesn't make sense. What was he doing with the information and how'd a guy like Hall get tied up with that bunch?"

"If you'll shut up and listen, I'll tell you."

From what they now knew, Leaphorn explained, Hall, Poher, and Jackson had arrived on the Reservation separately almost two months ago. A fingerprint check had been enlightening. Poher was relatively unknown. One arrest on suspicion of conspiracy to rob a bank, some East Coast Mafia associations, but no convictions. Jackson was another story. He was also known as Amos Raven, and Big Raven and George Thomas, with a long and violent juvenile record dating back into the late thirties in Los Angeles, and one adult conviction for armed robbery, and a half-dozen arrests for questioning in an assortment of crimes of violence—all Mafia-connected.

"A Relocation Indian. Jackson seems to have been born in Los Angeles." Leaphorn laughed. "California Navajo. That's what had me hung up. I was expecting him to act like The People and all he knew about The People he must have got out of a book."

"Case Studies in Navajo Ethnic Aberrations, for one," McKee said, "by John Greersen."

"Anyway," Leaphorn continued, "Jackson had apparently been picked for this assignment simply because he was a Navajo and looked like one. His job must have been to help Hall set up his equipment and to make sure that nobody knew what was going on. It wouldn't have seemed difficult, for the very reason the military chose this route for its overland missile. The country was almost completely deserted. Hall set up in Many Ruins Canyon complex, which The People avoid because of the Anasazi ghosts, and Jackson scared the few stragglers out by pretending to be a witch."

"Except Horseman," McKee said.

"Yeah. Except Horseman." Leaphorn's voice was flat.

"It wasn't your fault," McKee said.

"Remember what I said to Jackson at the trading post? I said if Horseman don't come out we'll come in looking for him. So Jackson brought him out for us and laid him out where we couldn't miss him."

"Use your head, Joe. There was no way you could have stopped it from happening."

"I was slow figuring it out," Leaphorn said. "I smelled something about Jackson. But I figured him to act like a Navajo and he was acting like a white man."

"Thanks a lot," McKee said.

"If he was a Navajo, no matter what he was doing in there, killing Horseman would have screwed it up for him. He would have gone off somewhere and had a sweat bath, and then he would have found himself a Singer and got himself cured and forgot about it."

Leaphorn told McKee about the Enemy Way and about finding the place where Jackson had built the road up Ceniza Mesa.

"He had put one of the radar sets up there and then he was improving his road so he could get it down fast, without using the winch. When he missed his hat, he knew someone had seen him, so he moved the radar back over to the plateau. I didn't know about the radar but it was beginning to be clear by then that there had to be a lot of money involved somewhere. You put it together—a lot of money and a killing. It's not natural and it's not Navajo."

"All right," McKee said. "I'll buy that. But how did Hall get into it?"

"I don't know," Leaphorn said. "I hear the federals are looking into a little West Coast electronics company with Mafia ownership. I think Hall did some work for them before—something legitimate." He looked at McKee pensively. "Didn't that business about Jackson wanting you to write the letter tell you something?"

"It told me he didn't want anybody coming in there looking for us," McKee said. "What else?"

"Think about it," Leaphorn said. "If you have a bunch of computer tapes giving you the exact performance of the other guy's ballistic missile system, it's worth a bunch of money. But it's worth a lot more if the other side doesn't suspect you've got it. Right?"

"Because if he suspects he changes the system," McKee said. "Eddie said something about that. About the letter being worth a lot of money."

A nurse came in then, a Navajo girl, in the uniform of the Indian Service Hospital. She scolded Leaphorn for staying too long, took McKee's temperature and gave him a capsule and a drink of water.

When McKee awoke again, there was a tray beside his bed with a covered dish of food on it, and beside the dish was an envelope.

He turned the envelope in his good hand, aware before he

opened it of the familiar feeling of his common sense struggling with his perennial incurable optimism. The note inside was from Ellen Leon. Tomorrow, it began, the doctor would let her come to visit him. It was not just fourteen blunt words in blue ink on blue paper. It was a long letter.

DANCE HALL OF THE DEAD

For Alex Atcitty and Old Man Madman and all the others who agree that Custer had it coming

AUTHOR'S NOTE

In this book, the setting is genuine. The Village of Zuñi and the landscape of the Zuñi reservation and the adjoining Ramah Navajo reservation are accurately depicted to the best of my ability. The characters are purely fictional. The view the reader receives of the Shalako religion is as it might be seen by a Navajo with an interest in ethnology. It does not pretend to be more than that.

Sunday, November 30, 5:18 p.m.

SHULAWITSI, THE LITTLE FIRE GOD, member of the Council of the Gods and Deputy to the Sun, had taped his track shoes to his feet. He had wound the tape as Coach taught him, tight over the arch of the foot. And now the spikes biting into the packed earth of the sheep trail seemed a part of him. He ran with perfectly conditioned grace, his body a machine in motion, his mind detached, attending other things. Just ahead where the trail shifted down the slope of the mesa he would stop—as he always did—and check his time and allow himself four minutes of rest. He knew now with an exultant certainty that he would be ready. His lungs had expanded, his leg muscles hardened. In two days when he led Longhorn and the Council from the ancestral village to Zuñi, fatigue would not cause him to forget the words of the great chant, or make any missteps in the ritual dance. And when Shalako came he would be ready to dance all the night without an error. The Salamobia would never have to punish him. He remembered the year when he was nine, and Hu-tu-tu had stumbled on the causeway over Zuñi Wash, and the Salamobia had struck him with their yucca wands and everyone had laughed. Even the Navajos had laughed, and they laughed very little at Shalako. They would not laugh at him.

The Fire God half fell onto the outcropping of rock that was his regular resting place. He glanced quickly at his watch. He had used eleven minutes and fourteen seconds on this lap—cutting eleven seconds off his time of yesterday. The thought gave him satisfaction, but it faded quickly. He sat on the outcrop, a slender boy with black hair falling damp across his forehead, massaging his legs through the cotton of his sweat pants. The memory of the laughing Navajos had turned his thoughts to George Bowlegs. He approached these thoughts gingerly, careful to avoid any anger. It was always to be avoided, but now it was strictly taboo. The Koyemshi had appeared in the village two days ago, announcing in each of the four plazas of Zuñi that eight days hence the Shalako would come from the Dance Hall of the Dead to visit their people and bless them. This was no time for angry thoughts. Bowlegs was his friend, but Bowlegs was crazy. And he had reason to be angry with him if the season did not forbid it. George had asked too many questions, and since George was a friend he had given more answers than he should have given. No matter how badly he wanted to be a Zuñi, to join the Fire God's own Badger Clan, George was still a Navajo. He had not been initiated, had not felt the darkness of the mask slip over his head, and seen through the eyes of the kachina spirit. And therefore there were things that George was not allowed to know and some of those things, the Fire God thought glumly, he might have told George. Father Ingles didn't think so, but Father Ingles was a white man.

Behind him, above the red sandstone wall of the mesa, a skyscape of feathery cirrus clouds stretched southward toward Mexico. To the west over the Painted Desert, they were flushed with the afterglow of sunset. To the north this reflected light colored the cliffs of the Zuñi Buttes a delicate rose. Far below him in the shadow of the mesa, a light went on in the camper near the site of the anthropologist's dig. Ted Isaacs cooking supper, the Fire God thought. And that was another thing not to think about, to avoid being angry with George. It had been George's idea to see if they could find some of the things made by the Old People in the Doctor's box of chips and beads and arrowheads. He would make use of it on a hunting fetish, George had said. Maybe make one for both of them. And the Doctor had been furious, and now Isaacs would not let anyone come anymore to watch him work. Crazy George.

The Fire God rubbed his legs, feeling a tightening in the

thigh muscles as breeze dried the sweat. In seventeen more seconds he would run again, cover the last mile down the mesa slope to where George would be waiting with his bicycle. Then he would go home and finish his homework.

He ran again, moving first at a slow jog and then faster as the stiffness left. Sweat again dampened the back of his sweat shirt, darkening the stenciled letters that said "Property of Zuñi Consolidated Schools." Under the angry red sky he ran, into the thickening darkness, thinking of crazy George, his oldest and best friend. He thought of George collecting cactus buttons for the doper at the hippie commune, and eating them himself in search of visions, of George going to the old man at the edge of Zuñi to learn how to become a sorcerer, and how angry the old man had been, of George wanting to quit being a Navajo so he could be a Zuñi. George was certainly crazy but George was his friend, and here now was his bicycle and George would be waiting.

The figure which stepped from behind the boulders in the red darkness was not George. It was a Salamobia, its round yellow-circled eyes staring at him. The Fire God stopped, opened his mouth, and found nothing to say. This was the Salamobia of the mole kiva, its mask painted the color of darkness. And yet it was not. The Fire God stared at the figure, the muscular body in the dark shirt, the bristling ruff of turkey feathers surrounding the neck, the black and empty eyes, the fierce beak, the plumed feathered topknot. Black was the color of the Mole Salamobia, but this was not the mask. He knew that mask. His mother's uncle was the personifier of the Mole Salamobia and the mask lived at a shrine in his mother's uncle's home. But if it was not the mask . . .

The Fire God saw then that the wand rising in the hand of this Salamobia was not of woven yucca. It glittered in the red light of the twilight. And he remembered that Salamobia, like all of the ancestor spirits which lived at the Zuñi masks, were visible only to members of the Sorcery Fraternity, and to those about to die.

2

Monday, December 1, 12:20 p.m.

LIEUTENANT JOE LEAPHORN was watching the fly. He should have been listening to Ed Pasquaanti, who, perched on a swivel chair behind the desk marked "Chief of Police, Zuñi" was talking steadily in a quick, precise voice. But Pasquaanti was discussing the jurisdictional problem and Leaphorn already understood both the problem and why Pasquaanti was talking about it. Pasquaanti wanted to make sure that Leaphorn and McKinley County Deputy Sheriff Cipriano ("Orange") Naranjo and State Policeman J. D. Highsmith understood that on the Zuñi reservation the Zuñi police would be running the investigation. And that was fine with Leaphorn. The sooner he got away from here, the happier he'd be. The fly had distracted him a moment or two earlier by landing on his notebook. It walked now, with the sluggishness of all winter-doomed insects, up the margin of the paper toward his finger. Would a Zuñi fly deign to tread upon Navajo skin? Leaphorn instantly regretted the thought. It represented a slip back into the illogical hostility he had been struggling against all morning—ever since he had been handed, at the Ramah chapter house, the message which had sent him over here.

Typical of the radio messages Leaphorn received from Shiprock, it said a little too little. Leaphorn was to drive over to Zuñi without delay to help find George Bowlegs, fourteen, a Navajo. Other details would be available from Zuñi police, with whom Leaphorn was instructed to cooperate.

The radioman at the Ramah communications center

grinned when he handed it over. "Before you ask," he said, "yes, this is all they said. And no, I don't know a damn thing about it."

"Well, hell," Leaphorn said. He could see how it would work. A thirty-mile drive over to Zuñi to find out that the kid had stolen something or other and had disappeared. But the Zuñis wouldn't know a damn thing about the boy. So then there would be the thirty-mile drive back to the Ramah reservation to find out where to look for him. And then . . . "You know anything about this George Bowlegs?" he asked.

The radioman knew about what Leaphorn had expected he would. He wasn't sure, but maybe the boy was the son of a guy named Shorty Bowlegs. Shorty had moved back from the Big Reservation after something went wrong with a woman he'd married over there around Coyote Canyon. This Shorty Bowlegs was a member of the High Standing House clan, and one of the boys of Old Woman Running. And once, after he had come back from Coyote Canyon, he had applied for a land use allocation with the grazing committee here. But then he had moved off somewhere. And maybe this was the wrong man, anyway.

"O.K., then," Leaphorn said. "If anybody wants me, I'll be at the police station in Zuñi."

"Don't look so sour," the radioman said, still grinning. "I don't think the Zuñis been initiating anybody into the Bow Society lately."

Leaphorn had laughed at that. Once, or so Navajos believed, initiates into the Zuñi Bow priesthood had been required to bring a Navajo scalp. He laughed, but his mood remained sour. He drove down N.M. 53 toward Zuñi a little faster than he should, the mood bothering him because he could find no logical reason to explain it. Why resent this assignment? The job that had taken him to Ramah had been onerous enough to make an interruption welcome. An old Singer had complained that he had given a neighbor woman eight hundred dollars to take into Gallup and make a down payment on a pickup truck, and the woman had spent his money. Some of the facts had been easy enough to establish. The woman had retrieved almost eight hundred dollars of her pawn from a Gallup shop on the day in question and she hadn't given any money to the car lot owner. So it should have been simple, but it wasn't. The woman said the Singer owed her the money, and that the Singer was a witch, a Navajo Wolf. And then there was the question of which side of the boundary fence they'd been standing on when the money changed hands. If she was standing where she said she had been, they were on Navajo reservation land and under tribal-federal jurisdiction. But if they stood where the Singer claimed, they were over on nonreservation allocation land and the case would probably be tried under the New Mexico embezzlement law. Leaphorn could think of no way to resolve that problem and ordinarily he would have welcomed even a temporary escape from it. But he found himself resenting this job—hunting a fellow Navajo at the behest of Zuñis.

Pasquaanti's voice rattled on. The fly took a tentative step toward Leaphorn's hard brown knuckle, then stopped. Leaphorn suddenly understood his mood. It was because he felt that Zuñis felt superior to Navajos. And he felt this because he, Joe Leaphorn, had once—a long time ago—had a Zuñi roommate during his freshman year at Arizona State about whom he had developed a silly inferiority complex. Therefore his present mood wasn't at all logical, and Leaphorn disliked illogic in others and detested it in himself. The fly walked around his finger and disappeared, upside down, under the notebook. Pasquaanti stopped talking.

"I don't think we're going to have any jurisdictional problems," Leaphorn said impatiently. "So why don't you fill us in on what we're working on?" It would have been more polite to let Pasquaanti set his own pace. Leaphorn knew it, and he saw in Pasquaanti's face that the Zuñi knew he knew it.

"Here's what we know so far," Pasquaanti said. He shuffled a Xeroxed page to each of them. "Two boys missing and a pretty good bet that one of them got cut."

Two boys? Leaphorn scanned the page quickly and then, abruptly interested, went back over every sentence carefully. Two boys missing. Bowlegs and a Zuñi named Ernesto Cata, and the Cata boy's bicycle, and a "large" expanse of blood soaked into the ground where the bicycle had been left.

"It says here they're classmates," Leaphorn said. "But Bowlegs is fourteen and Cata is listed as twelve. Were they in the same grade?" Leaphorn wished instantly he'd not asked the question. Pasquaanti would simply remind them all that Bowlegs was a Navajo—thereby explaining the gap in academic performance.

"Both in the seventh grade," Pasquaanti said. "The Cata boy'd be thirteen in a day or two. They'd been close friends two, three years. Good friends. Everybody says it."

"No trace of a weapon?" Naranjo asked.

"Nothing," Pasquaanti said. "Just blood. The weapon could have been anything that will let the blood out of you. You never saw so much blood. But I'd guess it wasn't a gun. Nobody remembers hearing anything that sounded like a shot and it happened close enough to the village so *somebody* would have heard." Pasquaanti paused. "I'd guess it was something that chopped. There was blood sprayed on the needles of piñon there as well as all that soaked into the ground, so maybe something cut a major artery while he was standing there. Anyway, whoever it was must have taken the weapon with him."

"Whoever?" Leaphorn said. "Then you're not all that sure Bowlegs is the one?"

Pasquaanti looked at him, studying his face. "We're not sure of nothing," he said. "All we know is down there. The Cata boy didn't come home last night. They went out looking for him when it got daylight and they found the blood where he left his bicycle. The Bowlegs kid had borrowed the bike and he was supposed to bring it back there to that meeting place they had. O.K.? So the Bowlegs boy shows up at school this morning, but when we find out about the borrowed bike and all and send a man over there to talk to him, he's gone. Turns out he got up during his social studies class and said something to the teacher about feeling sick and cut out."

"If he did the killing," Naranjo said, "you'd think he'd have run right after he did it."

"Course we don't know there *was* a killing yet," Pasquaanti said. "That could be animal blood. Lot of butchering going on now. People getting ready for all that cooking for Shalako."

"Unless maybe Bowlegs was smart enough to figure no one would suspect him unless he did run," Naranjo said. "So he came to school and then he lost his nerve and ran anyway."

"I don't think it got typed up there in the report, but the kids said Bowlegs was looking for Cata when he got to school, asking where he was and all," Pasquaanti said.

"That could have been part of the act," Leaphorn said. He was glad to find he was thinking like a cop again.

"I guess so," Pasquaanti said. "But remember he's just fourteen years old."

Leaphorn tapped the page. "It says here that Cata had gone out to run. What was it? Track team or something?"

The silence lasted maybe three seconds—long enough to tell Leaphorn the answer wouldn't be track team. It would be something to do with the Zuñi religion. Pasquaanti was deciding exactly how much he wanted them to know before he opened his mouth.

"This Cata boy had been selected to have a part in the religious ceremonials this year," Pasquaanti said. "Some of those ceremonials last for hours, the dancing is hard, and you have to be in condition. He was running every evening to keep in condition."

Leaphorn was remembering the Shalako ceremonial he'd attended a long time ago—back when he'd had a freshman Zuñi roommate. "Was Cata the one they call the Fire God?" he asked. "The one who is painted black and wears the spotted mask and carries the firebrand?"

"Yeah," Pasquaanti said. "Cata was Shulawitsi." He looked uncomfortable. "I don't imagine that has anything to do with this, though."

Leaphorn thought about it. Probably not, he decided. He wished he knew more about the Zuñi religion. But that wouldn't be his problem anyway. His problem would be finding George Bowlegs.

Pasquaanti was fumbling through a folder. "The only picture we have of the boys so far is the one in the school yearbook." He handed each of them a page of photos, two of the faces circled with red ink. "If we don't find them quick, we'll get the photographer to make us some big blowups off the negatives," he said. "We'll get copies of the pictures sent over to the sheriff's office and the state police, and over to the Arizona state police, too. And if we find out anything we'll get the word to you right away so you won't be wasting your time." Pasquaanti got up. "I'm going to ask Lieutenant Leaphorn to sort of concentrate on trying to find out where George Bowlegs got to. We'll be working on trying to find Ernesto and the bicycle, and anything else we can find out."

It occurred to Leaphorn that Pasquaanti, with his jurisdiction properly established, was not offering any advice about how to find Bowlegs. He was presuming that Naranjo and Highsmith and Leaphorn understood their jobs and knew how to do them.

"I'll need to know where Bowlegs lived, and if anybody's been there to see if he went home."

"It's about four miles out to where Shorty Bowlegs has his hogan and I'm going to have to draw you a little map," Pasquaanti said. "We went out but we didn't learn anything."

Leaphorn's expression asked the question for him.

Pasquaanti looked slightly embarrassed. "Shorty was there. But he was too drunk to talk."

"O.K.," Leaphorn said. "Did you find any tracks around where you found the blood?"

"Lot of bicycle tracks. He'd been going there for months to start running. And then there was a place where somebody wearing moccasins or some sort of heelless shoes had been standing around. Looks like he waited quite a while. Found a place where he sat under the piñon there. Crushed down some weeds. And then there was the tracks of Ernesto's track shoes. It's mostly rock in that place. Hard to read anything."

Leaphorn was thinking that he might go to this spot himself, that he could find tracks where a Zuñi couldn't. Pasquaanti was looking at him, suspecting such thoughts. "You didn't find anything that told you much, then?" Leaphorn asked.

"Just that our boy Ernesto Cata had a lot of blood in him," Pasquaanti said. He smiled at Leaphorn, but the smile was grim.

Monday, December 1, 3:50 p.m.

THE TIRE BLEW about halfway back from Shorty Bowlegs' place, reconfirming Leaphorn's belief that days that begin badly tend to end badly. The road wound through the rough country behind Corn Mountain—nothing more than a seldom-used wagon track. One *could* follow it through the summer's growth of weeds and grama grass if one paid proper attention. Leaphorn hadn't. He had concentrated on making some sense of what little he had learned from Bowlegs instead of on his driving. And the left front wheel had slammed into a weed-covered pothole and ruptured its sidewall.

He set the jack under the front bumper. Bowlegs had been too drunk for coherent conversation. But apparently he had seen George this morning when the boy and his younger brother left on the long walk to catch the school bus. The elder Bowlegs didn't seem to have the faintest idea when George had returned to the hogan Sunday night. That could mean either that it was after Shorty had gone to sleep, or that Shorty had been too drunk to notice.

Leaphorn pumped the jack handle, feeling irritated and slightly sorry for himself. By now Highsmith would be cruising comfortably down Interstate 40, having filed his descriptions of George Bowlegs and Ernesto Cata in the channels which would assure that highway patrolmen would eye young Indian hitch-hikers with suspicion. And Orange Naranjo would be back in Gallup and equally done with it once his report was circulated in the proper places. Pasquaanti would have given up on finding any tracks by now and would simply be waiting. There would be nothing much else to do in Zuñi. The word would have spread within an hour through every red stone home in the beehive village and across the reservation that one of the sons of Zuñi was missing and probably dead and that the Navajo boy who was always hanging around was wanted by the police. If any Zuñi saw George Bowlegs anywhere, Pasquaanti would know it fast.

The jack slipped on the slope of the pothole. Leaphorn cursed with feeling and eloquence, removed the jack, and began laboriously chipping out a firmer base in the rocky soil with the jack handle. The outburst of profanity had made him feel a little better. After all, what the sergeant and the deputy and the Zuñi cop were doing was all that it made any sense for them to do. If Bowlegs headed for Albuquerque or Phoenix or Gallup, or hung around Zuñi territory, he would almost certainly be picked up quickly and efficiently. If he holed up somewhere in Navajo country, that would be Leaphorn's problem—and it was nobody's fault that it was a much tougher one, solvable only by persistent hard work. Leaphorn reset the jack, reinserted the handle, stretched his cramped muscles, and looked down the wagon track at the expanse of wooded mesas and broken canyon country stretching toward the southern horizon. He saw the beauty, the patterned cloud shadows, the red of the cliffs, and everywhere the blue, gold, and gray of dry country autumn. But soon the north wind would take the last few leaves and one cold night this landscape would change to solid white. And then George Bowlegs, if he was hiding somewhere in it, would be in trouble. He would survive easily enough until the snow came. There were dried berries and edible roots and rabbits, and a Navajo boy would know where to find them. But one day an end would come to the endless sunshine of the mountain autumn. An arctic storm front would bulge down out of western Canada, down the west slope of the Rockies. Here the altitude was almost a mile and a half above sea level and there was already hard frost in the mornings. With the first storm, the mornings would be subzero. There would be no way to find food with the snow blowing. On the first day, George Bowlegs would be hungry. Then he would be weak. And then he would freeze.

Leaphorn grimaced and turned back to the jack. It was then he saw the boy standing there shyly, not fifty feet away, waiting to be noticed. He recognized him instantly from the yearbook photograph. The same rounded forehead, the same wide-set, alert eyes, the same wide mouth. Leaphorn pumped the jack handle. "Ya-ta-hey," he said.

"Ya-ta-hey, uncle," the boy said. He had a book covered with butcher paper in his hand.

"You want to help change this wheel? I could use some help."

"O.K.," the boy said. "Give me the trunk key and I'll get the spare."

Leaphorn fished the keys out of his pocket, realizing now that this boy was too young to be George Bowlegs. He would be Cecil, the younger brother.

Cecil brought the spare while Leaphorn removed the last lug nuts. Leaphorn was thinking hard. He would be very careful.

"You're a *Navajo* policeman," the boy said. "I thought at first it was the Zuñi patrol car."

"The car belongs to the Dinee," Leaphorn said. "Just like you and I." Leaphorn paused, looking at Cecil. "And just like George, your brother." A flicker of surprise crossed the boy's face, and then it was blank.

"We are all of The People," Leaphorn said.

The boy glanced at him, silent.

"It would be a good thing if George talked to a Dinee policeman," Leaphorn said. He stressed the word "Dinee," which meant "The People."

"You're hunting him." The boy's voice was accusing. "You think like the Zuñis said at school—that he ran away because he killed that Ernesto."

"I don't even know the Zuñi boy is dead. All I know now is what the Zuñi policeman told me," Leaphorn said. "I wonder what your brother would tell me."

Cecil said nothing. He studied Leaphorn's face.

"I don't think George ran away because he killed the Cata boy," Leaphorn said. "If he ran away maybe it was because he was afraid the Zuñi policeman would lock him in jail." Leaphorn removed the left front wheel and carefully fit the spare on the lug nuts, not looking at Cecil. "Maybe that was a smart thing to do. Maybe not. If he didn't kill the Cata boy, then running away wasn't smart. It made the Zuñis think maybe he was the one. But if he did kill the Cata boy, maybe it was smart and maybe it wasn't. Because probably they will catch him and then it will be worse for him. And if they don't catch him, he will have to run all the rest of his life." Leaphorn reached for the lug wrench, looking at Cecil now. "That is a bad way to live. It would be better to spend a few years in jail and get it over with. Or maybe spend some time in a hospital. If that boy is dead, and if George was the one who killed him, it was because there is something wrong inside his head. He needs to have it cured. The authorities would put him in a hospital instead of the jail."

The silence ticked away. A gust of breeze moved down the hillside, ruffling the grama grass. It was cold.

Cecil licked his lips. "George didn't run because he was afraid of the Zuñi police," he said. "That wasn't why."

"Why then, nephew?" Leaphorn asked.

"It was the kachina." The boy's voice was so faint that Leaphorn wasn't sure he had heard it. "He ran away from the kachina."

"Kachina? What kachina?" It was a strange sensation, more than an abrupt change of subject; more like an unexpected shift from real to unreal. Leaphorn stared at Cecil. The word "kachina" had three meanings. They were the ancestor spirits of the Zuñi. Or the masks worn to impersonate these spirits. Or the small wooden dolls the Zuñis made to represent them. The boy wasn't going to say anything more. This kachina business was just something that had come off his tongue—something to avoid telling what he knew.

"I don't know its name," Cecil said finally. "It's a Zuñi word. But I guess it would be the same kachina that got Ernesto."

"Oh," Leaphorn said. He tested the tightness of the lug

nuts, lowered the jack, giving himself time to think. He rested his hip on the fender and looked at Cecil Bowlegs. The crumpled sack that jutted from the boy's jacket pocket would be his lunch sack—empty now. What would Cecil find in that hogan to take to school for lunch?

"Did a kachina get Ernesto Cata? How did you find out?"

Cecil looked embarrassed.

The boy was lying. That was obvious. And no boy that age was good at it. Leaphorn had found that listening carefully to lies is sometimes very revealing of the truth. "Why would the kachina get after Ernesto? Do you know the reason?"

Cecil caught his lower lip between his teeth. He looked past Leaphorn, thinking.

"Do you know why George is running away from this kachina?"

"I think it's the same reason," Cecil said.

"You don't know the reason, but whatever it is, it would make the kachina go after both of them?"

"Yeah," Cecil said. "I think that's the way it is."

Leaphorn no longer thought Cecil was lying. George must have told him all this.

"I guess, then, from what you tell me, that Ernesto and George must have done something that made the kachina mad."

"Ernesto did it. George just listened to him. Telling is what breaks the taboo and Ernesto told. George just listened." Cecil's voice was earnest, as if it was very important to him that no one think his brother had broken a Zuñi taboo.

"Told what?"

"I don't know. George said he didn't think he should tell me. But it was something about the kachinas."

Leaphorn pushed himself away from the fender and sat down on the dead grass, folding his legs in front of him. What he had to find out was fairly simple. Did George know the Cata boy was dead when George and Cecil left for school this morning? If he knew that, it would almost certainly mean that George had either killed Ernesto, or had seen him killed, or had seen the killer disposing of the body. But if he asked Cecil straight out, and the answer was negative, Leaphorn knew he would have to discount the answer. Cecil would lie to protect his brother. Leaphorn fished out his cigarettes. He didn't like what he was about to do. My job is to find George Bowlegs, he told himself. It's important to find him. "Do you sometimes smoke a cigarette?" he asked Cecil. He extended the pack.

Cecil took one. "Sometimes it is good," he said.

"It's never good. It hurts the lungs. But sometimes it is necessary, and therefore one does it."

Cecil sat on a rock, inhaled deeply, and let the smoke trickle out of his nostrils. Obviously it wasn't his first experience with tobacco.

"You think Cata broke a taboo, and the kachina got Cata for doing it, and is after George." Leaphorn spoke thoughtfully. He exhaled a cloud of smoke. It hung blue in the still sunlight. "Do you know when George got home last night?"

"After I was asleep," Cecil said. "He was there when I woke up this morning, getting ready to catch the school bus."

"You boys like school better than I did," Leaphorn said. "When I was a boy, I would have told my daddy probably no school today because one of the students got killed yesterday. Maybe he'd let me stay home. Worth trying, anyway." The tone was casual, bantering, exactly right, he felt. Maybe it would elicit an unguarded admission, and maybe it wouldn't. If not, he'd simply try again. Leaphorn was a man of immense patience.

"I didn't know about it yet," Cecil said. "Not till we got to school." He was staring at Leaphorn. "They didn't find the blood until this morning." Cecil's expression said he was wondering how this policeman could have forgotten that, and then he knew Leaphorn hadn't forgotten. The boy's face was briefly angry, then simply forlorn. He looked away.

"To hell with it," Leaphorn said. "Look, Cecil. I was trying to screw you around. Trying to trick you into telling me more than you want to tell me. Well, to hell with that. He's your brother. You think about it and then you tell me just what you'd want a policeman to know. And remember, it won't be just me you're telling. I've got to pass it on—most of it, anyway—to the Zuñi police. So be careful not to tell me anything you think would hurt your brother."

"What do you want to know? Where George is? I don't know that."

"A lot of things. Mostly, a way to find George, because when I can talk to him he can give us all the answers. Like did he see what happened to Cata? Was he there? Did he do it? Did somebody else do it? But I can't talk to George until I figure out where he went. You say he didn't tell you this morning that something had happened to Cata. But he gave you the idea that a kachina was after both of them. What did he say?"

"It was kind of confused," Cecil said. "He was excited. I guess he borrowed Ernesto's bike after school and he took it back to where Ernesto was running and he was waiting there for Ernesto." Cecil stopped, trying to remember. "It was getting dark, and I guess it was then he saw the kachina coming. And he ran away from there and walked home. He didn't say it that way exactly, but that's what I think happened. When we got to school today, he was going to find out about the kachina."

"You didn't see George after he got off the bus?"

"No. He went looking for Ernesto."

"If you were me, where would you look for him?"

Cecil said nothing. He looked down at his shoes. Leaphorn noticed that the sole on the left one had split from the upper and they had been stuck together with some sort of grayish glue. But the glue hadn't held.

"O.K.," Leaphorn said. "Then has he got any other friends there at school? Anybody else who I should talk to."

"No friends there at school," Cecil said. "They're Zuñis." He glanced at Leaphorn, to see if he understood. "They don't like Navajos," he said. "Just make jokes about us. Like Polack jokes."

"Just Ernesto? Everybody says Ernesto and George were friends."

"Everybody says George is kind of crazy," Cecil said. "It's because he wants to . . ." The boy stopped, hunting words. "He wants to do things, you know. He wants to try everything. One time he wanted to be a witch, and then he studied about Zuñi sorcery. And one time he was eating cactus buttons so he would have dreams. And Ernesto thought all that was fun, and he made George worse than he was about it. I don't think Ernesto was a friend. Not really a friend." Cecil's face was angry. "He was a goddam Zuñi," he said.

"How about anybody else? Anybody that might know anything."

"There's those white men who are doing all that digging for the arrowheads. George used to go there a lot and watch that one man dig. Used to hang around there most of the summer and then after school started, too. Him and that Zuñi. But Ernesto stole something, I think, and they ran 'em off."

Leaphorn had noticed the anthropology site and had asked Pasquaanti about it. It was less than a mile from where the blood had been found.

"Like stole what? When did that happen?"

"Just the other day," Cecil said. "I think Ernesto stole some of that flint they dug up. I think it was arrowheads and stuff like that."

Leaphorn started to ask why they would want to steal flint artifacts but bit off the question. Why did boys steal anything? Mostly to see if they could get away with it.

"And then there's those Belacani living over in the old hogans behind Hoski Butte," Cecil said. "George liked that blond girl over there and she was trying to teach him to play the guitar, I think."

"White people? Who are these Belacani?"

"Hippies," Cecil said. "Bunch of them been living over there. They're raising some sheep."

"I'll talk to them," Leaphorn said. "Anyone else?"

"No," Cecil said. He hesitated. "You been to our place, just now. My father. Was he . . ." Embarrassment overcame the need to know.

"Yeah," Leaphorn said. "He'd been drinking some. But I think it'll be all right. I think he'll be asleep by the time you get home." And then he looked away from the pain and the shame in Cecil's face.

Monday, December 1, 4:18 p.m.

TED ISAACS RAN the shovel blade carefully into the dusty earth. The pressure on the heel of his hand told him that the resistance to the blade was a little light, that he was digging slightly above the high-calcium layer which Isaacs now knew—with absolute certainty—was the Folsom floor. He withdrew the blade and made a second stroke—a half-inch deeper—his hand now registering the feel of the metal sliding along the proper strata.

"Twenty," he said, dumping the earth on the pile on the sifter screen. He leaned the shovel against the wheelbarrow and began sorting the soft earth through the wire with a worn trowel. He worked steadily, and fast, pausing only to toss away clumps of grama grass roots and the tangles of tumbleweeds. Within three minutes nothing was left on the screen except an assortment of pebbles, small twigs, old rabbit droppings, and a large scorpion—its barbed tail waving in confused anger. Isaacs fished the scorpion off the wire with a stick and flicked it in the direction of his horned lark. The lark, a female, had been his only companion for the past two days, flirting around the dig site feasting on such tidbits. Isaacs wiped the sweat with his sleeve and then sorted carefully through the pebbles. He was a tall, bony young man. Now the sun was low behind Corn Mountain and he worked hatless—the white skin high on his forehead contrasting sharply with the burned brown leather of his face. His hands worked with delicate speed, blunt, calloused fingers eliminating most of the stones automatically, rejecting others after a quick exploratory touch, finally pausing with a chip no larger than a toenail clipping. This chip Isaacs examined, squinting in concentration. He put it into his mouth, cleaned it quickly with his tongue, spit, and reexamined it. It was a chip of agate flint—the third he had found this morning. He fished a jeweler's glass from the pocket of his denim shirt. Through the double lens, the chip loomed huge against the now massive ridges of his thumbprint. On one edge there was the scar he knew he would find—the point of percussion, the mark left a hundred centuries ago when a Folsom hunter had flaked it off whatever tool he had been making. The thought aroused in Isaacs a sense of excitement. It always had, since his very first dig as part of an undergraduate team—an exhilarating sense of making a quantum leap backward through time.

Isaacs stuffed the glass back in his pocket and extracted an envelope. He wrote "Grid 4 north, 7 west" on it in a small, neat hand, and dropped in the flake. It was then he noticed the white panel truck jolting up the ridge toward him.

"Crap," Isaacs said. He stared at the truck, hoping it would go away. It didn't. It kept bumping inexorably toward him, following the tracks his own truck-camper had left through the grama grass. And finally it stopped a polite fifty feet below the area marked by his network of white strings. Stopped gradually, avoiding the great cloud of dust which Dr. Reynolds in his perpetual hurry always produced when he drove his pickup up to the site.

The door of the carryall bore a round seal with a stylized profile of a buffalo, and the man who got out of it and was now walking toward Isaacs wore the same seal on the shoulder of his khaki shirt. The man had an Indian face. Tall, though, for a Zuñi, with a lanky, rawboned look. Probably a Bureau of Indian Affairs employee—which meant he could be anything from an Eskimo to an Iroquois. Whoever he was, he stopped several feet short of the white string marking the boundary of the dig.

"What can I do for you?" Isaacs said.

"Just looking for some information," the Indian said. "You have time to talk?"

"Take time," Isaacs said. "Come on in."

The Indian made his way carefully across the network of strings, skirting the grids where the topsoil had already been removed. "My name's Leaphorn," he said. "I'm with the Navajo Police."

"Ted Isaacs." They shook hands.

"We're looking for a couple of boys," Leaphorn said. "A Navajo about fourteen named George Bowlegs and a twelve-year-old Zuñi named Ernesto Cata. I understand they hang around here a lot."

"They did," Isaacs said. "But not lately. I haven't seen them since . . ." He paused, remembering the scene, Reynolds's yell of outrage and anger and Cata running from Reynolds's pickup as if hell itself pursued him. The memory was a mixture of amusement and regret. It had been funny, but he missed the boys and Reynolds had made it clear enough in his direct way that he didn't think much of Isaacs's judgment in letting them hang around. ". . . not since last Thursday. Most afternoons they'd come by after school," Isaacs said. "Sometimes they'd stay around until dark. But the last few days . . ."

"Have any idea why they haven't been back?"

"We ran 'em off."

"Why?"

"Well," Isaacs said. "This is a research site. Not the best place in the world for a couple of boys to be horsing around."

Leaphorn said nothing. The silence stretched. Time ticking silently away made Isaacs nervous but the Indian seemed unaware of it. He simply waited, his eyes black and patient, for Isaacs to say more.

"Reynolds caught them screwing around in his truck," Isaacs said, resenting the Indian for making him say it.

"What did they steal?"

"Steal? Why, nothing. Not that I know of. They didn't take anything. One of 'em was at Dr. Reynolds's truck and Reynolds yelled at him to get the hell away from his stuff and they ran away."

"Nothing missing?"

"No. Why are you looking for them?"

"They're missing," Leaphorn said. Again the silence, the Indian's face thoughtful. "You're digging up artifacts here, I guess," he said. "Could they have gotten off with any of that stuff?"

Isaacs laughed. "Over my dead body," he said. "Besides, I would have missed it." The very thought made him nervous. He felt an urge to check, to hold the envelope marked "Grid 17 north, 23 west," to feel the shape of the broken lance point under his fingers, to know it was safe.

"You're absolutely sure, then? Could they have stolen anything at all?"

"Reynolds thought they might have got something out of his toolbox, I think, because he checked it. But nothing was gone."

"And no artifacts missing? Not even chips?"

"No way," Isaacs said. "I keep what I find in my shirt pocket here." Isaacs tapped the envelopes. "And when I knock off at dark I lock it up in the camper. Why do you think they stole something?"

The Indian didn't seem to hear the question. He was looking toward Corn Mountain. Then he shrugged. "I heard they did," he said. "What are you digging here? Some sort of Early Man site?"

The question surprised Isaacs. "Yeah. It was a Folsom hunting camp. You know about the Folsom culture?"

"Some," Leaphorn said. "I studied a little anthropology at Arizona State. They didn't know much about Folsom then, though. Didn't know where he came from, or what happened to him."

"How long since you studied?"

"Too long," Leaphorn said. "I've forgotten most of it."

"You heard of Chester Reynolds?"

"I think he wrote one of my textbooks."

"Probably that was *Paleo-Indian Cultures in North America.* It's still a standard. Anyway, Reynolds worked out a set of maps of the way this part of the country looked back at the end of the last Ice Age—back when it was raining so much. From that he worked out the game migration routes at the very end of the Pleistocene period. You know. Where you'd find the mastodons and ground sloths and the saber-tooth cats and the longhorn bison, because of surface water and climate when this country started drying up. And from that he worked out the methods for calculating where the Folsom hunters were likely to have their hunting camps. That's what this was." Isaacs gestured across the gridwork of strings waffling the grassy ridge. "That flat place down there was a lake then. Folsom could sit up here on his haunches and see everything that came to water—either at the lake or north toward the Zuñi Wash."

Isaacs accepted a cigarette from Leaphorn. He sat on the frame of the sifter screen, looking tired and excited. And he talked. He talked as a naturally friendly man will talk when confronted—after days of enforced silence—with a good listener. He talked of how Reynolds had found this site and a dozen others. And of how Reynolds had given the sites to selected doctoral candidates, arranged foundation grants to finance the work. He talked of Reynolds's modification theory—which would solve one of the great mysteries of American anthropology.

Leaphorn, who had always been fascinated by the unexplained, remembered the mystery from Anthropology 127. Folsom hunting camps had been found all over the central and southwestern states—their occupancy generally dating from as early as twelve thousand to as late as nine thousand years ago. During this era at the tag end of the Ice Age they seemed to have had this immense expanse of territory to themselves. They followed the bison herds, living in small camps where they chipped their lance points, knives, hide scrapers, and other tools from flint. These lance points were their trademark. They were leaf-shaped, small, remarkably thin, their faces fluted like bayonets, their points and cutting edges shaped by an unusual technique called "pressure flaking." Making such a point was difficult and time consuming. Other Stone Age people, later and earlier, made larger, cruder points, quick and easy to chip out and no less efficient at killing. But Folsom stuck to his beautiful but difficult design century after century and left anthropology with a puzzle. Was the lance point part of a ritual religion—its shape a magic offering to the spirit of the animals that fed Folsom with their meat? When the glaciers stopped melting, and the great rain ended, and the country dried, and the animal herds diminished, and survival became a very chancy thing, Folsom camps disappeared from the earth. Had Folsom Man been trapped by this time-consuming ritualism which delayed his adaptation to changing conditions and caused his extinction? Whatever the reason, he vanished. There was a gap when the Great Plains seem to have been virtually empty of men, and then different hunting cultures appeared, killing with long, heavy lance points and using different stone-working techniques.

"Yeah," Isaacs said. "That's about the way the books explain it. But thanks to Reynolds, they're going to have to rewrite all those books."

"You going to prove something else happened?"

"Yeah," Isaacs said. "We damn sure are." He lit another cigarette, puffed nervously. "Let me tell you what those bastards did. Two years ago, when Reynolds started working on this, he read a paper on his theory at the anthro convention and some of those stuffy old academic bastards walked out on him." Isaacs snorted. "Got up and walked right out of the general assembly session." He laughed. "Nobody's done that since the physical anthropologists walked out on the paper announcing the original Folsom discovery, and that was back in 1931."

"Pretty serious insult, I guess," Leaphorn said.

"The worst kind. I wasn't there but I heard about it. They say Reynolds was ready to kill somebody. He's not used to that kind of treatment and he's not the kind of man you push on. They said he told some of his friends there that he'd make those people accept his theory if it took the rest of his life."

"What's the Reynolds theory?"

"In brief, Folsom Man didn't die out. He adapted. He began making a different kind of lance point—some of those that we've been crediting to entirely different cultures. And, by God, we're going to prove it right here." Isaacs's voice was exultant.

It seemed to Leaphorn a hard case to prove. "Any chance of talking to Reynolds? Will he be back?"

"He's coming in this evening," Isaacs said. "Come on down to the camper. You can wait for him there, and I'll show you what we're finding."

The camper was parked amid a cluster of junipers—a plywood box of a cabin built on the bed of a battered old Chevy pickup truck. The inside was fitted with a narrow bunk, a linoleum-topped worktable, a small pantry, and an array of metal filing cabinets on one of which sat a portable butane cooking burner. Isaacs unlocked a cabinet, extracted a tray of grimy envelopes, counted them carefully, and then put all but one back. He motioned Leaphorn to the only stool and opened the envelope. He poured its contents carefully into his hand and then extended his open palm to Leaphorn. In it lay four chips of flint and a flat rectangle of pink stone. It was perhaps three inches long, an inch wide, and a half-inch thick.

"It's the butt end of a lance point," Isaacs said. "The type we call 'parallel flaked'—the type we always thought was made by a culture that followed Folsom." He pushed it with a finger. "Notice it's made out of petrified wood—silicified bamboo, to be exact. And notice these chips are the same stuff. And now"—he tapped the side of the stone with a fingernail—"notice that it isn't finished. He was still smoothing off this side when the tip snapped off."

"So," Leaphorn said slowly, "that means he was making it up there at your Folsom hunting camp and that he didn't just come along and drop it. But he still could have been making it a couple of thousand years after the Folsoms were gone."

"It was on the same stratum of earth," Isaacs said. "That's interesting, but in this sort of formation it doesn't prove anything. What's more interesting is this. There isn't any of this silicified bamboo anywhere near here. The only deposit we know of is over in the Galisteo Basin south of Santa Fe—a couple of hundred miles. Around here there's plenty of good flint—schist and chalcedony and other good stuff not half a mile from here. It's easy to shape, but it's not pretty. The other cultures used what was handy and to hell with how it looked. Folsom would find himself a quarry of clear, fancy-colored stuff and carry chunks of it all over the country to make his lance points." Isaacs pulled another envelope out of the file. "One more thing," he said. He emptied about a dozen flakes of pinkish stone into his palm and extended it. "These are pressure flakes. Typical and unmistakable workshop debris from a Folsom camp. And they're out of the same silicified petrification."

Leaphorn raised his eyebrows.

"Yeah," Isaacs said. "That gets to be quite a coincidence, doesn't it? That two different bunches of hunters, two thousand years apart, would work the same quarry and then carry the stuff two hundred miles to work on it."

"I think you might call that real fine circumstantial evidence," Leaphorn said.

"And we're going to find enough of it so they'll have to believe it," Isaacs said. "I'm sure it happened here. The date's right. Our geologist tells us that high-calcium layers were only formed about nine thousand years ago. So these were very late Folsoms." Isaacs's eyes were looking at a scene very distant in time. "There weren't many left. They were starving. The glaciers were long gone and the rains had stopped and the game herds were going fast. It was getting hotter, and desert was spreading, and the culture they had lived by for three thousand years was failing them. They had to make a big kill at least every four or five days. If they didn't, they'd be too weak to hunt and they'd die. There just wasn't enough time anymore to make those fancy points that broke so easily." Isaacs glanced at Leaphorn. "Want some coffee?"

"Fine."

Isaacs began preparing the pot. Leaphorn tried to guess his age. Late twenties, he thought. No older than that, although his face sometimes had a wizened, old-man look about it. That was partly from the weathering. But something had aged him. Isaacs was conscious, Leaphorn had noticed earlier, of his teeth. They were slightly buck, and they protruded a little, and Isaacs called attention to them with an unconscious habit: he often had his hand to his face, shielding them. Now with the pot on the fire, he leaned against the wall, looking at Leaphorn. "It's always been presumed that they couldn't adapt so they died. That's the textbook dogma. But it's wrong. They were human, and smart; they had the intelligence to appreciate beauty and the intelligence to adapt."

Through the small window over the burner Leaphorn could see the red flare of the sunset. Red as blood. And was that blood under the piñon tree the blood of Ernesto Cata? And if so, what had happened to his body? And where under that garish evening sky could George Bowlegs be? But there was no possible profit in pondering that question now.

"I wonder, though," Leaphorn said. "Would changing your lance point make that much difference?"

"Probably not, by itself," Isaacs said. "But quite a bit. I can make a very rough version of a Folsom point in two or three hours on the average. They're so thin that you break a lot—and so did the Folsom Men. But you can whack out a big parallel-flaked point in maybe twenty minutes, and it's just as good as the ones Stone Age man used."

Isaacs fished a box of sugar cubes and a vacuum bottle cup out of a drawer and put them on the table beside Leaphorn. "We think he developed the Folsom point with all that symmetry in it as a sort of ritual offering to the animal spirit. Made it just as beautiful as he could make it. You're a Navajo. You know what I mean."

"I know," Leaphorn said. He was remembering a snowy morning on the Lukachukai plateau, his grandfather touching the barrel of his old 30-30 with sacred pollen, and then the chant—the old man's clear voice calling to the spirit of the male deer to make this hunt for the winter's meat right and proper and in tune with natural things; giving it the beauty of the Navajo Way.

"Reynolds figured—and he's right—that if Folsom was willing to change his lance point, he'd be willing to adapt in every other way. Under the old way, they'd be sitting in camp all day turning out maybe five or six of those fluted points, and maybe breaking ten or twelve to make a kill. They couldn't afford that anymore."

"Couldn't afford the beauty." Leaphorn laughed. "I went to a Bureau of Indian Affairs high school that had a sign in the hall. It said, 'Tradition Is the Enemy of Progress.' The word was give up the old ways or die." He didn't mean it to sound bitter, but Isaacs gave him a quizzical look.

"By the way," Isaacs said. "Have you asked the people over at Jason's Fleece about those boys?"

"Jason's Fleece? Is that the hippie place?"

"They hung around there some," Isaacs said. "If they ran away from home, maybe they're over there. There's a girl over there that's a good friend of theirs. Nice girl named Susanne. The boys liked her."

"I'll go talk to her," Leaphorn said.

"That Bowlegs boy's a funny kid," Isaacs said. "He's sort of a mystic. Interested in magic and witchcraft and all that sort of thing. One time he was looking bad and I asked him about it and he said he was fasting so that his totem would talk to him. Wanted to see visions, I think. And one time they asked me if I could get them any LSD, and if I'd ever been on an acid trip."

"Could you?"

"Hell, no," Isaacs said. "Anyway, I wouldn't. That stuff's risky. Another thing, if it helps any." Isaacs laughed. "George was studying to be a Zuñi." He laughed again and shook his head. "George is sort of crazy."

"You mean studying their religion?"

"He said Ernesto was going to get him initiated into the Badger Clan."

"Could that happen?"

"I don't know," Isaacs said. "I doubt it. I think it's like a fish saying it's going to become a bird. The only time I ever heard of such a thing was back at the end of the nineteenth century when they adopted an anthropologist named Frank Cushing into the tribe."

Outside there was a sound of a motor whining in second gear—driving too fast over the bumpy track.

"Reynolds?"

Isaacs laughed. "That's the way the silly bastard drives."

Reynolds was not what Leaphorn had expected. Leaphorn had expected, he realized, sort of a reincarnation of the stooped, white-haired old man who had taught Leaphorn's cultural anthropology section at Arizona State. The typical scholar. Reynolds was medium-sized and medium everything. Perhaps fifty, but hard to date. Brown hair turning gray in spots, a round, cheerful face with the field anthropologist's leathery complexion. Only his eyes set him apart. They were notable eyes. Protected by a heavy brow ridge above and a lump of cheekbone below, they stared from their sockets with sharp, unblinking bright blue alertness. They gave Leaphorn, during the brief handshake of introduction, the feeling that everything about his face was being memorized. And a moment later they were studying with equal intensity the chips Isaacs had found that day. Joe Leaphorn, Navajo policeman, had been sorted and stored out of the way.

"Which grid?" Reynolds asked.

Isaacs touched three fingers to the map. "These."

"Washed down. Old erosion. See any of them in place?"

"Got 'em off the sifter screen," Isaacs said.

"You noticed they're silicated. Same stuff as the parallel flaked?"

"Right."

"You're not missing anything?"

"I never do."

"I know you don't." Reynolds favored Isaacs with a glance that included fondness, warmth, and approval. It developed in a second into a smile that transformed Reynolds's leathery face into a statement of intense affection, and from that, in the same second, into sheer, undiluted delight.

"By God," he said. "By God, it really looks good. Right?"

"Very good, I think," Isaacs said. "I think this is going to be it."

"Yes," Reynolds said. "I think so." He was staring at Isaacs. "Nothing's going wrong with this dig. You understand that? It is going to be done exactly right." Reynolds spaced the words, spitting each one out.

A good hater, Leaphorn thought. Maybe a little crazy. Or maybe just a genius.

Reynolds's gaze now included Leaphorn, the bright blue eyes checking their memory. "Mr. Isaacs is one of the three or four best field men in the United States," he said. The smile clicked on and off, the leather turned hard. "What Mr. Isaacs is doing here is going to make some stubborn people face the truth."

"I wish you luck," Leaphorn said.

Isaacs's face had done something Leaphorn wouldn't have believed possible. It had assumed an expression of embarrassed pleasure and managed to flush red through the sunburn. It made Isaacs look about ten years old.

"Mr. Leaphorn is looking for a couple of boys," he said. "He stopped by to ask if I'd seen them."

"Was one of them that Zuñi kid that was screwing around my truck?" Reynolds asked. "The one that ran off when I yelled at him?"

"That's the one," Leaphorn said. "I'd heard they stole something here."

Reynolds's bright eyes flicked instantly to Isaacs. "Did they steal something?"

"No," Isaacs said. "I told him that. Nothing's missing."

Reynolds was still staring at Isaacs. "Were you letting two of them hang around here? I only saw one."

"The Zuñi boy and a Navajo named George Bowlegs," Leaphorn said. "They're friends and they're both gone. Did they steal something from you, Dr. Reynolds?"

"That Zuñi boy was poking around my truck. But nothing was missing. I don't think he stole anything. Frankly, I ran him off because it was beginning to look like this is a critically important site." Reynolds glanced at Isaacs. "It's damn sure no place to have unauthorized persons underfoot—especially not children."

"Was there anything in the pickup they might have stolen? Anything valuable?"

Reynolds thought about it. Impatience flashed across his face and was gone. "Is it important?"

"Those boys are missing. We think one of them was hurt. We need to know why they disappeared. Might help figure out where they are."

"Let's look, then," Reynolds said.

Outside the red sky was fading into darkness, and the early stars were out. Reynolds fished a flashlight out of the glovebox of a green GMC pickup. He checked the remaining contents—a hodgepodge of maps, small tools, and notebooks. "Nothing missing here," he said.

It took a little longer to check the toolbox welded behind the cab. Reynolds sorted carefully through the clutter—pliers, wire cutters, geologist's pick, hand ax, a folding trenching shovel, and a dozen other odds and ends. "There's a hammer missing, I think. No. Here it is." He closed the box. "All accounted for."

"On the day you ran the boys off, did you have any artifacts in the truck?"

"Artifacts?" Reynolds was facing the sunset. It gave his skin a redness. The blue eyes memorized Leaphorn again.

"Arrowheads, lance points, anything like that?"

Reynolds thought about the question. "By God, I did. Had my box with me. But why would they want to steal a piece of rock?"

"I heard one of the boys stole an arrowhead," Leaphorn said. "Was anything missing from the box?"

Reynolds's laugh was more a snort. "You can be damned sure there wasn't. That box had stuff in it from all eight of the digs I'm watching. Nothing very important, but stuff we're working on. If a single flake was taken out of there, I'd know it. It's all there." He frowned. "Who told you he'd stolen some artifacts?"

"It's thirdhand," Leaphorn said. "The Navajo boy has a little brother. He told me."

"That's funny," Reynolds said.

Leaphorn said nothing. But he thought, Yes, that's very funny.

Monday, December 1, 8:37 p.m.

THE MOON NOW HUNG halfway up the sky, the yellow of its rising gone and its face turned to scarred white ice. It was a winter moon. Under it, Leaphorn was cold. He sat in the shadow of the rimrock watching the commune which called itself Jason's Fleece. The cold seeped through Leaphorn's uniform jacket, through his shirt and undershirt, and touched the skin along his ribs. It touched his calves above his boottops, and his thighs where the cloth of his trouser legs stretched taut against the muscles, and the backs of his hands, which gripped the metal of his binoculars. In a moment, Leaphorn intended to deal with the cold. He would get up and climb briskly down to the commune below him and learn there whatever it was possible for him to learn. But now he ignored the discomfort, concentrating in his orderly fashion on this minor phase of the job of finding George Bowlegs.

A less precise man by now would have written off as wasted effort the mile walk from the point where he had parked his carryall and the climb to this high point overlooking the commune. It didn't occur to Leaphorn to do so. He had come here because his hunt for George Bowlegs logically led him to the commune. And before he entered it, he would study it. The chance that Bowlegs was hiding there seemed to Leaphorn extremely slight. But the chance existed and the operating procedure of Lieutenant Joe Leaphorn in such cases was to minimize the risk. Better spend whatever effort was required to examine the ground than chance losing the boy again by carelessness.

At the moment Leaphorn was examining, through the magnification of the binocular lenses, a denim jacket. The jacket hung on the corner post of a brush arbor beside a hogan some two hundred yards below where Leaphorn sat. The hogan was a neat octagon of logs built as the Navajo Way instructed, its single entrance facing the point of sunrise and a smoke hole in the center of the roof. Behind it Leaphorn could see a plank shed and behind the shed a pole corral that contained huddled sheep—probably about twenty. Leaphorn presumed the sheep belonged to the occupants of the commune, who currently numbered four men and three women. The allotment of land on which the sheep grazed belonged to Frank Bob Madman and the hogan, from which a thin plume of smoke now rose into the cold moonlight, belonged by Navajo tradition to the ghost of Alice Madman.

Leaphorn had learned this, and considerably more, by stopping at a hogan about four miles up the wagon track. With the young Navajo couple who lived there he had discussed the weather, the sagging market for wool, a Tribal Council proposal to invest Navajo funds in construction of livestock ponds, the couple's newborn son, and—finally—the group of Belacani who lived in the hogan down the wagon track. He had been told that Frank Bob Madman had abandoned the hogan almost three years before. Madman had gone to Gallup to buy salt and had returned to find that his wife of many years had died in his absence. ("She'd had a little stroke before," Young Wife said. "Probably had a big one this time.") There had been no one there to move Alice Madman out of the hogan so that her ghost—at the moment of death—might escape for its eternity of wandering. Therefore the chindi had been caught in the hogan. Madman had got a Belacani rancher over near Ramah to bury the body under rocks. He had knocked a hole in one wall and boarded up the smoke hole and the entrance, as was customary with a death hogan, to keep the ghost from bothering people. These duties performed, Madman had taken his wagon and his sheep, and left. Young Wife believed he had gone back to his own clan, the Red Foreheads, somewhere around Chinle. And then, a year ago last spring, the Belacani had arrived. There had been sixteen of them in a school bus and a Volkswagen van. They had moved into the Madman place, living in the death hogan and in two big tents. And then more had arrived until, by the end of summer, thirty-five or forty had lived there.

The number had declined during the winter and in the coldest part of the year, in the very middle of the Season When the Thunder Sleeps, there had been another death in the hogan of the ghost of Alice Madman. The population had stabilized during the spring and declined sharply again with the present autumn, until only four men and three women were left.

"The death?" Leaphorn asked. "Who was it? How did it happen?"

It had been a young woman, a very fat girl, a very quiet girl, sort of ugly. Somebody had said Ugly Girl had something wrong with her heart. Young Wife, however, thought it was too much heroin, or maybe the ghost of Alice Madman.

"Some of them were on horse then," Young Husband said. "Probably she got an overdose of the stuff. That's what we heard." Young Husband shrugged. He had spent twelve months with the First Cav in Vietnam. Neither heroin nor death impressed him. He discussed these whites with an impersonal interest tinged with amusement, but with the detailed knowledge of neighbors common to those who live where fellow humans are scarce. In general, Young Husband rated the residents of Jason's Fleece as generous, ignorant, friendly, bad mannered but well intentioned. On the positive side of the balance, they provided a source of free rides into Ramah, Gallup, and once even to Albuquerque. On the negative, they had contaminated the spring above the Madman place with careless defecation last summer, and had started a fire which burned off maybe fifty acres of pretty good sheep graze, and didn't know how to take care of their sheep, which meant they might let scabies, or some disease, get started in the flock. Yes, the visitors had included a Navajo boy who sometimes came by himself and sometimes came with a Zuñi boy.

The other visitors were Belacani, mostly young, mostly long-haired. Young Wife was both amused and curious. What were they after? What were any of them after?

"They call their place Jason's Fleece," Leaphorn said. "Do you know the story about that? It's a hero story, like our story of the Monster Slayer and Born of Water, the twins who go to find the Sun. In the whiteman story Jason was a hero who hunted across the world for a golden fleece. Maybe it stood for money. I think it was supposed to stand for whatever it is people have to find to live happy."

"I heard of it," Young Husband said. "Supposed to be a sheep skin covered up with gold." He laughed. "I think you're more likely to find scabies on the sheep they're raising."

Leaphorn smiled slightly at the recollection, stared at the denim jacket, and decided the jacket looked too large to be the one Bowlegs was wearing when he left school. He shifted his field of vision slowly, past the thin plume of vapor rising from the smoke hole of the hogan, past the plank shed, past the brush arbor, then back again. There was a table under the arbor, partly in darkness. On it, cooking utensils reflected spots of moonlight. Beyond it something in the darkness which might be a saddle and something hanging which could only be a deer carcass. Leaphorn examined it. Something at the corner of his vision tugged at his attention. The shape of a shadow contradicting his memory of the way the shadows had been formed under this arbor. He shifted the binoculars slightly. Projected onto the hard bare earth behind the hogan by the slanting light from the moon was the shadow of the pole which held up this corner of the shelter, and the shadow of part of the table, and beside that the shadow of a pair of legs. Someone was standing under the arbor. The shadow of the legs was motionless. Leaphorn frowned at it. The young neighbors had said only seven Belacani lived here now. He had seen two men and two women drive away in the school bus. He had seen one man and one woman—Susanne, judging from the description he had of her from Isaacs—go into the hogan. He had presumed the remaining man was also inside. Was this him standing so silently under the arbor? But why would he stand there in the icy moonlight? And how had he got there without Leaphorn seeing him? As he considered this, the figure moved. With birdlike swiftness it darted out of the arbor to the side of the hogan, disappearing into the shadow. It crouched, pressed against the logs. What the devil was it doing? Listening? It seemed to be. And then the figure straightened, its head moving upward into the slanting moonlight. Leaphorn sucked in his breath. The head was a bird's. Round, jaylike feather plumes thrusting backward, a long, narrow sandpiper's beak, a bristling ruff of feathers where the human neck would be. The head was round. As it turned away from profile, Leaphorn saw round eyes ringed with yellow against the black. He was seeing the staring, expressionless face of a kachina. Leaphorn felt the hairs bristling at the back of his neck. What was it his roommate had said of these spirits of the Zuñi dead? That they danced forever under a lake in Arizona; he remembered that. The man-bird was moving again, away from the hogan to disappear through the darkness among the piñons. "The way it's told," he heard the roommate's voice saying, "they're invisible. But you can see them if you're about to die."

Monday, December 1, 9:11 p.m.

THE GIRL NAMED SUSANNE spoke with a slight stammer. It caused her to pause before each sentence—her oval, freckled face assuming a split second of earnest concentration before she shaped the first word. At the moment she was saying that maybe George Bowlegs was simply ditching school, that George sometimes played hooky to go deer hunting, that probably he was doing this now.

"Maybe that's so," Leaphorn said. He felt an amused attraction to this girl. She would be better at it someday, perhaps, but she would never be one of those who developed a skill at deception. He let the silence stretch. The blanket hanging against the log wall of the hogan opposite him was a good Two Gray Hills weave worth maybe three hundred dollars. Had Frank Bob Madman left it behind when this hogan was abandoned to its malevolent ghost? Or had these young Belacani bought it somewhere and brought it with them? The man called Halsey moved very slightly in his rocking chair, back and forth, his face hidden, except for the forehead, behind the black binding of a book. Halsey's boots were dirty but they were very good boots. Halsey interested Leaphorn. Where had he come from? And what did he hope to find here where the whiteman had never before found anything?

"Anyway," Susanne said, "I'm d-d-d-dead sure he didn't do anything to Ernesto. They were like brothers."

"I heard that," Leaphorn said. "Ted Isaacs told me—"

The young man with the shaved head said, *"No!"* The

word was loud, startled, obviously not addressed to anything Leaphorn had been saying. It was the first word Leaphorn had heard the man speak. ("This is Otis," Susanne had said. "He's sick today." And Otis had turned glittering, unfocused eyes toward Leaphorn, staring up from the mattress on the hogan floor, saying nothing. It was not an unfamiliar look. Leaphorn had seen it in jail drunk tanks, in hospital wards, produced by wine and marijuana, by alcohol and peyote buttons, by the delirium of high fever, by LSD, by the venom of a rattlesnake bite.)

"No," Otis said again, more softly this time, simply confirming his rejection of some inner vision.

Susanne put her hand on the pale, bony arch of Otis's bare foot. "It's O.K., Oats," she said. "It's cool now. No problem."

Halsey leaned forward in his rocking chair, his face emerging past the book. He studied Otis and then glanced at Leaphorn, eyes curious. ("This is Halsey," Susanne had said. "He sort of holds this place together." Under his mustache Halsey grinned, challenging and combative, and extended his hand. "I never met a Navajo fuzz before," Halsey had said.) Whatever form Otis's nightmare took, it left his face drawn and bloodless, his eyes shocked.

"Is he on peyote?" Leaphorn asked. "If he is, they're usually all right after a couple of hours. But if it's not peyote, maybe a doctor should take a look at him."

"It couldn't be peyote," Halsey said, grinning again. "That stuff's illegal, isn't it?"

"It depends," Leaphorn said. "The way the Tribe sees it, it's O.K. if it's used for religious purposes. It's part of the ceremonial of the Native American Church and some of The People belong to that. The way it works, we don't notice people using peyote if they're using it in their religion. I'm guessing Otis here is a religious man."

Halsey caught the irony and its implications. His grin became slightly friendly. Otis's eyes were closed now. Susanne was stroking the arch of his right foot. "It's all right now," she was saying. "Oatsy, it's cool." The sympathy in her face confirmed Leaphorn's guess about this young woman. She would tell him all she knew about George Bowlegs for the same reason she now tried to bring Otis back from his grotesque psychedelic nightmare.

"Isaacs said the same thing you do," Leaphorn said. "That George wouldn't hurt the Zuñi boy. But that's not the point. It looks like somebody did hurt the Zuñi. Maybe killed him. We think George can tell us something about what happened."

Susanne was now stroking Otis's ankle. Her face was blank. "I don't know where he is," she said.

"I talked to George's little brother today," Leaphorn said. "The boy tells me George is running because he is afraid of something. *Really afraid.* The little brother says George isn't afraid of us, of the police, because he didn't do anything wrong. What's George afraid of?"

Susanne was listening carefully, the stubbornness fading.

"I don't know," Leaphorn continued. "I can't guess. But I can remember being afraid when I was a kid. You ever been really scared? Do you remember how it was?"

"Yes," Susanne said. "I remember."

Like yesterday, Leaphorn thought. Or maybe today. "You get panicky and maybe you run," he said. "And if you run it's worse, because you feel like the whole world is chasing you and you're afraid to stop."

"Or there's no place to stop," she said. "Like where would George go to get help? Do you know about his daddy? Being drunk all the time? And most of the time George having to worry about what they're going to eat?"

"Yeah," Leaphorn said. "I've been out there."

"Sometimes there isn't any home to go home to." Susanne seemed to say it to Otis, who wasn't listening.

"The trouble with running out here this time of year is the weather. Today it's late autumn and sunny and no problem. Tomorrow maybe it's winter. Overnight snow and maybe five or six below zero and all of a sudden you don't have any food and no way to get any."

"Does it get that cold here? Below zero?"

"You're almost seven thousand feet above sea level here. Practically sitting on the Continental Divide. Last year it got to fifteen below at Ramah and nineteen below at Gallup. We had eleven exposure deaths on the reservation—that we know about."

"But I don't know where he is," she said.

"But just telling me what he said would help me find him," Leaphorn said. "Why did he leave school in the middle of the morning? Why did he come here? What made him run? *Anything* you remember will help. It will help George."

This time Susanne let the silence grow. She might tell me he didn't come here, Leaphorn thought. That was what she had planned. But she wouldn't lie. Not now.

"I don't know exactly," she said. "I know he was afraid of something. He asked if I could give him any food—stuff he could carry that would keep. He wanted to take some of that deer out in the shed. That was George's deer anyway. He brought it to us last week."

"Where was he going?"

"He didn't say."

"But he must have said something. Try to remember everything he said."

"He asked me if I knew anything about the Zuñi religion," Susanne said, "and I said not much. Just a little bit that Ted had told me about it." She paused, putting the memory back together. "And then he asked me if Ted had ever told me anything about the kachinas punishing people." She frowned. "And if I knew anything about kachina forgiveness."

"Forgiveness?"

"He used the word 'absolution.' He said, 'If a Zuñi taboo is broken, is there any way to get absolution?' I told him I didn't know anything about it." She looked at Leaphorn curiously. "Is there?"

"I'm not a Zuñi," Leaphorn said. "A Navajo isn't likely to know any more about the Zuñi religion than a white man will know about Shintoism."

"It seemed important to George. I could tell that. He kept talking about it."

"Forgiveness for him? Did he give you any idea who needed to be forgiven? Was it him? Or Ernesto?"

"I don't know," Susanne said. "I guessed it was for him, himself. But maybe it was for Ernesto."

"Any hint of what the forgiveness would be for? What sort of . . ." Leaphorn paused, trying for the right word. It wouldn't be crime. Would it be sacrilege? He let the sentence dangle and substituted: "Did he say what had happened to offend the kachinas?"

"No. I wondered, too, but it didn't seem the time to ask. He was all emotional. In a big hurry. I'd never seen George in a hurry before."

"So he took some venison," Leaphorn said. "How much did he take? And what else?"

Susanne flushed. She tugged the long, grimy sleeve of her sweater down over her knuckles.

"He didn't take anything," Halsey said. "He asked for it. He didn't get it. I figured he was running from the law, or something, the way he acted. People who live here do not cooperate with a fugitive; do not aid and abet; do not do a damn thing to give the fuzz any reason to be hassling us." He grinned at Leaphorn. "We are law-abiding."

"So he left here without any food," Leaphorn said.

"I made him take my old jacket," Susanne said. She was staring at Halsey, her expression an odd mixture of defiance and fear. "It was an old quilted blue rayon thing with a hole in the elbow."

"What time did he leave?"

"He got here early in the afternoon and I guess he left about ten minutes later—maybe three or three-fifteen."

"And he didn't say anything about where he was going?"

"No," Susanne said. She hesitated. "Not really, anyway. George was kind of a crazy kid. Full of funny ideas. He said he might be gone for a while because he had to find the kachinas."

Leaphorn stopped at the fence that sealed the Ramah-Ojo Caliente road off from Navajo allotment grazing lands. He turned off the ignition, yawned. In a moment he would climb from the truck, open the barbed-wire gate, and drive on to Ramah. But now he simply sat, slumped, surrendering to fatigue. He had heard of George Bowlegs about noon and now it was after midnight. Bowlegs, you little bastard, where are you? Are you sleeping warm? Leaphorn sighed, climbed from the carryall, walked with stiff legs to the gate, opened it, climbed back into the carryall, drove through the gate, climbed out again, shut the gate, climbed back into the truck, and pulled onto the county road in a shower of dust and gravel. He shivered slightly and turned the heater fan higher. Outside the air was absolutely still, the sky cloudless, the moon almost directly overhead. Tonight there would be a hard freeze. And where were George Bowlegs and Ernesto Cata? Dead? Cata perhaps, but it seemed suddenly unlikely. There was no possible reason for anyone to kill him. The blood might have had other sources. Probably this was a wasted day. There was nothing much except the blood. Two square yards of blood-stiff earth under a piñon and two boys missing. One of them, everybody said, was a crazy kid. What else was there? Something stolen from an anthropologists' camp—something so trivial it hadn't been missed. And something which looked like a Zuñi kachina snooping in the moonlight at a hippie commune. What the hell could that have been? He thought again about what his eyes had seen through the binoculars, reshaping the image in his memory. Had his eyes translated something that merely seemed strange under the tricky light into something his imagination suggested? Then what could it have been? A big felt hat oddly creased? No. Leaphorn sighed and yawned. His head was buzzing with his tiredness. He could no longer concentrate. He would sleep at the Ramah chapter house tonight. Tomorrow morning he would check with the Zuñi Police. They would tell him that Cata had come home during the night and confessed to a silly hoax. Leaphorn suddenly knew what the explanation would be. A sheep slaughtered for the Shalako feast. The boys saving its blood, using it for an elaborate joke, unconscious of the cruelty in it.

Where the road crossed the ridge overlooking the Ramah Valley, Leaphorn slowed, flicked on the radio transmitter. The operator at Ramah would be long abed but Leaphorn raised Window Rock quickly.

There were three messages for him. The captain wanted to know if he was making any progress on the affair of the embezzled payment for the pickup truck. His wife had called to ask that Leaphorn be reminded that he had a dental appointment in Gallup at 2 P.M. And the Zuñi Police Department had called and asked that Leaphorn be informed that Ernesto Cata had been found.

Leaphorn frowned at the radio. "Found? Is that all they said?"

"Let me check," the dispatcher said. "I didn't take the message." The dispatcher sounded sleepy. Leaphorn rubbed his hand across his face, suppressing a yawn.

"Found his body," the dispatcher said.

Tuesday, December 2, 7:22 a.m.

THE SUN, RISING OVER OSO RIDGE, warmed the right side of Joe Leaphorn's face and cast the shadow of his profile horizontally against the raw gray earth exposed by the landslide. He stood with his arms folded over his stomach, his ears aware of the scraping sound of the shovels but his eyes involved with the beauty of the morning. The view from this eroded ridge above Galestina Canyon was impressive. Sunlight struck the east faces of the Zuñi Buttes ten miles to the northwest. It reflected from the yellow water tower that marked the site where the government had built Black Rock to house its Bureau of Indian Affairs people. It flashed now from the wing of a light plane taking off from the Black Rock landing strip. Almost due north, three miles up the valley, it illuminated the early-morning haze of smoke emerging from the chimneys of Zuñi Village. Much nearer, a yard from the toe of Leaphorn's boot, it lit the scuffed sole of a small, low-cut shoe. The shoe protruded from the earth-and-stone rubble of the slide—a black shoe, laces down. It was a track shoe, five spikes under the ball of the foot, none under the heel because a runner's heel does not strike the ground. Part of the runner's heel was visible, and the Achilles tendon, and perhaps an inch of muscular calf. The earth covered the rest. Leaphorn's gaze rested on Zuñi Village. Halona, they called it. Halona Itawana, the Middle Ant Hill of the World. A hillock beside a bend in the now dry bed of the Zuñi River, a hillock of red stone houses jammed together to form the old village and surrounded now by a sprawling cluster of newer houses. Maybe six thousand Zuñis, Leaphorn thought, with something like 65,000 square miles of reservation, and all but a few hundred of them lived like bees in this single busy hive. Up to twenty-five or thirty people in some houses, he had heard. All the daughters of a family still living with their mother, living together with their husbands and their children in a sort of reversal of the Navajos' mother-in-law taboo. It made for the handful of Zuñis a bigger town than the Navajos had made with their 130,000 people. What force caused the Zuñis to collect like this? Was it some polarity of the force that caused his own Dinee to scatter, to search for loneliness, as much as for grass, wood, and water, as an asset for a hogan site? Was this why the Zuñi had survived as a people against five centuries of invasions? Was there some natural law, like the critical mass of nuclear physics, which held that X number of Indians compacted in X number of square yards could resist the White Man's Way by drawing strength from one another?

The plane—silenced by distance—banked toward the north, toward Gallup, or Farmington, or perhaps Shiprock or Chinle, and blinked a quick reflection of sun from a polished surface. Just to Leaphorn's left Ed Pasquaanti pushed at the handle of his shovel, hat off, cropped gray hair bristling. Beyond him, three other Zuñis worked methodically. Their last names were Cata, Bacobi, and Atarque. They were the father and uncles, respectively, of Ernesto Cata. They dug with deliberate speed, wordlessly. The earth pile receded, revealing another inch of Ernesto Cata's calf.

"Where did you find the bicycle?" Leaphorn asked. "If you haven't finished looking there, I could check around some." (He had offered once—five minutes ago, when he had first arrived—to help with the digging. "No, thanks," the uncle named Thomas Atarque had said. "We can handle it all right." The earth was Zuñi earth, the body under it Flesh of the Zuñi Flesh. Leaphorn sensed digging here, at this moment in time, was not for a Navajo. He wouldn't repeat the offer.)

"The bike was down there," Pasquaanti said. He pointed. "Pushed under the uphill side of that sandstone outcrop. I just looked around enough to find the tracks leading up this way. It was getting dark then."

The bicycle had been remarkably well hidden considering the circumstances. It had been pushed half under a sandstone overhang and then disguised with a cover of dead grass and weeds. Even with the camouflage gone, it was hard to see. Leaphorn looked at it, thinking first that whoever had hidden it had found this site at night. Only moonlight, and two nights ago it would have been a half-moon. The implications of that were clear enough. Whoever had brought Ernesto Cata's body here to be hidden under a tumbled slide of earth either knew this landscape well or had planned in advance. George Bowlegs would know it and—he thought defensively—a thousand Zuñis would know it. Leaphorn went methodically to work.

The bike had been rolled here up a deer trail. Leaphorn backtracked to a sheep path down the slope. The path angled downhill and northward, toward Zuñi Pueblo. He checked everything, working slowly. By the time he reached the cluster of trees where Cata had bled out his life, it was noon. In this small area he spent another three hours—much of it squatted on his heels studying the dusty ground.

There were five sets of recent tracks. He quickly eliminated the Goodyear rubber heel-marks left by Pasquaanti and the waffle-soled boots of the Cata uncle who had found the blood. That left cowboy boots, presumably George Bowlegs's, which had dismounted from the bicycle near the trees, Cata's five-spiked track shoes, and moccasins worn by whoever had pushed the bicycle away with Cata's body as its cargo. Leaphorn sat on a slab of sandstone and considered what these tracks told him. It wasn't much.

He could guess that the killing hadn't been premeditated—at least not completely. One who plans to carry a body a long distance uphill over rough ground does not wear moccasins if he has any respect for his feet. He wears something with sturdy soles and heels. The Man Who Wore Moccasins had waited among the junipers out of sight. He could have struck Cata from this ambush had there been an intention to kill. But he hadn't. The moccasins had stepped out into the open. Moccasins and track shoes had faced one another long enough for several shuffles and shifts of weight. They had stood very close. (Had Moccasins perhaps gripped Cata's arm?) Then Cata had taken three long-stride steps downhill, and fallen, and pumped his blood out onto the thirsty earth. Moccasins now wheeled the bike to the bloody place, loaded Cata upon it, and rolled it away. But it seemed highly unlikely he could have known the bicycle would be available. Not unless Moccasins was George Bowlegs. Could the boy have ridden here in cowboy boots, parked the bike, walked over to the rocks, and changed into moccasins? Obviously, he *could* have. Leaphorn could think of no reasons why he would have. He tried to imagine what Cata and Moccasins might have talked about as they stood toe-to-toe. There was not even ground for speculation.

Leaphorn lit a cigarette. A piñon jay emerged from the junipers in a flash of blue feathers and disappeared toward Corn Mountain. A thin blue line of smoke corkscrewed upward from Leaphorn's cigarette to ravel away in the cold air. North, a jet drew a white line across the sky. Behind it the sky was gray with a high overcast. Intermittently throughout the dusty autumn, such omens had threatened snow. And all autumn, after a summer of drought, the omens had lied. Leaphorn studied the sky, his face dour. He was finding no order in his thoughts, none of that mild and abstract pleasure which the precise application of logic always brought to him. Instead there was only the discordant clash of improbable against unlikely, effect without cause, action without motive, patternless chaos. Leaphorn's orderly mind found this painful. The roughness of the sandstone pressed into his buttocks now but he ignored this, as he ignored his hunger, willing his thoughts away from these sensations, frowning across the brushy slopes at Corn Mountain, thinking.

Leaphorn came from the Taadii Dinee, the Slow-Talking People Clan. The father of his mother was Nashibitti, a great singer of the Beautyway and the Mountainway, and other curing rites, and a man so wise that it was said the people of Beautiful Mesa added Hosteen to his name when he was less than thirty—calling him Old Man when he was far too young to be a grandfather. Leaphorn had been raised at the knee of Hosteen Nashibitti when Nashibitti was old in years as well as wisdom. He had grown up among the sheepmen and hunters of Beautiful Mesa, families who descended from families who had elected to die when Kit Carson's horsemen came in 1864.

Thus the handed-down tribal memories which surrounded Leaphorn's boyhood were not, like those of most Navajos of his generation, the grandfather tales of being herded into captivity, of the Long Walk away from the sacred mountains to the concentration camp at Fort Stanton, of smallpox, and the insolent Apaches, and of misery, indignity, and finally the Long Walk home. Instead, the tales of Nashibitti were of the redder side of tragedy: of two brothers with bows against a troop of mounted riflemen; of sabered sheep, burning hogans, the sound of axes cutting down the peach orchards, the bodies of children in the snow, the red of the flames sweeping through the cornfields, and, finally, the litany of starving families hunted through the canyons by Kit Carson's cavalry. The boy who would become Hosteen Nashibitti and the grandfather of Leaphorn was delivered of a dying mother in such a hungry canyon. He had been raised with his ears filled with his uncle's accounts of brutal cruelty and sublime bravery; of how Carson had claimed to be a friend of the Navajos, of how Carson, led by the hated Utes, had ridden through the peaceful cornfields like death on horseback. But somehow, Nashibitti had never learned this bitterness. When he was initiated at the Yeibichai on the last night of the Night Way Ceremonial, the secret war name they gave him had been He Who Asks Questions. But to Leaphorn, seventy years later, he had been One Who Answers. It had been Nashibitti who had taught Leaphorn the words and legends of the Blessing Way, taught him what the Holy People had told the Earth Surface People about how to live, taught him the lessons of the Changing Woman—that the only goal for man was beauty, and that beauty was found only in harmony, and that this harmony of nature was a matter of dazzling complexity.

"When the dung beetle moves," Hosteen Nashibitti had told him, "know that something has moved it. And know that its movement affects the flight of the sparrow, and that the raven deflects the eagle from the sky, and that the eagle's stiff wing bends the will of the Wind People, and know that all of this affects you and me, and the flea on the prairie dog and the leaf on the cottonwood." That had always been the point of the lesson. Interdependency of nature. Every cause has its effect.

Every action its reaction. A reason for everything. In all things a pattern, and in this pattern, the beauty of harmony. Thus one learned to live with evil, by understanding it, by reading its cause. And thus one learned, gradually and methodically, if one was lucky, to always "go in beauty," to always look for the pattern, and to find it.

Leaphorn stabbed the cigarette butt against the rock, grinding it out with an angry gesture. There was no pattern here. Cata was dead without reason. George Bowlegs had not run when he should have run and then he had fled when he shouldn't have. Leaphorn stood and brushed off the seat of his khaki trousers, still thinking. What bothered him most, he realized, were not these large and important incongruities. It was smaller ones. Why had Cecil Bowlegs told him that Cata had stolen artifacts from the Early Man dig? There was no reason for Cecil to lie, and no reason for the anthropologists to lie in denying such a loss. Why did Cecil think George was running from a vengeful kachina if George had told Susanne he would be *hunting* a kachina? And what was that strange thing Leaphorn has seen at Jason's Fleece with the body of a man and the head of a bird? Could someone be wearing one of the masks of the Zuñi kachina religion? To do so for a purpose outside the religion would surely be the worst sort of sacrilege. There was no possible answer to any of these questions.

Leaphorn began walking rapidly down the slope toward Zuñi Village. The body would be there by now, the cause of death known. He would find out about that. And when there was time he would learn more about the Zuñi religion. But before he did that, he would get Shorty Bowlegs sober enough to talk—even if he had to lock him up to do it.

Tuesday, December 2, 6:11 p.m.

THE HEADLIGHTS on Joe Leaphorn's Law and Order Division van lost themselves one moment in a blinding gust of reddish-gray dust and the next in the whiteness of a flurry of dry snowflakes. Driving required catching glimpses between gusts and flurries of the twisting, bumpy wagon track and—when it became abruptly invisible—remembering where the wheels would find it. With one tire already blown yesterday on this chancy trail to Shorty Bowlegs' hogan—and no spare left—Leaphorn was taking it very slowly. He was in no particular hurry. He had no real hope that Shorty Bowlegs, if Shorty Bowlegs was sober enough to talk more coherently now, could tell him anything very useful. It was simply that Bowlegs was the last untapped possibility. After Bowlegs there would be no place left to go. This was the ultimate dead end of the Cata affair and Leaphorn knew himself too well to consider avoiding it. All other possible sources of information had been tapped and the incongruities remained. They would give him no peace. A boy had been killed without reason. Leaphorn's rational mind would not accept this. Not even the grasshopper took wing without reason. His mind would worry at the rough edges of this like a tongue at a broken tooth. It would reject Cata killed without cause, George Bowlegs fleeing the scene of this crime a day later than reason said he should have fled the whole irrational business.

Leaphorn turned the carryall down the last slope toward the Bowlegs place. It slid with a bone-jarring thump into a rut.

Leaphorn pronounced an explicit Navajo indecency which took in darkness, weather, himself, the Zuñi tribe in general, and Ed Pasquaanti in particular. He swung the truck across the bare and beaten ground to park.

The headlights lit the Bowlegs brush arbor, flashed for a second on a pole sheep corral down the slope, flicked past the doorway of the Bowlegs hogan and the blue-shirted form in its doorway, and stopped finally, as Leaphorn set the hand brake, focused on the gray-green foliage of a juniper. Leaphorn turned off the ignition but not the lights. He was relieved. Bowlegs was not only awake, but sober enough to be standing in the doorway, curious about his visitor.

Leaphorn shook out a cigarette, lit it, and waited. Navajo custom and good manners required the wait. The tradition had been born in the old days so that the ghosts which swarmed the reservation and followed travelers would wander impatiently away and not follow the guest into the host's hogan. Today it survived as much out of the respect for privacy of a scattered rural people as from the waning threat of the chindi. Without thinking of why he did it, Lieutenant Joe Leaphorn would wait in his truck until Shorty Bowlegs had put on his trousers or otherwise prepared to receive a visitor. And when Bowlegs was ready he would stand outside his hogan door so that Leaphorn would know it.

Leaphorn waited now. The wind shook the truck. It spoke in a dozen voices, whistling, hooting, rasping past cracks and corners and bends of metal. The defroster fan had died with the motor and his breath quickly misted the windshield. Outside spots of white showed where the dusting of dry snow drifted against rocks and eddied into the windbreak of the junipers. The flakes were still tiny, but there were more of them now, wind-driven through the headlight beams. When this squall line passed, a real snowstorm might develop. And it was desperately needed. Leaphorn waited, thinking of hungry cattle, dry stock tanks, and the penalties of drought; thinking of the long day behind him, of Cata's body on the table at the Black Rock BIA hospital—the doctor cleaning the sand from that great chopped wound which had almost severed head from body. An ax, perhaps, or a machete, swung with great force.

The funeral had been within the hour. First a funeral Mass at the mission church in the village and then the ceremonial of the Badger kiva at the open grave. He had watched it from a distance, feeling that he was an intruder into something sad and private and sacred. Who, he wondered suddenly, would be the Fire God for the Shalako ceremonials now that the Fire God was dead? Leaphorn had no doubt that there would be a new Shulawitsi dancing flawless attendance on the Council of the Gods when the ceremonials began. He thought of that, and of where George Bowlegs might be taking shelter on this miserable night, and then—abruptly—he was thinking that it was taking far too long for Shorty Bowlegs to reappear at his hogan doorway.

Leaphorn pushed the van door open against the pressure of the wind, pulled his windbreaker collar around his face, and stepped out, staring at the hogan. It was totally dark now. Had it been when he drove up? Leaphorn remembered only his headlights flashing past its entrance, the figure frozen in that flicker of light. He had presumed it was Bowlegs looking out to see who was driving up on this bitter night. But now there was no sign of light around the plank door, none around the small uneven window Bowlegs had cut through the logs of his southeast wall. Would Bowlegs have gone back inside, blown out his kerosene lamp, and left his visitor sitting outside in the cold? Leaphorn thought back, remembering the Bowlegs of yesterday as a friendly man—too drunk to understand what Leaphorn was saying, or for coherent answers, but smiling a wide, wet smile, trying to get Leaphorn to sit, to join him in a drink, trying to be helpful.

Leaphorn stood a moment beside the carryall, staring at the dark humped shape of the hogan, aware of the shrieking curses of the wind, of the evil ghosts of a thousand generations of Dinee who rode the night. And then he reached back inside the cab. He fished a flashlight out of the glove compartment and lifted his 30-30 from the rifle rack across the back window. Ten feet from the hogan door he stopped.

"Ya-ta-hey," he shouted. "Shorty Bowlegs, ya-ta-hey."

The wind whipped a mixture of dust and snow around the hogan, around Leaphorn's feet. The plank door moved, tapping at its crude casement. He stared at the door. In the dim reflection from the headlights he could barely detect the motion. He flicked on the flashlight. The door was formed of five vertical planks, braced with one-by-four-inch board. Under the yellow light it hung motionless. The wind gusted again, hooting through the hogan's stovepipe smoke hole and speaking in a quarrelsome chorus of voices around the cracks and crevices of its logs. Now the door moved. Outward, then inward, tapping against its latch.

"Hello," Leaphorn shouted. "Shorty?"

The wind voices of the hogan sank abruptly in pitch and volume, answering him with silence. Leaphorn moved beside the hogan wall. He pumped a shell into the 30-30 chamber, held the rifle on his right arm. With his left hand he pulled up the doorlatch and jerked outward. The wind helped, sucking the door open and banging it back against the log wall opposite Leaphorn.

Inside nothing moved. The flashlight beam reflected from the galvanized tin of a washtub against the back wall, lit a scattered jumble of cooking pots and food supplies, and lingered on clothing (boy-sized bluejeans, three shirts, a nondescript blue cloth, assorted underwear) which hung from the hogan's blanket rope. Behind the clothing, shadows moved on the rough log wall. Anything there? Nothing visible. Leaphorn moved the light clockwise through the hogan. It passed three empty bedrolls, all in disarray, passed a battered metal chest with its drawers hanging open, passed a rope-tied bundle of sheep hides, and stopped finally on the arm of a man. The arm extended limply on the packed earthen floor, the dark wrist thrust out of a sleeve that was khaki (not dark blue), the fingers relaxed, their tips touching the earth.

A stinging flurry of dry snowflakes whipped past Leaphorn's face. Again the wind spoke loud around the hogan, raising an obbligato mixture of hoots and shrieks. The flashlight now lit black hair—neatly parted, a braid tied with a string, a cloth headband which had been a faded pink but now was dyed—like the hair beneath it—a fresh bloody crimson.

Without knowing it, Leaphorn had been holding his breath. Now that he had found Shorty Bowlegs, he released it with a sound something like a sigh. He stood for a moment looking carefully past the hogan, studying the dim, wind-twisted shapes of the piñons and junipers which surrounded it, examining the shape of the outbuildings. Listening. But the wind made listening useless.

He stepped into the hogan and squatted on his heels. He stared first at the face that had been Bowlegs' and then examined the hogan. Shorty Bowlegs had been killed with a blow struck from behind with something heavy and sharp. The same weapon that had killed Cata? Swung by the figure in the blue shirt (a man, he thought, without knowing why he thought it) he had seen at the doorway. And where was that man now? Not more than five minutes away, but with wind, snow, dust, and darkness making both ears and eyes useless, he might as well be on another planet. Leaphorn cursed himself. He had seen this killer, and he had sat daydreaming in his truck while the man walked away.

Leaphorn tested the blood on Bowlegs' hair with a tentative fingertip. Sticky. Bowlegs had been struck at least thirty minutes before Leaphorn's arrival. The killer had apparently killed Bowlegs first and then ransacked the hogan. Had he come to kill Bowlegs and, with that done, searched the family's belongings? Or had he come to make the search and killed Bowlegs to make it possible? To search for what? Everything that Bowlegs had accumulated in perhaps forty years of living was littered on the hogan floor. Add it together—the clothing, the supplies, the sheepherder's tools—and it might have cost five hundred dollars, new, at inflated trading post prices. Now it was worn, used. By whiteman's standards, Leaphorn thought, Bowlegs had a net worth of maybe one hundred dollars. The white world's measure of his life. And what would the Navajo measure be? The Dinee made a harder demand—that man find his place in the harmony of things. There, too, Shorty Bowlegs had failed.

Outside the hogan, Leaphorn snapped off the carryall headlights and began a search in gradually widening circles. He worked slowly, conscious that the killer—unlikely as it seemed—might still be near. He looked for tracks—human, horse, or vehicle—using his flashlight sparingly in places where they might be preserved from the wind. He found nothing very conclusive. His own van's tires showed up in several places where the gusts had not erased them but no other vehicle had apparently come near the hogan recently. Having established that, he made a careful inspection of the pen in a shallow arroyo below the hogans which had served as the Bowlegs stables. Two horses had been kept there. The tracks of one—poorly shod—were only a few hours old. The other had apparently not been around for perhaps a day. Leaphorn squatted on the loamy earth, hunched against the icy wind, thinking about what that might mean.

The wind rose and fell, now whipping the limbs of the junipers into frantic thrashing, now dying into an almost silent lull. Leaphorn snapped off the light and crouched motionless. The wind had carried an incongruous sound. He listened. It was buried now under the thousand sounds of the storm. And then he heard it again. A bell. And then another, slightly lower in pitch. And a third with a tinny tinkle. Leaphorn moved swiftly toward a gnarled juniper barely visible in the darkness, toward the sound. He stood behind the tree, waiting. The bells approached, and with them the sound of a horse. The dim shape of a white goat tinkled past the tree, followed by a straggling stream of goats and then an almost solid mass of sheep. Finally, there came the horse, and on it a small shape, huddled against the cold.

Leaphorn stepped from behind the juniper.

"Ya-ta-hey," he shouted. "Cecil?"

9

Tuesday, December 2, 10:15 p.m.

IT WAS ALMOST TWO HOURS LATER when Leaphorn reached Zuñi and left Cecil with a young Franciscan brother at Saint Anthony's school. He had told Cecil as gently as he could that someone had struck his father on the back of the head and that Shorty Bowlegs was dead. He had radioed New Mexico State Police at Gallup to make this homicide a matter of record and the dispatcher had promised to notify Zuñi Police and the McKinley County sheriff's office. That would assure that the routine would be properly followed, although Leaphorn was sure that whoever had killed Shorty Bowlegs would not be stupid enough to be captured at a roadblock. With these official duties done, Leaphorn had helped Cecil unsaddle the horse and secure the sheep in the brush corral. He had left Cecil in the cab of the truck then, with the motor running and the heater on high, while he recovered the boy's bedroll and odds and ends of spare clothing from the hogan. He put these—a single shirt, three pairs of cheap socks, and underwear—in an empty grocery sack. He handed the sack through the truck window.

"I didn't find any pants."

"Just got these I got on," Cecil said.

"Anything else you want out of there?"

Cecil stared over his shoulder at the hogan. Leaphorn wondered what he was thinking. Two hours ago when he had left to bring in the sheep that humped shape had been home. Warm. Occupied by a man who, drunk or not, was his father.

Now the hogan was cold, hostile to him, occupied not by Shorty Bowlegs but by Shorty's ghost—a ghost which would in Navajo fashion embody only those things in his father's nature which were weak, evil, angry.

"Ought to get George's stuff out of there, I guess," Cecil said. He paused. "What do you think—would they have ghost sickness on them yet? And I've got a lunchbox. You think we should leave that stuff?"

"I'll get 'em. And tomorrow we'll get somebody to come out here and take care of the body and fix up the hogan. There won't be any ghost sickness."

"Just the lunchbox for me," Cecil said. "That's all I got."

It occurred to Leaphorn, back inside the hogan, that this would be an unusually complicated death. No relatives around to arrange for disposal of the body, and to break a hole through a hogan wall to release Shorty's ghost for its infinite wandering, and to nail shut the door as a warning to all that here stood a hogan contaminated by death, and—finally—to find the proper Singer, and arrange the proper Sing, to cure any of those who might have been somehow touched and endangered by this death. More important, there was no surrounding family to absorb the survivors—to engulf a child with the love of uncles and aunts and cousins, to give Cecil the security of a new hogan and a new family. The family to do this must be somewhere on the Ramah reservation. It would be part of Shorty's family. Since Cecil's mother was no good, it would be better to return him to the outfit of his father's mother. The people at the Ramah chapter house would know where to find them. And for Leaphorn there then remained the matter of finding Cecil's big brother.

In the hogan, he found surprisingly little trace of George. A spare shirt, too ragged even for George to wear, and a few odds and ends similarly rejected. Nothing else. Leaphorn added this lack of George's belongings to the absence of the second Bowlegs horse from the corral and came to the obvious conclusion. George had come back to this hogan the day that horse had left its latest tracks at the corral. That was yesterday, the day after Cata had died. George had picked up his spare clothing and the horse. He must have been here not long after Leaphorn had made his fruitless first call on Shorty.

On his way out of the hogan, Leaphorn saw what must be Cecil's lunchbox. It was one of those tin affairs sold in the dime stores. Its yellow paint was decorated with a picture of Snoopy atop his doghouse. It lay open now beside the hogan wall. Leaphorn picked it up.

Inside the box were a dozen or so papers, once neatly folded but now pawed through and left in disarray. The top one was filled with penciled subtraction problems and bore the notation "GOOD!" in red ink. The paper under it was titled "Paragraphs" in the upper left corner. Above the title a gold star was pasted.

Leaphorn refolded the papers. Under them were a small blue ball with a broken bit of rubber band attached, a spark plug, a small horseshoe magnet, a ball of copper wire wound neatly on a stick, an aspirin bottle half filled with what looked like dirty iron filings, the wheel off a toy car, and a stone figure a little larger than Leaphorn's thumb. It was the elongated shape of a mole carved from a piece of antler. Two thin buckskin thongs secured a tiny chipped-flint arrowhead to its top. It was obviously a fetish figure, probably from one of the Zuñi medicine fraternities. It certainly wasn't Navajo.

In the van, Cecil was looking through the windshield. He took the box without a word and put it on his lap. They jolted past the hogan with Cecil still staring straight ahead.

"I'm going to leave you at Saint Anthony's Mission tonight," Leaphorn said. "Then I'm going to find George and get both of you boys away from here. I'm going to get you to your father's family unless you feel there's somewhere else that would be better."

"No," Cecil said. "There's no place else."

"Where'd you get that fetish?"

"Fetish?"

"That little bone mole."

"George gave it to me."

"What does your other horse look like?"

"The other horse? It's a bay. Big, with white stockings."

"When George came and got the horse, what else did he take?"

Cecil said nothing. His hands gripped the lunchbox. Between the boy's fingers Leaphorn could make out the inscription: "Happiness is a strong kite string."

"Look," Leaphorn said. "If he didn't take the horse, who did? And who took his things? Don't you think we should find him now? Don't you think he'd be safer? For God's sake, think about it for a minute."

The carryall tilted up the slope above the hogan, grinding in second gear. A fresh assault of wind howled past its windows. The snow had stopped now and the vehicle was submerged in a sea of swirling dust. Cecil suddenly began shaking. Leaphorn put his hand on the boy's shoulder. He was overcome with a wild surge of anger.

"He got the horse yesterday evening," Cecil said. His voice was very small. "It was about dark, after I talked to you. My father, he was asleep, and I went out to see about the sheep and when I got back the rifle was gone and I found the note." Cecil was still staring straight ahead, his hands gripping the tin box so hard that his knuckles whitened. "And I guess he took his knife, and the stuff he kept in a leather pouch he made, and a part of a loaf of bread." Cecil fell silent, the catalog completed.

"Where'd he say he was going?"

"The note's in here with my stuff," Cecil said. He unlatched the box and sorted through the papers. "I thought I put it in here," he said. He shut the box. "Anyway, I remember most of it. He said he couldn't explain it to me exactly but he was going to find some kachinas. He said he had to talk to them. He couldn't pronounce the name of the place. He tried to say it but all I remember was it started with a 'K.' And when he was riding off he said he'd be gone several days to where this kachina was, taking care of the business he had. And if he couldn't get it done there, then he'd have to go to Shalako over at Zuñi and then he'd be home. And he said not to worry about him."

"Did he say anything about Ernesto Cata?"

"No."

"Or give any hint where he was looking for this kachina?"

"No."

"Was that all he said?"

Cecil didn't answer. Leaphorn glanced at him. The boy's eyes were wet.

"No," Cecil said. "He said to take care of Dad."

Wednesday, December 3, 10 a.m.

JOE LEAPHORN WAS having trouble concentrating. It seemed to him that a single homicide (as the death of Cata) could be thought of as a unit—as something in which an act of violence contained beginning and end, cause and result. But two homicides linked by time, place, participants and, most important, motivation presented something more complex. The unit became a sequence, the dot became a line, and lines tended to extend, to lead places, to move in directions. One-two became one-two-three-four. . . . Unless, of course, the deaths of the Zuñi boy and the drunken Navajo were the sum of some totality. Could this be?

This question was the focus of Leaphorn's concentration. Did the killing of Cata and of Shorty Bowlegs make sense in themselves? Or must they be part of something larger? And if the sequence was incomplete, where did the line between Cata and Bowlegs point? The question cried for every gram of Leaphorn's attention. His head ached with it.

But there were distractions. The FBI agent was talking. Once again a fly was patrolling the Zuñi Police Department office. And outside a truck whined down the asphalt of N.M. 53 with something noisily wrong with its gearbox. Leaphorn found himself thinking of the late Ernesto Cata, who had (as the Zuñis would say it) completed his path after thirteen years of life, who had been the personifier of the Fire God, an altar boy at Saint Anthony's Church, a baptized Christian, a Catholic communicant, a member of a Zuñi kiva fraternity born into the

Badger Clan, who would almost certainly have become one of the "valuable men" of the Zuñi religion had not someone, for some reason, found it expedient to kill him.

The voice of Agent John O'Malley intruded itself on Leaphorn's consciousness. He raised his eyebrows at the FBI to simulate attention.

"... ask enough people," O'Malley was saying. "We tend to find that someone finally remembers seeing something helpful. It's a matter of patiently . . ."

Leaphorn found his attention diverted again. Why, he was thinking, were FBI agents so often exactly like O'Malley? He saw that the white man who sat behind O'Malley had noticed the eyebrow gesture, had interpreted it for exactly what it was, and was grinning at Leaphorn a friendly, sympathetic, lopsided grin. This man was maybe fifty, with a pink, freckled, sagging, hound dog face and a shock of sandy hair. O'Malley had introduced him simply as "Agent Baker." As O'Malley must have intended, this left the impression that Baker was another FBI agent. It had occurred to Leaphorn earlier that Baker was not, in fact, an agent of the Federal Bureau of Investigation. He didn't look like one. He had bad teeth, irregular and discolored, and an air of casual sloppiness, and something about him which suggested a quick, inquisitive, impatient intelligence. Leaphorn's extensive experience with the FBI suggested that any of these three characteristics would prevent employment. The FBI people always seemed to be O'Malleys—trimmed, scrubbed, tidy, able to work untroubled by any special measure of intelligence. O'Malley was still talking. Leaphorn looked at him, wondering about this FBI policy. Where *did* they find so many O'Malleys? He had a sudden vision of an office in the Department of Justice building in Washington, a clerk sending out draft notices to all the male cheerleaders and drum majors at U.S.C., Brigham Young, Arizona State, and Notre Dame, ordering them to get their hair cut and report for duty. He suppressed a grin. Then it occurred to him that he had seen Baker before. It had been in Utah, in the office of the San Juan County sheriff, in the wake of an autopsy which showed that a Navajo rodeo performer had died of an overdose of heroin. Baker had been there, looking sloppy and amused, offering the sheriff credentials from the Narcotics Control Division of the Justice Department's Bureau of Narcotics and Dangerous Drugs. That had been a long time ago. It had been followed by reports of arrests made in Flagstaff, and by a variety of vaguish rumors of the sort which circulate among the brethren of the law, rumors suggesting that Mr. Baker had pulled quite a coup, that he was smarter than one should expect and apparently more ruthless as well.

So Baker is a narc. Leaphorn's mind instantly sought the proper place and perspective for this new bit of information. A narcotics agent was involving himself in the deaths of Ernesto Cata and Shorty Bowlegs. Why? And why had O'Malley tried to conceal this fact from local officers? On the surface both answers were obvious. Baker was here because some federal authority somewhere suspected illicit drugs were involved in this affair. And O'Malley hadn't introduced Baker properly because he didn't want the Navajo Police, or the Zuñi Police, or the New Mexico State Police, or the McKinley County Sheriff's Office to know a narc was at work here. But the answers raised new questions. What had aroused this federal suspicion of drugs? And who had cut the locals out of the picture? Which agency did they think would be leaking?

Leaphorn examined the FBI agent. ". . . if there's any physical evidence which leads us anywhere we'll find it," O'Malley was saying. "There's always something. Some little thing. But you people know this part of the country better than we do—and you know the local people. . . ." O'Malley was a handsome man, square-jawed, long-faced, the unhealthy whiteman pallor tanned away, the light hair sunburned lighter, the mouth a quick affair of lips and cheek muscles and white teeth. Was he green enough to believe that none of the men in the room would know that Baker was a narc? Or was he arrogant enough not to care if they detected the insult?

Leaphorn glanced at Pasquaanti, who was gazing at O'Malley with placid and inscrutable interest. The Zuñi's face told Leaphorn nothing. Highsmith was slumped in his chair, fiddling with his state police uniform cap, his legs stretched in front of him and his eyes invisible to Leaphorn. Orange Naranjo's stern old face was turned toward the window, his black eyes bored and restless. Leaphorn watched him. Saw him briefly turn to examine Baker, watch O'Malley, glance back toward the window. Some vague hint of anger among the wrinkles suggested to Leaphorn that Naranjo, too, remembered who Baker was. Naranjo's job, as assigned by O'Malley, was to cover the non-Navajo periphery of the Zuñi reservation, talking to ranchers, road crews, telephone linemen, anyone who might have noticed anything. Leaphorn wondered how hard he would work at it. "We would be interested if someone had seen any strangers, anything unusual, maybe a light plane flying low, maybe who knows what. . . ."

"Yeah," Naranjo said.

"Country this empty, people notice strangers," O'Malley said. Leaphorn had glanced quickly at Naranjo, curious about how he would react to this inanity.

"Yeah," Naranjo had said, looking slightly surprised.

O'Malley now looked at Leaphorn. It had been made clear earlier that the agent was not happy with Lieutenant Leaphorn. Leaphorn should not have prowled around in the Bowlegs hogan after he had found the Bowlegs body. He shouldn't have returned to the hogan at daylight this morning in his fruitless hunt for any tire tracks, footprints, or fragments that the wind might have left. Leaphorn should have backed carefully away and not interfered with the work of the experts. None of this had been said, but it had been implied in the questions with which O'Malley had interrupted Leaphorn's terse account of what had happened at the Bowlegs hogan.

"Baker and I'll head out to the Bowlegs place now," O'Malley said, "and see if there's any prints, or anything for the lab to work on. It would be helpful, Lieutenant, if you'd check among your people living around here and see what you can pick up. Sort of like Naranjo's going to do. O.K.?"

"O.K.," Leaphorn said.

O'Malley paused at the door. "We'd sure like to talk to George Bowlegs," he said to Leaphorn.

The silence Baker and O'Malley left behind them lasted maybe ten seconds. Highsmith rose, stretched, and adjusted his visored cap.

"Well, shee-it," he said. "Time to put the tired body back

behind the wheel and run errands for the Effy-Bee-Eye." He grinned down at Naranjo. "Country as empty as this, people notice strangers. Bet that never occurred to you before, Orange?"

Naranjo made a wry face. "Oh, well," he said. "He's probably all right when you get to know him."

Highsmith reached for the doorknob, then paused. "Any you birds know anything that makes it look like narcotics is mixed up in this?"

Leaphorn laughed.

"You mean besides Baker being a Treasury man?" Naranjo asked.

"I was wondering about Baker," Pasquaanti said. "He didn't look like FBI." He paused. "And now I'm wondering why O'Malley didn't tell us who he was."

"They found out about that treaty you Zuñis made with the Turks to become the global center of opium production," Highsmith said. "They don't want the Zuñi Police Department to know they're investigating."

"It's like my daddy always told me," Pasquaanti said. "Never trust no goddam Induns. That right, Lieutenant?"

"That's right," Leaphorn said. "My grandmother had a motto hanging there in the hogan when I was a kid. Said 'Beware All Blanket-Asses.' "

Naranjo put on his hat, which, despite the season, was straw.

"Somebody should have warned Custer," he said.

Highsmith was out the door now. "That motto," he shouted back at Leaphorn. "How did she spell Blanket-Ass in Navajo?"

"Capital B," Leaphorn said.

Outside the sun beat down from a dark blue sky. The air was still and cold and very dry.

"The weather's decided to behave itself," Highsmith said. "Last night I thought winter was finally going to get here."

"I don't like these late winters," Naranjo said. "Too damn dry and then when it does come, it's usually a son of a bitch."

Pasquaanti was leaning on the doorsill. Naranjo climbed into his car. "Well," he said, "I guess I'll go chasing around seeing if I can find . . ." The rest of it was drowned by the roar of Highsmith's engine as the state policeman made a backing turn and then shot away down New Mexico Highway 53.

Leaphorn put his carryall into gear and followed. He turned eastward, toward the intersection with the Ojo Caliente road, toward the commune which called itself Jason's Fleece. He had told O'Malley and Pasquaanti about the note George Bowlegs left for Cecil. O'Malley hadn't been interested. Pasquaanti had looked thoughtful, and finally had shaken his head and said that he'd heard Bowlegs was kind of a crazy kid, but offered no hint of explanation. Leaphorn decided he would tell Susanne of the note, and then talk to Isaacs about it, hoping for some forgotten crumb of information which might point in the direction Bowlegs had taken. The knobby rubber of his mud tires produced a spray of gravel on the county road and then a rooster tail of dust as he jolted down the wagon track toward the commune. He was thinking that while Bowlegs was hunting his kachina, something was almost certainly hunting Bowlegs. Joe Leaphorn, who almost never hurried, was hurrying now.

Wednesday, December 3, 12:15 p.m.

A YOUNG MAN with peeling sunburn and blond hair tied in a bun was working with a portable welding torch in the commune school bus. The noise it was making had covered the sound of Leaphorn's carryall rolling to a stop and he was obviously startled when he saw the policeman.

"She's busy," he told Leaphorn. "I don't think she's around here. What kind of business do you have with her?"

"Private kind," Leaphorn said mildly. "That is, unless you're a friend of George Bowlegs. We're trying to find where the Bowlegs boy got off to." Behind Hair in Bun, the blanket covering the door of the hogan of Alice Madman's ghost moved. A face appeared, stared at Leaphorn, disappeared. A second later, Halsey pushed past the blanket and emerged.

"You're a cop," Hair in Bun said.

"Like it says there," Leaphorn said, waving in the direction of the Navajo Police seal on the carryall door, "I'm Navajo fuzz." Halsey's expression had amused him and he repeated it loudly enough for Halsey to hear.

"Ya-ta-hey," Halsey said. "Sorry, but that kid you're hunting ain't been back."

"Well, then," Leaphorn said, "I'll just talk to Susanne a little more and see if she's remembered anything that might help."

"She hasn't," Halsey said. "We'll get word to you if anything comes up. No use you wasting your time."

"Don't mind," Leaphorn said. "It beats working. What you fixing on that bus?" The question was addressed to Hair in Bun. The man stared at him.

"Loose seat," Halsey said.

"Be damned," Leaphorn said. "You're welding it back instead of bolting it down? Like to see how you're doing that." He moved toward the bus door.

Hair in Bun stepped into the doorway, pulled his hands out of the bib of his overalls, and let them hang by his sides. Leaphorn stopped.

"I've got a one-track mind," he told Halsey. "The only thing I want to do is talk to Susanne and see if we can figure out a way to find that boy. But if Susanne is off somewhere, I'll kill some time by looking around some." He looked at Hair in Bun. "Starting with this bus," he said. The voice remained mild.

"I think she's over by the windmill," Halsey said. "I'll take you over there."

The path wandered maybe 150 yards down into a narrow wash and then up its sand-and-gravel bottom toward the wall of the mesa from which Leaphorn had watched the commune two nights earlier. Just under the mesa, an intermittent seep had produced a marshy spot. Some grazing leaser had drilled a shallow well, installed a windmill to pump a trickle of water into a sheep watering tank. A Russian olive beside the tank was festooned with drying shirts, jeans, overalls, and underwear. Susanne was sitting in its shade, watching them approach.

"Did you find him? Did George come home?"

"No. I was hoping we could go over it all again and maybe you'd remember something that would help."

"I don't think there's anything to remember." She shook her head. "I just don't think he told me anything except what I could remember Monday."

"Like I told you," Halsey said.

Leaphorn ignored him. "You said George asked you if you knew anything about the Zuñi religion," Leaphorn said. "Can you remember anything more about that part of the conversation?"

Behind him, Halsey laughed.

"Really. Really, I can't." She was looking past him at Halsey. "I just remember he asked me if I knew anything and I told him just what little Ted had told me about it. I'd help if I could."

"O.K.," Halsey said. "Come on, Navajo policeman, let's go."

Leaphorn turned. Halsey was standing in the path, hands in the pockets of the army fatigue jacket he was wearing, looking amused and insolent. He was a big man, tall and heavy in the shoulders. Leaphorn let his anger show in his voice.

"I'm just saying this once. This girl and I are going to talk awhile without you interrupting. We can talk here, or we can talk in the sheriff's office in Gallup. And if we go to Gallup, you and that illegal deer carcass will go along. Possession of an untagged mule deer carcass out of season will cost you maybe three hundred dollars and a little time in jail. And then you're going to go to Window Rock and talk to the Tribe's people about what the hell you're doing on Navajo land without a permit."

"It's public domain land," Halsey said. "It's off the reservation. Bureau of Land Management land."

"Our map shows it's on the res," Leaphorn said. "But you can argue with the magistrate about that. After you get clear of the sheriff at Gallup."

"O.K.," Halsey said. He looked past Leaphorn at Susanne—a long, baleful stare—turned on his heel, and walked rapidly down the draw toward the commune.

"But I still don't remember anything," Susanne said. She was looking after Halsey, her lower lip caught in her teeth.

Leaphorn leaned his hips against the steep arroyo bank behind him and watched Halsey out of sight. "How could anybody possibly find him?" Susanne added. "Either he ran away for good or pretty soon he'll come home. There's no use chasing him. I've been thinking about what you told me about the cold weather." She looked at him defiantly. "I don't think I really believe George will freeze. If the foxes and coyotes and things like that don't freeze, I bet George wouldn't. He's just as at home out there as they are. What you were telling me was just crap, wasn't it? Just something to get me to talk about him?"

"I wanted you to talk about him, yes," Leaphorn said. "And from what I hear, George is smart and tough. But we did have those eleven people freeze last winter. Some of them were old, and one was sick, and one had been thrown by his horse, but some of them were mature, healthy men. Just too much snow, too cold, too far from shelter."

"I'll bet they were drunk," Susanne said.

Leaphorn laughed. "O.K. If you made a bet like that, I guess you'd win. Three of them were drunk. I wouldn't worry much about George if he had plenty of food. If he isn't hungry, and a snowstorm catches him, he can keep a fire going."

"He'll get food," Susanne said. "He killed that deer for us, you know. And he must be just about the greatest deer hunter. He's been keeping his family supplied with meat since he was just a little boy. And he knows everything about deer."

"Like what?"

"Like . . . I don't know. What was it he was telling me?" She made a nervous gesture with her hands, recalling it. "Like deer have their eyes so far on the sides of their heads they can see a lot better behind them than we can. They can see except almost directly behind them. But then he said that deer are mostly color blind and . . . what was it he said? . . . they don't recognize shapes very well to the sides of them because they don't have stereoscopic vision as good as we do. Anyway, he said they see things like motion and flashes of reflections better than us . . . but it's mostly two dimensional. He told me that one day he was standing real still in plain view with two mule deer about seventy-five yards away staring at him. And just to test them, he opened his mouth. Didn't make any noise or anything. Just opened his mouth. And both deer ran away."

"They're very far-sighted," Leaphorn said.

"So I think, if he gets hungry, he'll kill a deer," she said.

"With what?"

"Didn't he stop and get his daddy's rifle?"

"Did he say he would?"

Susanne's expression said she hadn't meant to tell him that. "I guess maybe he did," she said slowly. "Or maybe I just presumed he would."

"Did he tell you anything else about deer hunting?"

"Lots of things. He was teaching Ernesto how to hunt, and

Ernesto was teaching him the Zuñi way of hunting. I think he was, whatever that is. Anyway, they talked about hunting a lot." She made a wry face. "Frankly, I learned more about it than I need to know."

"Like what else?" Leaphorn asked. "If Bowlegs was living off the land, knowing how much he knew about hunting deer could be useful."

"Like deer don't look up. So if you can get up on a cliff or something above them they won't see you." She stuck up a second finger. "Like they have a great sense of smell." A third finger went up. "And a great sense of hearing." She laughed. "So if you're up on that boulder, they won't see you but they smell you and hear you breathing. But they don't smell so well in extremely dry weather, and hardly anything if it's raining or heavy fog, or if the wind is blowing hard. But for miles if there's normal humidity and just a breeze." A fourth finger went up. "And like they don't notice natural sounds much, so if you're moving you're supposed to move right down the deer trail where they'd expect to hear noise, and you move in a sort of stop-and-go pace"—she made vaguish hand motions—"like the deer do themselves if there's a lot of leaves and stuff." She stopped, remembering, frowning. "George said the only noise that scares them is something strange, the wrong kind of noise or coming from the wrong place."

She looks tired and thin, Leaphorn was thinking. What the hell is she doing here with this hard bunch? She's too young. Why don't white people take care of their children? Then he thought of George Bowlegs. And why don't Navajos take care of their children?

"You said Ernesto was teaching him the Zuñi way to hunt," Leaphorn said. "What was that?"

"Maybe they were just joking," she said. "I guess it was religion, though. There was a poem, a little song. You're supposed to sing it when you go after mule deer. George was trying to memorize it in Zuñi, and it was hard because he is just beginning to speak Zuñi. I had them translate it and I wrote it down in my notebook."

"I'd like to see it," Leaphorn said. He would like very much to see the notebook, he thought. And so would Baker. What else had she jotted down in it?

"I can just about remember part of it." She paused.

"Deer, Deer, Strong Male Deer,
I am the sound you hear running in your
hoofprints,
I following come, the sound of running.
Sacred favors for you I bring.
My arrow carries new life for you."

Her voice, small and fluting, stopped abruptly. She glanced sidewise at Leaphorn, flushed. "There's a lot more of it, I think, and I probably got it wrong. And then there's a prayer when the deer falls. You take his muzzle in your hands and you put your face against his nostrils and you inhale his breath, and you say, 'Thank you, my father. This day I have drunken in the sacred wind of your life.' I think that's beautiful," she said. "I think the Zuñis have a beautiful . . ." Her voice trailed off. She put her head down, her hands over her face. "Ernesto was so happy," she said, the voice muffled by her hands. "Happy people shouldn't have to die."

"I don't know," Leaphorn said. "Maybe death should only be for the very old. The people who are tired and want some rest." Susanne wasn't making any sound. She sat with her head down, her face in her hands. Leaphorn talked about it quietly. He told her how the Navajo mythology dealt with it, how Monster Slayer and Child Born of Water took the weapons they had stolen from the Sun and how they killed the Monsters who brought death to the Dinee, but how they decided to spare one kind of death. "We call it Sa," Leaphorn said. "The way my grandfather told me the story, the Hero Twins found Sa sleeping in a hole in the ground. Born of Water was going to kill him with his club but Sa woke up, and he told the twins that they should spare him so that those who are worn out and tired with age can die to make room for others being born." He intended to keep talking just as long as she needed him to talk so that she could cry without embarrassment. She wasn't crying for Ernesto Cata, really, but for herself, and for George Bowlegs, and all the lost children, and all the lost innocence. And now she was wiping her face with the back of her hand, and now with the sleeve of her overlarge shirt.

How old is she? Leaphorn wondered. In her late teens, probably. But her age seemed crazily mixed. As green as spring, as gray as winter. How had she come here? Where had she come from? Why didn't the white man take care of his daughter? Was he, like Shorty Bowlegs, hiding from his children in a bottle?

"I hope all that about hunting helps but I don't see how it could," she said. "I think you should wait for him to come home again."

"I haven't told you about that," Leaphorn said. "There isn't any home for George anymore. You knew his dad was an alcoholic, I guess. Well, now his dad is dead."

"My God!" Susanne said. "Poor George. He doesn't know yet?"

"Not unless—" Leaphorn checked himself. "No," he said. "He hasn't been back."

"He was ashamed of his dad," Susanne said. "Ashamed of him being drunk all the time. But he liked him, too. You could tell that. He really loved him."

"So did Cecil," Leaphorn said.

"It's different when they're drunks, I think," Susanne said. "That's like your father being sick. He can't really help it. You can still love them then and it's not so bad." She paused. Her eyes were wet again but she ignored it. "Now he doesn't have anything. First he loses Ernesto and now he loses his dad."

"He has a brother," Leaphorn said. "An eleven-year-old brother named Cecil. He's got Cecil, but until we can find George, Cecil doesn't have him."

"I didn't know he had a brother," Susanne said. "Not until you mentioned it. He never said anything about him." She said it as if she found it incredible, as if she suddenly didn't quite understand George Bowlegs. She stood up, put her hands in the pockets of her jeans, nervously took them out again. They were small hands, frail, grimy, with broken nails. "I have a sister," she said. "Fourteen in January. Someday, I'm going back and get her." Susanne was looking down the wash. "When I have some money someday I'll go back and go to the school at lunch hour and I'll take her away with me."

"And bring her here?"

Susanne looked at him. "No. Not bring her here. Find someplace to take her."

"Isn't she better off with your parents?"

"Parent," Susanne corrected absently. "No. I don't know. I don't think so." The voice trailed away. "If you don't really think George would freeze, then you want to find him because you think he killed Ernesto? Is that it? Or somebody thinks he killed Ernesto?"

"I guess somebody thinks he might have. Or that he was close enough to where it happened to have got a look at who did it. Me, I think he can tell me enough so we'll know what happened, and why it happened."

"I can't remember anything else," Susanne said. She glanced at him and then at her hands. She tugged the cuff down to her knuckles, looked at her fingernails, then hid them in fists, then put the fists in her pockets. Leaphorn let the silence last, looking at her. She was much too thin, he thought, the skin stretched too tight over fragile bones.

"There's a problem, though, if I don't find him. Or *maybe* there is. The way Shorty Bowlegs died was somebody hit him over the head in his hogan last night. Whoever it was was looking for something. Searched through everything in the hogan. O.K. Think about it a little bit. Somebody kills the Cata boy. Two days later somebody kills George's dad and searches George's hogan." He looked at her. "What do you think? I'm nervous about George. Two killings, very much alike, and George is the only thing that connects the two of them."

"You mean George's father was killed. And you think somebody might be . . ."

Leaphorn shrugged. *"Quien sabe?* His friend gets killed, George disappears, his daddy gets killed, what's next? It makes me nervous."

"I didn't know his dad had been killed. I thought he just died."

"After George talked to you Monday, he went to their hogan. When Cecil got home Monday night, he found their horse was gone and their .30-30, and some of George's clothes. And George had left a note. He told Cecil he had some business with a kachina, or kachinas, and he was going to take care of it, and he'd be gone several days. Now, does that suggest anything to you? Did he say anything here about that?"

Susanne was frowning. "He was in a hurry. I remember that. Sweating like he'd been running." She squeezed her eyes shut, concentrating. "He said he wanted to get some venison. And when Halsey said no, George and I went out of the hogan. Then he started asking me about the Zuñi religion. I remember what he said, and what I said."

She opened her eyes and looked at Leaphorn. "I already told you that, about telling him I only knew what little Ted told me. And then he asked me if the Council of the Gods forgave people for breaking taboos. I said I didn't know anything about it. And then he said something about going to a dance hall, or to a dance, or something like that." She frowned again. "I think I must have misunderstood him. It sounded something like that, but that doesn't make much sense."

"Dance hall? I don't seem to . . ."

"It was something about a dance hall. I remember because I thought it sounded crazy at the time."

"I'll do some asking around," Leaphorn said. "Another thing. I don't think you should stay here anymore. I don't think it's safe."

"Why not?"

"It's not much more than just a feeling," Leaphorn said. "But George didn't have very many people close to him. And now two of them are dead. So that leaves you, and maybe Ted Isaacs, and as far as anybody knows, that's about all."

There was more to the feeling than that. There was the hostility of Halsey and Hair in Bun, and there was Mr. Baker grinning in the background, smelling heroin in the wind. And O'Malley's uncasual remark about low-flying planes. Whether or not Halsey's commune was a cover for delivery of Mexican narcotics flown up across the Sonoran desert, there were narcotics around. The condition of the man called Otis testified to that. It would be only a matter of time before Baker moved in.

"By the way," Leaphorn said. "How's Otis?"

"He's gone. Halsey took him into the bus station at Gallup yesterday."

"Was he better?"

"Maybe a little," Susanne said. "I don't think so." She paused. "Look," she said, "do you think Ted might be in any danger?"

"I don't know," Leaphorn said. "I wouldn't have figured Shorty Bowlegs was in any danger. Either somebody had a reason for killing him that we don't know about, or somebody was looking for George and he got in the way. To tell the truth, after that I'm nervous about *anybody* connected with George. That includes you."

"Have you warned Ted? You ought to warn him. Tell him to go back to Albuquerque. Tell him to get away from here." She looked distraught.

"I will," Leaphorn said. "I'm telling you, too. Get away from here."

"I can't," Susanne said. "But he could. There's no reason he can't."

"You can, too," Leaphorn said. "Go. What keeps you here?"

She moved her shoulders, opened her hands, a gesture of helplessness. "I don't have anyplace to go."

"Go back to your family."

"No. There isn't any family."

"Everybody's got a family. You said you had a parent. There must be grandparents, uncles." Leaphorn's Navajo mind struggled with the concept of a child with no family, found it incredible, and rejected it.

"No family," Susanne said. "My dad doesn't want me back." She said it without emotion, a comment on the weather of the human heart. "And the only grandmother I know about lives somewhere back east and doesn't speak to my dad and I've never seen her. And if I've got uncles I don't know about them."

Leaphorn digested this in silence.

"I guess *here's* my family," she said with a shaky laugh.

"Halsey, and Grace and Bad Dude Arnett, and Lord Ben, and Pots, and Oats, until Oats left. That and the rest of them, that's my family."

"You sleep with Halsey?"

"Sure," she said, defiant. "You earn your keep. Do some of the washing, and some of the cooking, and sleep with Halsey."

"He has the money, I guess. Made the deal with Frank Bob Madman for the allotment, and started this place, and buys the groceries."

"I think so. I don't know for sure. Anyway, I don't have any. I have these clothes I've got on, and a dress with a stain on the skirt, and another pair of jeans, and some underwear, and a ballpoint pen. But I don't have any money."

"No money at all? Not enough for a bus ticket someplace?"

"I don't have a penny."

Leaphorn pushed himself away from the arroyo wall and looked downstream. No one was in sight.

"How about Ted Isaacs?" he said. "You like him. He likes you. You could sort of look after one another until I can find George."

"No."

"Why not?"

"I don't know why I talk to you like this," Susanne said. "I never talk to anyone like this. No, because Ted is going to marry me. Someday."

"Why not now?"

"He can't marry me now," Susanne said. "He's got to finish that project and when he does he'll be just about famous, and he'll get a good faculty appointment, and he'll have everything he's never had before. No more being dirt poor and no more being nobody anybody ever heard of."

"O.K. Then why can't you just go over there and stay at his camper? I bet you don't eat much and you could help him dig."

"Dr. Reynolds wouldn't let him." She paused. "I used to work over there a lot but Dr. Reynolds talked to Ted about it." Her expression said she hoped Leaphorn would understand this. "I'm not a professional, and I don't know anything about excavation really. It looks simple but it's actually extremely complicated. And this is going to be a really important dig. It's going to make them rewrite all their books about Stone Age man, and I might mess something up. My just being there, an amateur who doesn't know anything, might make people wonder about how well it was done. And anyway, the establishment will be looking for things to criticize. So really, it's better if I stay away until it's finished." It came out with the sound of something memorized.

"Isaacs told you all that before we had two killings," Leaphorn said. "That sort of changes things. We'll go get your stuff and we don't need to tell Halsey anything except that I'm taking you with me."

"Halsey won't like it," Susanne said. But she followed him down the path.

Wednesday, December 3, 3:48 p.m.

IN ANOTHER TWO or three minutes the lower edge of the red sun would sink behind the strata of clouds hanging over western Arizona. Now the oblique angle of its late afternoon rays were almost parallel to the slope of the hillside toward Zuñi Wash. They projected the moving shadow of Ted Isaacs almost a thousand feet down the hillside, and beside it stretched the motionless shadow of Lieutenant Joseph Leaphorn. Every juniper, every bushy yellow chamiso, every outcrop of stone streaked the yellow-gray of the autumn grass with a stripe of dark blue shadow. And beyond the hillside, beyond the gridwork of twine that marked the Isaacs dig, two miles across the valley, the great bulk of Corn Mountain loomed, its broken cliffs sharply outlined in the reds and pinks of reflected sunlight and the blacks of shadows. It was one of those moments of startling beauty which as a matter of habit Joe Leaphorn took time to examine and savor. But he was preoccupied.

"Oh, God damn it," Isaacs said. "God damn it to hell." He threw another shovelful of earth onto the sifter frame, slammed the shovel against the wheelbarrow, and wiped his forehead against the back of his hairy forearm. He began working the dirt furiously through the wire, then threw down the trowel; sat on the edge of the sifter and looked at Leaphorn, his expression belligerent.

"I don't see how she could really be in any danger," he said. "That's just sheer damned guesswork." Isaacs's voice was angry. "Not even hardly guesswork. Just a sort of crazy intuition."

"I guess that's about right. Just a guess," Leaphorn said. He squatted now, sinking to his heels. A pair of golden eagles coasted down the air currents over the Zuñi River, hunting any rodent that moved. Leaphorn noted this without enjoying it. He found Isaacs's reaction interesting. Not what he expected.

Isaacs pinched the skin over the bridge of his nose between a grimy thumb and finger, shook his head. "George's dad got killed the same way Ernesto did, you say? Hit over the head." He shook his head again and then looked up at Leaphorn. "It does sound like somebody's crazy unless you can figure some reason for it." Across the slope toward Zuñi, smoke of supper cooking was beginning to make its evening haze over the hill that was Halona, the Middle Place of the World. "Maybe it's those goddamned Indians," Isaacs said. "Some kind of feud between the Zuñis and the Navajos, maybe. Could it be something like that?" His tone said he knew too much anthropology to believe it.

"No. Not likely," Leaphorn said. But he thought about it, as he had before. Would Ernesto's family strike out in revenge, presuming young Bowlegs had killed their son and nephew? From what Leaphorn knew of the Zuñi Way, such an act would be utterly unlikely. There hadn't been a homicide at Zuñi in modern times and damned few, Leaphorn suspected, in the history of these people. As far as he could remember, everything in their religion and philosophy militated against violence. Even internal, unexpressed anger was a taboo during their ceremonial periods, for it would destroy the effectiveness of rituals and weaken the tribal link with the supernatural. And when there had been some sort of killing, way back somewhere in the dimness of time, the Zuñis had settled the affair by arranging for gifts to be given the family that lost a member and having the guilty party initiated into the proper medicine society to cure him.

"I don't think there's any chance at all there's any revenge mixed up in this," he said. Still, if he didn't find George, if nothing cleared up this affair, then someday in the future he would try to learn if there had been a new initiation into whatever Zuñi cult would be responsible for curing the sickness of homicide. He probably wouldn't learn anything, but he would try.

"You really think maybe there's some danger for Susie?" Isaacs asked. "Look," he said. "I can't keep her here. Can't you put a guard out there, or something? Or put her someplace where she's safe? You're the law. You're supposed to keep people from getting hurt."

"I'm Navajo law and that gal's white, and I don't even know for sure whether those hogans are on Navajo land. And even if I did know for sure, all I've got is an uneasy feeling. The way it works out, Susanne's just not my baby."

Isaacs stared at Leaphorn. "I think she'll be all right," he said. His face said he was trying hard to believe it.

"There's another thing, too. Just between us, it wouldn't surprise me any if there were some arrests out there one of these days soon. If she's out there, she's going to get herself locked up."

"Narcotics?"

"Probably."

"Those damned crazy bastards!"

"I thought maybe you wouldn't want her pulled in on that," Leaphorn said.

"I don't want her out there at all," Isaacs said. "But right now I can't do a goddam thing. . . ." He stopped.

"Well," Leaphorn said. "I didn't mean to take up so much of your time. I just had the wrong impression." He got up, started to walk away. Isaacs's hand caught his elbow.

"Aren't you going to do anything about her? Look . . ."

"Yeah," Leaphorn said. "I'm going to go try to find George Bowlegs and try to get these killings cleared up. When that gets done you won't have to worry about her getting hit on the head. There's nothing I can do about getting her clear of a narcotics raid. In fact, I can think of a couple of people who'd be pissed off if they knew I was talking to anybody about it."

"I *wish* I could do something. . . ." Isaacs's voice trailed off. His expression was tortured.

"I sort of got the impression that she'd be willing to marry you," Leaphorn said. "That part of it's no business of mine, but then you could—"

The expression on Isaacs's face stopped him. Leaphorn shrugged. "O.K., forget it. I forget sometimes that white men got a different way of thinking about things than us Induns. One more thing: you're another one who might be in line for a hit on the head. You should—"

"Damn you," Isaacs said. His voice was barely under control. "What do you think? You think I don't care? You think I don't love her?" His voice was rising to a yell. "Let me tell you something, you self-righteous son of a bitch. I never had anything until Susie came by here last summer. I never had a girl, clothes, no money, no car, nor no time for women, and none of them would look at me twice anyway. And then here was Susie, ragged and all, and living at the commune, but you can tell what she is underneath all that. She's quality, that's what she is . . . quality. And you know what? Right from the first, we liked one another. She was fascinated by what we're doing here, and by God, she was fascinated by me." His tone suggested he couldn't believe this himself. "She couldn't stay away and I couldn't stand it if she did."

"But she did quit coming by here," Leaphorn said. "She hasn't been here in more than a week. You told me that, didn't you?"

Isaacs sat down again on the wheelbarrow, slumped, looking utterly tired and utterly defeated.

"That's something else you don't understand." He indicated the string-gridded dig site with a half-hearted wave. "About what this dig here is. We're proving the Reynolds theory here. I already told you that. But yesterday and today, I've been getting everything we dreamed we'd ever get. Not just the Folsom workshop chips mixed in with the parallel-flaked stuff. That was about as much as we'd ever dared hope for and I've been getting that all day. But we got the hard evidence, too." He pulled a handful of envelopes from his bulging shirt pocket. "I'm finding Folsom artifacts and parallel-flaked stuff coming out of the same blanks. It's more of that petrified marsh bamboo. Miocene stuff. Out of those formations south of Santa Fe." He spilled the contents of one of the envelopes onto his palm and extended it.

Three large pieces of flint and a score of chips and flakes, all pink or salmon-colored. Leaphorn leaned forward to examine it, noticing between the heavily calloused ridges on Isaacs's palm an angry red blister, and noticing that the hand was shaking.

"Pick it up and take a close look," Isaacs said. "See that grain? Now look at this piece here. He was making something like what we've been calling a Yuma point out of this one." Isaacs's cracked, dirty fingernail indicated the series of ridges where the flint had been flaked away. "But he pressed too hard, or something, and his blank broke. So . . ." Isaacs fished another pinkish stone from his palm. "He started making this one. Notice the leaf shape? He had a roughed-out Folsom point, but when he punched out the fluting, this one snapped, too."

"Having a bad day," Leaphorn said.

"But look," Isaacs said. "Damn it. Use your eyes. Look at the grain in this petrified wood. It's the same. Notice the discoloration in this piece." He indicated with his fingernail a streak of dark red. "Notice how that same streak picks up in this one where he was trying to make the Folsom point. It's the very same damned piece of flint."

"It sure as hell looks like it. Can you prove it?"

"I'm sure a minerologist with a microscope can prove it."

"You found them right together?"

"Right in the same grid," Isaacs said. He pointed to it. "Seventeen W, right there on the top of the ridge, right where a guy might be sitting watching for game down at the river while he chipped himself out some tools. And there was more of the same stuff in two of the adjoining grids. The guy must have broken one, dropped it right where he was sittin' there, and went to work on the other one."

"And broke it, and dropped it, too," Leaphorn said.

"And because he did, we blow the hell out of a tired old theory of Early Man and make anthropology admit the traditional disappearing man story won't hold water anymore."

"Has Reynolds got the good news yet?"

"Not until he comes back from Tucson this weekend," Isaacs said. "And that's what I was starting to explain to you. Reynolds is probably the one guy in the world who would give a graduate student a break like this. You probably know how it works. The professor who finds the site, and scares up the digging money, and plans the strategy—it's his dig. The graduate students do the shovel work and the sorting, but the professor makes all the decisions and he publishes the report under his name, and if his students are lucky, maybe he puts their name in a footnote, or maybe he doesn't. But with Reynolds, it's the other way around. He tells you how to do it and what to look for and he turns you loose. And then whatever you find you publish yourself. There's a dozen people around the country who have made their reputations that way because of him. He gives away the glory and all he expects in return is that you do him a scientific job." He looked at Leaphorn, his face bleak. "By that I mean a perfect job. Perfect."

"What do you mean?"

"I mean you don't make a single mistake. You don't screw up anything. Your records are exactly right. Nothing happens that would let any other scientist in any way cast any doubt on what you've found." Isaacs laughed, a grim, manufactured sound. "Like you don't let a couple of kids hang around your dig site. Like you don't let a girl hang around. You work from daylight until dark seven days a week and you don't let a damn thing distract you."

"I see," Leaphorn said.

"Reynolds let me know he was disappointed when he saw Susie here," Isaacs said. "And he raised bloody hell over the boys."

"So that sort of gives you a choice between Reynolds, who's done you a bunch of favors, and that girl, who needs some help."

"No. That's not it." Isaacs sat on the wheelbarrow rim. He looked away from Leaphorn, out across the valley. The sun had dipped behind the cloudbank now and the breeze was suddenly picking up. It riffled through his hair.

"These rocks I got here mean the rest of my life," he said slowly. "It means I get past the Ph.D. committee with no sweat, and I get the degree. And instead of being one of a hundred new Ph.D.s fighting it out for maybe three or four decent faculty places around the country, I have my pick. I have the reputation, and a book to write, and the status. And when I walk into the American Anthropological Association meetings, instead of being some grubby little pissant of a graduate assistant at some little junior college, why I'm the man who helped fill in the missing link. It's the kind of thing that lasts you all of your life."

"All I was suggesting that you do," Leaphorn said, "was bring Susanne here and keep an eye on her until this business settles down."

Isaacs still stared out toward the Zuñi Buttes. "I thought about it before. Just to get her away from that place. But here's the way it would work. Reynolds would figure it was the last proof he needed that I wasn't the man for this dig. He'd pull me off and put somebody else on it. He may do it anyway because of those boys being here. And that would blow my dissertation research, and the degree, and the whole ball game."

He swung toward Leaphorn, his anger blazing again. "Look," he said. "I don't know how it was with you. Maybe pretty thin. Well, my folks, such as I had, were all east Tennessee white trash. Never been a one of them went to college. Never a one had a pot to piss in. Just poor trash. My dad had run off somewhere, according to my mother, and I wouldn't even swear she knew who he was. With me it was living with a drunken uncle in a sharecropper shack, and chopping cotton, and every year pleading for him to let me go back to school when fall got there so I could finish high school. And after that being janitor and dishwasher in a frat house at Memphis State, and even trying to get into the army just to get onto the GI Bill and find out what it was like to eat regular." Isaacs fell suddenly silent, thinking about it.

"You know how long I been shoveling out here? Damn near six months. I get out here by the time the light gets good enough. And I'm digging until dark. Reynolds got a three-thousand-dollar grant and he split it among eight sites. This one's sprawled out all up and down this hill so he gave me a little more. He gave me four hundred dollars. And I borrow money here and there and buy that old truck and build the cabin on it and try to keep eating on about fifty dollars a month and hope to God the loan sharks won't figure out where I am and take the truck back. And I don't begrudge a minute of it because this is the first chance an Isaacs had to be anything but dirt." Isaacs stopped. He was still staring at Leaphorn, his jaw muscles working. "And when I get it made, I'm going to take about two thousand dollars or whatever it costs and I'm going to get these beaver teeth pushed back into my face. It's the sort of thing that you get done when you're about twelve years old, if anybody gives a damn, and it's probably too late now to fix 'em, but by God, by God, I'm going to try."

On his way back down the slope Leaphorn noticed that Susanne was no longer waiting in the carryall. It didn't surprise him. Even watching his conversation with Isaacs from a distance, it would have been easy enough for the girl to see that she'd guessed right—that Ted Isaacs wasn't eager to have her move in. So she hadn't waited for the embarrassment of hearing about it. Leaphorn thought about where the girl might have gone and about all the things that go into choices. He thought about how the whiteman mind of Ted Isaacs sorted things out so that Susanne was on one side of the scale and everything else he wanted on the other, and about the weighting of values that would cause Susanne to be rejected. Then he shook his head and changed the theme. He skipped back nine thousand years to a naked hunter squatting on Isaacs's ridge, laboriously chipping out a lance point, breaking it, calmly dropping it, working on another one, breaking it, calmly dropping it. Leaphorn had trouble with the second part of this scene. His imagination insisted on having his Folsom Man shout an angry Stone Age curse and throw the offending flint down the slope. Way down the slope where no anthropologist would find it ninety centuries later.

Wednesday, December 3, 5 p.m.

FATHER INGLES of the Order of Saint Francis was a wiry, tidy, tough-looking little man, his face a background of old pockmarks overlaid with two generations of damage by sun and wind. Leaphorn found him sitting on the low wall surrounding the cemetery behind the Saint Anthony's Mission church. He was talking to a youngish Zuñi. "Be with you in a minute," Father Ingles said. He and the Zuñi finished working down a list of names—members of the Catholic Youth Organization girls' basketball team who would be making the bus trip to Gallup to meet the Navajo Sawmill Jills and the Acoma Bravettes in a holiday tournament. Now, with that job finished and the Zuñi gone, he still sat on the wall, huddled in a castoff navy windbreaker, looking across the graves at nothing in particular and telling Leaphorn in a slow, soft voice what he knew of the Shorty Bowlegs family.

Leaphorn knew Ingles by reputation. He had worked for years out of Saint Michael's Mission near Window Rock and was known among the Window Rock Navajos as Narrowbutt in deference to his bony hindquarters. He spoke Navajo, which was rare among white men, and had mastered its complex tonalities so thoroughly that he could practice the Navajo pastime of spinning off puns and absurdities by pretending to slightly mispronounce his verbs. Now he talked somberly. He had told Leaphorn about the family of Ernesto Cata, and now he told him about Shorty Bowlegs. Much of this Leaphorn already knew. After a while, when enough time had passed to make this conversation absolutely comfortable, Leaphorn would ask the questions he had come to ask. Now he was content to listen. It was something Joe Leaphorn did very well.

"This George, now. He's an aggravating little devil," Ingles was saying. "I don't think I ever saw a kid with a funnier turn of mind. Quick. Quick. Quick. About half genius and half crazy. The kind of a boy that if you can make a Christian out of him will make you a saint. Full of mysticism—most of it nonsense and all muddled up—but something in him driving him to know more than a natural man is supposed to know. He'll probably end up writing poetry, or shooting himself, or being a drunk like his father. Or maybe we'll still bag him and we'll have a Saint Bowlegs of Zuñi."

"Had he been coming to church here?"

"For a while," Ingles said. He laughed. "I guess you'd say he studied us, in competition with witchcraft and sorcery and the Zuñi religion, and plain old starve-a-vision mysticism." The priest frowned. "You know, I'm not being fair to the boy, talking about him like this. George was looking for something because he was smart enough to see he didn't have anything. He knew all about what his mother had done and that's a cruel thing for a child. And of course he could see his dad was a drunk, and maybe that's even worse. He was away from his family, so he was denied the Navajo Way, and he didn't have anything to replace it."

"What did he know about his mother?"

"I've heard two variations. They lived over around Coyote Canyon someplace with her outfit. One way, she took to hitching rides into Gallup for drinking bouts with men. Or she moved out on Bowlegs and in with two brothers—and they were supposed to be witches. Take your pick. Or mix 'em up and take what you like of both. Anyway, Bowlegs didn't get along with his wife's people so he came back to his own folks at Ramah and then he got a job over here herding Zuñi sheep."

"Let's skip back just a little. You said the gossip was she moved in with two brothers who were witches. You remember any more about that? Who said it? Anything at all specific?"

"Guess I heard it two or three places. You know how gossip is. All fifth or sixth hand, and who knows where it started?" Ingles peered out across the cemetery, thinking. Moments passed. Ingles had lived among Navajos long enough to let time pass without strain. He fished a cigar out of his inside shirt pocket, offered it wordlessly to Leaphorn, who shook his head, bit off the tip, lit it, and exhaled a thin blue plume of smoke into the evening air. "Can't remember anything specific," he said. "Just that somebody told me the boy's mother was living with a couple of witches. You think it might be important?"

"No," Leaphorn said. "I just make a point not to overlook witch talk like that. We don't have much trouble on the reservation but that's where a lot of it starts."

"You believe in witches?"

"That's like me asking you if you believe in sin, Father," Leaphorn said. "The point is you gradually learn that witch talk and trouble sort of go together."

"I've noticed that myself," Ingles said. "You think there's a connection here?"

"I don't see how."

Ingles ejected another blue plume into the air. They watched it drift down the wall. "Anyway, by then George's dad was going after the bottle pretty hard and so maybe George's interest in coming around the church was just running away from drinking. Anyway, he didn't stay interested long."

"You didn't get him baptized?"

"No. From what Ernesto told me, George started getting interested in the Zuñi Way instead. Comparing their origin myth with the Navajo and with our Genesis, that sort of thing. Ernesto used to bring him in to talk to me. He'd ask me about the difference between the Zuñi kachina and our saints. Things like that."

Father Ingles punctuated another silence with more smoke.

"Very similar in a way. As we see it, when a Christian completes the good life his soul joins the community of saints. When the Zuñi completes his path, his spirit joins the village of the kachinas and he becomes one of them."

"What I know of the Zuñi religion is a little bit out of the anthropology books, a little hearsay, and a little from a roommate I used to have. It's not much, and part of it's probably wrong."

"Probably," Ingles said. "The Zuñis found out a long time ago that some outsiders looked on their religion as a sort of sideshow. And after that, most of them wouldn't talk about it to the anthropologists, and some of those who did were deliberately misleading."

"Right now I wish *I* knew a little more about it," Leaphorn said. "George told his little brother that he was going to find a kachina, or maybe it was *some kachinas.* He didn't seem to know exactly where to find them, but he must have had some idea because he said he'd be gone several days."

Ingles frowned. "Find some kachinas? He couldn't have meant the kachina dolls, I guess?"

"I don't think so. I think he, or he and Ernesto together, had done something to offend the kachinas—or thought they had, or some crazy damn thing like that—and George wanted to do something about it."

Ingles laughed. "That sounds about like George," he said. "That sounds exactly like him." He shook his head. "But where would he go? Did he say anything else?"

"He said if he didn't get his business done, he'd have to come back to Zuñi for Shalako. And he took one of the Bowlegs horses, if that helps any, and their rifle. To kill a deer for eating, I'd guess. And a girl he knew told me he said something about going to a dance hall. Can you make any connection out of all that?"

Ingles made a clucking sound with his tongue against his teeth. "You know what it might be?" he said. "It might be he's trying to find Kothluwalawa." The priest laughed and shook his head. "I don't know whether that makes any sense, but with George sense isn't all that important."

"Kothluwalawa?" Leaphorn asked. "Where's that?" The priest's amusement irritated him. "He was going somewhere you can go on a horse."

Ingles sensed the anger. "It's really not as impossible as it sounds. We tend to think of heaven as being up in the sky. The Zuñis also have a geographical concept for it, because of the nature of their mythology. Do you know that myth?"

"If I did, I don't remember much of it now."

"It's part of the migration mythology. The Zuñis had completed their emergence up through the four underworlds and had started their great journey hunting for the Middle Place of the Universe. Some children of the Wood Fraternity were carried across the Zuñi River by the older people. There was sort of a panic and the children were dropped. As they were washed downstream, instead of drowning they turned into water animals—frogs, snakes, tadpoles, so forth—and they swam downstream to this place we're talking about. According to the mythology, it's a lake. Once they got there, the children changed from water animals and became kachinas, and they formed the Council of the Gods—the Rain God of the North, the Rain God of the South, the Little Fire God, and the rest of them. Originally a hundred or so, I think."

"Sort of like the Holy People of the Navajo," Leaphorn said.

"Not really. Your Holy People—Monster Slayer, Changing Woman, Born of Water, and all that—they're more like a cross between the Greek hero idea and the lesser Greek gods. More human than divine, you know. The kachinas aren't like anything in Navajo or white culture. We don't have a word for this concept, and neither do you. They're not gods. The Zuñi have only one God, Awonawilona, who was the creator. And then they have Shiwanni and Shinwanokia—a man-and-woman team created by God to create the Sun, and Mother Earth, and all living things. But the kachinas are different. Maybe you could call them ancestor spirits. Their attitude toward humans is friendly, fatherly. They bring blessings. They appear as rain clouds."

"I'd heard some of that," Leaphorn said. "So this Kothluwalawa where Bowlegs said he was going is a lake somewhere down the Zuñi Wash?"

"It's not that simple," Ingles said. "I have four books about the Zuñis in my office—each one written by an ethnologist or anthropologist who was an authority. They have it located in four different places. One of them has it down near the confluence of Zuñi Wash and the Little Colorado, over in Arizona, not far from Saint Johns. And one of them says it's down south near the old Ojo Caliente village. And another of them puts it up in the Nutria Lake area northeast of here. And I've heard a couple of other places, most often a little natural lake just across the Arizona border. And I know that *some* Zuñis think of it as being located only in metaphysics, beyond time and space."

Leaphorn said nothing.

"What made me think of Kothluwalawa was that business of the dance hall. If you translate that word to English it means something like 'Dance Hall of the Dead,' or maybe 'Dance Ground of the Spirits,' or something like that." Ingles smiled. "Rather a poetic concept. In life, ritual dancing for the Zuñi is sort of a perfect expression of . . ." He paused, searching for the word. "Call it ecstasy, or joy, or life, or community unity. So what do you do when you're beyond life, with no labors to perform? You spend your time dancing."

The priest blew another blue cloud of cigar smoke over the cemetery, and they sat there, Navajo policeman and Franciscan missionary, watching the cloud dissipate over the Zuñi graves. In the west the sky had turned garish with sunset. What George Bowlegs was hunting, Leaphorn thought, was a concept so foreign to The People that their language lacked a word for it. There was no heaven in the Navajo cosmos, and no friendly kachina spirit, and no pleasant life after death. If one was lucky, there was oblivion. But for most, there was the unhappy malevolent ghost, the chindi, wailing away the eons in the darkness, spreading sickness and evil. He thought about what Ingles had said. This Kothluwalawa might be the word Cecil remembered that started with a *K*.

"I think what's important is not where this Zuñi heaven is located," Leaphorn said. "What's important is where George thinks it's located."

"Yes," Ingles said. "The same thought occurred to me."

"Where would he think it is?"

Ingles thought about it. "I bet I know. I bet it would be that little lake just across the border. It's used a lot for religious purposes. The religious people make prayer retreats to shrines over there, and they go several times a year to catch frogs and so forth. I think it would be my first guess. If George was asking around about it, that's where he'd most likely be told it was located. And now I have a question for you. Why are you hunting the boy? Do you think he killed Ernesto and his own father, too? If you think that, then I think you're wrong."

Leaphorn thought about the answer. "He could have killed Cata. He must have been somewhere near when it happened. And then he ran. And he *could* have killed Shorty. But there doesn't seem to be any reason. I guess that's the trouble. Nobody seems to have a reason." Leaphorn's tone made a question. He looked at the priest.

"To kill Ernesto? Not that I know anything about," Ingles said. "He was a good kid. Served Mass for me. Had a lot of friends. No enemies that I know of. What kid that age has enemies? They're too young for that."

"Cecil Bowlegs told me that Ernesto and George had stolen something." Leaphorn spoke slowly. This was the sensitive point. It had to be said very carefully. "It was supposed to have been something from that anthropological dig north of Corn Mountain. Ernesto was a Catholic. He was an altar boy. If he stole something he knew he had to give it back before he could make a good confession. Is that right?"

Ingles was grinning at him. "What you are saying is, 'You're his confessor. Did he confess anything to you that would explain why somebody killed him?' That's what you are asking me, but you know I can't reveal what I'm told in the confessional."

"But Cata's dead now. Nothing you tell me now is going to hurt that boy. Maybe it would help George Bowlegs."

"I'm thinking about it," Ingles said. "You know, I've been a priest almost forty years and it never came up before. Probably I won't tell you anything, but let's think a minute about the theology we've got ourselves involved in here."

"Just negative information might help. Just knowing that he didn't steal anything important. Cecil Bowlegs told me it was some arrowheads from the dig site, but it wasn't that. They checked and told me they weren't missing any artifacts. In fact, they weren't missing anything."

Ingles sat silently, his teeth worrying his lower lip, his mind worrying the problem. "To be a mortal sin, the offense has to be serious," he said. "What you're describing wouldn't have been more than a very minor imperfection. Something a boy would do. Something a boy with a less scrupulous conscience than Ernesto wouldn't even think of confessing."

"Now that he's dead can't you tell me?" Leaphorn said. "A tool? A piece of paper? Can you tell me what?"

"I think I can't," Ingles said. "Probably I shouldn't even tell you that it was inconsequential. Nothing of value. Nothing that would tell you anything at all."

"I wonder why, then, he wanted to confess it. Did *he* think it was important?"

"No. Not really. It was Saturday afternoon. I was hearing confessions. Ernesto wanted to talk to me, very privately, about something else. So he got in line. And then, since he was in the confessional anyway, I heard his confession and gave him absolution. Confession is a sacrament," Ingles explained. "God gives you grace for it, even if there's no sin to be absolved."

"Saturday. Last Saturday? The day before he was killed?"

"Yes," Father Ingles said. "Last Saturday. He was my server Sunday at Mass but I didn't talk to him. That was the last time Ernesto and I had a talk."

Ingles slid suddenly from the wall. "I'm getting cold," he said. "Let's go in."

Through the heavy wooden door, Ingles bowed in the direction of the altar and pointed Leaphorn toward the back pew.

"I don't know what I've said that's helpful," he said. "That George Bowlegs' dad was a drunk—which I guess you already knew. That Ernesto Cata hadn't done anything bad enough to cause anyone to kill him—or even scold him much, for that matter."

"Would it help any if you told me what Cata wanted to talk to you about? I mean before he confessed his sins?"

Ingles chuckled. "I doubt it," he said. "It was hardly the material for murder."

"But could you tell me what it was?"

"I don't think I'd tell a Zuñi," Ingles said. "But you're a Navajo." He smiled. "Ernesto thought maybe he had violated a

Zuñi taboo. But he wasn't sure, and he was nervous about it, and he didn't want to admit anything to anyone in his kiva yet, and he just wanted to talk to a friend about it," Ingles said. "I was that friend."

"What taboo?"

"Children . . . anyone not yet old enough to be initiated into the Zuñi religion society aren't supposed to be told about the personifiers," Ingles said. "You know about that?"

"Something about it."

"Well, in Zuñi mythology, the Council of the Gods—or whatever you want to call the spirits of those drowned children—would come back to the village each year. They'd bring rain, crops, blessings of all sorts, dance with the people, and teach them the right way of doing things. But it always happened that some of the Zuñis would follow them when they left to return to the Dance Hall of the Dead. And when you followed, you died. This was too bad, and the kachinas didn't want it to keep happening, so they told the Zuñis that they would come no more. Instead the Zuñis should make sacred masks representing them, and valuable men of the kivas and the various fetish societies would be selected to impersonate various spirits. The kachinas would come only in spirit. They would be visible, I've been told, to certain sorcerers. But anyone else who saw them would die. Now, this arrangement between the kachinas and the Zuñis was a secret arrangement. Only those initiated into the religion were to know of it. The children were not to be told."

Leaphorn's attention had been split. He heard Ingles's slow, precise voice, but his eyes were studying the murals that spread down the walls of the mission. Against the blank white plaster were the Dancing Gods of the Zuñis, most of them man-sized and manlike, except for the grotesque masks, which gave them heads like monstrous birds. Only one was smaller, a figure of black spotted with red, and one was much larger—just over their heads by the railing of the choir loft was the giant figure of the Shalako, a nine-foot-high pyramid topped by a tiny head and supported by human legs. This was the "messenger bird" of the gods.

"That's what Ernesto was worried about," Ingles was saying. "He'd told George that he would be the personifier of Shulawitsi and he was worrying about whether that had broken the taboo. There." The priest pointed at the small black figure leading the procession of kachinas down the wall. "The little black one in the spotted mask is Shulawitsi, the Little Fire God. He's always impersonated by a boy. It's terribly hard work—exercises, running, physical conditioning, memorizing chants, memorizing dances. It's the highest possible honor a child can receive from his people, but it's an ordeal. They miss a lot of school."

"Telling George about it—*had* that violated the taboo?"

"I don't know, really," Father Ingles said. "George would have been initiated two or three years ago if he was a Zuñi—so he wasn't a child in the way the myth means and he certainly would have already known that kachinas in the Shalako ceremonials are being impersonated by the men who live here. But on the other hand, he hadn't been formally initiated into the cult secrets. The way it's explained in the myth, this Zuñi boy tells the little children deliberately, to spoil the ceremonial for them, because he's angry—and the anger is part of the taboo violation. It is forbidden to harbor any anger in any period of ceremonialism. Anyway, the Council of the Gods send the Salamobia to punish the boy." Ingles pointed to the fourth kachina in the mural—a muscular figure armed with a whip of yucca, its beaked head surmounted by a pointed plume of feathers, its eyes ferocious. Leaphorn's eyes had lingered on it earlier, caught by something familiar. Now he knew what it was. This was the same beaked mask he had seen two nights earlier, reflecting the moonlight behind the hogan at Jason's Fleece.

"What was the punishment?" Leaphorn asked.

"The Salamobia chopped off his head with a machete—right in the plaza out here—and played football with it." Ingles laughed. "Most of the Zuñi mythology is humane and gentle but that one's as bad as one of the Grimms' fairy tales."

"Do you know how Ernesto was killed?"

Ingles looked surprised. "He bled to death, didn't he? I presumed he'd been knifed."

"Someone chopped him across the neck with a machete," Leaphorn said. "They almost cut his head off."

Thursday, December 4, 10:30 a.m.

LEAPHORN HAD BEEN up since dawn, making his third visit to the Bowlegs hogan. Around the brush corral he had examined the hoofprints of the horse George Bowlegs had taken, memorizing the nature of the horseshoes and every split and crack in the hooves. The body of Shorty Bowlegs was gone now. Buried by one of the Zuñis for whom he had herded, Leaphorn guessed, or taken by O'Malley for whatever postmortem magic the FBI laboratory technologists might wish to perform in Albuquerque. The livestock was gone, too, but the worldly goods of Shorty Bowlegs remained inside—made untouchable to Navajos by ghost sickness. Their disarray had been increased by a third search, this one by the federals.

Leaphorn stood at the doorway and thoughtfully inspected the jumble. Something held him here—a feeling that he was forgetting something, or overlooking something, leaving something undone. But whatever it was, it eluded him now. He wondered if O'Malley had found anything informative. If the case broke and the Albuquerque FBI office issued a statement explaining how the arrest had been made, Leaphorn wouldn't be told. He'd read about it in the Albuquerque *Journal* or the Gallup *Independent.* Leaphorn considered this fact without rancor as something natural as the turn of the seasons. At the moment six law-enforcement agencies were interested in the affair at Zuñi (if one counted the Bureau of Indian Affairs Law and Order Division, which was watching passively). Each would function as its interests dictated that it must. Leaphorn himself, without conscious thought, would influence his actions to the benefit of the Dinee if Navajo interests were at stake. Orange Naranjo, he knew, would do his work honestly and faithfully with full awareness that his good friend and employer, the sheriff of McKinley County, was seeking reelection. Pasquaanti was responsible first to laws centuries older than the whiteman's written codes. Highsmith, whose real job was traffic safety, would do as little as possible. And O'Malley would make his decisions with that ingrained FBI awareness that the rewards lay in good publicity, and the sensible attitude that other agencies were competitors for that publicity.

Leaphorn wasted a few moments considering why the FBI would accept jurisdiction in such a chancy affair. Usually the FBI would move into marginal areas only if someone somewhere was sure his batting average could be helped by a successful prosecution. Or if the case involved whatever held high agency priority of the season—and that these days would be either radical politics or narcotics. The presence of Baker said narcotics figured somewhere, and the attitude of O'Malley seemed to suggest that Baker had leads the federals weren't willing to share. Leaphorn pondered what these leads might be, drew a total blank, climbed back into his carryall, and started the motor. Behind him, in the rearview mirror, he noticed the plank door of Shorty Bowlegs's hogan move. Shorty's malicious ghost, perhaps, or just the same gusty morning breeze that whipped an eddy of dust around the logs.

Following the directions Father Ingles had given him, Leaphorn picked up the gravel road that led to the Zuñi Tribal Sawmill back in the Cibola National Forest, continued on it to the Fence Lake road, turned northward past the prehistoric Yellow House Ruins to N.M. 53. The highway, as usual, was empty. As he approached the Black Rock airstrip a single-engine plane took off, banked above the highway in front of him, and climbed over Corn Mountain, heading eastward. Passing through the old village of Zuñi he slowed, thinking he might make the three-block detour to the Zuñi police station to learn if anything had developed overnight. He suppressed the impulse. If anything important had happened, it would have been known at the communications center at the Ramah chapter house, where he had spent the night. And he wasn't in the mood for talking to O'Malley or to Baker, or to Pasquaanti, or to anyone. O'Malley had told him to find Bowlegs. He would find Bowlegs if he could because his curiosity demanded it. And now for the first time since he'd been here there was something to work on. A direction. George had left his family hogan with the horse Monday night. The distance to the lake would be maybe fifty miles. If George had taken the most direct route he would angle across the Zuñi reservation, probably pick up the Zuñi Wash about at the Arizona state line, and then follow this southwestward toward U.S. Highway 666. The country was rough, sloping irregularly away from the Continental Divide, which rose to almost eight thousand feet east of the reservation, toward that great inland depression which the maps called the Painted Desert. But the only barriers were natural ones. No more than two or three fences, Leaphorn guessed, in a day-and-a-half horseback ride.

Leaphorn's plan was simple. He would drive as close as he could get to the location of the lake and then begin looking for Bowlegs's tracks. He felt good about it, anticipating the pleasure of some solid accomplishment after three days of frustrations.

On the radio, a slightly nasal disk jockey was promoting a sky-diving exhibition at the Yah-Ta-Hey Trading Post and playing country-western records. Leaphorn flicked the tuning knob, got a guttural voice speaking alternately in English and Apache. He listened a moment, picking up an occasional word. It was a preacher from the San Carlos Apache reservation, one hundred miles to the south. "The good book says it to us," the man was saying. "The inheritance of the sinner is as the waterless desert." Leaphorn turned down the volume. A good line, he thought, for a year of drought.

The narrow asphalt narrowed even more, its gravel shoulders turning to weeds, and N.M. 53 abruptly became Arizona 61 at the border. Something was nagging at the corner of Leaphorn's consciousness, a vague thought which evaporated when he tried to capture it. It made him uneasy.

At the intersection with U.S. Highway 666, Leaphorn saw Susanne. She was standing north of the junction, a flour sack on the ground beside her, looking small and cold and frail, and pretending—after the first quick glance—not to notice the Navajo Police carryall. Leaphorn hesitated. He didn't want company today. He had looked forward to a day alone to restore the spirit. On the other hand, he was curious. And he found himself remarkably fond of this girl. He didn't want her to simply disappear. He pulled the carryall off the pavement and stopped beside her.

"Where you going?"

"I'm hitchhiking," she said.

"I see that. But where?"

"North. Up to Interstate Forty." She shook her head. "I guess I don't really know exactly. I'm going to decide whether to go east or west after I get to the Interstate."

"I think I know how to find George," Leaphorn said. "That's where I'm going now. To try. If you've got time you could help."

"I couldn't help."

"You're his friend," Leaphorn said. "He's almost certain to see me before I see him. He'll figure I'm after him so he'll hide. But if he sees you, he'll know it's all right."

"I wish I was sure it was all right myself," she said. But when he opened the door, she put the flour sack behind the seat and got into the cab beside him. He did a U-turn and started southward down 666. The sign at the intersection said ST. JOHNS 29 MILES.

"We're going south toward the place where Zuñi Wash goes under the highway," Leaphorn said. "About fifteen or sixteen miles. Before we get there, there's a ranch gate. We're going to pull in there and put this truck out of the way someplace handy, and then do some walking."

Susanne said nothing. The hilltop view stretched twenty miles. The country was mostly undulating hills but far to the south the great tableland of the Zuñi reservation extended, broken low mesas with scrubby brush timber on top and barren erosion below.

As he had guessed, Susanne had had no breakfast. He pointed to the grocery sack he had picked up at the store in Ramah.

"What happened to you yesterday? When Isaacs came to talk to you, you were gone."

"I went back to the commune. It was just the way I told you, wasn't it? Ted couldn't do anything? And my being there just made it harder for him?"

Leaphorn decided not to comment on that.

"So why did you change your mind about staying at the commune?"

"Halsey changed it for me. He said I was attracting too much police."

He noticed she was eating hungrily. Not just no breakfast, he thought. Probably no supper, either. She had folded up the cuff of her denim shirt and from it the frayed gray sleeve of a wool undershirt extended, covering the back of her narrow, fragile hand. As she ate, rapidly and wordlessly, Leaphorn saw that the skin between the thumb and forefinger of her right hand bore the puckered white of old scar tissue. It was an ugly, disfiguring shape. Whatever had caused it had burned through the skin right into the muscle fiber.

"So Halsey kicked you out?"

"He said to get my stuff together and this morning he gave me a ride out to the highway." She looked out of the window, away from him. "I was right about Ted, wasn't I? There wasn't anything he could do."

"You were right about that situation," he said. "Isaacs explained it the same way you did. He said Reynolds would fire him if anybody stayed there with him."

"There's just no way he could possibly do it," she said. "This is Ted's really big hope. He's going to be famous after this. You know, he's never been nothing but poor. Him and his whole family. And this is Ted's chance. He's never had a thing."

It sounded, Leaphorn thought, as if Susanne was trying to persuade both of them.

"He just couldn't do it," she said. "No way he could do it."

Leaphorn found the ranch gate Father Ingles had described about a mile and a half up the slope from Zuñi Wash. A weather-bleached sign was nailed to the post. The message it had once proclaimed—"Posted, Keep Out" or "Shut the Gate"—had long since been erased by the sandblasting of spring dust storms. Three coyote skins hung beside it, the gray dead hair riffling in the breeze.

"Why do they do that?" Susanne asked. "Stick 'em up on the fence?"

"The coyotes? I guess it's for the same reason white men put an animal's head on their wall. Shows everybody you got the machismo to kill him." The Navajo word for Hosteen Coyote was *ma ii.* He was the trickster, the joker, the subject of a thousand Navajo jokes, children's stories, and myths. He was often man's ally in the struggle to survive, and always the bane of a society which herded sheep. A Navajo would kill a lamb-killer if he could. It was a deed done with proper apology—not something to be flaunted on a roadside fence.

Leaphorn drove very slowly, keeping his wheels off the dirt track to cut the risk of raising dust. Each time the track branched toward another stock-watering windmill or a salt drop, Leaphorn chose the route that led toward the low escarpment of the Zuñi plateau. Father Ingles had said the lake was five or six miles in from the highway and below the mesa. It was a smallish natural playa that filled with draining runoff water in the rainy season and then dried slowly until the snow melt recharged it in the spring. Finding it would be relatively easy in a country where deer, antelope, and cattle trails would lead to any standing water.

The last dim trail dead-ended at a rusty windmill. Leaphorn pulled the carryall past it into a shallow arroyo and parked it amid a tangle of junipers.

The lake proved to be less than a mile away. Leaphorn stood among the rocks on the ridge above it and examined it carefully through his binoculars. Except for a killdeer hopping on its stiltlike legs in the shallows, nothing moved anywhere around the cracked mud shore. Leaphorn studied the landscape methodically through the glasses, working from near distance first, and then moving toward the horizon, seeing absolutely nothing.

"Are you sure that's it?" Susanne asked. "I mean, for a sacred lake you expect something bigger."

The question irritated Leaphorn.

"Didn't Thomas Aquinas teach you white people that an

infinite number of angels can dance on the head of a pin?"

"I don't think I heard about that," Susanne said. "I cut out of school in the tenth grade."

"Umm . . . well, the point is it doesn't take much water to cover a lot of spirits. But as far as *we're* concerned, it doesn't matter whether this is Kothluwalawa. What matters is whether George thinks it is. And *that* only matters if he came here and we can find him."

"I don't think he'd come here," she said doubtfully. "Why would he? Can you think of any reason?"

"All I know about George is what people tell me," Leaphorn said. "I hear he's sort of a mystic. I hear he's sort of crazy. I hear he's unpredictable. I hear he wants to become a member of the Zuñi tribe, that he wants to be initiated into their religion. O.K. Let's say some of that is true. Now, I *also* hear that Ernesto was his best friend. And that Ernesto was afraid he had broken a taboo by telling George more than you're supposed to tell the uninitiated about the Zuñi religion." Leaphorn paused, thinking about how it might have happened.

"Now. Let's say George left the bicycle where he was supposed to meet Ernesto and he wanders off somewhere. When he gets back, the bicycle is gone and so is Ernesto. That's natural enough. He thinks Ernesto didn't wait and he missed him. But he also notices that great puddle of blood. It would have been fresh then. It would have scared him. The next day he comes to school, looking for Ernesto. And he finds out Ernesto is missing. That's exactly the way it happened. Now, everybody tells me George is sort of crazy. Let's say he decides the kachinas have punished Ernesto for the broken taboo. George would have heard the legend about the boy who violated the secrecy rule and had his head cut off by the warrior kachinas. Maybe he wants to come here to ask the Council of the Gods to absolve him of any of the blame. Or maybe he came because here's where Ernesto's spirit will be coming to join the ancestors." Even as Leaphorn told it, it sounded unlikely.

"Remember," he said, "George asked you about whether the kachinas would absolve guilt. And remember he told Cecil he had to find the kachinas—that he had business with them."

"*Maybe* it's the way George would think," Susanne said. She glanced down at Leaphorn and then down at her hands. She pulled the cuff down over the scar. "He was way out in a lot of ways. He and Ernesto were always talking about witches and werewolves and sorcery and having visions and that sort of thing. With Ernesto you could tell it was mostly just talk. But with George I think it was real."

"If he plans to be here when Ernesto's spirit arrives, we have a good chance of catching up with him. That would be sometime tomorrow. Maybe at dawn."

"What do you mean?"

"It takes five days' travel after death for the spirit to reach the Dance Hall of the Dead," Leaphorn said. "The Zuñis try to have the burial of one of their people within the same cycle of sun in which he died—so they had the funeral for Ernesto the same day they dug his body out from under that little landslide on the mesa. Had a quick funeral for him at the Catholic church and then after that the priests and the valuable men of his kiva held their graveside ceremonial. But in a way the funeral's not really over. They put five sets of fresh clothing in the burial shroud with the body. And on the fifth day he gets here—if this really is the place—and he passes the guarding spirits on the shore, and he joins the Council of the Gods and becomes a kachina."

"So you think George will be here tomorrow?"

Leaphorn laughed. "I don't know if I really think it, or whether I just can't think of any other possibility."

"Maybe he wants to be here to sort of say good-bye or something. I think Ernesto was the only friend he ever had. Maybe he wants to make some sort of crazy gesture."

"Like suicide?"

Susanne looked at Leaphorn with eyes too old for her face. "He might do something like that, I think. He wanted bad to be a Zuñi and I guess Ernesto was his only hope—if there ever was a hope. But it wasn't just that." Her teeth caught her lower lip, then released it. "He was so lonely. I think it must be bad to be a Navajo if being lonely bothers you."

The thought had never occurred to Leaphorn. He considered it, looking across the broken expanse of grass, brush, and erosion which faded away to empty blue distance across the pond. "Yeah," he said. "Like a mole that hates the dark."

"Were *you* thinking he might come here to kill himself? Or do Navajos do that?"

"Not much. Except with the bottle," Leaphorn said. "It's a little slower than a gun."

Around the lake Leaphorn found antelope tracks, some old moccasin imprints in the dried mud, and the various traces left by coyotes and porcupines and red fox—the myriad species of small mammals that standing water attracts in arid country. The moccasin marks pretty well eliminated any doubt that this playa had some religious significance even if it wasn't the Sacred Lake. Except for ritual events, Zuñis were no more likely to be wearing moccasins than were Navajos or FBI agents. But there were no signs of the hoofprints of George's horse, or of the boots that George would have been wearing. The only tracks of horses he found were old and almost erased, perhaps by the same windstorm that had howled around Shorty Bowlegs's hogan the night he was killed, and they didn't match the hoofprints Leaphorn had memorized there. Pastured horses, he guessed, watering here.

He worked his way away from the lake, searching in an expanding circle along game trails and sandy drainage bottoms. Susanne followed, asking a few questions at first, then falling silent. By 2 P.M. Leaphorn was absolutely certain that George Bowlegs hadn't come to this lake. He sat under a juniper, offered the girl a cigarette and smoked one himself, as he tried to imagine where else George might go to find his kachinas. There didn't seem to be an answer. He finished the cigarette and resumed the search. Within five minutes he found, clear and unmistakable, the shape of the left forefoot of George's horse. It was in the bare earth where the bulk of a rabbit bush shielded it from the wind. Leaphorn then found the right front hoofprint in the open, so wind-erased that he would have missed it if he hadn't known where to look.

"So he did come," Susanne said. "But where do we look for him now?"

"He was here either before or during that little storm,"

Leaphorn said. "It must have been still light. So he made part of the trip Monday night after he left the note for Cecil and then finished the ride Tuesday."

And then what? Leaphorn examined the ground around the bush, picking up traces of hoof tracks in places where the ground cover or earth contour had offered some protection from the blasting wind. The short distance he scouted suggested that George had ridden up this ridge from the northeast—the direction of Zuñi Village. The boy had sat his horse for a considerable time behind a growth of piñon, and then had ridden some thirty yards along the ridge and away toward the southeast. Southeast there was the gray-green shape of the Zuñi escarpment. He had found the lake and then he had ridden away. Why? To wait? To wait for what? For Cata's spirit to arrive tomorrow for its descent into the underworld? Maybe. Leaphorn shook his head. Susanne was looking at him doubtfully.

"You're sure about him not taking food from the commune?" he asked.

"I'm sure," she said. "Halsey wouldn't let him have any."

"So he must have been hungry by the time he got here. The boy's hungry and he's proud of his ability as a deer hunter, and he's brought along his deer rifle. So I'd guess he'd go deer hunting." Otherwise, if he was waiting for Cata's spirit, he would have had two full days to pass without any food. There were no deer tracks here. The herds would still be back on the plateau, not yet driven down to low ground by snow and cold. If George was smart he'd head for the plateau, find a place with shelter, and hole up. And then he would find a herd territory and set up over a deer trail, and have meat to eat while he waited for whatever he waited for.

And because George Bowlegs knew how to find deer, Leaphorn knew how to find Bowlegs. That left the question of what to do with this skinny girl. Leaphorn looked at her speculatively, and explained the alternatives. They were simple enough. She could find her way back to the truck and wait for him there—perhaps until sometime late tomorrow. Or she could come along, which would involve a substantial amount of long-distance walking, and maybe spending a cold night on the plateau. "I don't know if it's dangerous," Leaphorn said. "I don't think George killed the Cata boy, but some people think so, and if he did maybe he'd want to shoot me because I'm hunting him. I doubt it, but then, as I said, everybody says he's sort of crazy. If he is crazy enough to take a shot at somebody, all he's got is a worn-out short-range 30-30. But actually, if he's good enough to stalk deer with that thing, I wouldn't want him stalking me." He paused. Was there anything he'd overlooked? He had a feeling there might be. "Another thing. He's almost sure to see us before we see him. Because we'll have to be moving and he probably won't be."

Susanne was smiling at him. "On the other hand," she said, "George likes me and he trusts me and he isn't going to shoot at me. I don't think he's going to shoot at anybody else either, and I'd rather come along than be at that truck all night by myself. And if I don't come along you'll never find him, because when he sees a strange man, he'll hide. But if he sees me, he'll come out and talk. I'd rather come along."

Leaphorn led the way down the ridge at a fast walk.

The route Bowlegs must have taken—the shortest and easiest way up the mesa—was a saddle-backed ridge which provided access up the mesa wall. He would track just long enough to confirm this and then head directly for the saddle. Susanne was hurrying along behind him.

"I'm kinda scared," she said. "I bet you are a little, too, aren't you? But I really *do* think George needs somebody to help him."

Exactly, Leaphorn thought. George, and Ted Isaacs, and the pale young man with nightmares, and a younger sister left somewhere back in cruel country, and a worldful of losers—they all need Susanne's help, and they'll get it if she can reach them. Which is what keeps her from being a loser, too. He walked fast, picking up the wind-faded hoofprint here and there, knowing Susanne would keep up, and trying without any luck at all to understand the choice Ted Isaacs had made.

15

Thursday, December 4, 2:17 p.m.

THEY FOUND THE TRACKS of George's horse on the saddleback slope, about where Leaphorn expected to find them.

"You're good at this, aren't you," Susanne said.

"I've been doing it a long time," Leaphorn said.

She was squatting on her heels at the deer trail beside him, inspecting the hoofprint. Her left hand continued to tug absently at her right cuff, pulling the frayed fabric over the scar. The reflex of a bruised spirit. How badly bruised? Leaphorn set his mind to building a set of circumstances under which this too-thin child-woman would have killed Ernesto Cata in some schizophrenic perversion of good purpose. His imagination managed that job, but failed at the next one—which attempted to place her in the Bowlegs hogan with a weapon raised over the head of a helpless drunk.

From the mesa top above them there came the raucous cry of a piñon jay. Leaphorn listened, heard nothing else. The breeze was dead now. Nothing moved. On the western horizon, somewhere over central Arizona, a grayish fringe of clouds had formed. Leaphorn wished he had listened to the weather forecast. He felt suddenly nervous. Had something startled the jay? Was George Bowlegs with his old 30-30 looking down at them from the rimrock? Had he guessed wrong about the boy? George couldn't have killed his father. He was a day's ride away from the hogan. But he could have killed Cata. Could he be not just a mixed-up way-out kid but literally insane? Living some fantasy of sorcery-witchcraft unreality that made murder just another part of the dream? The question occupied Leaphorn on the steep climb up the saddle over the lip of the mesa and caused him to move more slowly and cautiously as he went about his work. Even so, within an hour he had accumulated most of the information he needed.

In this season, this end of the mesa was the grazing territory for a herd of perhaps twenty to twenty-five mule deer. They watered at a seep under the rimrock and had two regular sleeping places—both on heavily brushed hummocks where updrafts would carry the scent of predators toward them. Within two hours he had a fair idea of the pattern the herd followed in its dawn, twilight, and nocturnal feedings. This feeding pattern, he explained to Susanne, was followed with almost machinelike rigidity by mule deer—varying only with changing weather conditions, wind, temperature, and food supplies.

"From what you tell me about George, he's going to know all this," Leaphorn said. "If he got up here when we think he did, he would have been trying to get one about dusk. He'd have done enough track reading to figure out where the deer browsed when they came out of their afternoon sleeping place. Then he'd set up an ambush and just wait."

The ravens led them to the spot. The guard bird rose, cawing an alert. A dozen feeders flapped skyward in his wake, noisy with alarm. And down the slope they found the small clearing where George had shot his deer.

The animal, a small two-year-old buck, still lay beside the trail in the shadow of an outcropping of cap rock boulders. Leaphorn stood on one of the boulders surveying the scene and feeling good about it. For the first time since he had heard of George Bowlegs, something seemed to be working out with that rational harmony Leaphorn's orderly soul demanded. He explained it to Susanne, showing her the scuff marks on the lichens where George had crouched on the boulders; explaining how, at dusk, the cooling air would be moving down the trail, taking George's scent away from the approaching herd and allowing him to perch almost directly over their route.

"From here we pick up his tracks and find where he spent last night. He'll have the horse hobbled somewhere close, so that should be easy. And if he's marking time until tomorrow . . ." Leaphorn's voice trailed off. His expression, which had been blandly satisfied, deteriorated into a puzzled frown. He broke the self-created silence by muttering something in Navajo. A moment ago this scene had clicked tidily into the framework his logic had built—a deer killed where, when, and how the deer should have been killed. Why hadn't he seen the glaring incongruity? Leaphorn's frown decayed into a glower.

Susanne was looking at him, surprised. "What's the matter?"

"You wait right here," he said. "I want a closer look at this."

He swung himself down off the boulders and squatted beside the carcass. It was stiff, dead not much less than a day. The smell of fresh venison and old blood rose into his nostrils. It was a fat, young, four-point buck, shot just behind the left shoulder from above and in front—a perfect shot for an instant kill and made, obviously, from the boulder at very short range. George had then rolled the buck on its back, removed the scent glands from its rear legs, tied off the anal vent, opened the chest cavity and the abdomen with a neat and precise incision through hide and muscles. He had rolled out the entrails, and then he had cut a long strip of hide and tied it to the buck's front ankles, presumably in preparation for hoisting the carcass from a tree limb to let it drain and cool away from ground rodents. But the carcass still lay there. Leaphorn scowled at it. He could have understood if George had simply sliced himself a substantial portion of venison and let the carcass lie. It would have gone against the grain, as Navajo and hunter, to waste the meat. But if he had been in a hurry George might have done it. Why this, though? Leaphorn rocked back on his heels and tried to recreate it.

The boy carefully scouting the herd without alerting it, checking its browsing routes, checking the wind drift, setting his ambush, waiting silently in the gathering darkness, picking the deer he wanted, firing the single precise shot in the proper place. Then bleeding his kill, taking each step in dressing the carcass, without sign of hurry. And then, with the job almost done, walking away and leaving the meat to spoil without even cutting himself a steak to roast.

"What are you doing?" Susanne asked. "Is something wrong?"

"Look around there and see if you can find the empty rifle shell."

"What would it look like?"

"Brass," Leaphorn said. "Smaller than a fountain pen cap." He poked through the entrails. The heart was missing, and the liver, and the gall bladder. The ravens had been at work, but they wouldn't have had time to finish off the large organs and would have avoided the bitter gall. It was useful to a Navajo only for ceremonial purposes, for medicine, to fend off witches. Leaphorn tried to remember if the gall of deer had any ritual use for the Zuñis. Something about a hunting fetish, he thought, but he didn't know much about their ceremonialism. He confirmed that George had taken no meat. At one point an incision had been made and some fat cut out. Why would George want tallow? Leaphorn could think of no answer. And why kill a deer for meat, start a neat butchering job, and then walk away with nothing but heart and liver? They'd said George was crazy but insanity wouldn't explain this.

Leaphorn rose from the crouch, noticing that his muscles were tired. He began with little hope or enthusiasm to determine what sort of story the tracks around this clearing would tell.

Deer tracks were everywhere. Near the carcass their frantic hoofs had churned the trail. George had walked here. The sign of his boots was plain over the hoof marks.

So was the print of the moccasin.

Leaphorn stared at this track—a soft, medium-sized, foot-shaped impression. And then his hand was fumbling at the flap of his pistol holster as the implications of what he was seeing became clear. He stood motionless, his eyes scanning the brush which surrounded this small opening, his hand on the butt of the pistol. The footprint had been made yesterday—after George had killed his deer but not long afterward. Someone had followed George here. In some unmeasurable fraction of a second, mind and memory fit pieces together. Leaphorn saw Cecil's battered tin lunchbox with keepsakes disordered by a searching hand. He heard Cecil's voice saying that the note from George had been left in the box. In that instant Leaphorn knew what he had been overlooking for thirty-six hours. The note was missing from the box because the man who killed Shorty Bowlegs had found it, and from it had calculated where George had gone, and had relentlessly tracked him to this spot.

Leaphorn cursed himself vehemently in Navajo. How could he have been so stupid? This is what his subconscious had been prodding him to remember. Had he remembered it too late? He glanced at the carcass. This person must have arrived as George was dressing the deer, which explained why George had abandoned the job unfinished. So where was George now? Had the man killed him and hidden the body?

"Here it is." Susanne's voice was behind him. "It's more like a lipstick than a fountain pen cap." She was holding up an empty cartridge between thumb and forefinger, grinning. (It wouldn't be an empty 30-30 from George's old rifle, Leaphorn thought. It would be .45 caliber, or .38, or 30-06, and it would proclaim that George Bowlegs had been shot to death at this spot yesterday about the same time Lieutenant Joseph Leaphorn had been wasting his time chatting with a Catholic priest in Zuñi.)

"Let's see it," Leaphorn said. Susanne dropped into his palm an empty 30-30 shell, its copper percussion cap dented, its mouth still smelling faintly of burned powder.

"It was right at the base of that big rock," Susanne said. "Was it from George's gun?"

"It was from George's rifle," Leaphorn said. "Now see if you can find another one. Look around the fringes of this clearing . . . around places where somebody could stand and look in here without being seen."

Susanne's face made a question. He didn't answer it. Instead he began the tedious job of finding how George had left this spot.

First he found the way George had arrived. He had come up the deer trail from below. It took another fifteen minutes to sort out the footprints and determine the way the boy had left. Leaphorn felt tremendous relief. George had left under his own power, walking directly away from the carcass and back around the boulder. There he had turned, crouched with his weight on the balls of his feet, facing back into the clearing. (Doing what? Listening? Watching? Had something alerted him?) From there the footprints led past a screen of piñons, past another stony outcrop, and up the slope into heavier timber.

Leaphorn spent another half hour at the clearing and learned little more. In her fruitless hunt for another empty cartridge (which Leaphorn no longer expected to find), Susanne startled a cottontail rabbit from his brush-pile den beyond the clearing and sent him bolting through the rocks. That sort of sound might have been what had alerted the boy. Whatever it had been, the boy had been nervous enough to take a covered, indirect route to the place where he had left his horse. From there he had ridden westward across the mesa.

Leaphorn sat on the trunk of a fallen ponderosa, fished out his emergency can of potted meat from his jacket pocket, and divided it with Susanne. While they ate he considered alternatives. He could continue trying to follow George's tracks, or he could wait and try to catch him at the lake tomorrow, or he could give up and go home. The odds of finding George now that he had been frightened looked dismal. The boy would either be running (but not very fast, because his horse would be nearly dead by now from hunger and exhaustion) or he would be hiding somewhere, very alert and very cautious. If Leaphorn had guessed right about the lake, the chance of catching George there looked a little better. At least they were the best odds available.

The sun was low now. The clouds in the west had risen up the horizon and were fringed with violent yellows. Slanting light was turning the alkali and calichi flats in the valley below from white and gray into rose and pink. Seventy miles southwestward, another cloud formation had formed over the dim blue shape of the White Mountains. This great vacant landscape reminded him of Susanne's remark about it being hard to be a Navajo if you minded being lonely. He wondered about George again. The boy's flight from the deer carcass seemed to suggest taut nerves more than panic. He had heard something, seen something, had been suddenly fearful, and had ducked away. He would hide somewhere safe, Leaphorn thought, rather than run wildly. And today his fears would have diminished with the light. George Bowlegs, Leaphorn decided, would still, right now, be on this mesa waiting for whatever he was waiting for at the Dance Hall of the Dead. But would the man who hunted him still be here? Leaphorn considered this. The man would have known he had flushed his bird. He needed to be a fairly competent tracker to find George's kill site. But once George was running, covering his tracks, he would have to be much better than that. He would have to be as good as Joe Leaphorn—and perhaps better than Leaphorn. As far as Leaphorn knew, there were no better trackers than himself. Certainly no Zuñi, or white man.

So what would the Man Who Wore Moccasins do? Leaphorn thought of the bloody head of Shorty Bowlegs, the ransacked hogan. He doubted if the man would give up. He would stay in a likely place with a long view and wait for the boy to make a move. Leaphorn looked toward Susanne, who was sprawled on her back, her face dusty and drawn with fatigue. Too tired to talk. He pushed himself to his feet, more tired himself than he'd been since as far back as he could remember.

"We've got a little bit of light left," he said. "I think we'll cut back toward that saddle where we climbed up here. That was George's way up and it's probably his way down. We'll find a place to get some rest somewhere near there. And in the morning we'll be in position to watch for him."

"You're not going to try to find him tonight?"

"I'm going to try to get some general idea of about where he might be," Leaphorn said. "And then we're going to rest."

On the rimrock above the saddle, Leaphorn stopped again. He got out his binoculars and spent five minutes examining the landscape. The saddle, as it had appeared from the lake, seemed to be the only easy way down. Beyond the saddle, south of the cliff on which Leaphorn stood, a shelf of land extended from the escarpment. The timber there was a thick jumble of mixed dry-country conifers. He had noticed it before, spotting it as ideal deer cover—the sort of place a deer herd would pick for a resting place. A single neck of land connected this great hill with the mesa. Against the rimrock, the deer could not be approached from above because of the overhung cliff. They could watch the backtrail, as resting deer always did, with no trouble. Rising air currents during the day would carry up to them the scent of any predator. And there were escape routes. The way down was steep but, unlike the mesa cliffs, not impossible. Leaphorn studied this site through the binoculars. It would be attractive to George for the same reason it would appeal to deer. It offered security without being a trap. George had seen it. He must have seen its advantages as a hiding place.

At the head of the saddle, they crossed the game trail which led down it. Susanne had revived slightly now. "There's our tracks," she said. "Your boots and my tennies. And there's George's horse's hoofprint that we saw going up."

"Yeah," Leaphorn said. If she was reviving, he wasn't.

"And here's one of those moccasin tracks," she said. "Like the one you showed me back at the deer."

"Where!"

"Right here. He stepped on your footprint."

Leaphorn squatted beside the track. The moccasin, going down the trail, had partially erased the heel mark Leaphorn had left that afternoon on the way up.

Susanne read something in his face. "Is that bad luck, or something? Someone stepping on your footprint?"

"I guess it depends," he said. He hadn't explained to her who must have left the prints at the carcass of the deer. There hadn't been any reason to frighten her. Now maybe he should tell her. The man who had been stalking George yesterday might now be stalking them. At least, he knew they were on the mesa. Leaphorn would decide what to tell her after they had found a place to spend the night.

By the time they reached the access route to the wooded peninsula of land below the rimrock, the western sky was the violent red of dying sunset. Due east there was the faint yellow glow where soon the full moon would be rising. Leaphorn stood at a gap in the rimrock, looking down the inevitable game path which led away into the brush.

"If I had hurried a little," he said, "I could see something." No tracks were visible in the dusk on the narrow trail. George might have avoided it, anyway, if he suspected he was followed. Far away and behind them, Leaphorn heard a yipping bark.

The calm cycle of day was ending. Now the hunting cycle began—the hours of the predator, the owl, and the bobcat, the coyote, and the wolf. There was no breeze at all, only the faint movement of the ground thermal, cold air sifting past him, sinking toward the valley far below. He was suddenly nervously aware that the Man Who Wore Moccasins knew they were on this mesa. Had the man found them? Had he watched them? Was he watching them now? The thought made Leaphorn conscious of a spot of itching skin between his shoulder blades. He decided to tell Susanne about the moccasin tracks. He would do it while they were eating. She should know.

"Susie," he said. "Keep your eyes open. I'm going down here just a little ways and see if I can see anything."

He took, as it turned out, exactly three steps.

Thursday, December 4, 6:08 p.m.

THE PAIN WAS LIKE being struck by a hammer. Leaphorn staggered a step backward. He gasped for air, conscious simultaneously of the loud double crack of the shot, of the great knot of pain in his abdomen, of the stink of burned powder. Behind him he heard Susanne scream. His left hand had moved, without his willing it to move, to his stomach. His right hand fumbled under his jacket for the pistol holstered on his hip—an action equally reflex. His eyes had seen the source of this attack at the very moment it had happened. They had registered a jet of motion from the rocks directly ahead of him, and the streak of the projectile toward him. It seemed impossible that he could have seen the bullet. It seemed impossible that the shot had come from the very face of the rocks. His right hand held his pistol now, but there was no target. No one was there. No one could be there. And then he was conscious of what his left hand was feeling. It had found, projecting from his shirt just above his navel, a tube of metal. Leaphorn stared down at it, incredulous at first and then trying to understand what he was seeing.

Projecting from his abdomen, the source of both the burned powder smell and his pain, was a cylinder of dull aluminum. A tangle of pink wool yarn was attached to its base. With a motion born of revulsion, Leaphorn jerked the cylinder away from his stomach. He flinched at the freshened pain. The cylinder was free from his flesh now, but caught on the tough khaki cloth of his shirt. He jerked it free. "What happened?" Susanne was shouting. "What's wrong?"

A steel hypodermic needle, half the diameter of a soda straw, jutted an inch from the front of the cylinder—red now with Leaphorn's blood. The cylinder was hot and stank of cordite. He stared at it without understanding. His finger found the barb which had caught in the cloth of his shirt. And then he knew what had stuck him. It was a hypodermic dart for stunning animals, used by zoos, game conservation officers, veterinarians, and animal biologists. He took six quick steps down the trail to the rocks. Carefully wedged into a crevasse, screened with dead leaves, was a black carbon dioxide pellet gun with a second tube attached to its top. A copper wire was tied to the trigger mechanism.

Susanne was beside him now, looking at the cylinder. "What is it?"

"I tripped some sort of booby trap," Leaphorn said. "And I got shot with this thing. It's what you shoot wild animals with when you want to capture them without killing them." Leaphorn unbuttoned his shirt and pulled apart the cloth enough to examine the wound. The puncture hole in the dark skin looked, to Leaphorn, incredibly small. Only a little blood seeped from it. But what sort of serum had it blasted into his flesh? Thinking of that added a measure of panic to the knot of pain. He wasn't ready to think about it for another second or two. "The way it works, the cylinder is fired by a compressed gas—or, in some guns, by gunpowder. And when it strikes the animal, there's another little powder charge in the cylinder. That explodes and forces the serum down the needle into—into whatever you're shooting."

"The serum? What would it be?" Susanne's eyes were enormous. "What will it do to you?"

By now Leaphorn was asking himself the same question. "We'll guess it's the same stuff they shoot into animals. So we've got to hurry." He looked around him almost frantically. He ran down the path and then cut back toward the cliff. "There," he said, pointing. "We'll get into that depression in the wall." He lost his footing twice scrambling up the mound of fallen stones under the rock wall of the mesa, and then sprawled onto the sand behind them. He inspected the site quickly. Given time he could have found something better, perhaps even a secure place to hide. Here whoever it was would find them, and it was too open from the front. But at least their rear and sides were protected. Nothing could reach them from above.

"What are—"

"Don't talk," Leaphorn said. "There isn't time." He handed her his pistol. "I'm going to be out of it in a minute, so listen. Here's how this thing works." He showed her how to aim, how the revolver fired, the dozen spare cartridges in his belt, and how to reload. "Whoever set that trap either heard it fire or he's going to come around and check, and he'll know he got somebody and he'll find us. You're going to have to stay alert. When he comes, shoot him." He felt a wave of nausea and raised his hand to rub his forehead. It took a concentrated effort of will to control the hand. "Try to kill him," Leaphorn said. His voice sounded thick in his ears now, and fierce with rage. "If you don't keep him away, I think he'll kill us. I think he's crazy."

It was hard now to control his tongue. "This stuff is paralyzing me. I think it wears off in a few hours and I'll be all right again. Don't let me smother if I fall over, or swallow my tongue or anything. And if I die, try to slip away in the dark. Find the highway." Talking now was an immense effort. His legs were numb. He wanted to move his feet. The message left his brain but nothing happened. "Don't get lost," he said. "Moon rises east, goes down west. Try . . ." His tongue would no longer rise from his teeth to form the sound.

When he could no longer talk, when he could do nothing, panic arrived . . . a frantic dream of suffocation, of drowning helplessly in his own fluids. He fought it down grimly, controlling his mind, as he could no longer control his body. The panic left as quickly as it had come. Left him calm, studying the effects of the drug. It seemed now to have included an almost total paralysis of all voluntary muscles without affecting involuntary actions—the blink of the eyes, the rhythmic expansion-contraction of the lungs. Leaphorn considered all this with an odd sort of detachment. He tried to remember what he had heard about this method of stunning animals. Paralytic drugs must block passage of the message from brain to muscle. Otherwise, if all muscles were paralyzed, breathing would cease. His mind still seemed clear—unusually clear, in fact—and his hearing was excellent. He simply could not move. It was as if his brain had been partly disconnected from his body—still receiving the sensory inputs of eyes and ears and nerve endings, but unable to react with commands to action.

How long would the paralysis last? He remembered a wildlife film he had seen on television—a rhino shot with such a dart for study by a biologist. What had they said about it? Several hours, he thought. How many is several? How would it affect a man? And what sort of drug had been used? No profit in speculation. He turned to other thoughts, impressed with how clearly his mind was working. Impressed, too, with how immense the rising moon looked emerging over the eastern horizon. Susanne had stopped trying to talk to him, recognizing that he could not respond. She sat beside him, her back to the dark. Where had the man got the rig? It would be easy enough, Leaphorn guessed. Veterinary-supply houses would have the dart guns and the serums. Maybe the drug would require a prescription. Leaphorn guessed that if it did, just about any rancher or game ranger or zoologist could manage to get the stuff.

He noticed, with mild surprise, that he could hear Susanne breathing. Faintly rasping intake, sighing exhalation. He could hear incredibly well. Somewhere on the cliff above, a night bird was moving. At some immense distance on the mesa a coyote yipped twice and then sang its warbling song. And somewhere to his front, somewhere behind the screen of rabbit brush and juniper on this rocky hill, there were the footsteps of a human. They were slow footsteps, carefully placed—the footsteps of a hunter stalking. Leaphorn found himself wishing almost casually that he could force his tongue to tell Susanne about this danger. At another level of consciousness he wondered about this lack of fear, this immense gain in ability to hear, and this odd feeling of detachment. He remembered a similar sensation from years ago at Arizona State when he and Tom Bob and Blackie Bisti and another Indian student had gone to a meeting of the Native American Church and he had sampled the bitterness of a ceremonial peyote button. He noticed that he could remember this incident with exact and detailed clarity. He was in the smoky room, acrid with some unfamiliar incense, seeing the sweat darkening the back of Blackie's shirt, everything. The stuffiness of rebreathed air, the drone of words, the grim face of the Kiowa preacher giving them their instructions. He listened to the sermon again, thinking now as he had then that it contained an odd mixture of Christianity, mysticism, and Pan-Indian nationalism. And now, as then, Leaphorn was quickly bored with it. And he left the smoky room, drifting out through time and space, and was again under the moon, which was approaching now, so close, so large, that its dark yellow form filled his entire skull with cold. He could no longer see around it. There was only moon in his field of vision, an immense disk of ice pulsing in the black sky. And then Susanne was speaking to him. Her whisper thundered around his head, the words indescribably slow. "Mr. Leaphorn, can you hear me? I think there is something out there. I think I hear something. Mr. Leaphorn! *Mr. Leaphorn!*" Her hand was on his chest, her face close to his, her hair blotting out the yellow disk, fear in her eyes, her face almost frantic. And more words. "Mr. Leaphorn. Please don't die." I won't, Leaphorn thought. I will never die.

But perhaps he would die. He could hear the footsteps of the hunter clearly. The hunter now stood behind the tangle of chamiso and juniper which the moonlight had turned from gray to silver. Now the hunter moved again, closer. He stopped behind the juniper with the broken limb. There now in the darkness diluted by the moonlight was the face of whatever it was that made these creaking footfalls. Obviously it was a bird. Perhaps a bird extinct since Folsom Man had hunted here. It was much larger than any physical bird, odd and angry. Its eyes stared, round and blank and dead, from a face that was black and yellow and blue, but mostly black. The eye sockets were empty, he saw. The bird's skull was hollow. And being hollow must be dead. Yet it moved. The rampant plume of feathers at its summit bristled with movement and its rigid beak angled outward past a juniper limb, reflecting the moonlight.

Beside him Susanne sucked in her breath and made a strangled sound. Leaphorn's pistol rose in her hand. It shattered the moon with a great flash of light and blast of sound. Now there was the smell of exploded powder. The echo rolled away around the mesa walls. Boom. Boom. Boom. Boom. Finally it melded into the other night sounds and faded away. The bird was gone now. Leaphorn could hear only the sound of crying. His nand fell from his leg and crashed into the ground. Leaphorn willed for a moment that it would rise again and restore itself to its perch away from the stony ground. But the hand simply lay there and Leaphorn retreated from it, and lost himself, falling, falling, falling into a glittering psychedelic dream in which the cold moon again pulsed in an inky void and a hunter sat naked on a ridge, working with infinite patience, chipping out lance points from pink ice, breaking them, dropping the broken parts onto the earth beside him, taking defeat after defeat without a show of anger.

Much later he became aware that Susanne had again fired the pistol. There was a thunder of sound all around him which forced the moon back into the sky. He was cold. Freezing, he thought. His hands were freezing. He managed some sort of sound, something between a sigh and a grunt. "You're all right," Susanne's voice whispered at his ear. "Your breathing sounds good, and your pulse seems O.K., and I think everything is going to be all right." She picked up his hand, turned it, looked at his wristwatch. "It's been almost four hours now, so maybe that stuff won't be working much longer." She stared into his face. "You can hear me, can't you? I can tell. You're getting awful cold. Your hands are like ice. I'm going to build a fire."

He focused every molecule of his will on an effort to say "No." He managed only a grunt. The psychedelic dream was gone for the moment and his mind was clear of hallucinations. She shouldn't build the fire. The Man Who Wore Moccasins might still be out there, waiting. By firelight, he might have light enough to shoot them. Again he managed a grunt, but the effort exhausted him. Susanne was away in the darkness. He could hear her moving. Gathering sticks. The moon had moved now, climbing up the sky and edging southward far enough behind the rim of the mesa so that the shadow extended ten yards beyond his feet. Outside the shadow, the landscape glittered gray and silver with moonlight. Nothing moved. His hearing still seemed to be unusually acute. From far, far away he heard the song of the coyote again, so dim by distance that it seemed to drift down from the stars. And then there was the sound, from much closer, of a hunting owl. The grotesque bird he had seen in his hallucination, the bird that had vanished after Susanne fired at it, must have been a kachina mask. Leaphorn thought about it. He recognized the mask. The bristling black ruff around the neck, the fierce plume of eagle feathers atop the head, the long tubular beak.

He had seen the mask before, in the moonlight behind the hogan at Jason's Fleece, and painted in the mural in the Zuñi mission. It was the Salamobia, the warrior who carried a whip-like sword of tight-woven yucca. He tried to summon from his memory what he knew of this kachina. There were two of them at Shalako ceremonials, dancing attendance on the other members of the Council of the Gods. But each of the six Zuñi kivas was represented by one—so the total must be six. So six such masks must exist. And each would be carefully guarded by the Zuñi who had been chosen by his kiva for the honor of personifying this figure. The mask would be kept in its own room, provided with food and water, and the spirit which resided within it honored by prayer.

Susanne was lighting the fire now. Having accepted that it was impossible to warn her, Leaphorn ignored this. What would be, would be. He would enjoy being warm again. Now, while he could, he would think. But no more of the mask. The genuine masks would be guarded, but anyone could make a counterfeit.

The flame spread through the pile of leaves and twigs, crackling, casting a flickering yellow light. The dart had been intended for George. Apparently not meant to kill him. At least not immediately. Why not? Was it because this person—like Leaphorn—wanted to talk to the boy?

And why had George taken the gall from the deer? Dried, it would be useful as medicine, for use in curing ceremonials. And why take the fat from under the deerskin? There was something Leaphorn should remember about that. Something to do with Zuñi hunting procedures. He had heard about it from his roommate. He and Rounder had compared Navajo and Zuñi origin myths, emergence myths, migration myths, methods of doing things. Part of it, he remembered, concerned hunting.

The Navajo myth cautions against killing any of the sixty or so beings which had joined the First People in their escape from the Fourth World to Earth Surface World, which limited hunting pretty well to deer, antelope, and a few game birds. The Zuñi legend told of the great war against Chakwena, the Keeper of the Game, which was won only after the Sun Father created the two Zuñi War Gods to lead them. There had been beer and talk far into the night. He forced his mind to recall it. Rounder, his moon face bland, telling them how Father Coyote had taught Clumsy Boy the prayers that would persuade the deer that the hunter brought not harm, but evolution into a higher being. The fire flared up through the dry wood and Leaphorn felt the heat against his face. He felt, again, that odd sense of being detached from himself. He was slipping into another hallucinogenic nightmare. The sound of the fire became a clamorous rattle and crackle. The stars were brighter than they should be on such a night of moon. Yikaisdahi, the Milky Way, the billion bright footprints left by spirits on their pathway across the sky, glittered against the night. Leaphorn forced himself to concentrate. He could see Rounder, slightly drunk, his two hands framing the beer mug on the table, his face earnest, chanting it in Zuñi, and then the translation:

"Deer, Deer.
I come following your hoofprints.
Sacred favors I bring as I run.
Yes, yes, yes, yes."

And then showing them, using the beer mug as the muzzle of the deer, how the Zuñi hunter breathed in the animal's last breath. And the prayer. How had it gone? Leaphorn remembered only that it was a statement of thanks that went with the drinking of the Sacred Wind of Life. And then the details of how the deer must be dressed, and of the making of the ball of deer fat and gall and blood from the heart and hair from the proper places, and some fetish offerings to be buried when the deer had fallen.

Suddenly Leaphorn could hear Rounder's drunken voice.

"Don't eat in the morning. The hungry hunter scents game against the wind." And he was seeing Rounder's placid face against the sky just above the brightness of So'tsoh—the North Star—between the constellations Ursa Major and Cassiopeia, which the Navajos called Cold Man of the North and his wife. Then the nightmare was on him again, worse than before. The sky filled with the chindi of the dead. They wore deerskin masks and their great beaks clacked. He saw Slayer of the Enemy Gods, standing on a rainbow bright against the sky, but above him towered something with a great blue face and a tall white forehead, its chest covered with prayer plumes, holding a great wand edged with obsidian. Leaphorn knew somehow that this was Uyuyewi, the Zuñi War God, and he felt a hopeless dread. Then there was a face against his, breathing his breath, taking the wind of his life as it left his nostrils. And next, the hand of Susanne on his face, her voice in his ear. "Mr. Leaphorn. It's all right. It's going to be good again. Don't be afraid."

There was cold gray light against the eastern horizon now. And the fire was nothing but hot embers, and Leaphorn's mind told his shoulder muscles to huddle against the cold. And they did huddle, and his hand, told to rub his icy shoulder, rubbed it. Leaphorn was suddenly wide awake, the hallucinations a memory. Susanne was curled by the fire, asleep, the pistol by her hand. Leaphorn tried his legs. They, too, moved to command. He felt a fierce joy. He was alive. He was sane. He tried to push himself to his feet. Made it. Staggered for two steps, and then fell against the stone cliff with a clatter. He could control some muscles well, others not so well. The noise awoke Susanne.

"Hey, you're O.K." She had dead leaves in her hair, dirt on her face. She looked absolutely exhausted and tremendously relieved.

It wasn't until after sunrise that Leaphorn had full control of all his muscles. His stomach bore a swollen red bruise where the dart had struck and fired its charge. He felt weak and sick. He suspected that would go away. He had planned to head for the lake, to try to reach it by sunrise—the sunrise of the fifth day, when Ernesto Cata's spirit would arrive to join the Council of the Gods. But while he could walk a little, he couldn't walk straight. So instead they had waited by the saddle on the slight chance that George Bowlegs had not been frightened by the sound of pistol shots during the night and would be passing by. George did not appear. Leaphorn exercised as quietly as he could, concentrated on regaining full use of his legs. And he thought about a diversity of things. About what Ernesto Cata had told Father Ingles, about the odd way in which George Bowlegs had behaved, about Zuñi hunting ritual, about Ted Isaacs's speculation on how a Stone Age hunter had made his lance points, and about Halsey and the pale young man named Otis whose psychedelic nightmares Leaphorn could now better appreciate. He thought about why whoever had set the trap for George Bowlegs had used a hypodermic gun instead of a shotgun, and of other matters. And when, finally, his right ankle would respond exactly as ordered, he told Susanne they would return to the deer carcass and then head back for the truck.

"We'll cut off enough venison for some breakfast," Leaphorn said.

They did that. And after he had made a fire on which to roast it, he examined the ground around the carcass. He found a place where a small hole had been cut into the earth beside the carcass. Buried in it was a still soft ball of clay, blood, tallow, gall, and deer hair, the fetish offering Rounder had described for the fallen animal. Leaphorn carried it back to the fire, sat on the boulder, and pulled it apart carefully. Inside the ball he found a turquoise bead, the broken tip of a stone lance point, and a small bit of abalone shell.

Friday, December 5, 2 p.m.

JOHN O'MALLEY MADE a tent out of his hands and looked past Leaphorn at something at the back of the Zuñi Tribal Courtroom. "To sum it up," he said, "we still don't know where to put our hands on George Bowlegs."

He shifted his eyes slightly to look at Leaphorn. He smiled. The action made a dimple in each cheek and crinkled the skin around his blue eyes. "I hope you'll stick to that chore. I'd put somebody on it to work with you if there was anybody. But everybody is working on something else. I think that kid knows something about why Cata and Shorty Bowlegs were killed. And I think he can tell us something about that commune." The eyes shifted away and the smile turned off. "We really wanted to talk to him today."

Leaphorn said absolutely nothing.

"Second, you think somebody else is hunting George. Maybe so," O'Malley said. "I don't doubt it. I can see why maybe some people would want to shut him up. But it looks like he's hard to catch." The smile came on again. "And it's too bad you getting shot by that coyote trap or whatever it was. We'll keep that syringe. Maybe we can track down where it came from and who bought the serum." The smile turned into a grin. "However, I think there's going to be enough charges to file when we get this broken so we may not need to worry about making a case on whoever committed that particular assault."

O'Malley folded the finger tent. The grin went away. He stood up.

"It might help," Leaphorn said quickly, "if you'd fill me in on what you've been learning."

O'Malley peered at him curiously.

"I gathered someone recognized Baker as a narcotics agent," O'Malley said. "He is." The silence stretched. That was all. Leaphorn realized with incredulous anger that this was all O'Malley was going to tell him.

"O.K. Then you think the commune is a cover for a narcotics drop—heroin or what have you," Leaphorn said. "And the killings were done to protect it?"

O'Malley said nothing.

"Is that right?" Leaphorn insisted.

O'Malley hesitated. Finally he said, "It's pretty obvious. But we haven't gotten everything we need yet to get the indictments. We need to talk to George. Among other things."

"Can I guess that Baker was working on this before the killings? That you've got enough so you don't have any doubts about it?"

O'Malley grinned again. "I'd say you could guess that."

"What have you got?"

The grin faded. "For a long time," O'Malley said, "our policy has been that every officer working a case is told everything he needs to know about the part he is working on. But we don't fill everybody in on everything that comes up if it doesn't have anything to do with the angle they're on. For example, I can tell you that we'd really like to talk to George today—but I don't guess that's likely?"

"Why today?"

"Tomorrow's this big Zuñi Shalako ceremonial. Thousands of people here—strangers from all over. It would be a good cover for somebody to come in and make a pickup."

"Anybody in particular?"

There was another pause while O'Malley thought about it. He unzipped the briefcase on his desk and pulled out a sheaf of photographs. Some were official police mug shots. Some were candid shots of the sort stakeouts collect through telescopic lenses. Leaphorn recognized Halsey in a photograph that seemed to have been taken on a college campus, and the pale boy called Otis in a police mug photo. There were five others he didn't recognize, including a balding fat man and a young man with an Indian face in a paratroop uniform. Leaphorn picked up this photograph and examined it.

"If you see any of these birds around tomorrow, I want to know about it," O'Malley said.

"This guy a Zuñi?"

"Yeah. He got the habit in Vietnam and he's been involved in dealing some since he got back."

Leaphorn put the photograph on the desk.

"That's the motive for the killings then?" he said. "Keeping a narcotics operation covered up? You got enough to be sure of that?"

"That's right," O'Malley said. "We're sure."

"O.K.," Leaphorn said. "So I'll just stick to finding George for you."

Pasquaanti wasn't in his office but his secretary—a small, cheerful girl with a very round face and a striking display of squash blossom jewelry—sent someone to find him after being persuaded it was important. Pasquaanti listened impassively while Leaphorn told him about seeing the kachina at the commune, about the ambition of George Bowlegs to become a Zuñi, about the note the boy had left for his brother, and about what had happened on the mesa. The Zuñi interrupted only once. He asked Leaphorn to describe the mask.

"It had a thick ruff of feathers around the neck," Leaphorn said. "Black. Probably crow or raven feathers. Had a beak maybe six inches long and round, like a broom handle. And the mask was rounded on top, with a sort of wand of feathers pointing quills-forward as a topknot. Then there was a design drawn on the cheek. I think it was a Salamobia mask."

"There are six of those," Pasquaanti said. He took out his fountain pen and made a quick sketch on notepaper. "Like this?"

"Yes. That's it."

"What color was the face?"

"The face? It was black."

Pasquaanti looked old. Leaphorn hadn't noticed that before.

"Mr. Leaphorn," he said. "I thank you for telling me this."

"Is there anything you can tell me?"

Pasquaanti thought about it. "I can tell you that the Salamobia you saw was not genuine. Black is the color of the Hekiapawa kiva, the Mole kiva. That mask is safe. It is always safe. So are the other masks. You can be sure of that."

"Then could someone have taken another mask?"

"There are two kinds of masks," Pasquaanti said. "Some are the actual kachina and the kachina spirit lives in them and they are fed and watered and taken care of with prayer plumes and everything they want. They are . . ." He paused, searching his English vocabulary for the right words. "Sacred," he said. "Very holy." He shook his head. Neither phrase was exactly right. "The other kind of mask is different. They are borrowed, and repainted to be used for different kachinas, and the spirit is not there."

"So perhaps someone might have taken one of those and changed it to look like a Salamobia?"

Pasquaanti considered this. His fingers folded and unfolded on the desk. "There are the bad among us," he said finally. "Some of us drink, and have learned the whiteman's greed, and aren't worth anything. But I don't think a Zuñi would take the mask of his family and use it like this."

The two men looked at each other silently. What Leaphorn described had been a hideous desecration. Worse, it had happened in the most holy period of the Zuñi liturgical year—in the days of sacred retreat just before Shalako. If this ceremonial was not properly done, rain did not fall, crops did not sprout, and sickness and bad luck were loosened across the land.

"One more thing," Leaphorn said. "I think George Bowlegs is wild to become a Zuñi. Maybe that's not possible, but he thinks it is. I think he went to your sacred lake because he wanted to talk to your Council of the Gods. And from what he told his little brother, I think he will come to Shalako and maybe he will do something. I think it would be good if your people watched for him."

"We will."

"And the man who wore the mask. He was smart enough to figure out where to look for George. He will be smart enough to figure it out again."

"We will watch for that man," Pasquaanti said. His voice was grim. It caused Leaphorn to remember something that Rounder had told him years ago: in Zuñi mythology, the penalty for sacrilege is death.

18

Saturday, December 6, 4:19 p.m.

LIEUTENANT JOSEPH LEAPHORN spent the afternoon on the ridge that overlooks the village of Zuñi from the south. He had picked the place carefully. It was a relatively comfortable spot, with soft earth under his buttocks and a sandstone slab for a backrest. A growth of chamiso and a gnarled piñon made it unlikely that anyone would see him and wonder what the devil he was doing there. And the view was ideal for his purpose. To his left his binoculars covered the old wagon trail that wandered up the Zuñi Wash from the southwest. To his right he looked down on a newly graded reservation road that angled under Greasy Hill at the edge of the village, swerved past the Zuñi cemetery, and ran southward. One or the other of these two roads would provide the most direct route from the mesa where George Bowlegs had killed his deer to the Shalako ceremonials in Zuñi Village. There were countless other ways Bowlegs might come—if come he did—including leaving his horse, walking to the paved highway, and hitchhiking. But Leaphorn could think of no other activity that offered better odds than did sitting here. And intercepting Bowlegs was only one of the reasons he was here. There was also the chance it offered him to think. He had a lot of thinking to do.

The swollen bruise on his abdomen reminded him of the first puzzle. Why had the trap been set to catch George Bowlegs but not to kill him? Cata and Shorty Bowlegs had been cut down without qualm or hesitation. Why not George?

Leaphorn leaned back against the rock, squirmed into an

easier position. Above him the sky was turning gray. The overcast had been building since noon. First it was nothing more than high-altitude humidity—a thin layer of stratospheric ice crystals which hung a glittering halo around the sun. Then a semiopaque grayness had crept in from north-northwest and the day gradually lost its light.

Why not George? Leaphorn felt the faintest trace of breeze on his cheek. Cold. It had been dead calm. The orgy of baking which caught up the women of Zuñi each Shalako season had reached its climax during the morning. Now most of the outdoor ovens were cooling. But a thin layer of blue smoke still hung in the air over the pueblo. It made a faint smear as far northwest as the Zuñi Buttes and eastward to the gaudy water tower at Black Rock. Even here, high over the valley and a half mile away, Leaphorn's nose caught the vague scent of baking bread and the perfume of burned piñon resin.

Already the wide shoulders of state road 53 were cluttered with cars and campers and pickups. The Zuñi people had come home from wherever they had wandered—college campuses, jobs in California and Washington. Those who called themselves the Flesh of the Flesh were drawn back to their birthplace for this great Coming Home of their ancestor spirits.

And with them came the curious, the tourists, dilettante Indian lovers, anthropologists, students, hippies, other Indians. Among the crowd would be the Zuñis' Brothers of the Pueblos: people from Acoma, Laguna, Zia, Hopi, Isleta, Santo Domingo, men who were priests of their own kivas, themselves connoisseurs of the metaphysics of nature, men with their own Dancing Gods who came to share in the ancient magic of their cousins. And, of course, the Navajos. In from the lonely hogans, with wives and children. Taller, rawboned, wearing their Levi's—looking on with a mixture of awe for great medicine made by these Callers of the Clouds, and the countryman's contempt for the dweller of towns.

Leaphorn sighed. Normally Zuñi Village held perhaps 3,500 of the 4,500 Zuñis. Tonight seven or eight thousand people would be crowded here. It would be, as O'Malley had said, the one time a stranger come to pay money or collect heroin would be least likely to be noticed. Leaphorn's anger at O'Malley had gone now, the victim of Leaphorn's habit of relating actions to causes. O'Malley would not be an agent of the FBI if his mind did not operate in a manner which conformed to FBI standards. Obviously someone in the agency had been interested in Halsey, or in Halsey's commune, before the killings. That would color O'Malley's thinking. And if O'Malley had no respect for Leaphorn as a policeman, Leaphorn must admit, in fairness, that he had no respect for O'Malley. He would think of other things. Why hadn't a shotgun been rigged into that trap set for Bowlegs? Or why hadn't the syringe been loaded with cyanide? Leaphorn considered the question, found no way to reach a conclusion, and skipped back to the beginning—back to Monday, when he had first arrived at Pasquaanti's office. From there he worked forward, examining each of the oddities that puzzled him.

There was a stir of activity in the village now—people gathering on the street that fronted along Zuñi Wash on the Old Village side. Leaphorn watched. Through his powerful navy-surplus binoculars he saw the figure of a boy, naked except for loincloth, crossing the footbridge behind a man in white buckskin. The boy wore a hood surmounted by a single feather. Mask and body were black, spotted with dots of red, blue, yellow, and white. The Little Fire God, Leaphorn knew—Shulawitsi entering the Old Village to make his ceremonial inspection of the sacred place before the entry of the Council of the Gods. Ernesto Cata was dead but the Little Fire God lived. The Badger Clan had provided another of its sons to personify this eternal spirit.

The afternoon wore on. Leaphorn watched the roads and pursued his thoughts. More activity in the village now. The sound of drums and flutes barely audible on the cold air. This would be the arrival of the Council of the Gods. They came dancing down Greasy Hill, past the white-painted village water tank. Some he could see through the magnifying lenses. The Fire God with a smoking cedar branch. Then Saiyatasha, the Rain God of the North, called Longhorn because of the great curved horn which jutted from the right side of his black-and-white mask. He was a burly man in white deerskin shirt and a blue-and-white kirtle, a bow in one hand and a deer-bone rattle in the other. And behind him Hu-tu-tu, who brought the rains from the south, his mask lacking the great horn. With Hu-tu-tu, the two Yamuhaktos, their round eye and mouth holes giving their masks an expression of silly, childlike surprise. And dancing attendance, two Salamobias—the same fierce beaked faces that Leaphorn remembered from his nightmare. In each hand they carried a heavy pointed whip wand of yucca blades. The crowd kept a respectful distance.

The procession disappeared into the village. The sun was lost now as the cloud cover steadily thickened. It was growing much colder. Below, two station wagons and a pickup truck pulled off the cemetery road and disgorged more than a dozen men and a load of paraphernalia. Several wore ceremonial kirtles and skullcaps of white doeskin. They would be the personifiers of the Shalako and their attendants. The group vanished beneath the slope.

Leaphorn reached into his pocket and extracted the turquoise bead, the abalone shell, and the broken flint lance tip. All were items to which both Navajo and Zuñi would attach ritual significance. Changing Woman had taught the Navajos the use of the gemstone and the shell in their curing ceremonies. They were appropriate fetish items for George to have offered to the spirit of the deer. And so was the flint tip. Leaphorn wasn't sure how the Zuñis valued such relics from older cultures but Navajos rated anything used by the Old People as potent medicine. As a boy, he used to hunt for these relics. He'd find them turned up amid the gravel in arroyo bottoms, uncovered on hillsides when the Male Rain pounded away the centuries of dust, and exposed among the clumps of buffalo grass when the Wind People carved potholes in the dry earth. He would give them to his grandfather and his grandfather would teach him another song from the Night Way, or a story of the Holy Ones. Perhaps George had found this lance point in like manner. Or perhaps he and Cata had stolen it from the dig site and it had—despite the certainty of Reynolds and Isaacs—somehow not been missed. That seemed unlikely, however. It was too fine a sample of Stone Age workmanship. Or perhaps . . .

The fragment of flint in Leaphorn's palm became a sort of

keystone. Around it the pieces of the puzzle of why Ernesto Cata had to die fell exactly into place. Suddenly Leaphorn knew why the trap set for George Bowlegs had not been a lethal trap, and what had happened in the hogan of Shorty Bowlegs, and why what George Bowlegs had told his brother about petty theft had been contradicted by Reynolds and Isaacs. He sat stock-still, sorting it very precisely in chronological order, checking for flaws, assigning to each of those deeds which had seemed so irrational a logical cause. He knew now why two murders had been committed. And he knew he couldn't prove it—could probably never prove it.

From below the hill came the noise of drum and rattle and a hooting sound. The Shalako emerged—the couriers of the Zuñi gods. The six huge ceremonial attendants. Leaphorn had forgotten how large they were. Ten feet tall, he guessed, to the ray of eagle feathers cresting their birdlike heads, so tall that the human legs supporting them under the great hooped skirts seemed grotesquely out of proportion. These immense birds would cross Zuñi Wash at sundown and be escorted to the houses that had been prepared for them. The sacred dancing and ceremonial feasting would continue until the following afternoon.

Leaphorn pushed himself to his feet, brushed the sand from his uniform, and began walking down the slope toward Zuñi Village. In that dim margin between day and night, the snow had begun. Heavy, wet, life-giving snow. Once again the Shalako had called the clouds and brought the water blessing to their people. One corner of Leaphorn's mind appreciated the harmony of this. Another urged him to hurry. Yesterday the killer had needed George Bowlegs alive. But if George Bowlegs came to Shalako, George Bowlegs would have to die.

Sunday, December 7, 2:07 a.m.

BY 1 A.M., LEAPHORN HAD DECIDED he wasn't likely to find George Bowlegs. He had prowled the village tirelessly, elbowing his way through the crowds jamming each of the ceremonial houses, watching, and studying faces. The very nature of the ritual magnified the difficulty. By tradition, not more than two of the Shalako could be entertained in a single house. Separate houses had to be prepared for Saiyatasha and his Council of the Gods, and for the ten Koyemshi, the sacred clowns. Three of these houses were in the oldest part of the village, on the crowded hill overlooking Zuñi Wash. Two were across the highway, where a newer portion of the village clustered around the Catholic school. Not only was the crowd thus fragmented, but it ebbed and flowed between these houses. Leaphorn had moved with it, watching the dark streets, checking the clusters of people around vehicles, pushing through the jam-packed viewing galleries and through the throngs eating lamb stew, canned peaches, and bakery cookies in the Zuñi kitchens, always looking for the face he had memorized from the Zuñi kitchens, always looking for the face he had memorized from the Zuñi school yearbook.

Once he had seen Pasquaanti, who seemed to have some ceremonial role at the Shalako house near Saint Anthony's school. Leaphorn had caught the Zuñi's attention, called him out into the darkness, and told him quickly and briefly his conclusions about who had killed Ernesto Cata. Pasquaanti had listened silently, commenting only with a nod. Later Leaphorn had noticed Baker, huddled in a bulky fur-collared coat, leaning against a post on the porch of the house where the Council of the Gods was dancing. Baker glanced at Leaphorn—a glance totally without recognition—and then had looked away. He obviously did not want to be seen talking to a man in the uniform of the Navajo Police. Leaphorn stood for a few moments well down the porch, curious. Beyond the porch, the yard was crowded with an assortment of vehicles. Baker looked either drunk or sleepy, perhaps both. He was watching a young man who stood in the back door of a camper talking to a young woman in a heavy mackinaw. Leaphorn felt a sudden impulse to walk up to Baker, grab him by the lapels, and tell him about Bowlegs, asking him to forget about this manhunt for an hour and help find the Navajo boy. Baker would be good at it, smart, fast, always thinking. But the impulse died a-borning. Baker would simply smile that silly smile and refuse to be distracted from whomever he was stalking. Leaphorn thought he would not like to be hunted by Baker.

At 1 A.M., when Leaphorn decided he wouldn't find Bowlegs, he was in the left gallery room of one of the Shalako houses on the hill. The bruise on his stomach ached with a steady throb. His eyes burned with tobacco smoke, incense, and stale air. He had finally worked his way up to the long window that looked down into the spectators jamming the benches and chairs in the dirt-floored room below him. He had scanned carefully every face visible through the opposite gallery. Now he leaned heavily on the sill and let mind and muscles relax. He was very tired. Almost directly below him and to his left, a wooden altar stood, its base bristling with rows of feathered prayer plumes. Next to it the drummers and flutists produced an intricate counterpointed rhythm which never seemed to repeat its complicated pattern. And on the floor, sunken four feet or more below ground level solely to permit this, the giant Shalako danced.

From where Leaphorn stood by the gallery window on the floor above, he was almost at eye level with the great bird. Its beak snapped suddenly—a half dozen sharp clacking sounds in perfect time with the drum. It hooted and its strange white-rimmed eyes stared for a moment directly into Leaphorn's. The policeman saw it with double vision. He saw it as a mask of tremendous technical ingenuity, a device of leather, embroidered cotton, carved wood, feathers, and paint held aloft on a pole, its beak and its movements manipulated by the dancer within it. But he also saw Shalako, the courier between the gods and men, who brought fertility to the seeds and rain to the desert when the people of Zuñi called, and who came on this great day to be fed and blessed by his people. Now it danced, swooping down the earthen floor, its great horns glittering with reflected light, its fan of topknot feathers bristling, its voice the hooting call of the night birds.

There was a sudden shift in the cadence of the music. The voices of the chanters rose in pitch. The Koyemshi had joined the Shalako on the floor. Mudheads, they were called. Their bodies were coated with a pinkish clay and their masks gave them heads distorted in shape, hairless, knobbed, with tiny rimmed eyes and puckered mouths. They represented the idiotic and deformed fruits of incest—that ultimate tribal taboo. The first Koyemshi, as Leaphorn remembered the mythology, were the offspring of a son and daughter of Shiwanni, the Sun Father. He had sent his children to help the Zuñi in their search for the Middle Place, but the boy had had intercourse with his sister. And the same night ten children were born. The first was normal and was to be the ancestor of the makers of rain. But the next nine were deformed and insane. Leaphorn considered this, his head buzzing with fatigue. The Mudheads represented evil and yet they were perhaps the most prestigious fraternity of this people. The men who represented the ten offspring were chosen to play this role for a year. They helped build the ceremonial houses and were involved in a year-long series of retreats, fastings, and ritual dancing. The assignment was so demanding of time that it wasn't unusual for a Mudhead to have to quit his job for a year and depend on the support of the villagers.

Leaphorn watched them dance. Despite the snow falling outside, they were nude except for black breechcloth and neck scarf, moccasins and mask. Their dance was intricate, a fast and exact placement of foot, their deerskin seed pouches slapping against sweat-damp ribs, their hands shaking feathered wands, their voices rising now in yells of triumph, and falling into the rhythmic recitation of the saga of their people.

Leaphorn scanned the crowd again. Below him there were mostly women—Zuñis in their ceremonial best, a scattering of Navajos, a blond girl, her face ashen with fatigue but her eyes bright with interest. To his right, two young Navajo men had edged their way near the window. They were discussing a young white man, who wore his hair in braids, had a red headband around his forehead and a heavy silver concho belt.

"I think he's an albino Indian," one said. "Ask him if he can say something in Navajo." The voice was loud enough for the white man to hear. "I think he's an Apache," the other Navajo said. "He looks too much like an Indian to be a Navajo."

They were drinking, Leaphorn saw. Not quite drunk, but drunk enough to slip over the boundary between humor and rudeness. If he weren't so tired, and otherwise occupied, he would move them out into the cold sobering air. Instead he would himself move from here, where George Bowlegs obviously wasn't, back to the Longhorn House for another check there. As he decided this, he saw George Bowlegs.

The boy was across the dance room, in the opposite gallery. He seemed to be standing on something, perhaps a chair, looking over the heads of those pressed against the windowsill—staring almost directly toward Leaphorn at the Shalako swooping down the dance floor. Leaphorn recognized him instantly. The generous mouth, the large expressive eyes, and the short-cropped hair. More than that. Even in that crowded gallery there was something about the boy that suggested the strange and the lonely. George stared at the dancing gods with eyes that were fixed and fascinated and a little crazy. He was no farther away than the width of the dance room. Perhaps a dozen yards.

Leaphorn began pushing his way back from the window, struggling through the packed humanity toward the passageway that ran behind the dance room to connect the two galleries. He moved as fast as he could, leaving a wake of jostled spectators, bruised feet, and curses. The passageway, too, was blocked with watchers. It took him two full minutes to fight his way through to the doorway. It was blocked as well. Finally he was in the right gallery. A Navajo woman was standing on the chair Bowlegs had used. He pushed his way through the crowd, looking frantically. The boy was nowhere.

Outside, Leaphorn thought. He must have gone out.

Outside the snow was falling heavily. Leaphorn pulled up his collar, gave his eyes a second to adjust, and peered into the darkness. A party of Anglos, loud and drunk, came around the corner toward the door where Leaphorn stood. And something—no more than a glimpse of movement—disappeared in the alleyway between the Shalako house and another of the cut stone houses of old Zuñi. Leaphorn followed at a trot. The alley was cut off from all light—utterly dark. Leaphorn ran down it and stopped at its mouth.

The alley opened into the unlit plaza just above the mission church. A small figure was now moving across it at a slow walk. Leaphorn stopped, peered through the sifting snow. Was it George? At that moment began a series of events which Leaphorn never quite straightened out in his memory. First, from the blackness of another alleyway, there came a wavering, hooting call. The walking figure stopped, turned, shouted something joyful which might have been the Navajo word for "yes!" And Leaphorn stood for some small measure of time, undecided. Whatever time he wasted—two ticks of his watch, or five—became time enough for George Bowlegs to die.

Leaphorn moved just as the boy's figure disappeared into the mouth of darkness. He moved frantically. His boots skidded on the wet snow and he fell heavily on his hands. And when he had scrambled again to his feet, he had lost another two or three seconds. It was then that he heard the sound. Actually, a double sound. Thump-crack. Loud but muffled. He pulled his pistol from his holster as he ran. At the alley opening he stopped, knowing he was too late. He was. George Bowlegs lay on his side just inside the alley. Leaphorn crouched beside him. And then there was another sound. This one a thump, followed by a muffled yell, followed by a scuffling, followed by silence. Leaphorn moved cautiously down the alley, hearing nothing now, seeing nothing. He pulled his flashlight from his coat pocket. The heavy snow ahead of him bore a single set of boot prints and then, at the empty doorway of an abandoned home, a jumble of footprints, and on the snow a plume of feathers. Leaphorn thought he recognized the plume. It was the decoration that had topped the fierce mask of the Salamobia.

Leaphorn flashed his light down the alley. The boot prints stopped here. Whoever had made them must have gone, or been taken, into the empty building. Leaphorn flashed his light through the doorway. There was fresh snow on the earthen floor. Part of it had sifted in through the broken roof and part had come from the feet of men. He flashed the light around, saw nothing, and ran back up the alley to where George Bowlegs lay. He knelt in the snow, his face against the boy's, hoping to feel a breath. The sacred wind of your life I breathe, Leaphorn thought. But the sacred wind was gone.

Snowflakes sifted through the beam of the flashlight, dusting the boy's tangled hair with white, clinging to an eyelash, melting on the still-warm face. Leaphorn gently turned the body and felt through the pockets of the ragged jacket. In the side pocket he found a case knife, a dime, some piñon nuts, a stub of pencil, a folding magnifying glass, the tiny figure of a bear carved from turquoise. He had seen the magnifying glass before, among the odds and ends in the ransacked hogan of Shorty Bowlegs. George must have stopped at the hogan on his way here from the mesa and found it abandoned. He would have seen the hole knocked in its wall, recognized the mark of the death hogan, and known that now he was even more alone than he had been.

It was then that Leaphorn noticed the prayer plume. George must have been carrying it in his hand, holding it out, offering it. And when the bullet struck, the boy had fallen on it. It was beautifully made, its willow butt smoothed and painted, its blue-and-yellow songbird feathers neatly arranged. And tied to the willow with a thong was the cold stone symmetry of a perfect Stone Age lance point. This one unbroken—slender, formed with parallel flaking, a relic from seven or eight thousand years in the past—a perfect offering to the gods.

Leaphorn took off his jacket and spread it carefully over the face of George Bowlegs. From somewhere in the dark across the plaza he heard the brief sound of flutes and chanting as a door opened and closed at one of the Shalako houses. Behind him there was the mutter of conversation. Three people, huddled in their coats against the snow, hurried across the plaza and disappeared in the alley toward the Shalako house he had left. No one seemed to have heard the muffled shot. No one except whoever had seized the killer and pulled him into the empty house. Leaphorn walked back down the alley, keeping against the wall and examining the footprints in the snow. The killer had been running. He wore boots. Size ten, Leaphorn guessed. Perhaps eleven. Apparently he had seen Leaphorn after he had fired the shot. But as he passed this doorway someone, something, had stopped him. Leaphorn studied the trampled snow, but already the tracks were softened and blurred by fresh-falling flakes.

Inside the empty building, Leaphorn took his time. There was no longer any reason to hurry and he meticulously sorted out what the snow tracks had to tell him. There had been three persons wearing moccasins. Leading from the alley into the doorway there were drag marks left by boot heels. The moccasins trailed snow through two empty rooms, left fresh tracks in a third, roofless room, and then departed over a fallen wall onto the street. Here the tracks indicated that two of the men bore a heavy burden. Leaphorn followed them for perhaps fifty yards. The tracks were fading fast and he lost them where they crossed a village street that had been heavily used. He was motivated only by a mild curiosity now. Everything was finished.

Back in the alley, he stared down at the body of George Bowlegs. Snow had whitened Leaphorn's coat and the boy's too-small denims. Leaphorn squatted and picked up the dead boy, his arms under the legs and shoulders. He guessed he was again violating O'Malley's procedures by moving the body. But he would not allow this boy to lie here alone in the icy darkness. He walked out of the alley, cradling the body, surprised at how light it seemed. And then stopped, conscious of a final irony. He was taking Bowlegs home. But where was home for this boy who had hunted heaven?

20

Sunday, December 7, 9 a.m.

INSIDE TED ISAACS'S homemade camper, it was an odd mixture of hot and cold. Outside, the landscape was a white wilderness of blowing snow, and the camper groaned and creaked with the buffeting gusts. The kerosene heater roared but icy air seeped through cracks and crevices, eddying around Leaphorn's snow-covered boots and up the legs of his trousers.

"I can't say I expected any company today," Isaacs said, "but I'm glad you came. When this lets up and they get the roads opened a little, I'm going to that commune and see about Susie. And I wanted to ask—"

"She left yesterday," Leaphorn said. "Halsey kicked her out. She went with me hunting for George Bowlegs Thursday and the last time I saw her she was at the Zuñi police station. That was about noon yesterday. The federal officers were talking to her."

"Where is she now?" Isaacs said. "Is she still there?"

"I don't know," Leaphorn said.

"My God!" Isaacs said. "I hope she isn't out in this snow." He looked at Leaphorn. "She didn't have anyplace to go."

"Yeah," Leaphorn said. "That's what I was telling you a couple of days ago." He didn't try to keep the anger from his voice. "Here, I came to bring you something." He fished the broken lance tip from his pocket and handed it to Isaacs.

"Parallel flaked," Isaacs said. "Where'd you fi . . ." His voice trailed off. He turned abruptly to the file case, jerked open a drawer, and rummaged. When he closed the drawer he had a second piece of flint in his hand.

"George Bowlegs had it," Leaphorn said. "He buried it where he killed a deer over southwest of here. Sort of a fetish offering."

Isaacs was staring at him.

"Does it match?" Leaphorn asked. "It does, doesn't it?"

"I think so." The anthropologist put both pieces on the Formica table, the broken butt he had slipped out of the envelope from the filing cabinet and the tip Bowlegs had buried. Both were of pinkish streaked silicified wood. Isaacs's fingers adjusted them. They fit perfectly.

Isaacs looked up, his face strained. "Man," he said. "If Reynolds finds out that boy got this, he'll kill me." He paused. "But how could he have gotten it? I never let him do any digging out there. Or any sorting, either. He couldn't have . . ."

"Cata gave it to him," Leaphorn said. "Cata stole it out of that box in the back of Reynolds's pickup truck, along with some other artifacts. Like I told you the last time I was out here. And he gave some of it to George."

"But Reynolds said nothing was missing," Isaacs said. He paused, staring at Leaphorn. "Wait a minute," he said. "He couldn't have gotten this out of Reynolds's truck. Reynolds couldn't have had it." He stopped again. Suddenly he looked sick.

"He couldn't have, but he did," Leaphorn said. "Reynolds was salting the site. Isn't that your word for it? Salting? Anyway, he was planting stuff for you to find."

"I don't believe it," Isaacs said. He sat down. His stricken face said he did believe it. His eyes were looking past Leaphorn at the wreckage of everything.

"Ernesto did his little bit of stealing just at the wrong time," Leaphorn said. "It spoiled a lot of work. Reynolds had gotten himself a supply of the sort of flint Folsom Man liked. That was easy enough. And then he prepared his evidence. I'd guess he made some bits and pieces of paralleled-flaked artifacts. He'd have saved the chips and the broken stuff and all. And then he started roughing out some pressure-flaked Folsom-type artifacts from the very same patterned flint. He didn't really need the fine finished product—which you say is hard to counterfeit. All he needed was the unfinished, broken stuff." Leaphorn paused, waiting for Isaacs to say something. Isaacs stared blindly at the wall. "Maybe the Reynolds theory is true," Leaphorn said. "It sounds sensible enough. But I guess Reynolds wasn't willing to wait to prove it. That ridicule must have infuriated him. He wanted to make his critics eat crow."

"Yeah," Isaacs said.

"I don't exactly know how he did it. Probably made himself some sort of tonglike gadget to hold the flint and punch them down to the hard layer where you were finding the stuff. He couldn't do it in advance because he had to place the planted stuff in the right location relative to the genuine artifacts you were finding."

"Yeah," Isaacs said. "He'd check in here a lot about sundown or so and we'd go over what I'd found and where I'd find it. And then while I was cooking supper, he'd take his flashlight and go out there and inspect the dig. That would be when he did it. And that's why everything seemed to fit so perfectly." Isaacs slammed his fist into his palm. "My God! It was perfect. Nobody could have even argued." He looked up at Leaphorn. "And then Cata stole some of the stuff he was planting. So Reynolds killed Cata?"

"Do you think that's enough reason for him to kill the boy?" Leaphorn asked. It was something that puzzled him.

"Of course," Isaacs said. "Hell, yes. Once he found out some of his artifacts were missing and Cata had 'em, I guess he'd have to do it." Leaphorn's doubt seemed to puzzle Isaacs. "Maybe you don't know how serious it would be to salt a site. My God! It's unthinkable. This whole science is based on everybody being beyond suspicion. When this gets out Reynolds will be worse than finished. Nobody will touch him, or his books, or trust anything he ever had anything to do with." Isaacs slumped on his stool, contemplating. "It's like—" he began. But he could think of no suitably hideous analogy.

Like murdering a boy, Leaphorn thought. Worse than that, obviously, in Isaacs's view. Even worse than three murders. In

Isaacs's scale of values, killing was a simple byproduct of the serious offense, something Reynolds would need to do to protect his reputation.

"It's just unthinkable," Isaacs concluded. "How did you figure it out?"

"Remember when you found the parts of those broken points right together? That bothered me. It would seem more natural when you've spent an hour trying to make something and all of a sudden it breaks to lose your temper and throw it half a mile. You don't just politely drop it at your feet. Not if it keeps happening."

"I guess that bothered me a little, too," Isaacs said. "Only I didn't let myself think about it."

"When Reynolds chased Cata away from the truck he must have checked right away and found some of his stuff was gone." Leaphorn fished the unbroken point from his pocket and handed it to Isaacs. "This had been taken, too, and probably other material. It was bad enough Cata having it. But *when* he got it was fatal. What if he got a guilty conscience and brought it back and gave it to you? You'd ask where he got it and when, and then you'd have known Reynolds was putting the stuff in the ground for you to find. Or if the site got to be famous—and Reynolds knew that would happen—then Cata was sure to talk."

"So he went out to kill Cata," Isaacs said. "Well, that makes sense."

"I think he just went out to get the stuff back. I think he rigged himself up a kachina mask so Cata wouldn't recognize him and planned to scare the boy into giving him the stuff. But the boy tried to get away from him."

"If you haven't arrested him yet, he's supposed to be in Tucson this weekend but he's coming back Monday," Isaacs said.

"He wasn't in Tucson. When Reynolds killed Cata he found the boy had just part of the missing stuff with him. The most damaging pieces were missing. And then he learned that Bowlegs had been here with him. So Bowlegs must have this most important fragment." Leaphorn tapped the broken lance tip. "You'd already found the butt and Bowlegs had the tip. So he had to go hunting for George. He had to catch him and make sure he got the tip back before he could kill him. Now Reynolds was covering up a murder, too. He wore the kachina mask when he was prowling around the commune seeing if George was there. If someone saw Reynolds, Reynolds was in trouble. If somebody reported seeing a kachina, you'd think they were crazy, or drunk, or just superstitious."

"But he didn't get George, did he?" Isaacs said suddenly. "He didn't get George?"

"He killed George last night," Leaphorn said. "He almost caught him Friday night, and when George came back to Zuñi, where we could pick him up, he simply had to kill him. I guess he figured that even if we found the artifact we'd have a hell of a time proving anything without George to testify."

"You'll need this, then." Isaacs pushed the broken point toward him. "That'll be some evidence, anyway. I'll bet you can hang him."

"We'll never find him," Leaphorn said. "I guess you'd say there's an old law that takes precedence over the white man's penal code. It says 'Thou shall not profane the Sacred Ways of Zuñi.' " He explained to Isaacs about the footprints in the alley. "I don't think anybody is ever going to know what happened to Reynolds. A few days from now, somebody will come across his pickup wherever he left it and he'll go into the records as a missing person."

He pushed the point back toward Isaacs.

"I don't need these," Leaphorn said. "The FBI has jurisdiction in this business and the FBI isn't interested in Indian superstitions and broken stones and all that. It's got another solution in mind."

Isaacs picked up the points, juggled them in his palm. Then he stared at Leaphorn.

"Do whatever you want to do," Leaphorn said. "I'm finished with all of this. I had just one little job. I screwed it up. I was supposed to find George Bowlegs. He's found, but not soon enough. I told the FBI man what I saw and what I heard last night. But I didn't tell him what I guessed. He didn't ask me, and I didn't tell him."

"What you're saying is that nobody but you and I and Reynolds knows this site was fixed," Isaacs said. "And you're saying Reynolds is dead. . . ."

"And I'm saying that when I leave here, I'm going to the Ramah chapter house and get back to work on a deal involving a down payment on a pickup truck."

Isaacs was still staring at him, wordlessly.

"Come on," Leaphorn said. "Can't you understand what I'm saying?" His voice was angry. He took the lance tip from Isaacs's palm, opened the jaws of the vise on the workbench, and held the flint between them while he screwed the vise closed. Under the pressure, the flint crumbled into fragments. "I'm saying," Leaphorn gritted through his teeth, "just how much do you want fame and fortune and a faculty job? A couple of days ago you wanted it worse than you wanted that girl of yours. How about now? You want it bad enough to lie a little? I'm saying nobody's going to guess this bastard of a dig was salted unless you tell them it was—and then maybe they won't believe you. Who in hell would believe the great Chester Reynolds would salt a dig? You think they'd believe a Navajo cop?" Leaphorn dusted the flint dust from his fingers. "A cop who doesn't have a shred of evidence?"

Joe Leaphorn opened the camper door and stepped out in the snow. "I'm trying to learn more about white men," he said. "You wanted all that worse than you wanted your woman. What else will you give up for it?"

He'd left his carryall on the shoulder of the highway. The motor was still warm and it started easily, the chains making a muted song where the wind had left clear spots on the pavement. He would make a circle up N.M. 53 to Interstate 40 in case Susie was trying to hitchhike, and if she was he'd give her a ride into Gallup and loan her the ten-dollar bill he had in his billfold. And maybe someday he would write a note to O'Malley and let him know who killed Ernesto Cata. But probably not.

LISTENING WOMAN

THE SOUTHWEST WIND picked up turbulence around the San Francisco Peaks, howled across the emptiness of the Moenkopi plateau, and made a thousand strange sounds in windows of the old Hopi villages at Shongopovi and Second Mesa. Two hundred vacant miles to the north and east, it sandblasted the stone sculptures of Monument Valley Navajo Tribal Park and whistled eastward across the maze of canyons on the Utah-Arizona border. Over the arid immensity of the Nokaito Bench it filled the blank blue sky with a rushing sound. At the hogan of Hosteen Tso, at 3:17 P.M., it gusted and eddied, and formed a dust devil, which crossed the wagon track and raced with a swirling roar across Margaret Cigaret's old Dodge pickup truck and past the Tso brush arbor. The three people under the arbor huddled against the driven dust. Tso covered his eyes with his hands and leaned forward in his rocking chair as the sand stung his naked shoulders. Anna Atcitty turned her back to the wind and put her hands over her hair because when this business was finished and she got Margaret Cigaret home again, she would meet the new boy from the Short Mountain Trading Post. And Mrs. Margaret Cigaret, who was also called Blind Eyes, and Listening Woman, threw her shawl over the magic odds and ends arrayed on the arbor table. She held down the edges of the shawl.

"Damn dirty wind," she said. "Dirty son-of-a-bitch."

"It's the Blue Flint boys playing tricks with it," Hosteen Tso said in his old man's voice. He wiped his eyes with the backs of his hands and looked after the whirlwind. "That's what my mother's father told me. The Blue Flint boys make the wind do that when they play one of their games."

Listening Woman put the shawl back around her shoulders, felt carefully among the assortment of bottles, brushes, and fetishes on the table, selected a clear plastic prescription vial, and uncapped it.

"Don't think about that," she said. "Think about what we're doing. Think about how you got this trouble in your body." She poured a measure of yellow corn pollen from the vial and swiveled her blind face toward where the girl was standing. "You pay attention now, daughter-of-my-sister. We're going to bless this man with this pollen. You remember how we do that?"

"You sing the song of the Talking God," Anna Atcitty said. "The one about Born of Water and the Monster Slayer." She was a pretty girl, perhaps sixteen. The legends GANADO HIGH SCHOOL and TIGER PEP were printed across the front of her T-shirt.

Listening Woman sprinkled the pollen carefully over the shoulders of Hosteen Tso, chanting in low, melodic Navajo. From the cheekbone to the scalp, the left side of the old man's face was painted blue-black. Another patch of blackness covered his bony rib cage over his heart. Above that, the colorful curved stick figure of the Rainbow Man arched over Tso's chest from nipple to nipple—painted by Anna Atcitty in the ritual tints of blue, yellow, green, and gray. He held his wiry body straight in the chair, his face stiff with sickness, patience, and suppressed pain. Listening Woman's chant rose abruptly in volume. "In beauty it is finished," she sang. "In beauty it is finished."

"Okay," she said. "Now I will go and listen for the earth to tell me what makes you sick." She felt carefully across the plank table, collecting the fetishes and amulets of her profession, and then found her walking cane. She was a large woman, handsome once, dressed in the traditional voluminous skirt and blue velvet blouse of the People. She put the last of the vials in her black plastic purse, snapped it shut, and turned her sightless eyes toward Tso. "Think about it now, before I go. When you dream, you dream of your son who is dead and of that place you call the painted cave? You don't have any witch in that dream?" She paused, giving Tso a chance to answer.

"No," he said. "No witches."

"No dogs? No wolves? Nothing about Navajo Wolves?"

"Nothing about witches," Tso said. "I dream about the cave."

"You been with the whores over at Flagstaff? You been laying with any kinfolks?"

"Too old," Tso said. He smiled slightly.

"Been burning any wood struck by lightning?"

"No."

Listening Woman stood, face stern, staring past him with her blind eyes. "Listen, Old Man," she said, "I think you better tell me more about how these sand paintings got messed up. If you're worried about people knowing about it, Anna here can go away behind the hogan. Then nobody knows but you and me. And I don't tell secrets."

Hosteen Tso smiled, very slightly. "Now nobody knows but me," he said, "and I don't tell secrets either."

"Maybe it will help tell why you're sick," Listening Woman said. "It sounds like witchery to me. Sand paintings getting messed up. If there was more than one sand painting at a time, then that would be doing the ceremonial wrong. That would be turning the blessing around. That would be witch business. If you been fooling around with the Navajo Wolves, then you're going to need a different kind of cure."

Tso's face was stubborn now. "Understand this, woman. A long time ago I made a promise. Some things I can't talk about."

The silence stretched, Listening Woman looking at whatever vision the blind see inside their skulls, Hosteen Tso staring out across the mesa, and Anna Atcitty, her face expressionless, waiting for the outcome of this contest.

"I forgot to tell you," Tso said. "On the same day the sand paintings got ruined, I killed a frog."

Listening Woman looked startled. "How?" she asked. In the complex Navajo metaphysics, the concept that would evolve into frogs was one of the Holy People. To kill the animals or insects which represented such holy thoughts violated a very basic taboo and was known to bring on crippling diseases.

"I was climbing among the rocks," Tso said. "A boulder fell down and crushed the frog."

"Before the sand paintings were messed up? Or after?"

"After," Tso said. He paused. "I talk no more about the sand paintings. I've told all that I can tell. The promise was to my father, and to the father of my father. If I have a ghost sickness, it would be a sickness from my great-grandfather's ghost, because I was where his ghost might be. I can tell you no more."

Listening Woman's expression was grim. "Why you want to waste your money, Old Man?" she asked. "You get me to come all the way out here to find out what kind of a cure you need. Now you won't tell me what I need to know."

Tso sat motionless, looking straight ahead.

Listening Woman waited, frowning.

"God damn it!" she said. "Some things I got to know. You think you been around some witches. Just being around them skinwalkers can make you sick. I got to know more about it."

Tso said nothing.

"How many witches?"

"It was dark," Tso said. "Maybe two."

"Did they do anything to you? Blow anything at you? Throw corpse powder on you? Anything like that?"

"No," Tso said.

"Why not?" Mrs. Cigaret asked. "Are you a Navajo Wolf yourself? You one of them witches?"

Tso laughed. It was a nervous sound. He glanced at Anna Atcitty—a look which asked help.

"I'm no skinwalker," he said.

"It was dark," said Listening Woman, almost mockingly. "But you said it was daytime. Were you in the witches' den?"

Tso's embarrassment turned to anger.

"Woman," he said, "I told you I couldn't talk about where it was. I made a promise. We will talk about that no more."

"Big secret," Mrs. Cigaret said. Her tone was sarcastic.

"Yes," Tso said. "A secret."

She made an impatient gesture. "Well, hell," she said. "You want to waste your money, no use me wasting my time.

If I don't hear anything, or if I get it wrong, it's because you wouldn't tell me enough to know anything. Now Anna will take me to where I can hear the voice-in-the-earth. Don't mess with the painting on your chest. When I get back I will try to tell you what sing you need."

"Wait," Tso said. He hesitated. "One more thing. Do you know how to send a letter to somebody who went on the Jesus Road?"

Listening Woman frowned. "You mean moved off the Big Reservation? Ask Old Man McGinnis. He'll send it for you."

"I asked. McGinnis didn't know how," Tso said. "He said you had to write down on it the place it goes to."

Listening Woman laughed. "Sure," she said. "The address. Like Gallup, or Flagstaff, or wherever they live, and the name of the street they live on. Things like that. Who do you want to write to?"

"My grandson," Tso said. "I have to get him to come. But all I know is he went with the Jesus People."

"I don't know how you're going to find him," Listening Woman said. She found her cane. "Don't worry about it. Somebody else can take care of getting a singer for you and all that."

"But there's something I have to tell him," Hosteen Tso said. "I have to tell him something before I die. I have to."

"I don't know," Listening Woman said. She turned away from Tso and tapped the brush arbor pole with her cane, getting her direction. "Come on, Anna. Take me up to that place where I can listen."

Listening Woman felt the coolness of the cliff before its shadow touched her face. She had Anna lead her to a place where erosion had formed a sand-floored cul-de-sac. Then she sent the girl away to await her call. Anna was a good student in some ways, and a bad one in others. But when she got over being crazy about boys, she would be an effective Listener. This niece of Listening Woman's had the rare gift of hearing the voices in the wind and getting the visions that came out of the earth. It was something that ran in the family—a gift of divining the cause of illness. Her mother's uncle had been a Hand-Trembler famous throughout the Short Mountain territory for diagnosing lightning sickness. Listening Woman herself—she knew—was widely known up and down this corner of the Big Reservation. And someday Anna would be famous too.

Listening Woman settled herself on the sand, arranged her skirts around her, and leaned her forehead against the stone. It was cool, and rough. At first she found herself thinking about what Old Man Tso had told her, trying to diagnose his illness from that. There was something about Tso that troubled her and made her very sad. Then she cleared her mind of all this and thought only of the early-evening sky and the light of a single star. She made the star grow larger in her mind, remembering how it had looked before her blindness came.

An eddy of wind whistled through the piñons at the mouth of this pocket-in-the-cliff. It stirred the skirt of Listening Woman, uncovering a blue tennis shoe. But now her breathing was deep and regular. The shadow of the cliff moved inch by inch across the sandy space. Listening Woman moaned, moaned again, muttered something unintelligible and lapsed into silence.

From somewhere out of sight down the slope, a half-dozen ravens squawked into startled flight. The wind rose again, and fell. A lizard emerged from a crevice in the cliff, turned its cold, unblinking eyes on the woman, and then scurried to its late-afternoon hunting stand under a pile of tumbleweeds. A sound partly obscured by wind and distance reached the sandy place. A woman screaming. It rose and fell, sobbing. Then it stopped. The lizard caught a horsefly. Listening Woman breathed on.

The shadow of the cliff had moved fifty yards down the slope when Listening Woman pushed herself stiffly from the sand and got to her feet. She stood a moment with her head down and both hands pressed to her face—still half immersed in the strangeness of the trance. It was as if she had gone into the rock, and through it into the Black World at the very beginning—when there were only Holy People and the things that would become the Navajos were only mist. Finally she had heard the voice, and found herself in the Fourth World. She had looked down through the emergence hole, peering at Hosteen Tso in what must have been Tso's painted cave. An old man had rocked on a rocking chair on its floor, braiding his hair with string. At first it was Tso, but when the man looked up at her she had seen the face was dead. Blackness was swelling up around the rocking chair.

Listening Woman rubbed her knuckles against her eyes, and shook her head, and called for Anna. She knew what the diagnosis would have to be. Hosteen Tso would need a Mountain Way Chant and a Black Rain Chant. There had been a witch in the painted cave, and Tso had been there, and had been infected with some sort of ghost sickness. That meant he should find a singer who knew how to do the Mountain Way and one to sing the Black Rain. She knew that. But she also thought that it would be too late. She shook her head again.

"Girl," she called. "I'm ready now."

What would she tell Tso? With the sensitized hearing of the blind, she listened for Anna Atcitty's footsteps. And heard nothing but the breeze.

"Girl," she shouted. "Girl!" Still hearing nothing, she fumbled against the cliff, and found her cane. She felt her way carefully back to the pathway toward the hogan. Should she tell Tso of the darkness she had seen all around as the voice spoke to her? Should she tell him of the crying of ghosts she had heard in the stone? Should she tell him he was dying?

Listening Woman's feet found the pathway. She called again for Anna, then shouted for Old Man Tso to come and lead her. Waiting, she heard nothing but the moving air. She tapped her way cautiously down the sheep trail, muttering angrily. The tip of her cane warned her away from a cactus, guided her around a depression and past an outcrop of sandstone. It tapped against a hummock of dead grass and contacted the little finger of the outstretched left hand of Anna Atcitty. The hand lay palm up, and the wind had drifted a little sand against it, and even to Listening Woman's sensitive touch, it felt like nothing more than another stick. And so she tapped her way, still calling and muttering, down the path toward the place where the body of Hosteen Tso lay sprawled beside his overturned rocking chair—the Rainbow Man still arched across his chest.

2

THE SPEAKER ON THE RADIO crackled and growled and said, "Tuba City."

"Unit Nine," Joe Leaphorn said. "You got anything for me?"

"Just a minute, Joe." The radio's voice was pleasantly feminine.

The young man sitting on the passenger side of the Navajo police carryall was staring out the window toward the sunset. The afterglow outlined the rough shape of the San Francisco Peaks on the horizon, and turned a lacy brushwork of high clouds luminescent rose, and reflected down on the desert below and onto the face of the man. It was a flat Mongolian face, with tiny lines around the eyes giving it a sardonic cast. He was wearing a black felt Stetson, a denim jacket, and a rodeo-style shirt. On his left wrist was a $12.95 Timex watch held by a heavy sand-cast silver watchband, and his left wrist was fastened to his right one with a pair of standard-issue police handcuffs. He glanced at Leaphorn, caught his eye, and nodded toward the sunset.

"Yeah," Leaphorn said. "I noticed it."

The radio crackled again. "Two or three things," it said. "The captain asked if you got the Begay boy. He said if you got him, don't let him get away again."

"Yes, Ma'am," the young man said. "Tell the captain the Begay boy is in custody."

"I got him," Leaphorn said.

"Tell her I want the cell with the window this time," the young man said.

"Begay says he wants the cell with the window," Leaphorn said.

"And the waterbed," Begay said.

"And the captain wants to talk to you when you get in," the radio said.

"What about?"

"He didn't say."

"But I'll bet you know."

The radio speaker rattled with laughter. "Well," it said. "Window Rock called and asked the captain why you weren't over there helping out with the Boy Scouts. When will you be in?"

"We're coming down on Navajo Route 1 west of Tsegi," Leaphorn said. "Be in Tuba City in maybe an hour." He flicked off the transmit button.

"What's this Boy Scout business?" Begay asked.

Leaphorn groaned. "Window Rock got the bright idea of inviting the Boy Scouts of America to have some sort of regional encampment at Canyon de Chelly. Kids swarming in from all over the West. And of course they tell Law and Order Division to make sure nobody gets lost or falls off a cliff or anything."

"Well," said Begay. "That's what we're paying you for."

Far to the left, perhaps ten miles up the dark Klethla Valley, a pinpoint of light was sliding along Route 1 toward them. Begay stopped admiring the sunset and watched the light. He whistled between his teeth. "Here comes a fast Indian."

"Yeah," Leaphorn said. He started the carryall rolling down the slope toward the highway and snapped off the headlights.

"That's sneaky," Begay said.

"Saves the battery," Leaphorn said.

"Pretty sneaky the way you got me, too," Begay said. There was no rancor in his words. "Parkin' over the hill and walkin' up to the hogan like that, so nobody figured you was a cop."

"Yeah," Leaphorn said.

"How'd you know I'd be there? You find out the Endischees was my people?"

"That's right," Leaphorn said.

"And you found out there was a Kinaalda for the Endischee girl?"

"Yeah," Leaphorn said. "So maybe you'd come to that."

Begay laughed. "And even if I didn't, it beat hell out of running all over looking for me." He glanced at Leaphorn. "You learn that in college?"

"Yeah," Leaphorn said. "We had a course on how to catch Begays."

The carryall jolted over a cattle guard and down the steep incline of the borrow ditch bank. Leaphorn parked on the shoulder and cut the ignition. It was almost night now—the afterglow dying on the western horizon and Venus hanging bright halfway up the sky. The heat had left with the light and now the thin high-altitude air was touched with coolness. A breeze stirred through the windows, carrying the faint sound of insects and the call of a hunting nighthawk. It died away, and when it came again it carried the high whine of engine and tires—still distant.

"Son-of-a-bitch is moving," Begay said. "Listen to that."

Leaphorn listened.

"Hundred miles an hour," Begay said. He chuckled. "He's going to tell you his speedometer needs fixing."

The headlights topped the hill, dipped downward, and then raced up the slope behind them. Leaphorn started his engine and flicked on his headlights, and then the red warning blinker atop the car. For a moment there was no change in the accelerating whine. Then abruptly the pitch changed, a brief squealing sound of rubber on pavement, and the roar of a car gearing down. It pulled off on the shoulder and stopped some fifty feet behind the carryall. Leaphorn picked his clipboard off the dash and stepped out.

At first he could see nothing through the blinding glare of the headlights. Then he made out the circled Mercedes trademark on the hood, and behind the ornament, the windshield. Every two seconds, the beam of his revolving warning blinker flashed across it. Leaphorn walked down the gravel toward the car, irritated by the rudeness of the high-beam lights. In the flashing red illumination he saw the face of the driver, staring at him through round gold-rimmed glasses. And behind the man, in the backseat, another face, unusually large and oddly shaped.

The driver leaned out the window. "Officer," he shouted. "Your car's rolling backward."

The driver was grinning a broad, delighted, anticipatory grin outlined in red by the blinker light. And behind the grinning man, the eyes in the narrow face still stared—dim but somehow avid—from the backseat.

Leaphorn spun and, blinded by glare, peered toward his carryall. His mind told him that he had set the hand brake and his eyes registered that the parked car was not rolling toward him. And then there was the voice of Begay screaming a warning. Leaphorn made a desperate, instinctive lunge for the ditch, hearing the squalling roar of the Mercedes accelerating, and then the thumping, oddly painless sound of the front fender striking his leg and spinning his already flying body into the roadside weeds.

A moment later he was trying to get up. The Mercedes had disappeared down the highway, trailing the diminishing scream of rapid acceleration, and Begay was beside him, helping him up.

"Watch the leg," Leaphorn said. "Let me see how it is."

It was numb, but it bore his weight. What pain he had was mostly in his hands, which had broken his fall on the weeds and dirt of the ditch bank, and his cheek—which somehow had picked up a long, but shallow, cut. It burned.

"Son-of-a-bitch tried to run you over," Begay said. "How about that?"

Leaphorn limped to the carryall, slid under the wheel, and flicked on the radio with one bleeding hand and the ignition with the other. By the time he had arranged for a roadblock at Red Lake, the speedometer needle had passed 90.

"Always wanted a ride like this," Begay was shouting over the sound of the siren. "The tribe got a liability policy in case I get hurt?"

"Just burial insurance," Leaphorn said.

"You're never going to catch him," Begay said. "You get a look at that car? That was a rich man's car."

"You get a look at the license? Or at that guy in the backseat?"

"It was a dog," Begay said. "Great big rough-looking dog. I didn't think about the license."

The radio cleared its throat. It was Tomas Charley reporting he was set up in a half block at the Red Lake intersection. Charley asked, in precise Navajo, whether to figure the man in the gray car had a gun and how to handle it.

"Play it like he's dangerous," Leaphorn said. "The bastard tried to run over me. Use the shotgun and if he's not slowing for you, shoot for the tires. Don't get hurt."

Charley said he didn't intend to and signed off.

"He might have a gun, come to think of it," Begay said. He held his cuffed wrists in front of him. "You oughta take this off in case you need help."

Leaphorn glanced at him, fished in his pocket for a key ring and tossed it on the seat. "It's the little shiny one."

Begay unlocked the cuffs and put them in the glove compartment.

"Why the hell don't you stop stealing sheep?" Leaphorn asked. He didn't want to remember the Mercedes roaring toward him.

Begay rubbed his wrists. "They're just white man's sheep. They don't hardly miss 'em."

"And slipping off from jail. Do that again and it's your ass!"

Begay shrugged. "Stop to think about it, though," he said. "And about the worst they can do to you for getting out of jail is get you back in again."

"This is three times," Leaphorn said. The patrol car skidded around a flat turn, swayed, and straightened. Leaphorn jammed down on the accelerator.

"That bird sure didn't want a ticket," Begay said. He glanced at Leaphorn, grinning. "Either that, or he just likes running over cops. I believe a man could learn to enjoy that."

They covered the last twenty miles to the Red Lake intersection in just under thirteen minutes and slid to a gravel-spraying stop on the shoulder beside Charley's patrol car.

"What happened?" Leaphorn shouted. "Did he get past you?"

"Never got here," Charley said. He was a stocky man wearing a corporal's stripes on the sleeves of his uniform shirt. He raised his eyebrows. "Ain't no place to turn off," he said. "It's fifty-something miles back up there to the Kayenta turnoff—"

"He was past that when I started chasing him," Leaphorn interrupted. "He must have pulled it off somewhere."

Begay laughed. "That dog in the back. Maybe that was a Navajo Wolf."

Leaphorn didn't say anything. He was spinning the car across the highway in a pursuit turn.

"Them witches, they can fly, you know," Begay said. "Reckon they could carry along a big car like that?"

It took more than half an hour to find where the Mercedes had left the highway. It had pulled off the north shoulder on the upslope of a hill—leaving the roadbed and plowing through a thin growth of creosote bush. Leaphorn followed the track with his flashlight in one hand and his .38 in the other. Begay and Charley trotted along behind him—Begay carrying Leaphorn's 30-30. About fifty yards off the highway, the car had bottomed on an outcrop of sandstone. After that, its path was blotched with oil spurting from a broken pan.

"Hell of a way to treat a car," Begay said.

They found it thirty yards away, rolled into a shallow arroyo out of sight from the highway. Leaphorn studied it a moment in the beam of his flashlight. He walked up to it cautiously. The driver's door was open. So was the trunk. The front seat was empty. So was the backseat. The front floorboards were littered with the odds and ends of a long trip—gum wrappers, paper cups, the wrapper from a Lotaburger. Leaphorn picked it up and sniffed it. It smelled of onions and fried meat. He dropped it. The nearest Lotaburger stand he could remember was at Farmington—about 175 miles east in New Mexico. The safety inspection sticker inside the windshield had been issued by the District of Columbia. It bore the name of Frederick Lynch, and a Silver Spring, Maryland, address. Leaphorn jotted it in his notebook. The car, he noticed, smelled of dog urine.

"He didn't leave nothing much back here," Charley said. "But here's a muzzle for a dog. A big one."

"I guess he went for a walk," Leaphorn said. "He's got a lot of room for that."

"Thirty miles to a drink of water," Charley said. "If you know where to find it."

"Begay," Leaphorn said. "Take a look in back and give me the license number."

As he said it, it occurred to Leaphorn that his bruised leg, no longer numb, was aching. It also occurred to him that he hadn't seen Begay since after they'd found the car. Leaphorn scrambled out of the front seat and made a rapid survey of the landscape with the flashlight. There was Corporal Charley, still inspecting the back seat, and there was Leaphorn's 30-30 leaning against the trunk of the Mercedes, with Leaphorn's key ring hung on the barrel.

Leaphorn cupped his hands and shouted into the darkness: "Begay, you dirty bastard!" Begay was out there, but he would be laughing too hard to answer.

THE FILE CLERK in the Tuba City subagency of the Navajo Tribal Police was slightly plump and extremely pretty. She deposited a yellow manila folder and three brown accordion files on the captain's desk, flashed Leaphorn a smile, and departed with a swish of skirt.

"You already owe me one favor," Captain Largo said. He picked up the yellow folder and peered into it.

"This will make two, then," Leaphorn said.

"If I do it, it will," Largo said. "I may not be that dumb."

"You'll do it," Leaphorn said.

Largo ignored him. "Here we have a little business that just came in today," Largo said from behind the folder. "A discreet inquiry is needed into the welfare of a woman named Theodora Adams, who is believed to be at Short Mountain Trading Post. Somebody in the office of the Chairman of the Tribal Council would appreciate it if we'd do a little quiet checking so he can pass on the word that all is well."

Leaphorn frowned. "At Short Mountain? What would anyone—"

Largo interrupted him. "There's an anthropological dig out there. Maybe she's friendly with one of the diggers. Who knows? All I know is her daddy is a doctor in the Public Health Service and I guess he called somebody in the Bureau of Indian Affairs, and the BIA called somebody in . . ."

"Okay," Leaphorn said. "She's out in Indian country and daddy's worried and would we look out after her—right?"

"But discreetly," Largo said. "That would save me a little work, if you'd take care of that. But it won't look like much of an excuse to ask Window Rock to let you off guarding those Boy Scouts." Largo handed Leaphorn the manila folder and pulled the accordion files in front of him. "Maybe there's an excuse in these," he said. "You can take your pick."

"I'll take an easy one," Leaphorn said.

"Here we have a little heroin stashed in the frame of a junk car over near the Keet Seel ruins," said Largo as he peered into one of the files. He closed the folder. "Had a tip on it and staked it out, but nobody ever showed up. That was last winter."

"Never any arrests?"

"Nope." Largo had pulled a bundle of papers and two tape cassettes out of another folder. "Here's the Tso-Atcitty killing," he said. "You remember that one? It was last spring."

"Yeah," Leaphorn said. "I meant to ask you about that one. Heard anything new?"

"Nada," Largo said. "Nothing. Not even any sensible gossip. Little bit of witch talk now and then. The kind of talk something like that stirs up. Not a damn thing to go on."

They sat and thought about it.

"You got any ideas?" Leaphorn asked.

Largo thought about it some more. "No sense to it," he said finally.

Leaphorn said nothing. There had to be sense to it. A reason. It had to fit some pattern of cause and effect. Leaphorn's sense of order insisted on this. And if the cause happened to be insane by normal human terms, Leaphorn's intellect would then hunt for harmony in the kaleidoscopic reality of insanity.

"You think the FBI missed something?" Leaphorn asked. "They screw it up?"

"They usually do," Largo said. "Whether they did or not, it's been long enough so we really ought to be checking around on it again." He stared at Leaphorn. "You any better at that than at bringing in prisoners?"

Leaphorn ignored the jibe. "Okay," he said. "You tell Window Rock you want me to work on the Atcitty case, and I'll run over to Short Mountain and check on the Adams woman too. And I'll owe *you* a favor."

"Two favors," Largo said.

"What's the other one?"

Largo had put on a pair of horn-rimmed bifocals and was thumbing his way owlishly through the Atcitty report. "I didn't hoorah you for letting that Begay boy get away. That's the first one." He glanced at Leaphorn. "But I'm not so damn sure this second one's any favor. Dreaming up reasons to borrow you from Window Rock so you can go chasing after that feller that tried to run you down. That's not so damned smart—getting mixed up in your own thing. We'll find that feller for you."

Leaphorn said nothing. Somewhere back in the subagency building there was a sudden metallic clamor—a jail inmate rattling something against the bars. Outside the west-facing windows of Largo's office an old green pickup rolled down the asphalt road into Tuba City, trailing a thin haze of blue smoke. Largo sighed and began sorting the Atcitty papers and tapes back into the file.

"Herding Boy Scouts is not so bad," Largo said. "Broken leg or so. Few snakebites. One or two of them lost." He glanced up at Leaphorn, frowning. "You got nothing much to go on, looking for that guy, anyway. You don't even know what he looks like. Gold-rim glasses. Hell, I'm about the only one in this building that doesn't wear 'em. And all you really know is that they were wire rims. Just seeing 'em with that red blinker reflecting off of 'em—that would distort the color."

"You're right," Leaphorn said.

"I'm right, but you're going to go ahead on with it," Largo said. "If I can find an excuse for you."

He tapped the remaining file with a blunt fingertip, changing the subject. "And here's one that's always popular—the vanishing helicopter," Largo said. "The feds love that one. Every month we need to turn in a report telling 'em we haven't found it but we haven't forgotten it. This time we've got a new sighting report to look into."

Leaphorn frowned. "A new one? Isn't it getting kinda late for that?"

Largo grinned. "Oh, I don't know," he said. "What's a few months? Let's see—it was December when we were running our asses off in the snow up and down the canyons, looking for it. So now it's August, and somebody gets around to coming into Short Mountain and mentioning he's seen the damn thing." Largo shrugged. "Nine months? That's about right for a Short Mountain Navajo."

Leaphorn laughed. Short Mountain Navajos had a long-standing reputation among their fellow Dinee for being uncooperative, slow, cantankerous, witch-ridden, and generally backward.

"Three kinds of time." Largo was still grinning. "On time, and Navajo time, and Short Mountain Navajo time." The grin disappeared. "Mostly Bitter Water Dinee, and Salts, and Many Goats people live out there," he said.

It wasn't exactly an explanation. It was absolution from this criticism of the fifty-seven other Navajo clans, including the Slow Talking Dinee. The Slow Talking Dinee was Captain Howard Largo's "born-to" clan. Leaphorn was also a member of the Slow Talking People. That made him and Largo something akin to brothers in the Navajo Way, and explained why Leaphorn could ask Largo for a favor, and why Largo could hardly refuse to grant it.

"Funny people," Leaphorn agreed.

"Lots of Paiutes live back in there," Largo added. "Lots of marrying back and forth." Largo's face had resumed its usual glumness. "Even a lot of marrying with the Utes."

Through the dusty window of Largo's office Leaphorn had been watching a thunderhead building over Tuba Mesa. Now it produced a distant rumble of thunder, as if the Holy People themselves were protesting this mixing of the blood of the Dinee with their ancient enemies.

"Anyway, the one who says she saw it wasn't really nine months late," Largo said. "She told a veterinarian out there looking at her sheep about it in June." Largo paused and peered into the folder. ". . . And the vet told the feller then that drives the school bus out there, and he told Shorty McGinnis about it back in July. And about three days ago, Tomas Charley was out there and McGinnis told *him.*" Largo paused, and looked up at Leaphorn through his bifocals. "You know McGinnis?"

Leaphorn laughed. "From way back when I was new and working out of here. He was sort of a one-man radar station/

listening post/gossip collector. I remember I used to think it wouldn't be too hard to catch him doing something worth about ten years in stir. He still have that place up for sale?"

"That place has been for sale for forty years," Largo said. "If somebody offered to buy it, it'd scare McGinnis to death."

"That sighting report," Leaphorn said. "Anything helpful?"

"Naw," Largo said. "She was driving her sheep out of a gully, and just as she came out of it, the copter came over just a few feet off the ground." Largo waved his hand impatiently at the file. "It's all in there. Scared the hell out of her. Her horse threw her and ran off and it scattered the sheep. Charley went to talk to her day before yesterday. Said she was still pissed off about it."

"Was it the right copter?"

Largo shrugged. "Blue and yellow or black and yellow. She remembered that. And pretty big. And noisy. Maybe it was, and maybe it wasn't."

"Was it the right day?"

"Seemed to be," Largo said. "She was bringing in the sheep because she was taking her husband and the rest of the bunch to a Yeibachi over at Spider Rock the next day. Charley checked on it and the ceremonial was the day after the Santa Fe robbery. So that's the right day."

"What time?"

"That's about right too. Just getting dark, she said."

They thought about it. Outside there was thunder again.

"Think we could have missed it?" Largo asked.

"We could have," Leaphorn said. "You could hide Kansas City out there. But I don't think we did."

"I don't either," Largo said. "You'd have to land it someplace where you can get someplace else from. Like near a road."

"Exactly," Leaphorn said.

"And if they left it near a road, somebody would have come across it by now." Largo extracted a pack of Winstons from his shirt pocket, offered them to Leaphorn, and then lit one for himself. "It's funny, though," he said.

"Yes," Leaphorn said. The strangest part of it all, he

thought, was how well the entire plan had stuck together, how well it had been coordinated, how well it had worked. You didn't expect such meticulous planning from a militant political group—and the Buffalo Society was as militant as they get. It had split off from the American Indian Movement after the AIM's seizure of Wounded Knee had fizzled away into nothing—accusing the movement's leaders of being gutless. It had mailed out a formal declaration of war against the whites. It had pulled a series of bombings, and two kidnappings that Leaphorn could remember, and finally this affair at Santa Fe. There, a Wells Fargo armored truck leaving the First National Bank of Santa Fe had been detoured down one of Santa Fe's narrow old streets by a man wearing a city policeman's uniform. Other Society members had simultaneously congealed downtown traffic to a motionless standstill by artfully placed detour signs. There had been a brief fight at the truck and a Society member had been critically wounded and left behind. But the gang had blasted off the truck door and escaped with almost $500,000. The copter had been reserved at the Santa Fe airport for a charter flight. It had taken off with a single passenger about the same moment the Wells Fargo truck had left the bank. It hadn't been missed, in the excitement, until the pilot's wife had called the charter company late that night worrying about her husband. Checking back the next day, police learned it had been seen taking off from the Sangre de Cristo Mountain foothills just east of Santa Fe about an hour after the robbery. It was seen, and definitely identified, a little later by a pilot approaching the Los Alamos airport. It had been headed almost due west, flying low. It had been seen—and almost definitely identified—about sundown by a Gas Company of New Mexico pipeline monitoring crew working northeast of Farmington. Again it was flying low and fast, and still heading west. A copter, this time identified only as black and yellow and flying low, had been reported by the driver of a Greyhound bus crossing U.S. 666 northwest of Shiprock. These reports had been coupled with the fact that the missing copter's full-tank range was only enough to fly it from Santa Fe to less than halfway across the Navajo Reservation and had caused the Navajo Police a full week of hard and fruitless searching.

The FBI report on this affair showed the copter had been reserved by telephone the previous day in the name of the local engineering company which often chartered it, that a passenger had emerged from a blue Ford sedan and boarded the copter without anyone getting much of a look at him, and that the Ford had thereupon driven away. A check disclosed that the engineering company had not reserved the copter and there was absolutely nothing else to go on. The FBI noted that while it had no doubt the copter had been used to fly away seven large sacks of bulky cash, the connection was purely circumstantial. Again, the planning had been perfect.

"Oh, well," Largo said. He removed his glasses, frowned at them, ran his tongue over the lenses, polished them quickly with his handkerchief, and put them on again. He lowered his chin and peered at Leaphorn through the upper half of the bifocals. "Here they are," he said, sliding the accordion files and the folder across the desktop. "Old heroin case, old homicide, old missing aircraft, and new 'herd the tourist' job."

"Thanks," Leaphorn said.

"For what?" Largo asked. "Getting you into trouble? *You* know what I think, Joe? This isn't smart at all, this getting personal about this guy. That ain't good business in our line of work. Whyn't you forget it and go on over to Window Rock and help take care of the Boy Scouts? We'll catch this fellow for you."

"You're right," Leaphorn said. He tried to think of a way to explain to Largo what he felt. Would Largo understand if Leaphorn described how the man had grinned as he tried to kill him? Probably not, Leaphorn thought, because he didn't understand it himself.

"I'm right," Largo said, "but you're going after him anyway?"

Leaphorn got up and walked to the window. The thunderhead was drifting eastward, trailing rain which didn't quite reach the thirsty ground. The huge old cottonwoods that lined Tuba City's single paved street looked dusty and wilted.

"It's not just getting even with him," Leaphorn said to the window. "I think a guy that laughs when he tries to kill someone is dangerous. That's a lot of it."

Largo nodded. "And a lot of it is that it doesn't make sense to you. I know you, Joe. You've got to have everything sorted out so it's natural. You got to know how come that guy left his car there and headed north on foot." Largo smiled and made a huge gesture of dismissal. "Hell, man. He just got scared and ran for it. And he didn't show up today hitchhiking because he got lost out there. Another day he'll come wandering up to some hogan begging for water."

"Maybe," Leaphorn said. "But nobody's seen him. And his tracks didn't wander. They headed due north—like he knew where he was going."

"Maybe he did," Largo said. "Figure it this way. This tourist . . . What's the name of the Mercedes owner? This Frederick Lynch stops at a bar in Farmington, and one of those Short Mountain boys wanders out of the same bar, sees his car parked there, and drives it off. When you stopped him, he just dumped the car and headed home on foot."

"That's probably right," Leaphorn said.

On the way out, Leaphorn met the plump clerk coming in. She had two reports relayed by the Arizona State Police from Washington and Silver Spring, Maryland. Frederick Lynch lived at the address indicated on his car registration form, and was not known to Silver Spring police. The only item on the record was a complaint that he kept vicious dogs. He was not now at home and was last reported seen by a neighbor seven days earlier. The other report was a negative reply from the stolen-car register. If the Lynch Mercedes had been stolen in Maryland, New Mexico, or anywhere else, the crime had not yet been reported.

THERE IS NO WAY that one man, or one thousand men, can search effectively the wilderness of stony erosion which sprawls along the Utah-Arizona border south of the Rainbow Plateau. Lieutenant Joe Leaphorn didn't try. Instead he found Corporal Emerson Bisti. Corporal Bisti had been born at Kaibito Wash and spent his boyhood with his mother's herds in the same country. Since the Korean War, he'd patrolled this same desert as a Navajo policeman. He went over Leaphorn's map carefully, marking in all the places where water could be found. There weren't many. Then Bisti went over the map again and checked off those that dried up after the spring run-off, or that held water only a few weeks after rainstorms. That left only eleven. Two were at trading posts—Navajo Springs and Short Mountain. One was at Tsai Skizzi Rock and one was a well drilled by the Tribal Council to supply the Zilnez Chapter House. A stranger couldn't approach any of these places without being noticed, and Captain Largo's patrolmen had checked them all.

By late afternoon, Leaphorn had pared the remaining seven down to four. At the first three watering places he had found a maze of tracks—sheep, horses, humans, dogs, coyotes, and the prints of the menagerie of small mammals and reptiles that teem in the most barren deserts. The tracks of the man who had abandoned the Mercedes were not among them. Nor were any of the dog tracks large enough to match those Leaphorn had found at the abandoned Mercedes.

Even with Bisti's markings on his map, Leaphorn almost missed the next watering place. The first three had been easy enough to locate—marked either by the animal trails that radiated from them or by the cottonwoods they sustained in a landscape otherwise too arid for greenery. But Bisti's tiny "x" put the fourth one in a trackless world of red Chinle sandstone.

The long-abandoned wagon track that led toward this spring had been easy to find. Leaphorn had jolted down it the seven point eight miles specified by Bisti's instructions and parked at a great outcropping of black shale as advised. Then he had walked two miles northeast by east toward the red butte which Bisti said overlooked the water hole. He found himself surrounded by carved rock without a trace of water or a hint of vegetation. He had searched in widening circles, climbing sandstone walls, skirting sandstone escarpments, engulfed in a landscape where the only colors were shades of pink and red. Finally he had scrambled to the top of a flat-topped pinnacle and perched there. He scanned the surroundings below him with his binoculars—looking for a trace of green, which would declare water, or for something that would suggest the geological fault that would produce a spring. Finding nothing helpful, he waited. Bisti had been a boy in this country. He would not be mistaken about water. Surface water in this desert would be a magnet for life. In time, nature would reveal itself. Leaphorn would wait and think. He was good at both.

The thunderhead that promised a shower to Tuba Mesa in the morning had drifted eastward over the Painted Desert and evaporated—the promise unfulfilled. Now another, taller thunderhead had climbed the sky to the north—over the slopes of Navajo Mountain in Utah. The color under it was blue-black, suggesting that on one small quadrant of mountainside the blessed rain was falling. Far to the southeast, blue and dim with distance, another towering cloud had risen over the Chuskas on the Arizona–New Mexico border. There were other promising clouds to the south, drifting over the Hopi Reservation. The Hopis had held a rain dance Sunday, calling on the clouds—their ancestors—to restore the water blessing to the land. Perhaps the kachinas had listened to their Hopi children. Perhaps not. It was not a Navajo concept, this idea of adjusting nature to human needs. The Navajo adjusted himself to remain in harmony with the universe. When nature withheld the rain, the Navajo sought the pattern of this phenomenon—as he sought the pattern of all things—to find its beauty and live in harmony with it.

Now Leaphorn sought some pattern in the conduct of the man who had tried to kill a policeman rather than accept a speeding ticket. Into what circumstances would such an action fit? Leaphorn sat, motionless as the stone beneath him, and considered a variation of Captain Largo's theory. The man with the gold-rimmed glasses was not Frederick Lynch. He was a Navajo who had killed Lynch, and had taken his car, and was running for cover in familiar country. A dead Lynch could not report his car stolen. And that would explain why Goldrims had headed so directly and confidently into the desert. As Largo had suggested, he was merely going home. He hadn't stopped for a drink at one of the nearer water holes because he had a bottle of water in the car, or because he had been willing to spend a hideously thirsty twenty-four hours rather than risk being tracked.

Leaphorn considered alternative theories, found none that made sense, and returned to Goldrims-is-Navajo. But what, then, about the dog? Why would a Navajo car thief take the victim's dog with him? Why would the dog—mean enough to require a muzzle—allow a stranger to steal his master's car? Why would the Navajo take the dog along with him at the risk of being bitten? Odder still, why had the dog followed this stranger?

Leaphorn sighed. None of the questions could be answered. Everything about this affair offended his innate sense of order. He began considering a Goldrims-is-Lynch theory and got nowhere with it. A pair of horned lark flicked past him and glided over a great hump of sandstone near the mesa wall. They did not reappear. A half hour earlier a small flight of doves had disappeared for at least five minutes in the same area. Leaphorn had been conscious of that point—among others—since seeing a young Cooper's hawk pause in its patrol of the mesa rim to circle over it. He climbed carefully from his perch. The birds had found the water for him.

The spring was at the bottom of a narrow declivity at a place where the sandstone met a harder formation of limestone. Thousands of years of wind had given this slot a floor of dust and sand, which supported a stunted juniper, a hummock of grama grass, and a few tumbleweeds. Leaphorn had circled within a hundred yards of this hole without guessing its presence, and had missed a sheep trail leading into it through the tough luck of encountering the path at the place where it crossed track-resistant limestone. Now he squatted on the sand and considered what it had to tell him. There were tracks everywhere. Old and new. Among the new ones, the cloven hoofs of a small flock of sheep and goats, the pawprints of dogs, at least three, and the prints of the same boots in which Goldrims had walked away from his abandoned Mercedes. Leaphorn examined a rim of sand in a bootprint near the water, fingered it, tested its moisture content, considered the state of the weather, and weighed in cool humidity in this shadowed place. Goldrims had been here not many hours ago—probably not long before noon. The dog was still with him. Those tracks, almost grotesquely large for a dog, were everywhere. The other dogs had been here about the same time. Leaphorn studied the sandy floor. He examined an indentation, made by an oblong rectangle eighteen inches long and eight inches wide. It was either fairly heavy, or had been dropped on the damp sand. He examined another place, much more vague, where some sort of pressure had smoothed the sand. He studied this from several angles, with his face close to the earth. He concluded, finally, that Goldrims might have rested a canvas backpack here. Not far from where the backpack had been, Leaphorn picked up a bead-sized ball of sand. It flattened between thumb and forefinger into a sticky, gritty red. A droplet of drying blood. Leaphorn sniffed it, touched it with his tongue, cleaned his fingers with sand, and trotted partway up the sloping wall of the pocket. He stood looking down on the basin. Across the shallow pool a section of sand was smooth—its collection of tracks erased.

Leaphorn did not think about what he might find. He simply dug, scooping the damp sand out with his hands and piling it to the side. Less than a foot below the surface, his fingers encountered hair.

The hair was white. Leaphorn rocked back on his heels, giving himself a moment to absorb his surprise. Then he poked with an exploring finger. The hair was attached to a dog's ear, which, when pulled, produced from the engulfing sand the head of a large dog. Leaphorn pulled this body from its shallow grave. As he did so he saw the foreleg of a second dog. He stretched the two animals side by side near the water, dipped his hat into the pool to rinse the sand from the bodies, and began a careful examination. They were a large brown-and-white male mongrel and a slightly smaller, mostly black female. The female had teeth gashes across its back but had apparently died of a broken neck. The male had its throat torn out.

Leaphorn put on his wet hat, tipped it back, and stood looking down at the animals. He stood long enough to feel the chill of evaporation on the back of his head, and to hear the call of a horned lark from somewhere back among the boulders, and the voice of an early owl from the mesa. And then he climbed out of the darkening basin and began walking rapidly back toward the place he had left his carryall.

The San Francisco Peaks made a dark blue bump against the yellow glare of the horizon. The cloud over Navajo Mountain was luminescent pink and the sandstone wilderness through which Leaphorn walked had become a universe of vermilion under this slanting light. Normally Leaphorn would have drunk in this dramatic beauty, and been touched by it. Now he hardly noticed it. He was thinking of other things.

He thought of a man named Frederick Lynch who had walked directly across thirty miles of ridges and canyons to a hidden spring. And when Leaphorn pushed this impossibility aside, his thoughts turned to sheepdogs and how they work, and fight, as a trained team. He thought of Lynch and his dog reaching the water hole, finding the flock there with the two dogs that had brought the sheep on guard. He tried to visualize the fight—the male dog staging a fighting retreat probably, while the female slashed at the flank. Then, with this diversion, the male going for the throat. Leaphorn had seen many such dog-fights. But he'd never seen the single dog, no matter how fierce, manage better than a howling defeat. What would have happened had the shepherd—probably a child—come along with his dogs? And what would this shepherd think tomorrow when he came and found his dead helpers? Leaphorn shook his head. Incidents like this kept the tales of skinwalkers alive. No boy would be willing to believe his two dogs could be killed by a single animal. But he could believe, without loss of faith in his animals, that a witch had killed them. A werewolf was more than a match for a pack of dogs. Nothing could face a skin-walker.

Leaphorn turned away from this unproductive thought, to the fact that Goldrims seemed not to be running away from his affair with the Navajo police, but hurrying toward something. But what? And where? And why? Leaphorn drew an imaginary line on an imaginary map from the place where Lynch had abandoned the car to the water hole. And then he projected it northward. The line extended between Navajo Mountain and Short Mountain—into the Nokaito Bench and onward into the bottomless stone wilderness of the Glen Canyon country, and across Lake Powell Reservoir. It ran, Leaphorn thought, not far at all from the hogan on Nokaito Bench where an old man named Hosteen Tso and a girl named Anna Atcitty had been killed three months ago. Leaphorn wound his way through the sandstone landscape, his khaki-uniformed figure dwarfed by the immense outcroppings and turned red by the dying light. He was thinking now about why these two persons might have died. By the time he reached his vehicle, he decided he would get to the Short Mountain Trading Post tomorrow. Tonight he would read the Tso-Atcitty file and try to find an answer to that question.

That evening at Tuba City, Leaphorn read carefully through the three reports Largo had given him. The heroin affair provoked little thought. A small plastic package of heroin, uncut and worth perhaps five thousand dollars at wholesale, had been found taped behind the dashboard of an old stripped car which had been rusting away for years about seven miles from the Keet Seel ruins. The find had been made as a result of an anonymous call received at the Window Rock headquarters. The caller had been a female. The heroin had been removed and the package refilled with powdered white sugar and replaced. The cache had been watched, closely for a week and then loosely for a month. Finally it was merely checked periodically. No one had ever tampered with the plastic package. That could be easily explained. Probably the buyer or seller had scented the trap and the cache had been written off as a loss. And because it could be easily explained, it didn't interest Lieutenant Joe Leaphorn.

The affair of the missing helicopter was more challenging. The original sighting reports were familiar, as was the map on which a line had been penciled to connect them and recreate the copter's path, because Leaphorn had studied them while the search was under way. The map's line curved and jiggled erratically. Significantly, it tended to stick to empty country, avoiding Aztec, Farmington, and Shiprock in New Mexico, and—as it entered the interior of the Big Reservation—skirting away from trading posts and water wells where people would be likely to see it.

There had been a definite, clear-cut sighting fifteen miles north of Teec Nos Pos and after that the line became sketchy and doubtful. It zigzagged, with question marks beside most of the sighting points. Leaphorn flipped through more recent reports of sightings—those which had accumulated gradually in the months since the hunt had been called off. For the first two months, someone had kept the map current, revising the line to match the fresh reports. But this fruitless project had been abandoned. Leaphorn fished out his ballpoint pen and spent a few minutes bringing the job up to date, which confirmed the existing line without extending it. It still faded away about one hundred miles east of Short Mountain—perhaps because the copter had landed, or perhaps because there simply were no people in the empty landscape to see it pass. Leaphorn put down the pen and thought. Almost forty men had hunted the copter, crisscrossing the Navajo Mountain–Short Mountain wilderness, questioning everybody who could be found to question, and finding absolutely nothing.

The sightings had been sorted into three categories: "definite-probable," "possible-doubtful," and "unlikely." The ghost and witchcraft talk was in the "unlikely" grouping. Leaphorn examined it.

One sighting involved a twelve-year-old girl, hurrying to get home before dark. A noise and a light in the evening sky. The sounds of ghosts crying in the wind. The sight of a black beast moving through the sky. The girl had run, crying, to her mother's hogan. No one else had heard anything. The investigating officer discounted it. Leaphorn checked the location. It was almost thirty miles south of the line.

The next sighting was from an old man, again hurrying back to his hogan to avoid the ghosts which would be coming out in the gathering darkness. He had heard a thumping in the sky and had seen a wolf flying—outlined black against the dim red afterglow on the stone face of a mesa wall. This, too, was south of the wildest zigzag of the line.

The others were similar. An old woman cutting wood, startled by a sound and a moving light overhead, and the noise returning four times from the four symbolic directions as she crouched in her hogan; a Dinnehotso schoolboy on a visit to a relative, watching a coyote on a cliff near the south shore of Lake Powell. He reported that the coyote disappeared and moments later he'd heard a flapping of wings and had seen something like a dark bird diving toward the lake surface and disappearing like a duck diving for a fish. And finally, a young man seeing a great black bird flying over the highway north of Mexican Water and turning itself into a truck as it passed him, and then flying again as it disappeared to the west. This report, picked up by an Arizona highway patrolman, bore the notation: "Subject reportedly drunk at time."

Leaphorn marked each sighting location on the map with a tiny circle. The flying truck was close enough to the line to fit the pattern and the diving coyote/bird would fit if the line was extended about forty miles westward and jogged sharply northward.

Leaphorn yawned and slid the map back into the accordion file. Probably the helicopter had landed somewhere, refueled from a waiting truck, and flown through the covering night to a hiding place well away from the search area. He picked up the Atcitty-Tso homicide file, with a sense of anticipation. This one, as he remembered it, defied all applications of logic.

He read swiftly through the uncomplicated facts. A niece of Hosteen Tso had arranged for Mrs. Margaret Cigaret, a Listener of considerable reputation in the Rainbow Plateau country, to find out what was causing the old man to be ill. Mrs. Cigaret was blind. She had been driven to the Tso hogan by Anna Atcitty, a daughter of Mrs. Cigaret's sister. The usual examination had been conducted. Mrs. Cigaret had left the hogan to go into her trance and do her listening. While she was in her trance, someone had killed the Tso and Atcitty subjects by hitting them on the head with what might have been a metal pipe or a gun barrel. Mrs. Cigaret had heard nothing. As far as could be determined, nothing was taken from either of the victims or from the hogan. An FBI agent named Jim Feeney, out of Flagstaff, had worked the case with the help of a BIA agent and two of Largo's men. Leaphorn knew Feeney and considered him substantially brighter than the run-of-the-mill FBI man. He knew one of the men Largo had assigned. Also bright. The investigation had been conducted as Leaphorn would have run it—a thorough hunt for a motive. The four-man team had presumed, as Leaphorn would have presumed, that the killer had come to the Tso hogan not knowing that the two women were there, that the Atcitty girl had been killed simply to eliminate a witness, and that Mrs. Cigaret had lived because she hadn't been visible. And so the team had searched for someone with a reason to kill Hosteen Tso, interviewing, sifting rumors, learning everything about an old man except a motive for his death.

With all Tso leads exhausted, the team reversed the theory and hunted for a motive for the murder of Anna Atcitty. They laid bare the life of a fairly typical reservation teenager, with a circle of friends at Tuba City High School, a circle of cousins, two and possibly three nonserious boyfriends. No hint of any relationship intense enough to inspire either love or hate, or motive for murder.

The final report had included a rundown on witchcraft

gossip. Three interviewees had speculated that Tso was the victim of a witch and there was a modest amount of speculation that the old man was himself a skinwalker. Considering that this corner of the reservation was notoriously backward and witch-ridden, it was about the level of witchcraft gossip that Leaphorn had expected.

Leaphorn closed the report and slipped it into its folder, fitting it beside the tape cassette that held what Margaret Cigaret had told the police. He slumped down in his chair, rubbed the back of his hand across his eyes, and sat—trying to recreate what had happened at the Tso hogan. Whoever had come there must have come to kill the old man—not the girl because it would have been simpler to kill her elsewhere. But what had caused the old man to be killed? There seemed to be no answer to that. Leaphorn decided that before he left for Short Mountain in the morning he would borrow a tape deck so that he could play back the Margaret Cigaret interview while he drove. Perhaps learning what Listening Woman thought had made Hosteen Tso sick might cast some light on what had made him die.

LISTENING WOMAN'S VOICE accompanied Joe Leaphorn eastward up Navajo Route 1 from Tuba City to the Cow Springs turnoff and then, mile after jolting mile, up the road to Short Mountain. The voice emerged from the tape player on the seat beside him, hesitating, hurrying, sometimes stumbling, and sometimes repeating itself. Leaphorn listened, his eyes intent on the stony road but his thoughts focused on the words that came from the speaker. Now and then he slowed the carryall, stopped the tape, reversed it, and repeated a passage. One section he replayed three times—hearing the bored voice of Feeney asking:

"Did Tso tell you anything else? Did he say anything about anyone being mad at him, having a grudge? Anything like that?"

And then the voice of Listening Woman: "He thought maybe it could be the ghost of his great-grandfather. That's because . . ." Mrs. Cigaret's voice trailed off as she searched for English words to explain Navajo metaphysics. "That's because Hosteen Tso, he made a promise . . ."

"Made a promise to his great-grandfather? That would have been a long time ago." Feeney didn't sound interested.

"I think it was something they did with the oldest sons," Mrs. Cigaret said. "So Hosteen Tso would have made the promise to his own father, and Hosteen Tso's father made it to his father, and—"

"Okay," Feeney said. "What was the promise?"

"Taking care of some sort of secret," Mrs. Cigaret said. "Keeping something safe."

"Like what?"

"A secret," Mrs. Cigaret said. "He didn't tell me the secret." Her tone suggested that she wouldn't have been improper enough to ask.

"Did he say anything about getting any threats from anyone? Have any quarrels? Did he—"

Leaphorn grimaced, and pushed the fast forward button. Why hadn't Feeney pursued this line of questioning? Because, obviously, the FBI agent didn't want to waste time on the talk of great-grandfather ghosts during a murder investigation. But it was equally obvious, at least to Leaphorn, that Mrs. Cigaret considered it worth talking about. The tape rushed squawking through ten minutes of questions and answers probing into what Mrs. Cigaret had been told about Tso's relationship with neighbors and relatives. Leaphorn stopped it again at a point near the end of the interview. He pushed the play button.

". . . said it hurt him here in the chest a lot," Mrs. Cigaret was saying. "And sometimes it hurt him in the side. And his eyes, they hurt him too. Back in the head behind the eyes. It started hurting him right after he found out that somebody had walked across some sand paintings and they stepped right on Corn Beetle, and Talking God, and Gila Monster, and Water Monster. And that same day, he was climbing and he knocked a bunch of rocks down and they killed a frog. And the frog was why his eyes—"

Feeney's voice cut in. "But you're sure he didn't say anything about anybody doing anything to hurt him? You're sure of that? He didn't blame it on any witch out there?"

"No," Mrs. Cigaret said. Was there a hesitation? Leaphorn ran it past again. Yes. A hesitation.

"Okay," Feeney said. "Now, did he say anything just before you left him and went over by the cliff?"

"I don't remember much," Mrs. Cigaret said. "I told him he ought to get somebody to take him to Gallup and get his chest x-rayed because maybe he had one of those sicknesses that white people cure. And he said he'd get somebody to write to his grandson to take care of everything, and then I said I'd go and listen and find out what was making his eyes hurt and what else was wrong with him and—"

Here the voice of Feeney cut in again, its tone tinged slightly with impatience. "Did he say anything about anyone stealing anything from him? Anything about fighting with relatives or—"

Leaphorn punched the off button, and guided the carryall around an outcrop of stone and over the edge of the steep switchback that dropped into Manki Canyon. He wished, as he had wished before, that Feeney hadn't been so quick to interrupt Mrs. Cigaret. What promise had Hosteen Tso made to his father? Taking care of a secret, Mrs. Cigaret had said. Keeping something safe. Tso hadn't told her the secret, but he might have told her much more than Feeney had let her report. And the sand paintings. Plural? More than one? Leaphorn had played that part over and over and she had clearly said "somebody had walked across some sand paintings." But there would be only a single sand painting existing at any one time at any curing ceremonial. The singer prepared the hogan floor with a background of fine sand, then produced his sacred painting with colored sands, and placed the patient properly upon it, conducted the chants and rituals, and then destroyed the painting, erased it, wiped away the magic. Yet she had said "some sand paintings." And the list of Holy People desecrated had been strange. Sand paintings recreated incidents from the mythic history of the Navajo People. Leaphorn could conceive of no incident which would have included both Gila Monster and Water Monster in its action. Water Monster had figured only once in the mythology of the Dinee—causing the flood that destroyed the Third World after his babies had been stolen by Coyote. Neither Gila Monster nor Talking God had a role in that episode. Leaphorn shook his head, wishing he had been there for the interrogation. But even as he thought it, he recognized he was being unfair to the FBI man. There would be no reason at all to connect incongruity in a curing sing with cold-blooded killing. And when he had talked to Listening Woman, Feeney had no way of knowing that all the more logical approaches to the case would dead-end. By the time Leaphorn pulled the carryall onto the bare packed earth that served as the yard of the

Short Mountain Trading Post, he had decided that his own fascination with the oddities in Mrs. Cigaret's story was based more on his obsession with explaining the unexplained than with the murder investigation. Still, he would find Mrs. Cigaret and ask the questions Feeney hadn't asked. He would find out what curing ceremonial Hosteen Tso had attended before his death, and who had desecrated its sand paintings, and what else had happened there.

He parked beside a rusty GMC stake truck and sat for a moment, looking. The FOR SALE sign which had been a permanent part of the front porch was still there. A midnight-blue Stingray, looking out of place, sat beside the sheep barn, its front end jacked up. Two pickups and an aging Plymouth sedan were parked in front. In the shade of the porch a white-haired matriarch was perched on a bale of sheep pelts, talking to a fat middle-aged man who sat, legs folded, on the stone floor beside her. Leaphorn knew exactly what they were talking about. They were talking about the Navajo policeman who had driven up, speculating on who Leaphorn was and what he was doing at Short Mountain. The old woman said something to the man, who laughed—a flash of white teeth in a dark shadowed face. A joke had just been made about Leaphorn. He smiled, and completed his quick survey. All was as he remembered it. The late-afternoon sun baked a collection of tired buildings clustered on a shadeless expanse of worn earth on the rim of Short Mountain Wash. Leaphorn wondered why this inhospitable spot had been chosen for a trading center. Legend had it that the Moab Mormon who founded the store about 1910 had picked the place because it was a long way from competition. It was also a long way from customers. Short Mountain Wash drained one of the most barren and empty landscapes in the Western Hemisphere. Legend also had it that after more than twenty hard years the Mormon became involved in a theological dispute concerning plural wives. He had picked up his own two and emigrated to a dissident colony in Mexico. McGinnis, then young and relatively foolish, had become the new owner. He had promptly realized his mistake. According to the legend, about thirty days after the purchase, he had hung out the THIS ESTABLISHMENT FOR SALE INQUIRE WITHIN sign that decorated his front porch for more than forty years. If anyone else had outsmarted John McGinnis, the event had not been recorded by reservation folklore.

Leaphorn climbed from the carryall, sorting out the questions he would ask McGinnis. The trader would know not only where Margaret Cigaret lived, but where she could be found this week—an important difference among people who follow sheep herds. And McGinnis would know if anything new had been heard about the mission helicopter, or about the reliability of those who brought in old reports, and everything about the lives and fortunes of the impoverished clans that occupied this empty end of the Rainbow Plateau. He would know why the Adams woman was here. Most important of all, he would know if a strange man wearing gold-rimmed glasses had been seen in the canyon country.

At this moment the screen door opened and John McGinnis emerged. He stood for a moment, blinking at Leaphorn through the fierce outside light, a stumpy, stooped, white-haired man swallowed up in new, and oversized, blue overalls. Then he squatted on the floor between the old woman and the man. Whatever he said produced a cackle of laughter from the woman and a chuckle from the man. Once again, Leaphorn guessed, he had been the subject of humor. He didn't mind. McGinnis would save him a lot of effort.

"I remember you," McGinnis said. "You're that Slow Talking Dinee boy who used to patrol out of Tuba City. Six, seven years ago." He had invited Leaphorn into his room at the rear of the store and gestured him to a chair. Now he poured a Coca-Cola glass half full from a bottle of Jack Daniel's, sloshed it around, and eyed Leaphorn. "The Dinee say you won't drink whiskey, so I ain't going to offer you any."

"That's right," Leaphorn said.

"Let me see, now. If I remember correct, your mama was Anna Gorman—ain't that right?—from way the hell over at Two Gray Hills? And you're a grandson of Hosteen Klee-Thlumie."

Leaphorn nodded. McGinnis scowled at him.

"I don't mean a goddam *clan* grandson," he said. "I mean a *real* grandson. He was the father of your mother? That right?"

Leaphorn nodded again.

"I knowed your granddaddy, then," McGinnis said. He toasted this fact with a long sip at the warm bourbon and then thought about it, his pale old man's eyes staring past Leaphorn at the wall. "Knowed him before he was Hosteen anything. Just a young buck Indian trying to learn how to be a singer. They called him Horse Kicker then."

"When I knew him he was called Hosteen Klee," Leaphorn said.

"We helped each other out, a time or two," McGinnis said, talking to his memories. "Can't say that about too many." He took another sip of bourbon and looked across the glass at Leaphorn—solidly back in the present. "You want to find that old Cigaret woman," he said. "Now, the only reason you'd want to do that is something must have come up on the Tso killing. That right?"

"Nothing much new," Leaphorn said. "But you know how it is. Time passes. Maybe somebody says something. Or sees something that helps us out."

McGinnis grinned. "And if anybody heard anything, it'd get to old John McGinnis. That right?" The grin vanished with a new thought. "Say, now, you know anything about a feller named Noni? Claims to be a Seminole Indian?" The tone of the question suggested that he doubted all claims made by Noni.

"Don't think so," Leaphorn said. "What about him?"

"He came in here a while back and looked the store over," McGinnis said. "Said he and a bunch of other goddam Indians had some sort of government loan and was interested in buying this hell hole. I figured to do that they'd have to deal with the Tribal Council for a license."

"They would," Leaphorn said. "But that wouldn't have anything to do with the police. They really going to buy it?" The idea of McGinnis actually selling the Short Mountain Post wasn't believable. It would be like the Tribal Council bricking up the hole in Window Rock, or Arizona selling the Grand Canyon.

"Probably didn't really have the money," McGinnis said. "Probably just come around looking to see if breaking in and stealing would be easy. I didn't like his looks." McGinnis scowled at his drink and at the memory. He put his rocking chair in motion, holding his elbow rigid on the chair arm and the glass rigid in his hand. In it, a brown tide of bourbon ebbed and flowed with the motion. "This Tso killing, now. You know what I hear about that?" He waited for Leaphorn to fill in the blank.

"What?" Leaphorn asked.

"Not a goddam thing," McGinnis said.

"Funny," Leaphorn said.

"It sure as hell is," McGinnis said. He stared at Leaphorn as if trying to find some sort of answer in his face. "You know what I think? I don't think a Navajo did it."

"Don't you?"

"Neither do you," McGinnis said. "Not if you've got as much sense as I hear you do. You Navajos will steal if you think you can get off with something, but I never heard of one going out to kill somebody." He flourished the glass to emphasize the point. "That's one kind of white man's meanness the Navajos never took to. Any killings you have, there's either getting drunk and doing it, or getting mad and fighting. You don't have this planning in advance and going out to kill somebody like white folks. That right?"

Leaphorn let his silence speak for him. McGinnis had been around Navajos long enough for that. What the trader had said was true. Among the traditional Dinee, the death of a fellow human being was the ultimate evil. He recognized no life after death. That which was natural in him, and therefore good, simply ceased. That which was unnatural, and therefore evil, wandered through the darkness as a ghost, disturbing nature and causing sickness. The Navajo didn't share the concept of his Hopi-Zuñi-Pueblo Indian neighbors that the human spirit transcended death in the fulfillment of an eternal kachina, nor the Plains Indian belief in joining with a personal God. In the old tradition, death was unrelieved horror. Even the death of an enemy in battle was something the warrior cleansed himself of with an Enemy Way ritual. Unless, of course, a Navajo Wolf was involved. Witchcraft was a reversal of the Navajo Way.

"Except maybe if somebody thought he was a Navajo

Wolf," McGinnis said. "They'd kill him if they thought he was a witch."

"You hear of anyone who thought that?"

"That's the trouble," McGinnis said cheerfully. "Nobody had nothing but good words to say about old Hosteen Tso." The cluttered room was silent again while McGinnis considered this oddity. He stirred his drink with a pencil from his shirt pocket.

"What do you know about his family?" Leaphorn asked.

"He had a boy, Tso did. Just one kid. That boy wasn't no good. They called him Ford. Married some girl over at Teec Nos Pos, a Salt Cedar I think she was, and moved over with her people and got to drinking and whoring around at Farmington until her folks run him off. Ford was always fighting and stealing and raising hell." McGinnis sipped at his bourbon, his face disapproving. "You could understand it if somebody hit *that* Navajo on the head," he said.

"He ever come back?" Leaphorn asked.

"Never did," McGinnis said. "Died years ago. In Gallup I heard it was. Probably too much booze and his liver got him." He toasted this frailty with a sip of bourbon.

"You know anything about a grandson?" Leaphorn asked.

McGinnis shrugged. "You know how it is with Navajos," he said. "The man moves in with his wife's outfit and if there's any kids they're born into their mother's clan. If you want to know anything about Tso's grandson, you're going to have to drive to Teec Nos Pos and start asking around among them Salt Cedar people. I never even heard Ford had any children until old Hosteen Tso come in here a while before he got killed and told me he wanted to write this letter to his grandson." McGinnis's face creased with remembered amusement. "I told him I didn't know he had a grandson, and he said that made two things I didn't know about him and of course I asked him what the other one was and he said it was which hand he used to wipe himself." McGinnis chuckled and sipped his bourbon. "Witty old fart," he said.

"What did he say in the letter?"

"I didn't write it," McGinnis said. "But let's see what I can remember about it. He come in one day. It was colder'n a wedge. Musta been early in March. He asked me what I charged to write a letter and I told him it was free for regular customers. And he started telling me what he wanted to tell this grandson and would I send the letter to him and of course I asked him where this boy lived and he said it was way off east somewhere with nothing but white people. And I told him he'd have to know more than that for me to know what to write on the front of the envelope."

"Yeah," Leaphorn said. When a marriage broke up in the matriarchal Navajo system, it wouldn't be unusual for paternal grandparents to lose track of children. They would be members of their mother's family. "Ever hear anything about Ford's wife?"

McGinnis rubbed his bushy white eyebrow with a thumb, stimulating his memory. "I think I heard she was a drunk, too. Another no-good. Works that way a lot. Birds of a feather." McGinnis interrupted himself suddenly by slapping the arm of the rocker. "By God," he said. "I just thought of something. Way back, must have been almost twenty years ago, there was a kid staying with Hosteen Tso. Stayed there a year or so. Helped with the sheep and all. I bet that was the grandbaby."

"Maybe," Leaphorn said. "If his mother really was a drunk."

"Hard to keep track of Navajo kids," McGinnis said. "But I remember hearing that one went off to boarding school at St. Anthony's. Maybe that'd explain what Hosteen Tso said about him going on the Jesus Road. Maybe them Franciscan priests there turned him Catholic."

"There's something else I want to know about," Leaphorn said. "Tso went to a sing not very long before he was killed. You know about that?"

McGinnis frowned. "There wasn't no sing. About last March or so? We had all that sorry weather then. Remember? Blowing snow. Wasn't no sings anywhere on the plateau."

"How about a little earlier?" Leaphorn asked. "January or February?" McGinnis frowned again. "There was one a little after Christmas. Girl got sick at Yazzie Springs. Nakai girl. Would have been early in January."

"What was it?"

"They did the Wind Way," McGinnis said. "Had to get a singer from all the way over at Many Farms. Expensive as hell."

"Any others?" Leaphorn asked. The Wind Way was the wrong ritual. The sand painting made for it would include the Corn Beetle, but none of the other Holy People mentioned by Hosteen Tso.

"Bad springs for sings," McGinnis said. "Everybody's either getting healthy, or they're too damn poor to pay for 'em."

Leaphorn grunted. There was something he needed to connect. They sat. McGinnis moved the glass in small, slow circles which spun the bourbon to within a centimeter of its rim. Leaphorn let his eyes drift. It was a big room, two high windows facing east and two facing west. Someone, years ago, had curtained them with a cotton print of roses on a blue background. Big as the room was, its furniture crowded it. In the corner, a double bed covered with quilts; beside it a worn 1940-modern sofa; beyond that, a recliner upholstered in shiny blue vinyl; two other nondescript overstuffed chairs; and three assorted chests and cabinets. Every flat surface was cluttered with the odds and ends accumulated in a long lifetime—Indian pottery, kachina dolls, a plastic radio, a shelf of books, and even—on one of the window sills—an assortment of flint lance points, artifacts which had interested Leaphorn since his days as an anthropology student at Arizona State. Outside, through the dusty glass window, he saw two young men talking beside one of the trading post's outbuildings. The building was of stone, originally erected, Leaphorn had been told, by a Church of Christ missionary early in McGinnis's tenure as trader and postmaster. It had been abandoned after the preacher's optimism had been eroded by his inability to cause the Dinee to accept the idea that God had a personal and special interest in humans. McGinnis then had partitioned the chapel into three tourist cabins. But, as one of his customers had put it, "it was as hard to get white-man tourists to go over that Short Mountain road as it was to get Navajos to go to heaven." The cabins, like the church, had been mostly empty.

Leaphorn glanced at McGinnis. The trader sat, swirling

his drink, his face lined and compressed by age. Leaphorn understood the old man's distaste for Noni. McGinnis didn't want a buyer. Short Mountain had trapped him in his own stubbornness, and held him here all his life, and the FOR SALE sign had been no more than a gesture—a declaration that he was smart enough to know he'd been screwed. And the asking price, Leaphorn had always heard, had been grotesquely high.

"No," McGinnis said finally. "There just wasn't any sings close around here at all."

"Okay," Leaphorn said. "So if there wasn't any sings, and Hosteen Tso told you he'd seen somebody step on two or three sand paintings last March, where would you figure that could have happened?"

McGinnis shifted his gaze from the bourbon to Leaphorn, peering at him quizzically. "No place," he said. "Shit. What kind of a question is that?"

"Hosteen Tso was there when it happened."

"No damned place," McGinnis said. He looked puzzled. "What the hell you going to have two or three sand paintings for at once?"

"It wouldn't be that Wind Way Chant," Leaphorn said. "Wrong painting."

"And the wrong clan. The Nakais are Red Foreheads. Wouldn't be no reason for Old Man Tso to go down there for the Wind Way." He took another sip of his bourbon. "Where'd you hear that crap?"

"Margaret Cigaret passed it on to the FBI when they were questioning her. When I leave here I'm going to go out to her place and find out more about it."

"She probably ain't home," McGinnis said. "Somebody said she was off somewhere. Visiting kin, I think. Somewhere up east of Mexican Water."

"Maybe she's back by now."

"Maybe," McGinnis said. His tone said he doubted it.

"I guess I'll go find out," Leaphorn said. He probably wouldn't find her at home, but "up east of Mexican Water" meant just about anywhere in a thousand square miles along the Arizona-Utah border. Leaphorn decided it was time to move the conversation toward what had really brought him here—the man in the gold-rimmed glasses. He moved obliquely.

"Those your lance points?" Leaphorn asked, nodding toward the window sill.

McGinnis pushed himself laboriously out of the chair and waddled to the window, brought back three of the flint points. He handed them to Leaphorn and lowered himself into the rocker again.

"Came out of that dig up Short Mountain Wash," he said. "Anthropologists say they're early Anasazi but they look kind of big to me for that. They musta found a hundred of 'em."

The points had been chipped out of a shiny black basaltic schist. They were thick, and crude, with only slight fluting where the butt of the point would be fastened into the lance shaft. Leaphorn wondered how McGinnis had got his hands on them. But he didn't ask. Obviously the anthropologists would guard such artifacts zealously, and obviously the way McGinnis had got them wouldn't stand scrutiny. Leaphorn changed the subject, angling toward his main interest.

"Anybody come in and tell you they found an old helicopter?"

McGinnis laughed. "That son-of-a-bitch is long gone," he said. "If it ever flew into this country in the first place." He sipped again. "Maybe it did come in here. The feds seemed to have that pinned down pretty good. But if it crashed, I'da had some of those Begay boys, or the Tsossies, or somebody in here long ago nosing around to see if there was a reward, or trying to pawn it to me, or selling spare parts, or something."

"Another thing," Leaphorn said. "Mrs. Cigaret said Tso was worried about getting a sickness from his great-grandfather's ghost. That mean anything to you?"

"Well, now," McGinnis said. "Now, that's interesting. You know who his great-grandfather was? He came from quite a line, Tso did."

"Who was it?"

"Course he had four great-grandfathers," McGinnis said. "But the one they talk about around here was a big man before the Long Walk. Lots of stories about him. They called him

Standing Medicine. He was one of them that wouldn't surrender when Kit Carson came through. One of that bunch with Chief Narbona and Ganado Mucho who fought it out with the army. Supposed to been a big medicine man. They claim he knew the whole Blessing Way, all seven days of it, and the Mountain Way, and several other sings."

McGinnis poured another dollop of bourbon into his glass—raising the level carefully to the bottom of the Coca-Cola trademark. "But I never heard anything about his ghost being any particular place—or bothering people." He sampled the freshened drink, grimaced. "God knows, though, he might be causing ghost sickness all over that country out there." It was time now, Leaphorn thought, for the crucial question.

"Last day or two you hear anything about a stranger with a big dog? A great big dog?"

"A stranger?"

"Or a Navajo, either."

McGinnis shook his head. "No." He laughed. "Heard a Navajo Wolf story this morning, though. Feller from back on the plateau said a skinwalker killed his nephew's sheepdogs at the Falling Rock water hole way out there on the plateau. But you're talking about a real dog, ain't you?"

"A real one," Leaphorn said. "But did this nephew see the witch?"

"Not the way I heard it," McGinnis said. "The dogs didn't come back with the sheep. So the next day the boy went to see about it. He found 'em dead and the werewolf tracks where they'd been killed." McGinnis shrugged. "You know how it goes. Pretty much the same old skinwalker story."

"Nothing about a stranger, then," Leaphorn said.

McGinnis eyed Leaphorn carefully, watching his reaction. "Well, now. We got us a stranger right here at Short Mountain. Got in early this morning." He paused with the storyteller man's talent for increasing the impact. "A woman," he said.

Leaphorn said nothing.

"Pretty young woman," McGinnis said, still watching Leaphorn. "Big sports car. From Washington."

"You mean Theodora Adams?" Leaphorn asked.

McGinnis didn't show his disappointment.

"You know all about her, then?"

"A little bit," Leaphorn said. "She's the daughter of a doctor in the Public Health Service. I don't know what the hell she's doing here. Or care, for that matter. What's she after? One of those anthropologists up the wash?"

McGinnis examined the level of bourbon in his glass, sloshed it gently, and examined Leaphorn out of the corner of his eye.

"She's trying to find someone who can take her up to Hosteen Tso's hogan," McGinnis said. He grinned then. He'd finally gotten a reaction out of Lieutenant Joe Leaphorn.

LOOKING FOR THEODORA ADAMS proved to be unnecessary. Joe Leaphorn emerged from the front door of the Short Mountain Trading Post and found Theodora Adams hurrying up, looking for him.

"You're the policeman who drives that car," she told him. The smile was brilliant, a flashing white arch of perfect teeth in a very tanned perfect face. "There's something you could do for me"—again the smile—"if you would."

"Like what?" Leaphorn asked.

"I have to get to the hogan of a man named Hosteen Tso," Theodora Adams said. "I've found a man who knows how to get there, but my car won't go over that road." She glanced ruefully at the Corvette Stingray parked in the shade of the barn. Two young men were tinkering with it now. And then the full force of her eyes was again on Leaphorn. "It's too low," she explained. "The rocks hit the bottom."

"You want me to take you to the Tso hogan?"

"Yes," she said. Her smile said "please" for her.

"Why do you want to go?"

The smile faded slightly. "I have some business there."

"With Hosteen Tso?"

The smile left. "Hosteen Tso is dead," she said. "You know that. You're a policeman." Her eyes studied Leaphorn's face, slightly hostile but mostly with frank, unabashed curiosity. Leaphorn remembered suddenly when he had first seen blue eyes like that. He had gone to the boarding school at Kayenta with his uncle and cousin and there had been a white woman there with blue eyes who had stared at him. He had thought, at first, that eyes as odd as that must be blind. That woman, too, had stared at him as if he were an interesting object. On that same day, he remembered, he had seen his first bearded man—something to a Navajo boy as curious as a winged snake—but somehow the unaccustomed rudeness of those pale eyes had affected him more. He had always remembered it. And the memory, now, affected his response.

"Who's your business with?"

"That's none of *your* business," Theodora Adams said. She took a half step away from him, stopped, turned back. "I'm sorry," she said. "Of course it's your business. You're a policeman." She made a deprecating face, and shrugged. "It's just that it's something very private. Nothing to do with the law and I simply can't talk about it." She smiled again, plaintively. "I'm sorry," she said.

Her expression told Leaphorn that the regret was genuine. She was a remarkably handsome girl, high-breasted, slender, dressed in white pants and a blue shirt which exactly matched the color of her eyes. She looked expensive, Leaphorn thought, and competent, and assured. She also looked utterly out of place at Short Mountain Trading Post.

"Do you know how to get to Tso's place?"

"That man was going to show me." She pointed to the two young men at her car, one under it now—apparently inspecting front-end damage—and the other squatted beside him. "But we couldn't get that damned Stingray over the rocks." She paused, her eyes intent on Leaphorn's. "I was going to pay him twenty-five dollars," she said. The statement hung there, not an offer, not a bribe, simply a statement for Leaphorn to consider and make what he wanted of. He considered it, and found it neatly done. The girl was smart.

"One thing I've got. Plenty of money," she said.

"The Navajo Tribal Police have a regulation against picking up hitchhikers," Leaphorn said. He turned it over in his mind. He would tell Largo his Theodora Adams was here and healthy. He would tell Largo where she wanted to go. He was almost sure Largo would tell him to take her to the Tso place, simply to find out what she wanted there. But maybe not. By asking Largo to find out about the welfare of Theodora Adams, Window Rock had, in an unofficial, unspoken way, made him responsible for it. Under the circumstances, Largo might not want her taken into that back country.

"Look," he said. "How much do you know about Hosteen Tso?"

"I know somebody killed him, if that's what you mean. Last spring."

"And we don't know who did it," Leaphorn said. "So we're interested in anybody who has business out there."

"My business doesn't have anything to do with crime," Theodora Adams said. She looked amused. "It doesn't have anything to do with the law, or with the police. It's just personal business. And if you're not willing to help me, I'll find somebody who will." And with that, she walked across the yard and disappeared into the trading post.

One of the disadvantages of the Short Mountain Trading Post location was that it was impossible for shortwave radio communication. To contact Tuba City, Leaphorn had to drive out of the declivity made by the wash, going high enough up the mesa so that his reception wasn't blanked out by the terrain. He found Captain Largo suitably surprised at the Adams woman's aim of visiting the Tso hogan.

"You want me to take her?" Leaphorn asked. "I'm going out to see the Cigaret woman and it's sort of on the way. Same direction anyway."

"No," Largo said. "Just find out what the hell she's doing."

"I'm pretty sure she's not going to tell me," Leaphorn said. "She already told me it was none of our business."

"You could bring her in here for questioning."

"Could I? You recommending that?"

The pause was brief—Largo remembering the reason for his original interest in Theodora Adams. "I guess not," he said. "Not unless we have to. Handle it your own way. But don't let anything happen to her."

The way Leaphorn had already decided to handle it would be to offer to drive Theodora Adams to the Tso hogan. If he did that there would be no conceivable way she could prevent him from learning why she had gone there. He would find the Adams woman and get on the road.

But when he got back to the trading post, it was after 10 P.M. and Theodora Adams was gone. So was a GMC pickup truck owned by a woman named Naomi Many Goats.

"I saw her talking to Naomi Many Goats," McGinnis said. "She came in here and got me to draw her a little map of how to get to the Tso place. And then she asked if you were headed back to Tuba City, and I told her you'd probably just gone off to do some radio talking because you was fixing to go out and talk to the Cigaret woman. So she got me to show her where the Cigaret hogan was on the map. Then she asked who she could hire to take her to the Tso place, and I said you never could tell with you Navajos, and the last thing I saw her doing was talking to Naomi."

"She get the Many Goats woman to drive her?"

"Hell, I don't know," McGinnis said. "I didn't see 'em leave."

"I'll guess she did," Leaphorn said.

"It occurs to me that I've been telling you a hell of a lot and you ain't been telling me nothing," McGinnis said. "Why does that girl want to go to the Tso hogan?"

"Tell you what," Leaphorn said. "When I find out, I'll tell you."

7

BY THE RELAXED STANDARDS of the Navajo Reservation, the first three miles of the road to the hogan of Hosteen Tso were officially listed as "unimproved—passable in dry weather." They led up Short Mountain Wash to the site where the anthropological team was excavating cliff ruins. The road followed the mostly hard-packed sand of the wash bottom, and if one was careful to avoid soft places, offered no particular hazard or discomfort. Leaphorn drove past the ruins a little after midnight. Except for a pickup and a small camping trailer parked in the shade of a cottonwood, there was no sign of life. From there, the road quickly deteriorated from fair, to poor, to bad, to terrible, until it was, in fact, no road at all, merely a track. It left the narrowing wash via a subsidiary arroyo, snaked its way through a half mile of broken shale and emerged on the top of Rainbow Plateau. The landscape became a roadbuilder's nightmare and a geologist's dream. Here, eons ago, the earth's crust had writhed and twisted. Nothing was level. Limestone sediments, great masses of gaudy sandstone, granite outcroppings, and even thick veins of marble had been churned together by some unimaginable paroxysm—then cut and carved and washed away by ten million years of wind, rain, freeze, and thaws. Driving here was a matter of following a faintly marked pathway through a stone obstacle course. It required care, patience, and concentration. Leaphorn found concentration difficult. His head was full of questions. Where was Frederick Lynch? Where was he going? His course northward from his abandoned car would take him near the Tso hogan. Was Theodora Adams's business at the hogan business with Frederick Lynch? That seemed logical—if anything about this odd business made any logic at all. If two white strangers appeared at about the same time in this out-of-the-way corner, one headed for the Tso hogan and the other aimed in that direction, logic insisted that more than coincidence was involved. But why in the name of God would they cross half a continent to meet at one of the most remote and inaccessible spots in the hemisphere? Leaphorn could think of no possible reason. Common sense insisted that their coming must have something to do with the murder of Hosteen Tso, but Leaphorn could conceive no link. He felt the irritation and uneasiness that he always felt when the world around him seemed out of its logical order. There was also a growing sense of anxiety. Largo had told him not to let anything happen to Theodora Adams. Most likely, Theodora Adams was somewhere ahead of him on this road, riding with a woman familiar with its hazards, who could drive it faster than could Leaphorn. Leaphorn remembered once again the face of Lynch grinning as he set Leaphorn up for the kill. He thought of the shepherd's dogs savaged by the animal Lynch had with him. This was what Theodora Adams was going to meet. Leaphorn jolted the carryall over a boulder faster than he should have, heard the bottom grate against stone, and cursed aloud in Navajo.

As he braked the carryall to a halt, he became aware that something was in the vehicle with him. Some sense of motion, or of unexplained sound, reached him. He unsnapped the holding strap over his pistol, drew the hammer quietly back to the half-cocked position, palmed it, and spun in the seat. Nothing. He peered over the back of the seat, the pistol ready. On the floor, cushioned by his sleeping bag, lay Theodora Adams.

"I hope you didn't get stuck," she said. "That's what happened to me—banging over the rocks like that."

Leaphorn flicked on the dome light and stared down at her, saying nothing. Surprise was replaced by anger, and this was quickly diluted by relief. Theodora Adams was safe enough.

"I told you we had a rule against riders," Leaphorn said. She pulled herself from the floor to the backseat, shook her head to untangle the mass of blond hair. "I didn't have any choice. That woman wouldn't take me. And that old man told me you were going out here anyway."

"McGinnis?"

Theodora Adams shrugged. "McGinnis. Whatever his name is. So there wasn't any reason for me not to come along."

It was a statement that could be argued, but not answered. Leaphorn rarely argued. He considered his impulse to order her out of the carryall, to be picked up on his way back. The impulse died quickly, anger overcome by the need to know why she was going to the Tso hogan. Her eyes were an unusually deep blue, or perhaps the color was accentuated by the unusual clarity of the whiteness that surrounded the iris. They were eyes that would not be stared down, which fixed on Leaphorn's eyes—unabashed, arrogant, slightly amused.

"Get in the front seat," Leaphorn said. He didn't want her behind him.

They jolted through the boulder field in silence and onto the smoother going of a long sandstone slope. Theodora Adams dug into her purse, extracted a folded square of notepaper and smoothed it on the leg of her pants. It was a pencil-drawn map. "About where are we?"

Leaphorn turned up the dash light and peered at it. "About here," he said. He was conscious of her thigh under his fingertip. Exactly, he knew, as she knew he would be.

"About ten miles?"

"About twenty."

"So we'll be there pretty soon?"

"No," Leaphorn said, "we won't." He down-geared the carryall over a hump of stone. The carryall rolled into the shadow of an outcrop, making her reflection suddenly visible on the inside of the windshield. She was watching him, waiting for the answer to be expanded.

"Why not?"

"Because first we're going to the Cigaret hogan. I'll talk to Margaret Cigaret. *Then* we'll decide whether to go to the Tso hogan." In fact, there was no reason to reach the Cigaret place before dawn. He had intended to find it and then park for some sleep.

"Decide?"

"You'll tell me what your business is. I'll decide whether we go on from there."

"Look," she said. "I'm sorry if I was rude back there. But you were rude too. Why don't we . . ." She paused. "What's your name?"

"Joe Leaphorn."

"Joe," she said, "my name is Judy Simons, and my friends all call me Judy, and I don't see why we can't be friends."

"Reach into your purse, Miss Simons, and let me see your driver's license," Leaphorn said. He pushed the handbag toward her.

"I don't have it with me," she said.

Leaphorn's right hand fished deftly into the handbag, extracted a fat blue leather wallet.

"Put that back." Her voice was icy. "You don't have any right to do that."

The driver's license was in the first plastic cardholder. The face that stared from the square was the face of the woman beside him, the smile appealing even when directed at the license bureau camera. The name was Theodora Adams. Leaphorn flipped the wallet shut and pushed it back into the handbag.

"Okay," she said. "It's none of your business, but I'll tell you why I'm going to the Tso place." The carryall tilted over the sloping stone. She clutched the door to keep from sliding down the seat against him. "But you'll have to promise to take me there."

She waited for an answer, staring at him expectantly. Leaphorn said nothing.

"I have a friend. A Navajo. He's been having a lot of trouble." Leaphorn glanced at her. Her smile disparaged her good Samaritan role. "You know. Getting his head together. So he decided to come home. And I decided I would come out and help him."

The voice stopped, the silence inviting comment. Leaphorn shifted again to cope with another steep slope.

"What's his name?"

"Tso. He's Hosteen Tso's grandson. The old man wanted him to come to see him."

"Ah," Leaphorn said. But was this grandson also Frederick Lynch? Was he Goldrims? Leaphorn was almost certain he was.

"Joe," she said. Her fingertip touched his leg. "You could drop me off at the Tso place and talk to Mrs. Cigaret on the way home. It won't take any longer."

"I'll think about it," Leaphorn said. Mrs. Cigaret probably wasn't home. And whatever Margaret Cigaret could tell him seemed trivial against the thought of confronting Goldrims—of taking the man who had tried, so gleefully, to kill him. "Is he expecting you?"

"Look," she said. "You're not going to take me there first. You're not going to do anything for me. Why should I tell you anything about my business?"

"We'll go there first," Leaphorn said. "But what's the hurry? Does he know you're coming?"

She laughed. There was genuine merriment in the sound, causing Leaphorn to take his eyes off the track he was following to look at her. It was a hearty laugh, a sound full of happy memories. "Yes and no," she said. "Or just yes. He knows." She glanced at Leaphorn, her eyes still amused. "That's like asking somebody if they know the sun's going to come up. Of course it's going to come up. If it doesn't, the world ends."

She is a formidable young woman, Leaphorn thought. He didn't want her with him when he first approached Hosteen Tso's place. Whether she liked it or not, she'd wait in the carryall while he determined who, or what, waited at the hogan.

HAD LEAPHORN'S TIMING been perfect, he would have arrived on the mesa rim overlooking the Tso hogan at dawn. In fact, he arrived perhaps an hour early, the moon almost down on the western horizon and the starlight just bright enough to confirm the dim shape of the buildings below. Leaphorn sat and waited. He sat far enough back from the mesa edge so that the downdrift of cooling air would not carry his scent. If the dog was there, Leaphorn didn't want it alerted. The dog had been very much on his mind as he found his way down the dark wagon track toward the hogan and up the back slope of this small mesa. Leaphorn doubted that it would be out hunting, but anything seemed possible in this peculiar affair. The thought of the dog had increased his caution and tightened his nerves. Now, sitting motionless with his back protected by a slab of stone, he relaxed. If the animal was prowling, he would hear it in time to react to an attack. The danger—if indeed there had been danger—was gone now.

Silence. In the dim, still, predawn universe, scent dominated sight and hearing. Leaphorn could smell the acrid perfume of the junipers just behind him, the aroma of dust and other scents so faint they defied identification. From somewhere far behind him there came a single, almost inaudible snapping sound. Perhaps a stone cooling and contracting from yesterday's heat, perhaps a predator moving suddenly and breaking a stick, perhaps the earth growing one tick older. The sound turned Leaphorn's thoughts back to the dog, to the eyes staring at him out of the car, to what had happened to the sheepdogs at the water hole, and to witch dogs, the Navajo Wolves, of his people's ancient traditions. The Navajo Wolves were men and women who turned from harmony to chaos and gained the power to change themselves into coyotes, dogs, wolves, or even bears, and to fly through the air, and to spread sickness among the Dinee. As a boy he had believed, fervently and fearfully, in this concept of evil. Two miles from his grandmother's hogan was a weathered volcanic upthrust which the People avoided. In a cave there the witches supposedly gathered to initiate new members into their clan of Wolves. As a sophomore at Arizona State, he had come just as fervently to disbelieve in the ancient ways. He had visited his grandmother, and gone alone to the old volcano core. Climbing the crumbling basalt crags, feeling brave and liberated, he had found two caves—one of which seemed to lead downward into the black heart of the earth. There had been no witches, nor any sign that anything used these caves except, perhaps, a den of coyotes. But he hadn't climbed down into the darkness.

Now for many minutes, Leaphorn's imagination had been suggesting a dim opalescence along the eastern horizon, and presently his eyes confirmed it. A ragged division between dark sky and darker earth, the shape of the Chuska Mountains on the New Mexico border. At this still point, another sound reached Leaphorn. He realized he had been aware of it earlier somewhere below the threshold of hearing. Now it became a murmuring which came and died and came again. It seemed to come from the north. Leaphorn frowned, puzzled. And then he realized what it must be. It was the sound of running water, the San Juan River moving over its rapids, sliding down its canyon toward Lake Powell. At this season the river would be low, the snow melt of the Rockies long since drained away. Even in this stillness Leaphorn doubted if the sound muffled by the depth of its canyon would carry far. One of the river bends must bring it to within a couple of miles of Tso's hogan.

Leaphorn's eye caught a flick of movement in the gray light below—an owl on the hunt. Or, he thought, sardonically, the ghost of Hosteen Tso haunting the old man's hogan. The east was brightening. Leaphorn eased himself silently from the stone and moved nearer the rim. The buildings were clearly visible. He examined the setting. Directly below him, drainage had eroded a cul-de-sac from the sandstone face of the mesa. This must be where Listening Woman had communed with the earth while her patient and her assistant were being murdered. He studied the topography. It was light enough now to make out the wagon track that connected the Tso hogan tenuously with the world of men. Down this track the killer must have come. The investigators had found only the tracks of Mrs. Cigaret's pickup, and no hoofprints. So, the killer had come on foot, visible from the hogan for more than three hundred yards. Tso and the girl must have watched death walking toward them. They had recognized no threat, apparently. Had they seen a friend? A stranger? Below Leaphorn's feet the track swerved toward the cliff, passing within a dozen yards of where Mrs. Cigaret had sat invisible behind a curtain of stone while the killer had walked past. What had he done then? He would have seen the ritual design painted on the old man's chest. That should have told him that Tso was undergoing a ceremonial diagnosis, that a Listener, or Hand Trembler, must be somewhere nearby. He might have believed the teenage girl was the diagnostician. But not if he was a local Navajo. Then he would have known the truck belonged to Listening Woman. Leaphorn studied the grounds below him, trying to recreate the scene. The killer apparently had left immediately after the killing. At least, nothing was known to be missing from Tso's belongings. He had simply walked away as he had come—down the track forty feet below Leaphorn's boot tips. Leaphorn retraced this line of retreat with his eyes, then stopped. He frowned, puzzled. At that same moment, he smelled smoke.

The east was streaked with red and yellow now, providing enough light to illuminate a wavering thin blue line emerging from the smoke hole in the Tso hogan. The man was there. Leaphorn felt a fierce excitement. He took out his binoculars, adjusted them quickly, and studied the ground around the hogan. If the dog was to be part of this contest he needed to know it. He could detect no sign of the animal. The few places where tracks might show bore only boot prints. There was no sign of droppings. Leaphorn studied places where a dog would be likely to urinate, where it might sprawl in the afternoon shade. He found nothing. He lowered the glasses and rubbed his eyes. As he did, the door of the hogan swung open and a man emerged.

He stood, one hand resting on the plank door, and stared out at the dawn. A largish man, young, wearing an unbuttoned blue shirt, white boxer shorts, and short boots not yet laced. Leaphorn studied him through the binoculars, trying to connect this man enjoying the beauty of the dawn with the grinning face seen through the windshield of the Mercedes. The hair was black, which was as he had remembered it. The man was tall, his figure foreshortened by the magnification of Leaphorn's binoculars and the viewing angle. Perhaps six feet, with narrow hips and a heavy muscular torso. The man examined the morning, showing more of his face now. It was a Navajo face, longish, rather bony. A shrewd, intelligent face reflecting only calm enjoyment of the morning. Discomfort in his chest made Leaphorn realize that he had been holding his breath. He breathed again. Some of the tension of the night had left him. He had hunted a sort of epitome of evil, something that would kill with reckless enjoyment. He had found a mere mortal. And yet this Navajo who stood below him inspecting the rosy dawn sky must be the same man who, just three nights ago, had run him down with a laugh. Nothing else made sense.

The man turned abruptly and ducked back into the hogan. Leaphorn lowered the binoculars and thought about it. No glasses. No gold-rims. That might simply mean that the man had them in his pocket. Leaphorn studied the layout of the buildings below him. He located a place where he could climb down the mesa without being seen and approach the hogan away from its east-facing entrance. Before he could move, the man emerged again. He was dressed now, wearing black trousers, with what looked like a purple scarf over his shoulders. He was carrying something. Through the binoculars Leaphorn identified two bottles and a small black case. What appeared to be a white towel hung over his wrist. The man walked rapidly to the brush arbor and put the bottles, the case and the towel on the plank table there.

Shaving, Leaphorn thought. But what the man was doing had nothing to do with shaving. He had taken several objects from the case and arranged them on the table. And then he stood motionless, apparently simply staring down at them. He dropped suddenly to one knee, then rose again almost immediately. Leaphorn frowned. He examined the bottles. One seemed to be half filled with a red liquid. The other held something as clear as water. Now the man had taken an object small and white and held it up to the light, staring at it. He held it in the fingers of both hands, as if it were heavy, or extremely fragile. Through the binoculars it appeared to be a broken piece of bread. The man was pouring the red liquid into a cup, adding a few drops of the clear, raising the cup in both hands to above eye level. His face was rapt and his lips moved slightly, as if he spoke to the cup. Abruptly Leaphorn's memory served him—something he had witnessed years ago and which had then dominated his thoughts for weeks. Leaphorn knew what the man was doing and even the words he was speaking: ". . . this is the cup of my blood, the blood of the new and everlasting covenant. It will be shed for you and for all men so that sins may be forgiven . . ."

Leaphorn lowered the binoculars. The man at the Tso hogan was a Roman Catholic priest. As the rules of his priesthood required of him each day, he was celebrating the Mass.

Back at the carryall, Leaphorn found the girl asleep. She lay curled on the front seat, her head cushioned on her purse, her mouth slightly open. Leaphorn examined her a moment, then unlocked the driver-side door, moved her bare feet, and slid under the steering wheel.

"You were gone long enough," Theodora Adams said. She sat up, pushed the hair away from her face. "Did you find the place?"

"We're going to make this simple and easy to understand," Leaphorn said. He started the engine. "If you'll answer my questions about this man, I'll take you there. If you start lying,

I'll take you back to Short Mountain. And I know enough to tell when the lying starts."

"He was there, then," she said. It wasn't really a question. The girl hadn't doubted he'd be there. But there was a new expectancy in her face—something avid.

"He was there," Leaphorn said. "About six foot, black hair. That sound like the man you expected?"

"Yes," she said.

"Who is he?"

"I'm going to raise hell about this," the girl said. "You don't have any right."

"Okay," Leaphorn said. "Do that. Who is he?"

"I told you who he is. Benjamin Tso."

"What does he do?"

"Do?" She laughed. "You mean for a living? I don't know."

"You're lying," Leaphorn said. "Tell me, or we go back to Short Mountain."

"He's a priest," the girl said. "A member of the Order of Friars Minor . . . a Franciscan." Her voice was resentful, perhaps at the information, perhaps at having been forced to reveal it.

"What's he doing here?"

"Resting. He was tired. He had a long trip."

"From where?"

"From Rome."

"Italy?"

"Italy." She laughed. "That's where Rome is."

Leaphorn turned off the ignition. "We stop playing these games," he said. "If you want to see this man, you're going to tell me about it."

"Oh, well," she said. "What the hell?" And having decided to talk, she talked freely, enjoying the narration.

She had met Tso in Rome. He had been sent there to complete his studies at the Vatican's American College and at the Franciscan seminary outside the city. She had gone with her father and had met Tso through the brother of her college roommate, who was also about to be ordained. Having met him, she stayed behind when her father returned to Washington.

"The bottom line is we're going to get married. To skip a little, he came out here to see about his grandfather and I came out to join him."

You've skipped a lot, Leaphorn thought. You've skipped the part about seeing something you can't have, and wanting it, and going after it. And the Navajo, a product of the hogan life, of the mission boarding school, and then of the seminary, seeing something he had never seen before, and not knowing how to handle it. It would have been strictly no contest, Leaphorn guessed. He remembered Tso's rapt face staring up at the elevated bread, and felt unreasonably angry. He wanted to ask the girl how she had let Tso struggle this far off the hook. Instead he said, "He giving up being a priest?"

"Yes," she said. "Priests can't marry."

"What brought him here?"

"Oh, he got a letter from his grandfather, and then, as you know, his grandfather got killed. So he said he had to come and see about it."

"And what brings you here?"

She glanced at him, eyes hostile. "He said to join him here."

Like hell he did, Leaphorn thought. He ran and you tracked him down. He started the carryall again and concentrated for a moment on steering. He doubted if he would learn anything more from Theodora Adams. Probably she and Tso were simply what they seemed to be. Rabbit and coyote. Probably Tso was simply a priest who had been inspired to escape from this woman by some instinct for self-preservation. To save what? Himself? His honor? His soul? And probably Theodora Adams was the woman who has everything pursuing the man made desirable because he is taboo.

Or perhaps Father Tso *was* Goldrims. If he was, Theodora Adams's role would be something more complex than sexual infatuation. But whatever her role, Leaphorn felt she was too tough and too shrewd to reveal more than she wanted to reveal.

The carryall jolted and groaned over the sloping track beneath the mesa and rolled across the expanse of packed earth that served as the yard of Hosteen Tso. The girl was out of the vehicle before it stopped rolling, running toward the hogan shouting, "Bennie, Bennie." She pulled open the plank door and disappeared inside. Leaphorn waited a moment, watching for the dog. There was no trace of it. He stepped out of the carryall as the girl emerged from the hogan.

"You said he was here," she said. She looked angry and disappointed.

"He was," Leaphorn said. "In fact, he is."

Tso had emerged from the screen of junipers west of the hogan and was walking slowly toward them, looking puzzled. The morning sun was in his eyes and he had not yet identified the girl. Then he did. He stopped, stunned. Theodora Adams noticed it too.

"Bennie," she said. "I tried to stay away." Her voice broke. "I just couldn't."

"I see," Tso said. His eyes were on her face. "Was it a good trip?"

Theodora Adams laughed a shaky laugh. "Of course not," she said. She took his hand. "It was awful. But it's all right now."

Tso glanced over her shoulder at Leaphorn. "The policeman brought you," he said. "You shouldn't have come."

"I had to come," she said. "Of course I'd come. You knew that."

Leaphorn was suddenly acutely embarrassed.

"Father Tso," he said. "I'm sorry. But I need to ask some questions. About your grandfather."

"Sure," Tso said. "Not that I know much. I hadn't seen him for years."

"I understand you got a letter from him. What did he say?"

"Not much," Tso said. "He just said he was sick. And wanted me to come and arrange a sing and take care of things when he died." Tso frowned. "Why would anyone want to kill an old man like that?"

"That's the problem," Leaphorn said. "We don't know. Did he say anything that would help? Do you have the letter?"

"It's with my stuff," Tso said. "I'll get it." He disappeared into the hogan.

Leaphorn looked at Theodora Adams. She stared back.

"Congratulations," Leaphorn said.

"Screw you," she said. "You—" She stopped. Tso was coming through the hogan doorway.

"It really doesn't say much, but you can read it," he said.

The letter was handwritten in black ink on inexpensive typing paper.

"My Grandson," it began. "I have the ghost sickness. There is no one here to talk to the singer and do all the things that have to be done so that I can go again in beauty. I want you to come and get the right singer and see about the sing. If you don't come I will die very soon. Come. There are valuable things I must give you before I die."

"I'm afraid it doesn't help much," Tso said.

"Your grandfather couldn't write, could he? Do you know who he would get to write it for him?"

"I don't know," Tso said. "Some friend, probably."

"How did he get your address?"

"It was just addressed care of the Franciscan abbot at the American College. I guess they asked the Franciscans over at St. Anthony's how to send it."

"When was it mailed?"

"I got it about the middle of April. So I guess it was mailed just before he got killed." Tso glanced down at his hands. He had obviously thought a lot about this. "I was busy with a lot of things then," he said. He glanced up at Leaphorn, looking for some sort of understanding of this failure. "And it was already too late, anyway."

"Bennie thought it could wait a little while," Theodora Adams said.

"I suppose I operated on Navajo time," Tso said. But he didn't smile at the old joke. "I hadn't seen the old man since I was eleven or twelve. I guess I thought it could wait."

Leaphorn said nothing. He was remembering Mrs. Cigaret's voice on the tape recording, recalling for Feeney what Hosteen Tso had told her. ". . . And he said he'd get somebody to write to his grandson." That's what Mrs. Cigaret had said. Get somebody to write. Hosteen Tso hadn't lived more than an hour after that. And yet the letter had been written. Who the hell could have done it? Leaphorn decided he'd go back to Short Mountain and talk to McGinnis again.

"You have any idea what those 'valuable things' he wanted to give you could be?" Leaphorn asked.

"No," Tso said. "I have no idea. Everything I found in the hogan wouldn't be worth a hundred dollars." Tso looked thoughtful. "But maybe he didn't mean money value."

"Maybe not," Leaphorn said. He was still thinking of the letter. If McGinnis hadn't written it, who the hell had?

MCGINNIS POURED the bourbon carefully, stopping exactly at the copyright symbol under the Coca-Cola trademark on the glass. That done, he glanced up at Leaphorn.

"Had a doctor tell me I ought to quit this stuff because it was affecting my eardrums and I told him I liked what I was drinking better'n what I was hearing."

He held the glass to the light, enjoying the amber as a wine-lover enjoys the red.

"Two things I can't even guess at," McGinnis said. "The first is who he got to write that letter for him, and the other is how come he didn't come back to me to write it for him after he found out the address." McGinnis considered this, his expression sour. "You might think it's because I'm a man who's known for knowing everybody's business. A gossip. But then all those people out here know I don't talk what I write in their letters for them. They've had many a year to learn that."

"I'm going to tell you exactly what was in that letter," Leaphorn said. He leaned forward in his chair, eyes intent on McGinnis's face. "I want you to listen. It said, 'My Grandson. I have ghost sickness. Nobody is here to get me a singer and do the things necessary so I can go again in beauty. I need you to come here and hire the right singer and see about things. If you don't come I will die soon. Come. There are valuable things I must give you before I die."

McGinnis stared into the bourbon, full of thought. "Go on," he said. "I'm listening."

"That's it," Leaphorn said. "I memorized it."

"Funny," McGinnis said.

"I'm going to ask you if that's about the same as the letter he was telling you he wanted written."

"I figured that's what you were going to ask," McGinnis said. "Let me see the letter."

"I don't have it," Leaphorn said. "This Benjamin Tso let me read it."

"You got a hell of a memory, then," McGinnis said.

"Nothing much wrong with it," Leaphorn said. "How about yours? You remember what he wanted you to write?"

McGinnis pursed his lips. "Well, now," he said. "It's kind of like I told you. I got a reputation around here for not gossiping about what people want put in their letters."

"I want you to hear something else, then," Leaphorn said. "This is a tape of an FBI agent named Feeney talking to Margaret Cigaret about what Hosteen Tso told her that afternoon just before he got killed." Leaphorn picked up the recorder and pushed the play button.

". . . say anything just before you left him and went over by the cliff?" the voice of Feeney asked.

And then the voice of the Listening Woman. "I don't remember much. I told him he ought to get somebody to take him to Gallup and get his chest x-rayed because maybe he had one of those sicknesses that white people cure. And he said he'd get somebody to write to his grandson to take care of everything, and then I said I'd go and listen—"

Leaphorn stopped the tape, his eyes still on McGinnis's.

"Well, well," McGinnis said. He started the rocking chair in motion. "Well, now," he said. "If I heard what I think I heard . . ." He paused. "That was her talking about just before old Tso got hit on the head?"

"Right," Leaphorn said.

"And he was saying he still hadn't got the letter written. So nobody could have written it—except Anna Atcitty, and that's damned unlikely. And even if she wrote it, which I bet my ass she didn't, the guy that hit 'em on the head would've had to gone and mailed it." He glanced at Leaphorn. "You believe that?"

"No," Leaphorn said.

McGinnis abruptly stopped the rocking chair. In the Coca-Cola glass the oscillation of the bourbon turned abruptly into splashing waves.

"By God," McGinnis said, his voice enthusiastic. "This gets mysterious."

"Yeah," Leaphorn said.

"That was a short letter," McGinnis said. "What he told me would make a long one. Maybe a page and a half. And I write small."

McGinnis pushed himself out of the rocker and reached for the bourbon. "You know," he said, uncapping the bottle, "I'm known for keeping secrets as well as for talking. And I'm known as an Indian trader. By profession, in fact, that's what I am. And you're an Indian. So let's trade."

"For what?" Leaphorn asked.

"Tit for tat," McGinnis said. "I tell you what I know. You tell me what you know."

"Fair enough," Leaphorn said. "Except right now there's damned little I know."

"Then you'll owe me," McGinnis said. "When you get this thing figured out you tell me. That means I gotta trust you. Got any problems with that?"

"No," Leaphorn said.

"Well, then," McGinnis said. "You know anything about somebody named Jimmy?" Leaphorn shook his head.

"Old Man Tso come in here and he sat down over there." McGinnis waved the glass in the direction of an overstuffed chair. "He said to write a letter telling his grandson that he was sick, and to tell the grandson to come right away and get a singer to cure him. And to tell him that Jimmy was acting bad, acting like he didn't have any relatives."

McGinnis paused, sipped, and thought. "Let's see now," he said. "He said to tell the grandson that Jimmy was acting like a damned white man. That maybe Jimmy had become a witch. Jimmy had stirred up the ghost. He said to tell his grandson to hurry up and come right away because there was something that he had to tell him. He said he couldn't die until he told him." McGinnis had been staring into the glass as he spoke. Now he looked up at Leaphorn, his shrunken old face expressionless but his eyes searching for an answer. "Hosteen Tso told me he wanted to put that down twice. That he couldn't die until he told that grandson something. And that after he told him, then it would be time to die. Looks like somebody hurried it up." He was motionless in the chair a long moment. "I'd like to know who did that," he said.

"I'd like to know who Jimmy is," Leaphorn said.

"I don't know," McGinnis said. "I asked the old fart, and all he'd say was that Jimmy was a son-of-a-bitch, and maybe a skinwalking witch. But he wouldn't say who he was. Sounds like he figured the grandson would know."

"He say anything about wanting to give the grandson something valuable?"

McGinnis shook his head. "Hell," he said. "What'd he have? A few sheep. Forty, fifty dollars' worth of jewelry in pawn here. Change of clothes. He didn't have nothing valuable." McGinnis pondered this, the only sound in the room the slow, rhythmic creaking of his rocker.

"That girl," he said finally. "Let me see if I guessed right about the way that is. She's after that priest. He's running and she's chasing and now she's got him." He glanced at Leaphorn for confirmation. "That about it? You left her out there with him?"

"Yeah," Leaphorn said. "You got it figured right."

They thought about it awhile. The old mantel clock on the shelf behind Leaphorn's chair became suddenly noisy in the silence. McGinnis smiled faintly over his Coca-Cola glass. But McGinnis hadn't seen it happen, hadn't seen the defeat of Father Benjamin Tso as Leaphorn had. Leaphorn had asked the priest a few more questions about the letter, and had established that Father Tso had seen nothing of Goldrims, and no sign of the dog. And then Theodora Adams had opened the back door of the carryall, and taken out her small duffel bag, and put it on the ground beside the vehicle. Benjamin Tso had looked at it, and at her, and had taken a long, deep breath and said, "Theodora, you can't stay." And Theodora had stood silently, looking first at him and then down at her hands, and her shoulders had slumped just a fraction, and Leaphorn had become aware from the tortured expression on the face of Father Tso that Theodora Adams must be crying, and Leaphorn had said he would "look around a little" and had walked away from this struggle of two souls, which was, as Miss Adams had told him, not the business of the Navajo Tribal Police. The struggle had been brief. When Leaphorn had completed his idle, fruitless examination of the ground behind the hogan, Father Tso was holding the girl against him, saying something into her hair.

"That's some woman," McGinnis said, mostly to himself. His watery old eyes were almost closed. Leaphorn had nothing to add to that. He was thinking of the expression on Father Tso's face when Tso had told him to leave the girl. The God Tso had worshipped was no more than a distant abstraction then. The girl stood against his side, warm and alive, though at this stage of the Fall of Father Tso lust hadn't been the enemy. Tso's enemy, Leaphorn thought, would be a complicated mixture. It would include pity, however sadly misplaced, and affection, and loneliness and vanity. Lust would come later, when Theodora Adams wanted it to come—and Tso would learn then how he had overestimated himself.

"Certain kind of woman likes what she can't have," McGinnis said. "They hate to see a man keep a promise. Some of 'em go after married men. But you take a real tiger like that Adams—she goes gets herself a priest." He sipped the bourbon, glanced sidewise at Leaphorn. "You know how that works with a Catholic priest?" he asked. "Before they're ordained, they get some time to think about the promises they're going to make—giving up the world, and women, and all that. And then when the time comes, they go up to the altar, and they stretch out on the floor, flat on their face, and they make the promise in front of the bishop. Psychologically it makes it mean as hell to change your mind. Just one step short of getting your balls cut off if you break a promise like that." McGinnis sipped again. "Makes it a hell of a challenge for a woman," he added.

Leaphorn was thinking of another challenge. It was obsessing him. Somewhere in this jumble of contradictions, oddities, coincidences, and unlikely events there must be a pattern, a reason, something that linked a cause and an effect, which the laws of natural harmony and reason would dictate. It had to be there.

"McGinnis," he said. He tried to keep his voice from sounding plaintive. "Is there anything you're not telling me that would help make sense out of this? This secret the old man was keeping—what could it have been? Could it have been worth killing for?"

McGinnis snorted. "There ain't nothing around here worth killing for," he said. "Put it all together and this whole Short Mountain country ain't worth hitting a man with a stick for."

"What do you think, then?" Leaphorn asked. "Anything that would help."

The old man communed with the inch of amber left in the Coca-Cola glass. "I can tell you a story," he said finally. "If you don't mind having your time wasted."

"I'd like to hear it," Leaphorn said.

"Part of it's true," McGinnis said. "And some of it's probably Navajo bullshit. It starts off about a hundred twenty years ago when Standing Medicine was headman of the Bitter Water Dinee and a man noted for his wisdom." McGinnis rocked back in his chair, slowly telling how, in 1863, the territorial governor of New Mexico decided to destroy the Navajos, how Standing Medicine had joined Narbona and fought Kit Carson's army until, after the bitter starvation winter of 1864, what was left of the group surrendered and was taken to join other Navajos being held at Bosque Redondo.

"That much is the true part," McGinnis said. "Anyhow, Standing Medicine shows up on the army records as being brought in in 1864, and he died at Bosque Redondo in 1865. And that gets us to the funny story." McGinnis tipped his head back and drained the last trickle of bourbon onto his tongue. He put the glass down, carefully refilled it to the copyright symbol, capped the bottle, and raised the glass to Leaphorn. "Way they told it when I was a young man, this Standing Medicine was known all around this part of the reservation for his curing. Maybe I told you about that already. But he knew every bit of the Blessing Way, and he could do the Wind Way, and the Mountain Way Chant and parts of some of the others. But they say he also knew a ceremonial that nobody at all knows anymore. I heard it called the Sun Way, and the Calling Back

Chant. Anyway, it's supposed to be the ceremonial that Changing Woman and the Talking God taught the people to use when the Fourth World ends."

McGinnis paused to tap the Coca-Cola glass—just a few drops on the tongue. "Now, you may have another version in your clan," he said. "The way we have it around Short Mountain, the Fourth World isn't supposed to end like the Third World did, with Water Monster making a flood. This time the evil is supposed to cause the Sun Father to make it cold, and the Dinee are supposed to hole up somewhere over in the Chuska range. I think Beautiful Mountain opens up for them. Then when the time is just right, they do this Sun Way and call back the light and warmth, and they start the Fifth World."

"I never heard a version quite like that," Leaphorn said.

"Like I said, maybe it's bullshit. But there's a point. There is a point. The way the old story goes, Standing Medicine figured this Way was the most important ceremonial of all. And he figured Kit Carson and the soldiers were going to catch him, and he was afraid the ritual would be forgotten, so . . ." McGinnis sipped again, watching Leaphorn, timing his account. "So he found a place and somehow or other in some magic way he preserved it all. And he just told his oldest son, so that Kit Carson and the Belacani soldiers wouldn't find it and so the Utes wouldn't find it and spoil it."

"Interesting," Leaphorn said.

"Hold on. We ain't got to the interesting part yet," McGinnis said. "What's interesting is that Standing Medicine's son came back from the Long Walk, and married a woman in the Mud clan, and this feller's oldest son was a man named Mustache Tsossie, and he married back into the Salt Cedar clan, and his oldest boy turned out to be the one we called Hosteen Tso."

"So maybe that's the secret," Leaphorn said.

"Maybe so. Or like I said, maybe it's all Navajo bullshit." McGinnis's expression was carefully neutral.

"And part of the secret would be where this place was where Standing Medicine preserved the Sun Way," Leaphorn said. "Any guesses?"

"My God," McGinnis said. "It's magic. And magic could be

up in the sky, or under the earth. Out in that canyon country it could be anywhere."

"It's been my experience," Leaphorn said, "that secrets are hard to keep. If fathers know and sons know, pretty soon other people know."

"You're forgetting something," McGinnis said. "Lot of these people around here are Utes, or half Utes. Lot of intermarrying. You got to think about how a die-hard old-timer like Hosteen Tso, and his folks before him, would feel about that. That sort of makes people close-mouthed about secrets."

Leaphorn thought about it. "Yeah," he said. "I see what you mean." The Utes had always raided this corner of the reservation. And when Kit Carson and the army had come, Ute scouts had led them—betraying hiding places, revealing food caches, helping hunt down the starving Dinee. Standing Medicine would have been guarding his secret as much from the Utes as from the whites—and now the Utes had married into the clans.

"Even if we knew what it was and where it is, it wouldn't help anyway," McGinnis said. "You probably got an old medicine bundle and some Yei masks and amulets hidden away somewhere. It's not the kind of stuff anybody kills you for."

"Not even if it's the way to stop the world from ending?" Leaphorn asked.

McGinnis looked at him, saw he was smiling. "That's what you birds got to do, you know," McGinnis said. "If you're going to solve that Tso killing, you got to figure the reason for it." McGinnis stared into the glass. "It's a damn funny thing to think about," he said. "You can just see it. Somebody walking up that wagon track, and the old man and that Atcitty girl standing there watching him coming, and probably saying 'Ya-ta-hey' whether it was friend or stranger, and then this feller taking a gun barrel or something, and clouting the old man with it and then running the girl down and clubbing her, and then . . ." McGinnis shook his head in disbelief. "And then just turning right around and walking right up that wagon track away from there." McGinnis stared over the glass at Leaphorn. "You just plain *know* a feller would have to have a real reason to do something like that. Just think about it."

Joe Leaphorn thought about it.

Outside there was the sound of hammering, of laughter, of a pickup engine starting. Leaphorn was oblivious to it. He was thinking. He was again recreating the crime in his mind. The reason for what had happened at the Tso hogan must have been real—desperate and urgent—even if it had been done by the sort of person who laughed as he ran over a strange policeman beside a lonely road. Leaphorn sighed. He would have to find out about that reason. And that meant he would *have* to speak with Margaret Cigaret.

"You were right about Mrs. Cigaret not being home," Leaphorn said. "I went by there to check. Nobody there and the truck's gone. You got any ideas where she is?"

"No telling," McGinnis said. "She could be anyplace. I'd guess visiting kin, like I told you."

"How did you know she wasn't home?"

McGinnis frowned at him. "That don't take any great brains," he said. "She come through here three or four days ago. Had one of the Old Lady Nakai's girls driving her truck. And she ain't been back." He stared belligerently at Leaphorn. "And I *knew* she didn't come home because the only way to get to her place from the outside is right past my place here."

"Three or four days ago? Can you remember which day?"

McGinnis thought about it. It took only a moment. "Wednesday. Little after I ate. About 2 P.M."

Wednesday. The Kinaalda where Leaphorn had arrested young Emerson Begay would have been starting about then. Begay was a member of the Mud clan. His niece was being initiated into womanhood at the ceremony.

"What's Mrs. Cigaret's clan?" Leaphorn asked. "Is she a Mud Dinee?"

"She's a born-to Mud," McGinnis said.

So Leaphorn knew where he could find Mrs. Cigaret. For a hundred miles around, every member of the Mud People healthy enough to stir would be drawn to the ritual reunion to share its blessing and reinforce its power.

"There's not many Mud Dinee around Short Mountain," McGinnis said. "Mrs. Cigaret's bunch, and the Nakai family, and the Endischee outfit, and Alice Frank Pino, and a few

Begays, and I think that's all of them."

Leaphorn got up and stretched. He thanked McGinnis for the hospitality and said he would go to the sing. He used the Navajo verb *hodeeshtal,* which means "to take part in a ritual chant." By slightly changing the guttural inflection, the word becomes the verb "to be kicked." As Leaphorn pronounced it, a listener with an ear alert to the endless Navajo punning could have understood Leaphorn to mean either that he was going to get himself cured or get himself kicked. It was among the oldest of old Navajo word plays, and McGinnis—grinning slightly—replied with the expected pun response.

"Good for a sore butt," he said.

THE WIND FOLLOWED Leaphorn's carryall half the way across the Nokaito Bench, enveloping the jolting vehicle in its own gritty dust and filling the policeman's nostrils with exhaust fumes. It was hot. The promise of rain had faded as the west wind raveled away the thunderheads. Now the sky was blank blue. The road angled toward the crest of the ridge, growing rockier as it neared the top. Leaphorn down-shifted to ease the vehicle over a corrugation of stone and the following wind gusted past him. He drove across the ridge line, blind for a moment. Then, with a shift in the wind, the dust cleared and he saw the place of Alice Endischee.

The land sloped northward now into Utah, vast, empty, and treeless. In Leaphorn the Navajo sensitivity to land and landscape was fine-tuned. Normally he saw beauty in such blue-haze distances, but today he saw only poverty, a sparse stony grassland ruined by overgrazing and now gray with drought.

He shifted the carryall back into third gear as the track tilted slightly downward, and inspected the place of Alice Endischee far down the slope. There was the square plank "summer hogan" with its tar-paper roof, providing a spot of red in the landscape, and beyond it a "winter hogan" of stone, and a pole arbor roofed with sage and creosote brush, and two corrals, and an older hogan built carefully to the prescription of the Holy People and used for all things sacred and ceremonial.

Scattered among the buildings Leaphorn counted seven pick-ups, a battered green Mustang, a flatbed truck, and two wagons. The scene hadn't changed since he had come there to find Emerson Begay, when the Kinaalda had only started and the Endischee girl had been having her hair washed in yucca suds by her aunts as the first step of the great ritual blessing. Now the ceremonial would be in the climactic day.

People were coming out of the medicine hogan, some of them watching his approaching vehicle, but most standing in a milling cluster around the doorway. Then, from the cluster, a girl abruptly emerged—running.

She ran, pursued by the wind and a half-dozen younger children, across an expanse of sagebrush. She set the easy pace of those who know that they have a great distance to go. She wore the long skirt, the long-sleeved blouse, and the heavy silver jewelry of a traditional Navajo woman—but she ran with the easy grace of a child who has not yet forgotten how to race her shadow.

Leaphorn stopped the carryall and watched, remembering his own initiation out of childhood, until the racers disappeared down the slope. For the Endischee girl, this would be the third race of the day, and the third day of such racing. Changing Woman taught that the longer a girl runs at her Kinaalda, the longer she lives a healthy life. But by the third day, muscles would be sore and the return would be early. Leaphorn shifted back into gear. While the girl was gone, the family would re-enter the hogan to sing the Racing Songs, the same prayers the Holy People had chanted at the menstruation ceremony when White Shell Girl became Changing Woman. Then there would be a pause, while the women baked the great ceremonial cake to be eaten tonight. The pause would give Leaphorn his chance to approach and cross-examine Listening Woman.

He touched the woman's sleeve as she emerged from the hogan, and told her who he was, and why he wanted to talk to her.

"It's like I told that white policeman," Margaret Cigaret said. "The old man who was to die told me some dry paintings had been spoiled, and the man who was to die had been there. And maybe that was why he was sick."

"I listened to the tape recording of you talking to the white policeman," Leaphorn said. "But I noticed, my mother, that the white man didn't really let you tell about it. He interrupted you."

Margaret Cigaret thought about that. She stood, arms folded across the purple velvet of her blouse, her blind eyes looking through Leaphorn.

"Yes," she said. "That's the way it was."

"I came to find you because I thought that if we would talk about it again, you could tell me what the white man was too impatient to hear." Leaphorn suspected she would remember he was the man who had come to this ceremonial three days before and arrested Emerson Begay. While Begay was not a member of the Cigaret family as far as Leaphorn knew, he was Mud clan and he was probably some sort of extended-family nephew. So Leaphorn was guilty of arresting a relative. In the traditional Navajo system, even distant nephews who stole sheep were high on the value scale. "I wonder what you are thinking about me, my mother," Leaphorn said. "I wonder if you are thinking that it's no use talking to a policeman who is too stupid to keep the Begay boy from escaping because he would be too stupid to catch the one who killed those who were killed." Like Mrs. Cigaret, Leaphorn refrained from speaking the name of the dead. To do so was to risk attracting the attention of the ghost, and even if you didn't believe this, it was bad manners to risk ghost sickness for those who did believe. "But if you think about it fairly, you will remember that your nephew is a very smart young man. His handcuffs were uncomfortable, so I took them off. He offered to help me, and I accepted the offer. It was night, and he slipped away. Remember, your nephew has escaped before."

Margaret Cigaret acknowledged this with a nod, then she tilted her head toward the place near the hogan door. There three women were pouring buckets of batter into the fire pit, making the ritual cake of the menstruation ceremony. Steam now joined the smoke. She turned toward them and away from Leaphorn.

"Put corn shucks over all of it," Mrs. Cigaret instructed them in a loud, clear voice. "You work around in a circle. East, south, west, north."

The women stopped their work for a moment. "We haven't got it poured in yet," one of them said. "Did you say we could put the raisins in?"

"Sprinkle them across the top," Mrs. Cigaret said. "Then arrange the corn-shuck crosses all across it. Start from the east side and work around like I said." She swiveled her face back toward Leaphorn. "That's the way it was done when First Man and First Woman and the Holy People gave White Shell Girl her Kinaalda when she menstruated," Mrs. Cigaret said. "And that's the way Changing Woman taught us to do."

"Yes," Leaphorn said. "I remember."

"What the white man was too impatient to hear was all about what was making the one who was killed sick," Mrs. Cigaret said.

"*I* would like to hear that when there is time for you to tell me, my mother."

Mrs. Cigaret frowned. "The white man didn't think it had anything to do with the killing."

"I am not a white man," Leaphorn said. "I am one of the Dinee. I know that the same thing that makes a man sick sometimes makes him die."

"But this time the man was hit by a gun barrel."

"I know that, my mother," Leaphorn said. "But can you tell me why he was hit with the gun barrel?"

Mrs. Cigaret thought about it.

The wind kicked up again, whipping her skirts around her legs and sending a flurry of dust across the hogan yard. At the fire pit, the women were carefully pouring a thin layer of dirt over newspapers, which covered the corn shucks, which covered the batter.

"Yes," Mrs. Cigaret said. "I hear what you are saying."

"You told the white policeman that you planned to tell the

old man he should have a Mountain Way sing and a Black Rain ceremony," Leaphorn said. "Why those?"

Mrs. Cigaret was silent. The wind gusted again, moving a loose strand of gray hair against her face. She had been beautiful once, Leaphorn saw. Now she was weathered, and her face was troubled. Behind Leaphorn there came a shout of laughter. The kindling of split piñon and cedar arranged atop the cake batter in the fire pit was flaming.

"It was what I heard when I listened to the Earth," Mrs. Cigaret said, when the laughter died out.

"Can you tell me?"

Mrs. Cigaret sighed. "Only that I knew it was more than one thing. Some of the sickness came from stirring up old ghosts. But the voices told me that the old man hadn't told me everything." She paused, her eyes blank with the glaze of glaucoma, and her face grim and sad. "The voices told me that what had happened had cut into his heart. There was no way to cure it. The Mountain Way sing was the right one because the sickness came from the spoiling of holy things, and the Black Rain because a taboo had been broken. But the old man's heart was cut in half. And there was no sing anymore that would restore him to beauty."

"Something very bad had happened," Leaphorn said, urging her on.

"I don't think he wanted to live anymore," Margaret Cigaret said. "I think he wanted his grandson to come, and then he wanted to die."

The fire was blazing all across the fire pit now and there was a sudden outburst of shouting and more laughter from those waiting around the hogan. The girl was coming—running across the sagebrush flat at the head of a straggling line. One of the Endischees was hanging a blanket across the hogan doorway, signifying that the ceremonial would be resumed inside.

"I have to go inside now," Mrs. Cigaret said. "There's no more to say. When someone wants to die, they die."

Inside, a big man sat against the hogan wall and sang with his eyes closed, the voice rising, falling and changing cadence in a pattern as old as the People.

"She is preparing her child," the big man sang. "She is preparing her child.

"White Shell Girl, she is preparing her,
With white shell moccasins, she is preparing her,
With white shell leggings, she is preparing her,
With jewelry of white shells, she is preparing her."

The big man sat to Leaphorn's left, his legs folded in front of him, among the men who lined the south side of the hogan. Across from them, the women sat. The hogan floor had been cleared. A small pile of earth covered the fire pit under the smoke hole in the center. A blanket was spread against the west wall and on it were arranged the hard goods brought to this affair to be blessed by the beauty it would generate. Beside the blanket, one of the aunts of Eileen Endischee was giving the girl's hair its ceremonial brushing. She was a pretty girl, her face pale and fatigued now, but also somehow serene.

"White Shell Girl with pollen is preparing her," the big man sang.

"With the pollen of soft goods placed in her mouth, she will speak.

"With the pollen of soft goods she is preparing her.
With the pollen of soft goods she is blessing her.
She is preparing her.
She is preparing her.
She is preparing her child to live in beauty.
She is preparing her for a long life in beauty.
With beauty before her, White Shell Girl prepares her.
With beauty behind her, White Shell Girl prepares her.
With beauty above her, White Shell Girl prepares her."

Leaphorn found himself, as he had since childhood, caught up in the hypnotic repetition of pattern which blended meaning, rhythm, and sound in something more than the total of all of them. By the blanket, the aunt of the Endischee girl was tying up the child's hair. Other voices around the hogan wall joined the big man in the singing.

"With beauty all around her, she prepares her."

A girl becoming a woman, and her people celebrating this addition to the Dinee with joy and reverence. Leaphorn found himself singing too. The anger he had brought—despite all the taboos—to this ceremonial had been overcome. Leaphorn felt restored in harmony.

He had a loud, clear voice, and he used it. "With beauty before her, White Shell Girl prepares her."

The big man glanced at him, a friendly look. Across the hogan, Leaphorn noticed, two of the women were smiling at him. He was a stranger, a policeman who had arrested one of them, a man from another clan, perhaps even a witch, but he was accepted with the natural hospitality of the Dinee. He felt a fierce pride in his people, and in this celebration of womanhood. The Dinee had always respected the female equally with the male—giving her equality in property, in metaphysics, and in clan—recognizing the mother's role in the footsteps of Changing Woman as the preserver of the Navajo Way. Leaphorn remembered what his mother had told him when he had asked how Changing Woman could have prescribed a Kinaalda cake "a shovel handle wide" and garnished with raisins when the Dinee had neither shovels nor grapes. "When you are a man," she had said, "you will understand that she was teaching us to stay in harmony with time." Thus, while the Kiowas were crushed, the Utes reduced to hopeless poverty, and the Hopis withdrawn into the secret of their kivas, the eternal Navajo adapted and endured.

The Endischee girl, her hair arranged as the hair of White Shell Girl had been arranged by the Holy People, collected her jewelry from the blanket, put it on, and left the hogan—shyly aware that all eyes were upon her.

"In beauty it is finished," the big man sang. "In beauty it is finished."

Leaphorn stood, waiting his turn to join the single file exiting through the hogan doorway. The space was filled with the smell of sweat, wool, earth and piñon smoke from the fire outside. The audience crowded around the blanket, collecting their newly blessed belongings. A middle-aged woman in a pants suit picked up a bridle; a teenage boy wearing a black felt "reservation hat" took a small slab of turquoise stone and a red plastic floating battery lantern stenciled HAAS; an old man wearing a striped denim Santa Fe Railroad cap picked up a flour sack containing God knows what. Leaphorn ducked through the doorway. Mixed with the perfume of the piñon smoke there now came the smell of roasting mutton.

He felt both hungry and relaxed. He would eat, and then he would ask around about a man with gold-rimmed glasses and an oversized dog, and then he would resume his conversation with Listening Woman. His mind had started working again, finding a hint of a pattern in what had been only disorder. He would simply chat with Mrs. Cigaret, giving her a chance to know him better. By tomorrow he wanted her to know him well enough even to risk discussing that dangerous subject no wise Navajo would discuss with a stranger—witchcraft.

The wind died away with evening. The sunset had produced a great flare of fluorescent orange from the still-dusty atmosphere. Leaphorn had eaten mutton ribs, and fry bread, and talked to a dozen people, and learned nothing useful. He had talked with Margaret Cigaret again, getting her to recreate as well as she remembered the sequence of events that led up to the Tso-Atcitty deaths, but he had learned little he hadn't already known from the FBI report and the tape recording. And nothing he learned seemed helpful. Anna Atcitty had not wanted to drive Mrs. Cigaret to her appointment with Hosteen Tso, and Mrs. Cigaret believed that was because she wanted to meet a boy. Mrs. Cigaret wasn't sure of the boy's identity but suspected he was a Salt Cedar Dinee who worked at Short Mountain. A dust devil had blown away some of the pollen which Mrs. Cigaret used in her professional procedure. Mrs. Cigaret had not, as Leaphorn had assumed, done her listening in the little cul-de-sac worn in the mesa cliff just under where Leaphorn had stood looking down on the Tso hogan. Leaphorn had guessed about that, knowing from the FBI report only that she had gone to a sheltered place against the cliff out of sight of the hogan; he had presumed she had been led by Anna Atcitty to the closest such place. But Mrs. Cigaret remembered walking along a goat trail to reach the sand-floored cul-de-sac where she had listened. And she thought it was at least one hundred yards from the hogan, which meant it was another, somewhat smaller drainage cut in the mesa cliff west of where Leaphorn had stood. Leaphorn remembered he had looked down into it and had noticed it had once been fenced off as a holding pen for sheep.

None of these odds and ends seemed to hold any promise, though sometime after midnight Leaphorn learned that the child who had reported seeing the "dark bird" dive into an arm of Lake Powell was one of the Gorman boys. The boy was attending the Kinaalda, but had left with two of his cousins to refill the Endischee water barrels. That involved a round trip of more than twelve miles and the wagon probably wouldn't be back before dawn. The boy's name was Eddie. He was the boy in the black hat and it turned out he wouldn't be back at all after loading the water barrels; he was going to Farmington.

Leaphorn sat through the night-long ceremonial, singing the twelve Hogan Songs, and the Songs of the Talking God, and watching sympathetically the grimly determined efforts of the Endischee girl not to break the rules by falling asleep. When the sky was pink in the east he had joined the others and chanted the Dawn Song, remembering the reverence with which his grandfather had always used it to greet each new day. The words, down through the generations, had become so melded into the rhythm that they were hardly more than musical sounds. But Leaphorn remembered the meaning.

"Below the East, she has discovered it,
Now she has discovered Dawn Boy,
The child now he has come upon it,
Where it was resting, he has come upon it,
Now he talks to it, now it listens to him.
Since it listens to him, it obeys him;
Since it obeys him, it grants him beauty.
From the mouth of Dawn Boy, beauty comes forth.
Now the child will have life of everlasting beauty.

Now the child will go with beauty before it,
Now the child will go with beauty all around it,
Now the child will be with beauty finished."

Then the Endischee girl had gone, trailed again by cousins, and nieces, and nephews, to run the final race of Kinaalda. The sun had come up and Leaphorn thought he'd try once more to talk to Mrs. Cigaret. She was sitting in her truck, its door open, listening to those who were about to remove the Kinaalda cake from the fire pit.

Leaphorn sat down beside her. "One thing still troubles me," he said. "You told the FBI man, and you have told me, that the man who was killed said that sand paintings were spoiled. Sand paintings. More than one of the dry paintings. How could that be?"

"I don't know," Mrs. Cigaret said.

"Do you know of *any* sing that has more than one sand painting at a time?" Leaphorn asked. "Is there any singer *anywhere* on the reservation who does it a different way?"

"They all do it the same way, if they do it the way the Talking God taught them to make dry paintings."

"That's what my grandfather taught me," Leaphorn said. "The proper one is made, and when the ceremonial is finished, the singer wipes it out, and the sand is mixed together and carried out of the hogan, and scattered back to the wind. That's the way I was taught."

"Yes," Margaret Cigaret said.

"Then, old mother, could it have been that you did not understand what the man who was your patient said to you? Could he have said one sand painting was spoiled?"

Mrs. Cigaret turned her face from the place where the Endischees had scraped away the hot cinders, and had brushed away a layer of ashes, and were now preparing to lift the Kinaalda cake from its pit oven. Her eyes focused directly on Leaphorn's face; as directly as if she could see him.

"No," she said. "I thought I heard him wrong. And I said so. And he said . . ." She paused, recalling it. "He said, 'No, not just one holy painting. More than one.' He said it was strange, and then he wouldn't talk any more about it."

"Very strange," Leaphorn said. The only place he knew of that a bona fide singer had produced genuine dry paintings to be preserved was at the Museum of Navajo Ceremonial Art in Santa Fe. There it had been done only after much soul-searching and argument, and only after certain elements had been slightly modified. The argument for breaking the rules had been to preserve certain paintings so they would never be lost. Could that be the answer here? Had Standing Medicine found a way to leave sand paintings so a ceremony would be preserved for posterity? Leaphorn shook his head.

"It doesn't make sense," Leaphorn said.

"No," Mrs. Cigaret said. "No one would do it."

Leaphorn opened his mouth and then closed it. It was not necessary to say the obvious. There was no reason to say, "Except a witch." In the metaphysics of the Navajo, these stylized reproductions of Holy People reliving moments from mythology were produced to restore harmony. But this same metaphysics provided that when not done properly, a sand painting would destroy harmony and cause death. The legends of the grisly happenings in witches' dens were sprinkled with deliberately perverted sand paintings, as well as with murder and incest.

Mrs. Cigaret had turned her face toward the fire pit. Amid laughter and loud approval, the great brown cake was being raised from the pit—carefully, to avoid breaking—and the dust and ashes brushed away.

"The cake is out," Leaphorn said. "It looks perfect."

"The ceremony has been perfect," Listening Woman said. "Everything was done just right. In the songs, everybody got the words right. And I heard your voice among the singers."

"Yes," Leaphorn said.

Mrs. Cigaret was smiling now, but the smile was grim. "And in a moment you will ask me if the man who was to die told me anything about skinwalkers, anything about a den of witches."

"I might have asked you that, old mother," Leaphorn said. "I was trying to remember if it is wrong to even ask about witches at a Kinaalda."

"It's not a good thing to talk about," Mrs. Cigaret said. "But in this case it is business, and we won't be talking much about witches, because the old man told me nothing about them."

"Nothing?"

"Nothing. I asked him. I asked him because I, too, wondered about the sand paintings," Mrs. Cigaret said. She laughed. "And all he did was get angry. He said he couldn't talk about it because it was a secret. A big secret."

"Did you ever think that the old man might himself be a skinwalker?"

Mrs. Cigaret was silent. At the hogan door, Mrs. Endischee was cutting portions from the rim of the cake and handing them out to relatives.

"I thought about it," Mrs. Cigaret said. She shook her head again. "I don't know," she said. "If he was, he doesn't hurt anybody now."

Just beyond the Mexican Water chapter house, where Navajo Route 1 intersects with Navajo Route 12, Leaphorn pulled the carryall onto the shoulder, cut the ignition, and sat. The Tuba City district office was 113 miles west, down Route 1. Chinle, and the onerous duty of helping provide Boy Scout security at Canyon De Chelly, lay 62 miles almost due south down Route 12. Desire pulled Leaphorn westward. But when he got to the Tuba City district office what could he tell Captain Largo? He had come up with absolutely nothing concrete to justify the time Largo had bought for him—and damned little that could be described even as nebulous. He should radio Largo that he was calling it all off and then drive to Chinle and report for duty. Leaphorn picked up the Tso-Atcitty file, flipped rapidly through it, put it down again, and picked up the thicker file about the search for the helicopter.

The recreated route of the copter still led erratically, but fairly directly, toward the vicinity of the Tso hogan. Leaphorn stared at the map, remembering that another line—drawn from an abandoned Mercedes to a water hole where two dogs had died—would, if extended, pass near the same spot. He flipped to the next page and began reading rapidly the description of the copter, the details of its rental, the pertinent facts about the pilot. Leaphorn stared at the name, Edward Haas.

HAAS had been stenciled in white on the red plastic of the battery lantern on the blanket in the Endischee hogan.

"Well, now," Leaphorn said aloud. He thought of dates and places, trying to make connections, and failing that, thought of what Listening Woman had said when he'd asked if Tso might have been a witch. Then he reached down, picked up the radio mike and checked in with the Tuba City headquarters. Captain Largo wasn't in.

"Just tell him this, then," Leaphorn said. "Tell him that a boy named Eddie Gorman was at the Endischee Kinaalda with one of those floating fishermen's lanterns with the name Haas stenciled on it." He filled in the details of description, family, and where the boy might be found. "Tell him I'm going to Window Rock and clear a trip to Albuquerque."

"Albuquerque?" the dispatcher asked. "Largo's going to ask me why you're going to Albuquerque."

Leaphorn stared at the speaker a moment, thinking about it. "Tell him I'm going to the FBI office. I want to read their file on that helicopter case."

SPECIAL AGENT GEORGE WITOVER, who ushered Leaphorn into the interrogation room, had a bushy but neat mustache, shrewd light-blue eyes, and freckles. He took the chair behind the desk and smiled at Leaphorn. "Well, Lieutenant—" He glanced down at the note the receptionist had given him. "Lieutenant Leaphorn. We understand you found a flashlight from the Haas helicopter." The blue eyes held Leaphorn's eyes expectantly. "Have a seat." He gestured to the chair beside the desk.

Leaphorn sat down. "Yes."

"Your Window Rock office called and told us a little about it," the man said. "They said you particularly wanted to talk to me. Why was that?"

"I heard somewhere that the man to talk to about the case was Agent George Witover," Leaphorn said. "I heard you were the one who was handling it."

"Oh," Witover said. He eyed Leaphorn curiously, and seemed to be trying to read something in his face.

"And I thought about the rule the FBI has about not letting anybody see case files, and I thought about how we have just exactly the same rule, and it occurred to me that sometimes rules like that get in the way of getting things done. So I thought that since we're both interested in that copter, we could sort of exchange information informally."

"You can see the report we made to the U.S. Attorney," Witover said.

"If you're like us, sometimes that report is fairly brief, and the file is fairly thick. Everything doesn't go into the report," Leaphorn said.

"What we heard from Window Rock was that you were at some sort of ceremonial, and saw the flashlight there with the name stenciled on it, but you didn't get the flashlight or talk to the man who had it."

"That's about it," Leaphorn said. "Except it was a battery lantern and a boy who had it."

"And you didn't find out where he'd gotten it?"

Leaphorn found himself doing exactly what he'd decided not to do. He was allowing himself to be irritated by an FBI agent. And that made him irritated at himself. "That's right," he said. "I didn't."

Witover looked at him, the bright blue eyes asking "Why not?" Leaphorn ignored the question.

"Could you tell me why not?" Witover asked.

"When I saw the lantern, I didn't know the name of the helicopter pilot," Leaphorn said, his voice cold.

Witover said nothing. His expression changed from incredulous to something that said: "Well, what can you expect?" "And now you want to read our file," he stated.

"That's right."

"I wish you could tell us a bit more. Any sudden show of wealth among those people. *Anything* interesting."

"In that Short Mountain country, if anybody has three dollars it's a show of wealth," Leaphorn said. "There hasn't been anything like that."

Witover shrugged and fiddled with something in the desk drawer. Through the interrogation room's single window Leaphorn could see the sun reflecting off the windows of the post office annex across Albuquerque's Gold Avenue. In the reception room behind him, a telephone rang once.

"What made you think I was particularly interested in this case?" Witover asked.

"You know how it is," Leaphorn said. "Small world. I just remember hearing somebody say that you'd asked to come out from Washington because you wanted to stay on that Santa Fe robbery."

Witover's expression said he knew that wasn't exactly what Leaphorn had heard.

"Probably just gossip," Leaphorn said.

"We don't know each other," Witover said, "but John O'-Malley told me you worked with him on that Cata homicide on the Zuñi Reservation. He speaks well of you."

"I'm glad to hear that." Leaphorn knew it wasn't true. He and O'Malley had worked poorly together and the case, as far as the FBI was concerned, remained open and unsolved. But Leaphorn was glad that Witover had suddenly chosen to be friendly.

"If I show you the file, I'd be breaking the rule," Witover said. It was a statement, but it included a question. What, it asked, do I get in return?

"Yes," Leaphorn said. "And if I found the helicopter, or found out how to find it, our rules would require me to report to the captain, and he'd inform the chief, and the chief would inform Washington FBI, and then they'd teletype you. It would be quicker if I picked up the telephone and called you directly—at your home telephone number—but that would break *our* rules."

Witover's expression changed very slightly. The corners of his lips edged a millimeter upward. "Of course," he said, "you can't be tipping people off on their home telephones unless there's a clear understanding that nobody talks about it later."

"Exactly," Leaphorn said. "Just as you can't leave files in here with me if you didn't know I'd swear it never happened."

"Just a minute," Witover said.

It actually took him almost ten minutes. When he came back through the door he had a bulky file in one hand and his card in the other. He put the file on the desk and handed Leaphorn the card. "My home number's on the back," he said.

Witover sat down again and fingered the cord that held down the file flap. "It goes all the way back to Wounded Knee," he said. "When the old American Indian Movement took over the place in 1973, one of them was a disbarred lawyer from Oklahoma named Henry Kelongy," He glanced at Leaphorn. "You know about the Buffalo Society?"

"We don't get cut in for much of that," Leaphorn said. "I

know what I hear, and what I read in *Newsweek.*"

"Um. Well, Kelongy was a fanatic. They call him 'The Kiowa' because he's half Kiowa Indian. Raised in Anadarko, and got through the University of Oklahoma law school, and served in the Forty-fifth Division in World War Two, and made it up to first lieutenant and then killed somebody in Le Havre on the way home and lost his commission in the court-martial. Some politics after that. Ran for the legislature, worked for a congressman, kept getting more and more militant. Ran an Indian draft-resisters group during the Vietnam war. So forth. Behind all this he was working as a preacher. Started out as a Church of the Nazarene evangelist, and then moved over into the Native American Church, and then started his own offshoot of that. Kept the Native American peyote ceremony, but tossed out the Christianity. Went back to the Sun God or whatever Indians worship." Witover glanced quickly at Leaphorn. "I mean whatever Kiowas worship," he amended.

"It's complicated," Leaphorn said. "I don't know much about it, but I think Kiowas used the sun as a symbol of the Creator." Actually, he knew quite a bit about it. Religious values had always fascinated Leaphorn, and he'd studied them at Arizona State—but just now he wasn't prepared to educate an FBI agent.

"Anyway," Witover continued, "to skip a lot of the minor stuff, Kelongy had a couple of brushes with the law, and then he and some of his disciples got active in AIM. We're pretty sure they were the ones who did most of the damage when AIM took over the Bureau of Indian Affairs office in Washington. And then at Wounded Knee, Kelongy was there preaching violence. When the AIM people decided to cancel things, Kelongy raised hell, and called them cowards, and split off."

Witover fished a pack of filtered cigarettes from his pocket, offered one to Leaphorn, and lit up. He inhaled, blew out a cloud of blue smoke. "Then we started hearing about the Buffalo Society. There was a bombing in Phoenix, with pamphlets left scattered around, all about the Indians killed by soldiers somewhere or other. And some more bombings here and there. . . ." Witover paused, tapping his fingertips on the desktop, thinking. "At Sacramento, and Minneapolis, and

Duluth, and one in the South—Richmond, I think it was. And a bank robbery up in Utah, at Ogden, and always pamphlets identifying the Buffalo Society and a bunch of stuff about white atrocities against the Indians." Witover puffed again. "And that brings us to the business at Santa Fe. A very skillful piece of business." He glanced at Leaphorn. "How much you know about that?"

"Nothing much that didn't apply to our part of it," Leaphorn said. "Hunting the helicopter."

"The afternoon before the robbery, Kelongy checked into the La Fonda and asked for a fifth-floor suite overlooking the plaza. You can see the bank from there. Then—"

"He used his own name?" Leaphorn was frowning.

"No," Witover said. He looked slightly sheepish. "We had a tail on him."

Leaphorn nodded, his expression carefully noncommittal. He was imagining Witover trying to write the letter explaining how a man had managed a half-million-dollar robbery while under Witover's surveillance.

"We've pretty well put together exactly what happened," Witover went on. He leaned back in the swivel chair, locked his fingers behind his head, and talked with the easy precision of one practiced in delivering oral reports. The Wells Fargo truck had pulled away from the First National Bank on the northwest corner of Santa Fe Plaza at three-ten. At almost exactly three-ten, barriers were placed across arterial streets, detouring traffic from all directions into the narrow downtown streets. As the armored truck moved away from downtown, traffic congealed in a monumental jam behind it. This both occupied police and effectively sealed off the sheriff's and police departments, both in the downtown district. A man in a Santa Fe police uniform and riding a police-model motorcycle put up a barrier in the path of the armored truck, diverting a van ahead of the truck, the truck itself and a following car into Acequia Madre street. Then the barrier was used to block Acequia Madre, preventing local traffic from blundering onto the impending robbery. On the narrow street, lined by high adobe walls, the armored truck was jammed between the van and the car.

Witover leaned forward, stressing his point. "All perfectly timed," he said. "At about exactly the same time, some sort of car—nobody can remember what—drove up to the Airco office at the municipal airport. The copter was waiting. Reserved the day before in the name of an engineering company—a regular customer. Nobody saw who got out of the car and got into the copter."

Witover shook his head and gestured with both hands. "So the car drove away, and the copter flew away, and we don't even know if the passenger was a man or a woman. It landed on a ridge back in the foothills north of St. John's College. We know that because people saw it landing. It was on the ground maybe five minutes, and we can presume that while it was on the ground, the money from the Wells Fargo truck was loaded onto it—and maybe it took on a couple more passengers."

"But how'd they get into the armored truck?" Leaphorn said. "Isn't that supposed to be damned near impossible?"

"Ah," Witover said. "Exactly." The pale-blue eyes approved Leaphorn's question. "The armored truck is designed with armed robbery in mind and therefore the people on the inside can keep the people on the outside out. So how did the robbers get in? That brings us to the Buffalo Society's secret weapon. A crazy son-of-a-bitch named Tull."

"Tull?" The name seemed vaguely familiar.

"He's the only one we got," Witover said. He grimaced. "It turns out Tull thinks he's immortal. Believe it or not, the son-of-a-bitch claims to think he's already died two or three times and comes back to life." Witover's eyes held Leaphorn's, gauging his reaction. "That's what he tells the federal psychiatrists, and the shrinks tell us they believe he believes it."

Witover got up, and peered through the glass down at Gold Avenue. "He sure as hell acts like he believes it," he continued. "All of a sudden the truckdriver finds himself blocked, front and rear, and Tull jumps out of the van and puts some sort of gadget on the antenna to cut off radio transmission. By the time he gets that done the guard and driver are bright enough to have figured out that a robbery attempt is in progress. But Tull trots around to the rear door and starts stuffing this puttylike stuff around the door hinges. And what the hell you think the guard did?"

Leaphorn thought about it. The guard would have been incredulous. "Yelled at him, probably."

"Right. Asked him what the hell he was doing. Warned him he'd shoot. And by the time he did shoot, Tull had the putty in—and of course it was some sort of plastic explosive with a radio-activated fuse. And then the guard didn't shoot until Tull had it worked in and was running away."

"Then bang!" Leaphorn said.

"Right. Bang. Blew the door off," Witover said. "When the police finally got there, the neighbors were giving first aid. Tull had a bullet through the lung, and the guard and the driver were in pretty bad shape from blast concussions, and the money was gone."

"There must have been a bunch of them," Leaphorn said.

"Altogether probably six. One to put out the detour signs to create the traffic jams, and whoever got on the helicopter, and Kelongy, and the one dressed as a cop who diverted the armored truck and followed it down Acequia Madre, and Tull and the guy driving the car behind the van. And each one of them faded away as his part of the job was done."

"Except Tull," Leaphorn said.

"We got Tull and an identification on the one who wore the police uniform and had the motorcycle. The driver and the guard got a good look at him. He's the guy who called himself Hoski up at Wounded Knee, and something else before then, and a couple of other names since. He's Kelongy's right-hand man."

"This Tull," Leaphorn said. "Was he in on that Ogden bank robbery? If I remember that one, didn't they pull it off because a crazy bastard walked right up to a gun barrel?"

"Same guy," Witover said. "No doubt about it. It was another money transfer. Two guards carrying bags and one standing there with a shotgun and Tull walks right up to the shotgun and the guard's too damned surprised to shoot. You just can't train people to expect something like that."

"Maybe it's a bargain, then," Leaphorn said. "They got a half-million dollars and you got Tull."

There was a brief silence. Witover made a wry face. "When Tull was in the hospital waiting to get the lung fixed up, we got bond set at $100,000—which is sort of high for a non-homicide. Figured they were tossing Tull to the wolves, so we made sure Tull knew how much they had from the bank, and how much they needed to bail him out." Witover's blue eyes assumed a sadness. "If they didn't bail him out, the plan was to offer him a deal and get him to cooperate. And sure enough, no bail was posted. But Tull wouldn't cooperate. The shrinks warned us he wouldn't. And he didn't. When no bail was posted, there was a theory that the Buffalo Society had lost the money and that Tull somehow knew it. That explained why they couldn't find the copter. It had crashed into Lake Powell and sank."

Leaphorn said nothing. He was thinking that the route of the copter, if extended, would have taken it down the lake. The red plastic lantern with HAAS stenciled on it was a floating lantern. And then there was the distorted story that its finder had seen a great bird diving into the lake.

"Yes," Leaphorn said. "Maybe that's it."

Witover laughed, and shook his head. "It sounded plausible. Tull got his lung healed, and they transferred him to the state prison at Santa Fe for safekeeping, and months passed and they talked to him again, told him why be the fall guy, told him it was clear nobody was going to bond him out, and Tull just laughed and told us to screw ourselves. And now"—Witover paused, his sharp blue eyes studying Leaphorn's face for the effect—"and now they show up and bail him out."

It was what Leaphorn had expected Witover to say, but he caused his face to register surprise. Goldrims must be Tull, new to freedom and running to cover before the feds changed their minds and got the bond revoked. That would explain a lot of things. It would explain the craziness. He calculated rapidly, counting the days backward.

"Did they bail him out last Wednesday?"

Witover looked surprised. "No," he said. "It was almost three weeks ago." He gazed at Leaphorn, awaiting an explanation for the bad guess.

Leaphorn shrugged. "Where is he now?"

"God knows," Witover said. "They caught us napping. From what we can find out, it was this one they call Hoski. He made a cash deposit in five Albuquerque banks. Anyway, Tull's lawyer showed up with five cashier's checks, posted bond, got the order, and the prisoner was sprung before anybody had time to react." Witover looked glum, remembering it. "So they didn't lose the money. There goes the theory that the copter sank in the lake. They leave him in all that time, and then all of a sudden they spring him," Witover complained.

"Maybe all of a sudden they needed him," Leaphorn said.

"Yeah," Witover said. "I thought of that. It could make you nervous."

THE RIGHT EYE OF JOHN TULL stared directly at the lens, black, insolent, hating the cameramen then, hating Leaphorn now. The left eye stared blindly upward and to the left out of its ruined socket, providing a sort of crazy, obscene focus for his lopsided head. Leaphorn flipped quickly back into the biographical material. He learned that when John Tull was thirteen he had been kicked by a mule and suffered a crushed cheekbone, a broken jaw, and loss of sight in one eye. It took only a glance at the photographs to kill any lingering thoughts that Tull and Goldrims might be the same. Even in the dim reflection of the red warning flasher, a glimpse of John Tull would have been memorable. Leaphorn studied the photos only a moment. The right profile was a normally handsome, sensitive face—betraying the blood of Tull's Seminole mother. The left showed what the hoof of a mule could do to fragile human bones. Leaphorn looked up from the report, lit a cigarette and puffed—thinking how a boy would learn to live behind a façade that reminded others of their own fragile, painful mortality. It helped explain why guards had been slow to shoot. And it helped explain why Tull was crazy—if crazy he was.

The report itself offered nothing surprising. A fairly usual police record, somewhat heavy on crimes of violence. At nineteen, a two-to-seven for attempted homicide, served at the Santa Fe prison without parole—which almost certainly meant a rough record inside the walls. And then a short-term armed-robbery conviction, and after that only arrests on suspicion and a single robbery charge which didn't stick.

Leaphorn flipped past that into the transcripts of various interrogations after the Santa Fe robbery. From them another picture of Tull emerged—wise and tough. But there was one exception. The interrogator here was Agent John O'Malley, and Leaphorn read through it twice.

O'MALLEY: You're forgetting they drove right off and left you.

TULL: I wanted to collect my Blue Cross benefits.

O'MALLEY: You've collected them now. Ask yourself why they don't come and get you. They got plenty of money to make bail.

TULL: I'm not worrying.

O'MALLEY: This Hoski. This guy you call your friend. You know where he is now? He left Washington and he's in Hawaii. Living it up on his share. And his share is fatter because part of it's your share.

TULL: Screw you. He's not in Hawaii.

O'MALLEY: That's what Hoski and Kelongy and the rest of them are doing to you, baby. Screwing you.

TULL: *(Laughs).*

O'MALLEY: You ain't got a friend, buddy. You're taking everybody's fall for them. And this friend of yours is letting it happen.

TULL: You don't know this friend of mine. I'll be all right.

O'MALLEY: Face it. He went off and left you.

TULL: God damn you. You pig. You don't know him. You don't even know his name. You don't even know where he is. He never will let me down. He never will.

Leaphorn looked up from the page, closed his eyes, and tried to recreate the voice. Was it vehement? Or forlorn? The words on paper told him too little. But the repetition suggested a shout. And the shouting had ended that particular interview.

Leaphorn put that folder aside and picked up the psychiatric report. He read quickly through the diagnosis, which concluded that Tull had psychotic symptoms of schizophrenic paranoia and that he suffered delusions and hallucinations. A Dr. Alexander Steiner was the psychiatrist. He had talked to Tull week after week following his bout with chest surgery and he'd established an odd sort of guarded rapport with Tull, surprisingly soon.

Much of the talk was about a grim childhood with a drunken mother and a series of men with whom she had lived—and finally with the uncle whose mule had kicked him. Leaphorn scanned rapidly through the report, but he lingered over sections that focused on Tull's vision of his own immortality.

STEINER: When did you find out for sure? Was it that first time in prison?

TULL: Yeah. In the box. That's what they called it then. The box. *(Laughs.)* That's what it was, too. Welded it together out of boiler plate. A hatch on one side so you could crawl in and then they'd bolt it shut behind you. It was under the floor of the laundry building in the old prison—the one they tore down. About five foot square, so you couldn't stand up but you could lay down if you lay with your feet in one corner and your head in the other. You know what I mean?

STEINER: Yes.

TULL: Usually you got into that for hitting a guard or something like that. That's what I done. Hit a guard. *(Laughs.)* They don't tell you how long you're going to be in the box, and that wouldn't matter anyway because it's pitch black under that laundry and it's even blacker in the box, so the only way you could keep track of the days passing is because the steam pipes from the laundry make more noise in the daytime. Anyway, they put me in there and bolted that place shut behind me. And you keep control pretty good at first. Explore around with your hands, find the rough places and the slick places on the wall. And you fiddle with the buckets. There's one with drinking water and one you use as a toilet. And then, all of a sudden, it gets to you. It's closing in on you, and there ain't no air to breathe, and you're screaming and fighting the walls and . . . and . . . *(Laughs.)* Anyway, I smothered to death in there. Sort of drowned. And when I came alive again, I was laying there on the floor, with the spilled water all cool and comfortable around me. I was a different person from that boy they put in the box. And I got to thinking about it and it came to me that wasn't the first time I'd died and come alive again. And I knew it wouldn't be the last time.

STEINER: The first time you died. Was that when the horse kicked you?

TULL: Yes, sir, it was. I didn't know it then, though.

STEINER: And then you feel as if you died again when this truck guard shot you at Santa Fe?

TULL: You can feel it, you know. There's a kind of a shock when the bullet hits—a numb feeling. And it hurts a little where it went in and came out. Lot of nerves in the skin, I guess. But inside, it just feels funny. And you see the blood running out of you. *(Laughs.)* I said to myself, "Well, I'm dyin' again and when I come alive in my next life, I'm going to have another face."

STEINER: You think about that a lot, don't you? Having another face?

TULL: It happened once. It'll happen again. This wasn't the face I had the first time I died.

STEINER: But don't you think that if they had taken you to the right kind of surgeon he could have straightened it out after you got kicked?

TULL: No. It was different. It wasn't the one I had.

STEINER: When you look in a mirror, though. When you look at the right side of your face, isn't that the way you always looked?

TULL: The right side? No. I didn't really look like that in my first life. *(Laughs.)* You got a cigarette?

STEINER: Pall Malls.

TULL: Thanks. You know, Doc, that's why the pigs is so wrong about my buddy. The one they call Hoski. They don't even know his real name. He's like me. He told me once that he's immortal too. Just let it slip out, like he wasn't supposed to tell anyone. But it don't make any difference to me if everybody knows. And there's another way I can tell he's like me. When he looks at me, he sees me. Me. You know. Not this goddamned face. He sees right through the face and he sees me behind it. Most people they look and they see this crazy eyeball, and they flinch, like they was looking at something sick and nasty. But—but my buddy . . . *(Laughs.)* I almost let his real name slip out there. The first time he looked at me, he didn't see this face at all. He just grinned and said "Gladtameetcha," or something like that, and we sat there and drank some beer, and it was just as if this face had peeled away and it was me sitting there.

STEINER: But the police think this man sort of took advantage of you. Left you behind and all that.

TULL: They think bullshit. They're trying to con me into talking. They think I'm crazy, too.

STEINER: What do you think about that?

TULL: You ought to see the Kiowa. He's the crazy one. He's got this stone. Claims it's a sort of a god. Got feathers and fur and a bone hanging from it. Hangs it from this goddamn bamboo tripod and sings to it. *(Laughs.)* Calls it Boy Medicine, and Taly-da-i, or some damn thing like that. I think it's a Kiowa word. He told us there at Wounded Knee that if those AIM people was willin' to start shootin' to kill, then this Boy Medicine would help them. The white man was goin' to be wiped out and the Buffalo would cover the earth again. *(Laughs.)* How about *that* for crazy shit?

STEINER: But isn't that the leader of the organization? The one you're supposed to be following?

TULL: The Kiowa? Shit. My buddy, he was workin' with him, and I'm workin' with my buddy. Following? We don't follow nobody. Not my buddy and me.

Leaphorn skipped back and reread the paragraph about the Kiowa. What was it they had learned in his senior graduate seminar on Native American Religions? The sun was personified by the Kiowas, as he remembered it, and the sun had lured a Kiowa virgin into the sky and impregnated her and she had borne an infant boy. Much like the Navajos' own White Shell Maiden, being impregnated by Sun and Water and bearing the Hero Twins. And the Kiowa maiden had tried to escape from the sun, and had lowered the boy to earth and escaped after him. But the sun had thrown down a magic ring and killed her. Then the boy had taken the ring, and struck himself with it, and divided himself into twins. One of the twins had walked into the water and disappeared forever. The other had turned himself into ten medicine bundles and had given himself to his mother's people as a sort of Holy Eucharist. Nobody seemed to know exactly what had happened to these bundles. Apparently they had been gradually lost in the Kiowas' endless cavalry war for control of the High Plains. After the battle of Palo Duro Canyon, when the army herded the rag-tag remainders of these Lords of the Plains back into captivity at Fort Sill, at least one of the bundles had remained. The army had made the Kiowa watch while the last of the tribe's great horse herd was shot. But according to the legend, this Boy Medicine still remained with his humiliated people. The Kiowas had tried to hold their great annual Kado even when captive on the reservation, but they had to have a bull buffalo for the dance. Warriors slipped away to the King Ranch in Texas to buy one, but they came back empty-handed. And after that, the old people taught, Boy Medicine had left the Kiowas and the last of the medicine bundles had disappeared.

Leaphorn thought about it. Could Kelongy actually have come into possession of one of the sacred medicine bundles? He had preached a revival of the Buffalo religion. He promised the return of utopia, the white men exterminated, and Native Americans again living in a free society. The Buffalo then would again spring from the earth in their millions and nurture the children of the sun.

Leaphorn became aware of heat against his finger—his cigarette burning too close to the skin. He took a final drag, stubbed it out, and studied the smoke trickling slowly upward from his lips. He felt a vague uneasiness. Some thought struggling to be remembered. Something nameless tugging at him. He tried to let it surface and found himself thinking vaguely of witchcraft, remembering incongruously something that had no connection at all with what he had been reading, remembering Listening Woman telling him that more than one of the holy sand paintings had been desecrated in the place where Hosteen Tso had been. And remembering that it had occurred to Listening Woman, as it had occurred to him, that Hosteen Tso might have been involved in some sort of perverted ritual of a coven of Navajo Wolves.

The door to the interrogation room opened. A youngish man in a seersucker suit came in, glanced curiously at Leaphorn, said "Excuse me," and left. Leaphorn stretched and yawned, put the Tull folder back into the accordion file that held it, and resumed his fishing expedition through the remaining material.

The helicopter pilot seemed straight. He had flown copters in Vietnam. He had a wife and two children. There was no criminal record. The only question the FBI had been able to raise about his character referred to "three trips to Las Vegas over the past two years, after two of which he told informants he had won small amounts of money."

Kelongy had a much thicker file, but it added nothing substantial to Leaphorn's knowledge. Kelongy was a violent man, and a bitter one, and a dreamer of deadly dreams. Three of the other "minimum of six" participants in the Santa Fe robbery remained nameless and faceless. There was a short file for a Jackie Noni, a young part-Potawatomi with a brief but violent police record, who apparently drove the car that blocked the armored truck.

That left Tull's buddy, the one the FBI called Hoski. There was nothing standard about Hoski.

The FBI had no real idea who he was. It listed him as Frank Hoski, also known as Colton Hoski, a.k.a. Frank Morris, a.k.a. Van Black. The only photograph in the file was a grainy blowup obviously taken with a telephoto lens in bad light. It showed a trim but slightly stocky man, face partially averted, coming through a doorway. The man's hair was black, or very dark, and he looked Indian, possibly Navajo or Apache, Leaphorn thought, or possibly something else. He reminded Leaphorn vaguely of the uneasiness that had been troubling him, but he could dredge up absolutely nothing. The legend under the photo guessed Hoski's weight at "about 190," and his height at about five foot eleven, his race as "probably Indian, or part Indian," and his identifying marks as "possible heavy scar tissue under hairline above right cheek."

Not much was known of Hoski's career. He had first appeared at Wounded Knee, where informers listed him as one of the "violents" and as a right-hand man of Kelongy. A man who fit his description and used the name Frank Morris was seen by witnesses at the Ogden robbery and FBI informers confirmed that Hoski and Morris were identical. What was known about him was mostly pieced together from FBI informers who had infiltrated AIM. He was believed to be a Vietnam war veteran. Three informers identified him as army, two of the three as a demolitions expert, the other as an infantry company radioman. He occasionally smoked cigars, was a moderate drinker, was pugnacious (having engaged in fistfights on three occasions with other AIM members), often told jokes, had once lived in Los Angeles, had once lived in Memphis, and possibly once lived in Provo, Utah. Had no known homosexual tendencies, had no known relationships with females, had only one known close friend, a subject identified as John Tull. He had been identified again, on a "most likely" basis, as the man wearing the police uniform who had diverted the Wells Fargo truck into the robbery trap at Santa Fe. He came into view again in Washington, D.C., where he was working as a janitor for a company identified as Safety Systems, Inc., which dealt in burglary alarms, locking systems, and other security devices.

Leaphorn opened the last section of the report. The FBI, he was thinking, was in an enviable situation relative to Hoski. They had spotted him without Hoski's knowing he was spotted. A string tied to a key man in the Buffalo Society would almost inevitably lead eventually to other members of the terrorist group. The agency would put its best people on the surveillance team. It wouldn't risk either tipping Hoski or allowing him to slip away.

Leaphorn read. The head of the team of the FBI's best people, assigned to keep Hoski on the FBI string, was George Witover. And that, of course, was why Witover had been sent back to the Albuquerque agency, and why Witover was willing to break a rule. Hoski had cut the string under Witover's eyes.

Leaphorn read on. Until the very end, Witover's operation had seemed to go flawlessly. Hoski had been located more than a month after the Santa Fe robbery. He followed a routine. Each weekday afternoon about 6 P.M., Hoski would emerge from his utility apartment, walk two blocks to a bus stop and catch a bus to his job at Safety Systems, Inc., where he was employed under the name Theodore Parker. On the premises, he would eat a midnight lunch, carried from his apartment in a sack, with a black fellow janitor. At about 4:30 A.M. he would leave the Safety Systems, Inc., building, walk five blocks to a bus stop and catch the bus back to his apartment. He would reemerge from the apartment in the early afternoon, to do grocery shopping, take care of his laundry at a neighborhood coin-operated laundromat, take long walks, or sit in a park overlooking the Potomac. The routine had rarely varied and never in any important degree—until March 23. On that date he was observed at the laundromat engaging in a lengthy conversation with a young woman, subsequently identified as Rosemary Rita Oliveras, twenty-eight, divorced, an immigrant from Puerto Rico. On March 30, the two had again met at the laundromat, engaged in conversation, and later gone for a wandering walk which lasted more than three hours. On April 1, a Saturday, Hoski had surprised his surveillance by emerging from his apartment before noon and walking to the boardinghouse where Mrs. Oliveras resided. The two thereupon walked to a cafe, lunched, and went to a movie. Subsequently Hoski spent most of his free time with Mrs. Oliveras. Otherwise, nothing changed.

The mail cover on Hoski continued turning up one outgoing letter every week, either left for the mailman or dropped in a letter slot. The letter was invariably addressed to an Eloy R. Albertson, General Delivery, West Covina, California, and invariably contained the same message: "Dear Eloy: Nothing new. Hoski."

No one had ever appeared at the West Covina post office to claim the letters.

The second variation in the pattern of Hoski's behavior came on March 11. A taxicab had pulled up to his address at about 1 P.M. and had taken Hoski to an urban renewal demolition district two blocks from the Potomac. He left the cab at a street corner, walked through a mixture of wind-driven rain and sleet to a telephone booth and made a brief call. He then walked down the street into the sheltered doorway of an abandoned storefront across the street from the Office Bar. Approximately twenty minutes later, at 2:11 P.M., a taxi discharged a passenger at the entrance of the Office Bar. The passenger was subsequently identified as Robert Rainey, thirty-two, a former activist in the Students for a Democratic Society, and a former AIM member, with a three-rap demonstration-related arrest record. He immediately entered the bar. The FBI agent watching Hoski notified his control that a meeting seemed impending. A second agent was dispatched. The second agent arrived twenty-one minutes after Rainey entered the bar. Informed that Hoski was still waiting across the street from the Office Bar, the second agent parked his van down the street. To avoid suspicion, he left the vehicle and took up a position out of sight in the doorway of an empty storefront. About three minutes after he did so, Hoski walked down the street to the doorway, spoke to the agent about "getting in out of the weather," and then walked back up the street and into the Office Bar. The second agent thereupon checked and discovered that the alley exit from this bar was closed off by a locked garbage-access gate. Since the second agent had been seen, the first agent entered the bar to determine whether Hoski was making a contact. Hoski was sitting in a booth with Rainey. The agent ordered a beer, drank it at the bar, and left—there being no opportunity to overhear the conversation between Hoski and Rainey. Hoski left the bar about ten minutes later, walked to the telephone booth at the end of the block, made a brief telephone call, and then returned to his apartment by bus. He emerged again, as was usual, to take a bus to his job.

"It is presumed that Rainey delivered a message," the report said.

Leaphorn rubbed his eyes. A messenger, of course, but how had the meeting been arranged? Not by mail, which was covered. Not by telephone, which was tapped. A note hand-delivered to Hoski's mail slot, perhaps. Or handed to him on a bus. Or a prearranged visit to a pay-phone information drop. There were any of a thousand ways to do it. That meant Hoski either knew he was being watched, or suspected he was, or was naturally cautious. Leaphorn frowned. That made Hoski's behavior relative to the meeting inconsistent. The bar was outside Hoski's regular territory, broke his routine, was sure to attract FBI attention. And so, certainly, was his behavior—the long wait outside the bar, all that. Leaphorn frowned. The frown gradually converted itself to a smile, to a broad, delighted grin, as Leaphorn realized what Hoski had been doing. Still grinning, Leaphorn leaned back in the chair and stared at the wall, reconstructing it all.

Hoski had known he was being followed and had gone to considerable pains to keep the FBI from knowing that he knew. The weekly letters to California, for example. No one would ever pick them up. Their only purpose was to assure the FBI that Hoski suspected nothing. And then the message had come. Probably a note to call a telephone number. From a pay phone. Hoski had picked an isolated bar and a meeting time which would guarantee low traffic and high visibility. He had picked a bar without a back entrance to assure that no one could enter without being seen by Hoski. He had notified the messenger of the meeting place only after he was in position to watch the front door. Then he had waited to watch the messenger arrive—and to watch the FBI reaction to the arrival and Hoski's other unorthodox behavior. Why? Because Hoski didn't know whether the messenger was a legitimate runner of the Buffalo

Society or an FBI informer. If the messenger was not FBI, the agency would quickly send someone to tail the messenger. Thus Hoski had waited for the second tail to arrive. And when the van had parked down the street, Hoski had walked over to make sure the driver was in fact FBI, watching from the doorway, and not someone with a key and business inside. Then, with the legitimacy of the messenger confirmed by the FBI reaction, he'd gone into the bar and received his message.

What next? Leaphorn resumed reading. The following day the agency had doubled its watch on Hoski. The day was routine, except that Hoski had walked to a neighborhood shopping center and, at a J. C. Penney store, had bought a blue-and-white-checked nylon windbreaker, a blue cloth hat, and navy-blue trousers.

The next day the routine shattered. A little after 3 P.M. an ambulance arrived at Hoski's apartment building. Hoski, holding a bloody bath towel to his face, was helped into the vehicle and taken to the emergency room at Memorial Hospital. The ambulance attendants reported that they found Hoski sitting on the steps just inside the entrance waiting for them. The police emergency operator revealed that a man had called fifteen minutes earlier, claimed he had cut himself and was bleeding to death, and asked for an ambulance. At the hospital, the attending physician reported that the patient's right scalp had been slashed. Hoski said he had slipped with a bottle in his hand and fallen on the broken glass. He was released with seventeen stitches closing the wound, and a bandage which covered much of his face. He took a cab home, called Safety Systems, Inc., and announced that he had cut his head and would have to miss work for two or three days.

At mid-morning the next day, he emerged from the apartment wearing the clothing purchased at J. C. Penney and carrying a bulging pillowcase. He walked slowly, with one rest at a bus stop, to the Bendix laundromat where he had routinely done his laundry. In the laundry, Hoski washed the contents of the pillowcase, placed the wet wash in a dryer, disappeared into the rest room for about four minutes, emerged, and waited for the drying cycle to be completed, and then carried the dried laundry in the pillowcase back to his apartment.

Two days later, a young Indian, who hadn't been observed entering the apartment building, emerged and left in a taxi. This had aroused suspicion. The following day, Hoski's apartment was entered and proved to be empty. Evidence found included a new blue-and-white-checked nylon windbreaker, a blue cloth hat, navy-blue trousers, and the remains of a facial bandage, which—since it was not stained by medications—was presumed to have been used as a disguise.

Leaphorn read through the rest of it rapidly. Rosemary Rita Oliveras had appeared two days later at Hoski's apartment house, and had called his employer, and then had gone to the police to report him missing. The FBI statement described her as "distraught—apparently convinced that subject is the victim of foul play." The rest of it was appendix material—interviews with Rosemary Rita Oliveras, the transcripts of tapped telephone calls, odds and ends of accumulated evidence. Leaphorn read all of it. He sorted the materials into their folders, fitted the folders back into the accordion file, and sat staring at nothing in particular.

It was obvious enough how Hoski had done it. When the FBI's reaction had proved the messenger legitimate, he had gone to a department store and bought easy-to-recognize, easy-to-match clothing. Then he had called a friend. (Not a friend, Leaphorn corrected himself. He had called an accomplice. Hoski had no friends. In all those months in Washington he had seen no one except Rosemary Rita Oliveras.) He had told the accomplice exactly which items to buy, and to have his face bandaged as if his right scalp had been slashed open. He had told him to come early and unobserved to the laundromat, to lock himself into a toilet booth, and to wait. When Hoski had appeared, this man had simply assumed Hoski's role—had carried the laundry back to Hoski's apartment and waited. And inside the men's room booth, Hoski had dressed in a set of clothing the man must have brought for him, and removed the bandage, and covered his sewn scalp with a wig or a hat, and vanished. Away from Washington, and from FBI agents, and from Rosemary Rita Oliveras. He must have been tempted to call her, Leaphorn thought. The only thing that Hoski hadn't planned on was falling in love with this woman. But he had.

Something in those telephone transcripts said he had. They were terse, but you found love somehow in what was said, and left unsaid. But Hoski hadn't contacted her. He had left Rosemary Rita Oliveras without a word. The FBI would have known if he had tipped her off. She was an uncomplicated woman. She couldn't have faked the frantic worry, or the hurt.

Leaphorn lit another cigarette. He thought of the nature of the man the FBI called Hoski; a man smart enough to use the FBI as Hoski had done and then to arrange that clever escape. What had that taken? Leaphorn imagined how it must have been done. First, the call to the ambulance to minimize the risk. Then the broken glass gripped carefully, placed against the cringing skin. The brain telling the muscle to perform the act that every instinct screamed against. God! What sort of man was Hoski?

Leaphorn turned back to the file. The last items were three poorly printed propaganda leaflets left at the scenes of various Buffalo Society crimes. The rhetoric was uncompromising anger. The white man had attempted genocide against the Buffalo People. But the Great Power of the Sun was just. The Sun had ordained the Buffalo Society as his avenger. When seven symbolic crimes had been avenged, white men everywhere would be stricken. The earth would be cleansed of them. Then the sacred buffalo herds and the people they nourished would again flourish and populate the land.

The crimes were listed, with the number of victims, in the order they would be avenged. Most of them were familiar. The Wounded Knee Massacre was there, and the ghastly slaughter at Sand Creek, and the mutilation of Acoma males after their pueblo stronghold fell to the Spanish. But the first crime was unfamiliar to Leaphorn. It was an attack on a Kiowa encampment in West Texas by a force of cavalry and Texas Rangers. The pamphlet called it the Olds Prairie Murders, said it came when the men were away hunting buffalo, and listed the dead as eleven children and three adults. That was the smallest casualty total. The death toll increased down the list, culminating with the "Subjugation of the Navajos." For that, the pamphleteer listed a death toll of 3,500 children and 2,500 adults. Probably, Leaphorn thought, as fair a guess as any. He put the pamphlet aside and found a sort of anxious uneasiness again intruding into his thoughts. He was overlooking something. Something important. Abruptly he knew it was related to what Mrs. Cigaret had told him. Something about where she had sat, with her head against the stone, while she had listened to the voices in the earth. But what had she said? Just enough to let Leaphorn know that he had guessed wrong about which of the cul-de-sacs in the mesa cliff she had used for this communion with the stone. She had not used the one closest to the Tso hogan. Anna Atcitty had led her up a sheep trail beside the mesa.

Leaphorn closed his eyes, grimaced with concentration, remembering how he had stood on the mesa rim, looking down on the Tso hogan, on the wagon track leading to it, on the brush arbor. There had been a cul-de-sac below him and another perhaps two hundred yards to his left, where sheep had once been penned. Leaphorn could see it again in memory—the sheep track angling gradually away from the wagon road. And then he was suddenly, chillingly aware of what his subconscious had been trying to tell him. If Listening Woman had sat there, she would have been plainly visible to the killer as he approached the hogan down the wagon track—and even more obvious as he left. Did that mean Mrs. Cigaret had lied? Leaphorn wasted hardly a second on that. Mrs. Cigaret had not lied. It meant the wagon road was not the way the killer had come and gone. He had come out of the canyon, and departed into it. And that meant that if he emerged again, he would find Father Tso and Theodora Adams just where he had found Hosteen Tso and Anna Atcitty.

THE NUCLEUS OF THE CLOUD formed about noon over the Nevada-Arizona border. By the time it trailed its dark-blue shadow across the Grand Canyon, it had built into a tower more than a mile from its sparkling white top to its flat, dark base. It crossed the southern slopes of Short Mountain at midafternoon, growing fast. Fierce internal updrafts pushed its cap above thirty thousand feet. There the mist droplets turned to ice, and fell, and melted, and were caught again in updrafts and soared into the frigid stratosphere, only to fall again—increasing in size with this churning and producing immense charges of static electricity which caused the cloud to mutter and grumble with thunder and produce occasional explosive bolts of lightning. These linked cloud with mountain or mesa top for brilliant seconds, and sent waves of echoes booming down the canyons below. And finally, the icy droplets glittering at the cloud-top against the deep-blue sky became too heavy for the winds, and too large to evaporate in the warm air below. Then thin curtains of falling ice and water lowered from the black base of the cloud and at last touched the ground. Thus, east of Short Mountain, the cloud became a "male rain."

Leaphorn stopped the carryall, turned off the ignition and listened to it coming. The sun slanted into the falling water, creating a gaudy double rainbow which seemed to move steadily toward him, narrowing its arch as it came in accordance with rainbow optics. There was sound now, the muted approaching roar of billions of particles of ice and water striking stone. The first huge drop struck the roof of Leaphorn's carryall. Plong! Plong-plong! And a torrent of rain and hail swept over the vehicle. The screen of falling water dimmed the landscape for a moment, the droplets reflecting the sun like a rhinestone curtain. And then the light was drowned. Leaphorn sat, engulfed in sound. He glanced at his watch, and waited, enjoying the storm as he enjoyed all things right and natural—not thinking for a moment about any of the unnatural affairs that involved him. He put aside the sense of urgency that had brought him down this wagon track much faster than it could wisely be driven. It took a fraction over seven minutes for the storm to pass Leaphorn's carryall. He started the engine and drove through the diminishing shower. A mile short of the Tso place, runoff water flashing down an arroyo had cut deeply into its bank. Leaphorn climbed out of the carryall and examined the road. A couple of hours with a shovel would make it passable again. Now it was not. It would be quicker to walk.

Leaphorn walked. The sun emerged. In places the sandstone landscape was littered with hail. In places the hot stone steamed, the cold rain water evaporating to form patches of ground mist. The air was cold, smelling washed and clean. The Tso hogan, as Leaphorn approached it, appeared deserted.

He stopped a hundred yards short of the buildings and shouted, calling first for Tso and then for the girl. Silence. The rocks steamed. Leaphorn shouted again. He walked to the hogan. The door stood open. He peered into its dark interior. Two bedrolls, side by side. Theodora Adams's overnight case and duffel bag. The scant luggage of Father Tso. A box of groceries, cooking utensils. Everything was neat. Everything in order. Leaphorn turned from the doorway and surveyed the surroundings. The rain had swept the ground clean of tracks, and nothing had been here since the rain had stopped. Father Tso and Theodora had left the hogan before the storm arrived. And they had been too far afield to return to its shelter when the rain began. But where could they go? Behind the hogan, the wall of the mesa rose. It was mostly cliff, but breaks made it easy enough to climb in half a dozen places. To the north, northwest and northeast, the ground fell away into a labyrinth of vertical-walled canyons which he knew drained, eventually, into the San Juan River. The track he had taken circled in from the south, through a wilderness of eroded stone. Tso and the girl had probably climbed the mesa, or wandered southward, though the canyons would make forbidding, and dangerous, walking.

A faint breeze stirred the air and brought the distant sound of thunder from the retreating storm. The sun was low now, warm against the side of Leaphorn's face. He looked down the wagon track toward the place where Listening Woman had seen her vision and had been, for some reason, herself unseen by a murderer. So the murderer had not used the only easy exit route. If he had climbed the mesa, it, too, would have offered him an open view of the woman. That left only the canyons. Which made no sense.

Leaphorn looked northward. A reasonably agile man could climb down off this bench to the canyon floor, but canyons would lead him nowhere. Only into an endless labyrinth—deeper and deeper into the sheer-walled maze.

Leaphorn turned suddenly, ducked through the hogan door, and sorted through Tso's supplies. His groceries included about twenty cans of meats, fruits, and vegetables, two-thirds of a twenty-pound sack of potatoes, and an assortment of dried beans and other staples. Tso had come, obviously, for a long stay. Leaphorn checked the girl's duffel bag, and the priest's suitcases, and found nothing that seemed helpful.

Then as he looked toward the hogan door, he saw marks on the floor which were almost too faint to register. They were visible only because of the angle of light between Leaphorn and the doorway. They were nothing more than the damp pawprints of a very large dog left on the hard-packed earthen floor. But they were enough to tell Leaphorn that he had failed in carrying out his instructions to take care of Theodora Adams.

Leaphorn studied the hogan floor again, his cheek to the packed earth as he examined the stirred dust against the light. But he learned little. The dog had evidently come here during the rain or immediately after it. And someone had been with the dog, since several of its damp footprints had been scuffed. That could have been Goldrims, or Tso and Adams, or perhaps all three. The dog might even have arrived pre-rain, and have run out into the rain, and returned wet-footed. And all had left while enough rain was still falling to erase their tracks.

He stood at the door. Too much coincidence. Leaphorn didn't believe in it. He believed nothing happened without cause. Everything intermeshed, from the mood of a man, to the flight of the corn beetle, to the music of the wind. It was the Navajo philosophy, this concept of interwoven harmony, and it was bred into Joe Leaphorn's bones. There had to be a reason for the death of Hosteen Tso, and it had to be connected with why Goldrims—or at least Goldrims's dog—had been drawn to the Tso hogan. Leaphorn tried to think it through. He knew Listening Woman had sensed some unusual evil behind the troubled spirit of Hosteen Tso. She had decided to recommend that a Mountain Way be performed for the old man, and that the Black Rain Chant also should be done. It was an unusual prescription. Both of the curing ceremonials were ritual re-creations of a portion of the myths that taught how the Dinee had emerged from the underworld and become human clans. The Mountain Way would have been intended to restore Hosteen Tso's psyche with the harmony that had been disrupted by his witnessing some sort of sacrilegious taboo violation—the disrespect to the holy sand paintings probably. But why the Black Rain Chant? Leaphorn should have asked her more about that. It was an obscure ritual, rarely performed. He remembered that its name came from the creation of rain. First Coyote had a role in it, Leaphorn recalled. And a fire played a part somehow. But how could that be involved with the curing of Hosteen Tso? He leaned against the hogan doorframe, recalling the lessons of his boyhood. Hosteen Coyote had visited Fire Man, and had tricked him, and had stolen a bundle of burning sticks and escaped with the treasure tied to his bushy tail. And in running, he had spread flames all across Dinetah, and the Holy Land of the People was burning, and the Holy People had met to consider the crisis. Something clicked suddenly into place. The hero of this particular myth adventure was First Frog. Hosteen Frog had used his magic, inflated himself with water, and—carried aloft by First Crane—had produced black rain to save Dinetah from fire. And Listening Woman had mentioned that Hosteen Tso had killed a frog—or caused it to be killed by a falling rock. Leaphorn frowned again. Killing a frog was a taboo, but a minor one. A personal chant would cure the guilt and restore beauty. Why had the death of this frog been weighed so heavily? Because, Leaphorn guessed, Tso associated it with the other, grimmer sacrilege. Had there been frogs near the place where the sand paintings were desecrated?

Leaphorn glanced again at the mesa, where his common sense suggested that Father Tso and Theodora Adams must have gone—and away from the dead-end waste of canyons which led absolutely nowhere except—if you followed them far—under the drowning waters of Lake Powell. Yet, Leaphorn thought, if the man who had killed Hosteen Tso had failed to see Listening Woman, he must have gone into the canyons. And if there was a secret place nearby where the sand paintings and the medicine bundle of the Way to Cure the World's End had waited out the generations, it might well be in a deep, dry cave and caves again meant the canyons. Finally, the mesa offered no water, and thus no possibility of frogs. Leaphorn—walking fast—headed for the canyon rim.

The branch canyon that skirted past the Tso hogan was perhaps eighty vertical feet from the cap rock to its sandy bottom. The trail that connected the two had been cut by goats at a steep angle and at the bottom Leaphorn found tracks which proved to him he had guessed right. The rocks were dry now and the humans—humanlike—had avoided the rainwater puddles between them. But the dog had not. At several places Leaphorn found traces left by its wet paws. They led down the narrow slot, and here a narrow strip of sand was wet. Two persons had stepped in it—perhaps three. Large feet and a small foot. Adams and Father Tso? Adams and Goldrims? Had the party included a third member, who had stepped from rock to rock and left no footprints? Leaphorn turned to the spring. It was little more than a seep, emerging from a moss-covered crack and dripping into a catch basin which Tso had probably dug out. There were no frogs here, and no sign of a rock slide. Leaphorn tasted the water. It was cold, with a slightly mineral taste. He drank deeply, wiped his mouth, and began walking as quietly as he could down the hard-packed sand of the canyon bottom.

LEAPHORN HAD BEEN WALKING almost three hours, slowly, cautiously, trying to follow tracks in the gathering darkness, when he heard the sound. It stopped him, and he held his breath, listening. It was a soprano sound, made by something living—human or otherwise. It came from a long distance, lasted perhaps three or four seconds, cut off abruptly in mid-note, and was followed by a confusion of echoes. Leaphorn stood on the sand of the canyon bottom, analyzing the diminishing echoes. A human voice? Perhaps the high-pitched scream of a bobcat? It seemed to come from the place where this canyon drained into a larger canyon about 150 yards below him. But whether it originated up or down the larger canyon, or across it, or above it, Leaphorn could only guess. The echoes had been chaotic.

He listened a moment longer and heard nothing. The sound seemed to have startled even the insects and the insect-hunting evening birds. Leaphorn began to run as quietly as he could toward the canyon mouth, the whisper of his bootsoles on the sand the only sound in an eerie silence. At the junction he stopped, looking right and left. He had been in the canyons long enough to develop an unusual and unsettling sense of disorientation—of not knowing exactly where he was in terms of either direction or landmarks. He understood its cause: a horizon which rose vertically overhead and the constant turning of the corridors sliced through the stone. Understanding it made it no more comfortable. Leaphorn, who had never been lost in his life, didn't know exactly where he was. He could tell he was moving approximately northward. But he wasn't sure he could retrace his way directly back to the Tso hogan without wasting steps. That uncertainty added to his general uneasiness. Far overhead, the clifftops still glowed with the light of the sunset's afterglow, but here it was almost dark. Leaphorn sat on a boulder, fished a cigarette out of a package in his shirt pocket, and held it under his nose. He inhaled the aroma of the tobacco, and then slipped it back into the pack. He would not make a light. He simply sat, letting his senses work for him. He was hungry. He put that thought aside. On earth level the breeze had died, as it often did in the desert twilight. Here, two hundred feet below the earth's surface, the air moved down-canyon, pressed by the cooling atmosphere from the slopes above. Leaphorn heard the song of insects, the chirping of rock crickets, and now and then the call of an owl. A bullbat swept past him, hunting mosquitoes, oblivious of the motionless man. Once again Leaphorn became aware of the distant steady murmur of the river. It was nearer now, and the noise of water over rock was funneled and concentrated by the cliffs. No more than a mile and a half away, he guessed. Normally the thin, dry air of desert country carries few smells. But the air at canyon bottom was damp, so Leaphorn could identify the smell of wet sand, the resinous aroma of cedar, the vague perfume of piñon needles, and a dozen scents too faint for identification. The afterglow faded from the clifftops.

Time ticked away, bringing to the waiting man sounds and smells, but no repetition of the shout, if shout it had been, and nothing to hint at where Goldrims might have gone. Stars appeared in the slot overhead. First one, glittering alone, and then a dozen, and hundreds, and millions. The stars of the constellation Ursa Minor became visible, and Leaphorn felt the relief of again knowing his direction exactly. Abruptly he pushed himself upright, listening. From his left, down the dark canyon, came a faint rhythm of sound. Frogs greeting the summer night. He walked slowly, placing his feet carefully, moving down the canyon toward the almost imperceptible sound of the frogs. The darkness gave him an advantage. While it canceled sight, the night magnified the value of hearing. If it had kept

Tso's secrets for a hundred years, the cave must be hidden from sight. But if there were people in it, they would—unless they slept—produce sound. The darkness would hide him, and he could move almost without noise down the sand of the canyon floor.

But there was also a disadvantage. The dog. If the dog was out in the canyon, it would smell him two-hundred yards away. Leaphorn assumed that the cave would be somewhere up the cliff wall, as caves tended to be, and in this damp air, his scent would probably not rise. If the dog was in the cave, Leaphorn could go undetected. Nevertheless, he drew his pistol and walked with it in his hand, its hammer held on half cock and the safety catch off. He walked tensely, stopping every few yards both to listen and to make sure that his breathing remained slow and low.

He heard very little: the faint sound of his own bootsoles placed carefully on the sand, the distant barking of a coyote hunting somewhere on the surface above, the occasional call of a night bird, and finally, as the evening breeze rose, the breathing of air moving around the rocks, all against the background music of frog song. Once he was startled by a sudden scurrying of a rodent. And then, midstride, he heard a voice.

He stood motionless, straining to hear more. It had been a man's voice—coming from somewhere down the canyon, saying something terse. Three or four quick words. Leaphorn looked around him, identifying his location. Just down the canyon bottom, he could make out the shape of a granite outcropping. The canyon bent here, turning abruptly to the right around the granite. To his left, at his elbow, the cliff wall split, forming a narrow declivity in which brush grew. Checking his surroundings was an automatic precaution, typical of Leaphorn—making sure that he could find this place again in daylight. That done, he renewed his concentrated listening.

He heard in the darkness the sound of running, and of panting breath. It was coming directly toward him. In a split second the adrenal glands flooded his blood. Leaphorn managed to thumb back the pistol hammer to full cock, and half raise the .38. Then looming out of the darkness came the bulk of the dog, eyes and teeth reflecting the starlight in a strange wet whiteness. Leaphorn was able to lunge sideways toward the split cliff, and jerk the trigger. Amid the thunder of the pistol shot, the dog was on him. It struck him shoulder-high. Because of Leaphorn's lunge, the impact was glancing. Instead of being knocked on his back, the animal atop him, he was spun sideways against the cliff. The beast's teeth tore at his jacket instead of his throat, and the momentum of its leap carried it past him. Leaphorn found himself in the crevasse, scrambling frantically upward over boulders and brush. The dog, snarling now for the first time, had recovered itself and was into the crevasse after him. Leaphorn pulled himself desperately upward, with the dog just below him—far enough below him to make Leaphorn's dangling legs safe by a matter of perhaps a yard. He gripped a root of some sort with his right hand and felt carefully with his left and found a higher handhold. He squirmed upward, reaching a narrow shelf. There the dog couldn't possibly reach him. He turned and looked down. In this crevasse, the darkness of the canyon bottom became total. He could see nothing below him. But the animal was there, its snarl had become a frustrated yipping. Leaphorn took a deep breath, held it a moment, released it—recovering from his panic. He felt the nausea of a system overloaded with adrenaline. There was no time for sickness, or for the anger which was now replacing fear. He was safe for the moment from the dog, but he was totally exposed to the dog's owner. He made a quick inventory of his situation. His pistol was gone. The animal had struck him as he swung it upward and had knocked it from his hand. He hadn't, apparently, hit the dog, but the blast of the shot must have at least surprised and deafened it—and given Leaphorn time. No worry about concealment now. He unhooked his flashlight from his belt and surveyed his situation. The dog was standing, its forepaws against the rock, just below him. It was as huge as Leaphorn expected. He was neither knowledgeable nor particularly interested in dogs, but this one, he guessed, was a mongrel cross between some of the biggest breeds; Irish wolfhound and Great Dane perhaps. Whatever the mix, it had produced a shaggy coat, a frame taller than a man's when the dog stood as it now stood, on its hind legs, and a massive, ugly head. Leaphorn inspected the declivity into which he had climbed. It slanted steeply upward, apparently an old crack opened by an earth tremor in the cliff. Runoff water had drained down it, debris had tumbled into it, and an assortment of cactus, creosote bush, rabbit brush, and weeds had taken root amid the boulders. It had two advantages—it offered a hiding place and was too steep for the dog to climb. Its disadvantage overrode both of these. It was a trap. The only way out was past the dog. Leaphorn felt around him for a rock of proper throwing size. The one he managed to pull loose from between the two boulders on which he was perched was smaller than he wanted—about the size of a small, flattened orange. He shifted the flashlight to his left hand and the rock to his right, and examined his target. The dog was snarling again. Its teeth and its eyes gleamed in the reflected light. He must hit it in the forehead, and hit it hard. He hurled the rock.

It seemed to strike the dog between its left eye and ear. The animal yelped and retreated down the slope.

At first he thought the dog had disappeared. Then he saw it, eyes reflecting the light, just outside the mouth of the crack. Still within accurate rock range. He fished behind him for another rock, and then quickly flicked off the light. On the canyon floor behind the dog he saw a glimmer of brightness—a flashlight beam bobbing with the walking pace of the person who held it.

"There's the dog," a voice said. "Don't put the light on it, Tull. The son-of-a-bitch has a gun."

The flashlight beam abruptly blinked out. Leaphorn eased himself silently upward. He heard the same voice talking quietly to the dog. And then a second voice:

"He must be up in that crack there," the man called Tull said. "The dog's treed him."

The first voice said, "I told you that dog would earn his keep."

"Up to now he's been a pain in the butt," Tull said. "The son-of-a-bitch scares me."

"No reason for that," the first voice said. "Lynch trained him himself. He was the pride of Safety Systems." The man laughed. "Or he was before I started slipping him food."

"Hell," Tull said. "Look what I just stepped on. It's his gun!

The dog took the bastard's gun away from him."

There was a brief silence.

"It's the right one all right. It's been fired," Tull said.

The flashlight went on again. Leaphorn's reaching hand was exploring an opening between the boulders. He pulled himself further into the slot, stood cautiously and looked downward. He could see a circle of yellow light on the sandy canyon bottom and the legs of two men. Then the light flashed upward, its beam moving over the rocks and brush below him. He ducked back. The beam flashed past, lighting the space in which he stood with its reflection. To the left of where he was crouching, and above him, an immense slab had split away from the face of the cliff. Behind it there would be better cover and the faint possibility of a route to climb upward.

The first voice was shouting up toward him.

"You might as well come on down," the voice said. "We'll hold the dog."

Leaphorn stood silent.

"Come on," the voice said. "You can't get out of there and if you don't come down we're going to get sore about it."

"We just want to talk to you," the Tull voice said. "Who the hell are you and what are you doing here?"

The voices paused, waiting for an answer. The words echoed up and down the canyon, then died away.

"It's a police-issued pistol," the first voice said. "Thirty-eight revolver. There's just one shot fired. The one we heard."

"A cop?"

"Yeah, I'd guess so. Maybe the one that came nosing around the old man's hogan."

"He's not going to come down," Tull said. "I don't think he's coming down."

"No," First Voice said.

"You want me to go up and get him?"

"Hell, no. He'd brain you with a rock. He's above you and you couldn't see it coming in the dark."

"Yeah," Tull said. "So we wait for morning?"

"No. We're going to be busy in the morning," First Voice said. There was silence then. The flashlight beam moved up the crevasse, back and forth, to Leaphorn's hiding place, and then above it. Leaphorn turned and looked up. Far above his head the yellow light reflected from sections of unbroken cliff. But the cleft, he saw, went all the way to the top.

Four cautious steps into the opening and the flash caught him. He scrambled desperately, blinded by the beam, toward the crevasse behind the slab. There was a sudden explosion of gunshots, deafening in the closed space, and the sound of bullets whining off the stones around him. Then he was behind the slab, panting, the flashlight beam reflecting off the cliff.

"What do you think?" Tull asked.

"Damn. I think we missed him."

"He's sure not going to come down now," Tull said.

"Hey, buddy," First Voice said. "You're stuck in a box. If you don't come down, we're going to set this brush on fire here at the bottom and burn you out. Hear that?"

Leaphorn said nothing. He was considering alternatives. He was sure that if he came out they would kill him. Would they build the fire? Maybe. Could he survive it? This slot would give him some protection from the flame, but the fire would roar up the crevasse much like a chimney, exhausting the oxygen. If the heat didn't kill him, suffocation would.

"Go ahead and start it," First Voice said. "I told you he's not coming down."

"Well, hell," Tull said. "Don't a fire draw a crowd out here?"

Voice One laughed. "The only light that'll get out of this canyon will reflect straight up," he said. "There's nobody in forty miles to see it, and by morning the smoke will be all gone."

"Here's some dry grass," Tull said. "Once it gets going, the damp stuff will catch. It's not that wet."

Leaphorn had made his decision without consciously doing so. He would not climb down to be shot. The men below him started the blaze in a mat of brush and canyon-bottom driftwood caught at the crevasse opening. In moments, the smell of burning creosote bush and piñon resin reached Leaphorn's nostrils. The fire below would be interfering with the men's vision. He looked down at them. The dog stood behind them, backed nervously away from the blaze, but still looking up—its pointed ears erect and its eyes reflecting yellow in the firelight. To its left stood a large man in jeans and a denim jacket. He was holding a military-model automatic rifle cradled over his arm and using the other hand to shield his face from the heat. The face looked lopsided, somehow distorted, and the one eye Leaphorn could see stared upward toward him curiously. Tull. The second man was smaller. He wore a long-sleeved shirt and no jacket, his hair was black and cut fairly short, and the firelight glittered off gold-rimmed glasses. And behind the glasses Leaphorn saw a bland Navajo face. The light was weak and flickering, the glimpse was momentary, and the gold-rimmed glasses might have tricked the imagination. But Leaphorn found himself facing the fact that the man trying to kill him looked like Father Benjamin Tso of the Order of Friars Minor.

15

THE PROBLEM WOULD BE FLAME, heat, and lack of oxygen. Behind this slab, the flames would not reach him unless they were drawn in by some freakish draft. That left heat, which could kill him just as surely. And suffocation. The light from the fire below grew, flickering at first and then steady. Leaphorn worked his way further behind the slab, away from the light. His bootsole suddenly splashed into water. The slab had formed a catch basin which had trapped the day's rain water as it poured down the cliff face. Behind him now the flames were making a steady roar as brush higher up the crevasse heated and exploded into fire. He pulled himself into the water. It was cool. He soaked his shirt, his pants, his boots. Through the slot behind him now he could see only fire. A gust of heat struck him, a searing torch on his cheek. He ducked his face into the water, held it there until his lungs cried for air. When he raised his face, he drew in a breath slowly and cautiously. The air was hot now, and his ears were filled with the roar of the fire. As he looked through slitted eyes, weeds in the lip of the slot wilted suddenly, then exploded into bright yellow flame. His denims were steaming. He splashed more water on them. The heat was intense, but his lungs told him it would be suffocation that would kill him unless he could find some source of oxygen. He climbed frantically between the cliff face and the inner surface of slab, working his way away from the fire. The first breath he took seared his lungs. But there was a draft now, sucking past his face. It came not from the flames but from somewhere below, pulled through the slot by the heat-caused vacuum. Leaphorn forced himself into the increasingly narrow gap—away from the furnace and toward this source of blessed air. Finally he could go no farther. His head was jammed in a vise of stone. The heat varied, now unbearably intense, now merely scalding. He could feel steam from his soaked pants legs hot on his inner thighs. The fire was making its own wind, sucking air—extremely hot air—past his face. If the draft changed, it would pull fire up this slot and char him like a moth. Or when his clothing dried and ignited, this draft of oxygen would turn him into a torch. Leaphorn shut this thought out of his mind and concentrated on another thought. If he stayed alive, he would get his rifle, and he would kill the dog and the man with the lopsided face and, most of all, he would kill Goldrims. He would kill Goldrims. He would kill Goldrims. And thus Joe Leaphorn endured.

The time came when the roar of fire diminished, and the draft of air around his face faded, and the heat rose to a furnace intensity. Leaphorn thought, then, that he would not survive. Consciousness slipped away. When it returned, the noise of burning was nothing more than a crackling, and he could hear voices. Sometimes they sounded faint and far away, and sometimes Leaphorn could understand the words. And finally the voices stopped, and time passed, and it was dark again. Leaphorn decided he would try to move, and found that he could, and inched his head out of the crevasse. His nostrils were filled with the smell of heat and ashes. But there was little fire. Most of the light here came from a log which had tumbled into the crack from above. It burned fitfully a hundred yards overhead. Leaphorn eased himself downward, toward the pool of water. It was warm now, almost hot, and much of it had evaporated. Leaphorn put his face into what remained and drank greedily. It tasted of charcoal. Hot as the fire had been it had not been enough to substantially raise the temperature of the massive living stone of the cliff which was still cool and made the temperature here bearable. In the flickering light, Leaphorn sat and inspected himself. He would have blisters, especially on one ankle where the skin had been exposed, and perhaps on his wrists and neck and face. His chest felt uncomfortable but there was no real pain. He had survived. The problem now was just as it had been—how to escape this trap.

He eased his way to the edge of the slab and peered around it. Below, logs and brush were still burning at a dozen places, and hot coals glowed at a hundred others. He could see neither dog nor man. Perhaps they were gone for good. Perhaps they were merely waiting for the fire to cool enough to climb the crevasse and make sure he was dead. Leaphorn thought about it. It must have seemed impossible, seen from below, for any living thing to survive in that flame-filled crevasse. Yet he couldn't quite convince himself that the two men would take the risk. He would try to climb out.

He burned himself a half-dozen times before he learned to detect and avoid the hot spots left by the fire. But by the time he was 150 feet above the canyon floor heat was no longer the problem. Now the cleft had narrowed but the climb was almost vertical. Climbing involved inching upward a few feet and then an extended pause to rest muscles aching with fatigue. The climb used up the night. He finally pulled himself onto the cap rock in the gray light of dawn and lay, utterly spent, with his face against the cold stone. He allowed himself a few minutes to rest and then moved into the cover of a cliffside juniper.

There he extracted his walkie-talkie from its case on his belt, switched on the receiver and sat, getting his bearings. His transmission range was perhaps ten miles—hopelessly short for reaching any Navajo Police receiver. But Leaphorn tried it anyway. He broadcast his location and a call for help. There was no response. The Arizona State Police band was transmitting a description of a truck. The New Mexico State Police transmitter at Farmington was silent. He could hear the Utah Highway Patrol dispatcher at Moab, but not well enough to understand anything. The Federal Law Enforcement channel was sending what seemed to be a list of identifications. The Navajo State Police dispatcher at Tuba City, like the ASP radio, was giving someone a truck description—a camper truck, a big one apparently, with tandem rear wheels.

Leaphorn had himself placed now. The mesa that overlooked the Tso hogan was on the southwestern horizon, perhaps three miles away. Beyond that was his carryall, with his rifle and a radio transmitter strong enough to reach Tuba City. But at least two canyons cut the plateau between him and the hogan. Getting there would take hours. The sooner he started the better.

If there was any life on this segment of the plateau it wasn't visible in the early morning light. Except for whitish outcrops of limestone, the cap rock was a dark red ingenous rock which supported in its cracks and crevasses a sparse growth of dry-country vegetation. A few hundred yards west, a low mesa blocked off the horizon. Leaphorn examined it, wondering if he'd have to cross it to reach his vehicle.

From the radio the pleasant feminine voice of the Tuba City dispatcher came faintly. It completed the description of the camper truck, lapsed into silence, and began another message. Leaphorn's mind was concentrating on what his eyes were seeing—seeking a way up the mesa wall. But it registered the word "hostages." Suddenly Leaphorn was listening.

The radio was silent again. He willed it to speak. The rim of the horizon over New Mexico was bright now with streaks of yellow. A morning breeze moved against his face. The radio spoke faintly, with the meaning lost in the moving air. Leaphorn squatted behind the juniper and held the speaker against his ear.

"All units," the voice said. "We have more information. All units copy. Confirming three men involved. Confirming all three were armed. Witnesses saw one rifle and two pistols. In addition to the Boy Scouts, the hostages are two adult males. They are identified as—Discontinue this. Discontinue this. All units. All police units are ordered to evacuate the area of the Navajo Reservation north of U.S. Highway 160 and east of U.S. Highway 89, south of the northern border of the reservation, and west of the New Mexico border. We have instructions from the kidnappers that if police are seen in that area the hostages will be killed. Repeating. All police units are ordered . . ."

Leaphorn was only half conscious of the voice repeating itself. Could this explain what Goldrims was doing? Had he been setting up a Buffalo Society kidnapping? Preparing its base—a hiding place for hostages? Why else would police be ordered out of this section of the reservation?

The radio completed its repetition of the warning and finished its interrupted description of the male adult hostages, both leaders of a troop of Scouts from Santa Fe. It launched into a description of the hostage boys.

"Juvenile subject one is identified as Norbert Juan Gomez, age twelve, four feet, eleven inches tall, weight about eighty pounds, black hair, black eyes. All juvenile subjects wearing Boy Scout uniforms.

"Juvenile subject two is Tommy Pearce, age thirteen, five feet tall, weight ninety, brown hair, brown eyes.

"Juvenile subject three . . ."

They all sound pretty much alike, Leaphorn thought. Turned into statistics. Changed by exposure to violence from children into juvenile subjects three, four, five, and six, to be measured in pounds and inches and color of hair.

"Juvenile subject eight, Theodore Middle initial F. Markham, age thirteen, five feet two inches, weight about one hundred pounds, blond hair, blue eyes, pale complexion."

Leaphorn converted juvenile subject eight into a pale blond boy he had noticed last summer watching a rodeo at Window Rock. The boy had stood at the arena enclosure, one foot on the bottom rail, his hair bleached almost white, his face peeling from old sunburn, his attention on the efforts of a Navajo cowboy trying to tie the forelegs of a calf he had bulldogged.

"Juvenile subject nine is Milton Richard Silver," the radio intoned, and Leaphorn's mind converted nine into Leaphorn's own nephew, who lived in Flagstaff, whose blue jeans were chronically disfigured with plastic model cement and whose elbows were disfigured from the scars of skateboard accidents. And that thought led to another one. Tuba City would remember he had gone to the Tso hogan. They'd be trying to reach him to call him out of the prohibited zone. But that didn't matter. Goldrims knew he was here. Knew he had been here before the warning. What mattered was to get moving. To get his rifle.

Leaphorn walked rapidly, flinching at first from the stiffness in calves and ankles. He considered dropping his equipment belt, leaving binoculars, radio, flashlight, and first-aid kit behind to save the weight. But though the radio and binoculars were heavy, he might need them. The radio had completed its descriptions of the hostage Scouts with juvenile subject eleven and was engaged in responding to questions and transmitting orders. From this Leaphorn pieced together a little more of what had happened. Three armed men, all apparently Indians, had appeared the night before at one of the many Boy Scout troop encampments scattered around the mouth of Canyon de Chelly. They had arrived in two trucks—a camper and a van. They had herded the two Scout leaders and eleven of the boys into the camper and had left two more adults and seven other Scouts tied and locked in the van.

Leaphorn frowned. Why take some hostages and leave others? And why that number? The question instantly answered itself. He remembered the propaganda leaflet in the FBI file at Albuquerque. First on the list of atrocities to be avenged was the Olds Prairie Murders, the victims of which had been three adults and eleven children. The thought chilled him. But why hadn't they taken three adults? Theodora Adams. Was she the third? The Buffalo Society evidently had planned to dramatize the deaths of eleven Kiowa children from a century ago by taking eleven Boy Scouts hostage. They'd known this would launch an international orgy of news coverage, would make for nationwide suspense. There would be television interviews with weeping mothers and distraught fathers. The whole world would be watching this one. The whole world would be asking if an Indian named Kelongy simply wanted to recall an old atrocity or if his sense of justice would demand a perfect balance. Leaphorn was wondering about this himself when he heard the dog.

It came from above him on the cap of the mesa—an angry, frustrated sound something between a snarl and a bark. He had forgotten the dog. The sound stopped him in his tracks. Then he saw the animal almost directly above him. It stood with its front paws on the very edge of the rimrock, shoulders hunched, teeth bared. It barked again, then turned abruptly and ran along the cliff away from him, then back toward him, apparently looking frantically for a way down. The creature was even bigger than he remembered it, looming in the yellow firelight of the night before. At any minute it would find a way down—a rock slide, a deer trail, almost any break in the cliff which would lead to the talus slope below. Leaphorn became aware of a cold knot of fear in his stomach. He looked around him, hoping to see something he could use for a club. He broke a limb from a dead juniper, although it was hopelessly inadequate to stop the animal. Then he turned and ran stiffly back toward the main-stem canyon. It was the only place where having hands could give him an advantage over an adversary with four legs and tearing canine teeth. He stopped at a twisted little cedar rooted into the rock about six feet from the lip of the cliff. Behind it he hurriedly unlaced his boots. He knotted the laces securely together, doubled them, and tied the strings around the trunk of the bush. Then he whipped off his belt, looped it, and tied it to the doubled bootstrings. As he tested its strength, he saw the dog. It had worked its way along a crack in the cap rock, and was bounding down the talus slope toward him, baying again. Last night it had attacked without a sound, as attack dogs are trained to strike, and even after it had cornered him had only snarled. But he must have hurt it with a rock and it had apparently forgotten at least a little of its training. Leaphorn hoped fervently that in its hate for him it had forgotten everything. He picked up his juniper stick and trotted out across the cap toward the dog, his untied boots flapping on his ankles. Then he stopped. The worst mistake would be going too far, waiting too long, and being caught away from the edge of the cliff. He stood, the stick gripped at his side, waiting. Within seconds, the dog appeared. It was perhaps a hundred fifty yards away, running full out, looking for him.

Leaphorn cupped his hands. "Dog," he shouted. "Here I am."

The animal changed direction with an agility that caused Leaphorn's jaw muscles to tighten. His idea wasn't going to work. In a matter of seconds he would be trying to kill that huge animal with a stick and his bare hands. Still, the cliff edge was his best hope. The dog was racing directly toward him now, no longer barking, its teeth bared. Leaphorn waited. Eighty yards now, he guessed. Now sixty. He had a sudden vision of his laceless boots tripping him, and the nightmare thought of falling, with the dog racing down on him. Forty yards. Thirty.

Leaphorn turned and ran desperately in his flapping boots toward the cedar. He knew almost at once that he had waited too long. The dog was bigger and faster than he had realized. It must weigh nearly two-hundred pounds. He could hear it at his heels. The race now seemed almost dreamlike, the looped belt hanging forever outside his reach. And then with a last leap his hand was grabbing the leather, and he felt the dog's teeth tearing at his hip, and his momentum flung him sideways around the bush, holding with every ounce of his strength to the belt, feeling the dog fly past him, its jaws still ripping at his hip—knowing with a sense of terror that their combined weight would pull his grip loose from the belt, or the nylon strings loose from the tree, and both of them would slide over the cliff and fall, the dog still tearing at him. They would fall, and fall, and fall, tumbling, waiting for the hideous split second when their bodies would strike the rocks below.

And then the teeth tore loose.

In some minuscule fraction of a second Leaphorn's senses told him he was no longer connected to the dog, that his grip on the belt still held, that he would not fall to his death. A second later he knew that his plan to send the animal skidding over the cliff had failed. The dog's hold on Leaphorn's hip had saved it. The animal's back legs had slid over the edge as it had turned, but its body and its front legs were still on the cap rock and it was straining to pull itself to safety.

There was no time to think. Leaphorn flung himself at the animal, pushing desperately at its front feet. The hind paws dislodged stones as the beast kicked for lodging. It snapped viciously at Leaphorn's hand. But the effort cost it an inch. Leaphorn pushed again at a forepaw. This time the dog's teeth snapped shut on his shirt sleeve. The creature was moving backward, pulling Leaphorn over the edge. Then the cloth tore loose. For a second the animal stood vertically against the cliff, supported by its straining front legs and whatever grip its hind paws had found on the stone face of the canyon wall. It was snarling, its straining efforts aimed not at saving itself but at attacking its victim. And then the hind paws must have slipped for the broad, ugly head disappeared. Leaphorn moved cautiously forward and looked over the edge. The animal was cartwheeling slowly as it fell. Far down the cliff it struck a half-dead clump of rabbit brush growing out of a crack, bounced outward, and set off a small rain of dislodged rocks. Leaphorn looked away before it struck the canyon bottom. But for luck, his body too might be suffering that impact. He pulled himself back to the cedar and inspected the damage.

His pants were bloody at the hip, where the dog's teeth had snapped through trousers, shorts, skin, and muscle and had torn loose a flap of flesh. The wound burned and was bleeding copiously. It was a hell of a place to fix. No possibility of a tourniquet, and putting on a pressure bandage would require securing it around both hip and waist. He took tape from his first-aid kit and bandaged the tear as best he could. His other wounds were trivial. A bitten place on his right wrist from which a small amount of blood was oozing, and a gash, probably caused by the dog's teeth, on the back of his left hand. He found himself wondering if the dog had been given rabies shots. The idea seemed so incongruous that he laughed aloud. Like giving shots to a werewolf, he thought.

The laugh died in his throat.

On the mesa, not far from where he had first seen the dog, sunlight flashed from something. Leaphorn crouched behind the cedar, straining his eyes. A man was standing back from the mesa rim, scanning the rocky shelf along the canyon with binoculars. Probably Goldrims, Leaphorn thought. He would have been following his dog. He would have heard barking, and now he would be looking for the animal and for its prey. Leaphorn contemplated hiding. With the dog out of the picture he might succeed, if he could find a place under the rim of the cap rock where he could hang on. And then he realized the man had already seen him. The binoculars were turned directly on Leaphorn's cedar. There would be no hiding. He could only run, and there was no place to run. He would climb down the cleft again. That would delay the inevitable and perhaps in the cover and loose boulders of that steep slope the odds would improve for an unarmed man. Improve, Leaphorn thought grimly, from zero to a hundred to one.

The man didn't seem to have a rifle, but Leaphorn kept under cover as well as he could in reaching the place where the canyon wall was split. As he lowered himself over the cap rock, he saw the man emerging on the talus slope under the mesa, using the same route the dog had taken. Leaphorn had maybe a five-minute lead, and he used it recklessly—taking chance after chance with his injured leg, with precarious handholds on fire-blackened brush, with footholds on stones that might not hold. He had no accurate sense of time. At any moment Goldrims might appear at the top of the slot above him and end this one-sided contest with a pistol shot. But the shot didn't come. Leaphorn, soot-blackened, reached the sheltered place where he had survived the fire. He would give Goldrims as much excitement as he could for his money. He would climb once again up behind that great slab of stone to the place where he had lain when the fire was burning. Goldrims would have to climb after him to kill him. And while he was climbing, Goldrims might leave himself momentarily vulnerable to something thrown from above.

A small cascade of stones slid down the cleft with a clatter. Goldrims was beginning his descent. It would be slower than his own, Leaphorn knew. Goldrims had no reason to be taking chances. That left a little time. Leaphorn looked around him for rocks of the proper size. He found one, about as big as a grapefruit. The binoculars would also make a missile, and so would the flashlight. He began to climb.

It was easy enough. The face of the cliff and the inner surface of the slab were less than a yard apart. He could brace himself between them as he worked his way upward. The surfaces were relatively smooth, the stone polished by eons of rain and blowing sand since some ancient earthquake had fractured the plateau. Above him Leaphorn saw the narrow shelf where he had jammed himself and huddled away from the fire. His heart sank. It was too narrow and too cramped to offer any hope at all of defense. He couldn't throw from there expecting to hit anything. And it offered no cover from below. Goldrims would simply shoot him and the game would be over.

Leaphorn hung motionless for a moment, looking for a way out. Could he squeeze his way to that source of air which had kept him breathing during the fire? He couldn't. The gap narrowed quickly and then closed completely. Leaphorn frowned. Then where had that draft of fresh air originated? He could feel it now, moving faintly against his face. But not from ahead. It came from beneath him.

Leaphorn moved downward, crabwise, as rapidly as he could shift his elbows and knees. It was cooler here, and there was dampness in the air. His boots touched broken rocks. He was at the bottom of the split. Or almost at the bottom. Here the stones were whitish, eaten with erosion. They were limestone, and seeping water had dissolved away the calcite. Below Leaphorn's feet the split sloped away into darkness. A hole. He kicked a rock loose and listened to it bouncing downward. From above and behind him came the sound of other rocks falling. Goldrims had noticed the crack behind the slab and was following him. Without a backward glance, Leaphorn scrambled downward into the narrow darkness.

THE WATCH HANDS and numerals were suspended, luminous yellow against the velvet blackness. It was 11:03 A.M. Almost fourteen hours since the dog had first attacked him on the canyon floor, more than twenty-four hours since he had eaten, and two hours since the thundering fall of the boulders Goldrims had dislodged to block his exit. Resting, Leaphorn had used those two hours to assess his situation and work on a plan. He wasn't happy with either. He was caught in a cave. Two quick inspections with his flashlight told him that the cave was extensive, that it sloped sharply downward, and that—like most large caves—it had been leached out of a limestone deposit by ground water. Leaphorn understood the process. Rain water draining through soil containing decaying vegetation became acidic. The acid quickly ate away the calcite in limestone, dissolving the stone and forming caverns. Here when the canyon formed it had drained away the water, and checked the process. Then an earth tremor had cracked open an entrance to the cave. Since air flowed through it, there must be another entrance. Leaphorn could feel the movement now: a cool current past his face. His plan was simple—he would try to find another exit. If he couldn't, he would return here and try to dig his way out. That would involve dislodging the boulders that Goldrims had rolled into the hole, causing them to tumble downward. Doing that without being crushed would be tricky. Doing it without noise would be impossible, and Goldrims would probably be waiting.

Leaphorn flicked on the flashlight again and began edging downward. As he did, a blast of air struck him, and with the concussion, a deafening explosion of sound. It knocked him from his feet and sent him tumbling down the limestone slope, engulfed in a Niagara of noise. He lay on the cool stone, his ears assaulted with slamming echoes and the sound of falling rock. What the hell had happened? His nostrils told him in a second as the stench of burned dynamite reached them. The flashlight had been knocked from his hand, but it was still burning just below him. He retrieved it and aimed its beam upward. The air above was a fog of limestone dust and blue smoke. Goldrims had dropped dynamite into the cave entrance to kill the policeman with concussion, or crush him, or seal him in. There'd be damn little hope now of getting out the way he'd come in. His hope, if there was hope, lay in finding the source of the air which had moved upward through this cavity.

Leaphorn moved cautiously downward, his ears still ringing with the aftereffects of the blast. At least there was no worry now of Goldrims or Tull following him. He was, from their point of view, dead or neutralized. The thought was small consolation, because Leaphorn's common sense told him such a theory was probably accurate.

The cavity sloped at about sixty degrees, angling toward the face of the canyon cliff. As he lowered himself deeper into it, it widened. At places now the space overhead rose at least a hundred feet. The luminous dial of his wrist watch read a little after three when he first detected reflected light. It originated from a side cavern which led upward and to his right. Leaphorn climbed up it far enough to conclude that the light leaked in from some sort of split in the canyon cliff. The approach to it was too narrow for anything larger than a snake to navigate. Leaphorn let his head slump against the stone and stared longingly toward the unattainable light. He felt no panic—only a sense of helpless defeat. He would rest for a while and then he would begin the long, weary climb back up to the entrance Goldrims had dynamited. There'd be almost no chance he could dig his way out. The blast must have dislodged tens of tons of stone. But it was the only possibility. He backed out of the crack into the cavern itself, and sat thinking. The silence was complete. He could hear his heart beating and the breath moving past his lips. The air was cool. It pressed against his left cheek, smelling fresh and clean. It should smell of burned dynamite, Leaphorn thought. Why doesn't it? It doesn't because at this time of day, air would be moving upward through the cave, pushing the fumes out. The air was still moving. Did that mean that the exit hadn't been entirely sealed by the blast? Leaphorn felt a stirring of hope. But no. The air was moving in the wrong direction. It was moving past his face into the crack—toward the light source. Leaphorn thought about what that implied, and felt another stirring of hope. There must be another source of air, deeper in the cavern. Perhaps this eroded cavity intersected with the cliff wall somewhere below.

At 6:19 P.M., Leaphorn reached a bottom. He squatted, savoring the unaccustomed feel of level flatness under his bootsoles. The floor here had been formed by sediment. It was calcite dissolved out of the limestone walls, but over the calcite there was a thin layer of gritty sand. Leaphorn examined it with the flashlight. It seemed to be the same sort of sand one would find at the canyon bottom outside—a mixture of fine particles of granite, silica, limestone, and sandstone. He flashed the light around. This flat surface seemed to extend from the declivity he had been descending along the length of this long, narrow compartment. The sand must have washed in from below or blown in on the wind. Either way, he should be able to see daylight. He turned off the flashlight and stood, seeing nothing but blackness. But there was still the moving air—the faint feeling of pressure against his face which seemed characteristic of this cave. He moved into the air movement now, as he had ever since he had entered the cave. For the first time, the going was relatively easy—a matter of walking instead of climbing. He saw that originally the cave had continued its downward plunge here—but an invasion of water had filled it with a sedimentary floor. The floor was level, but the ceiling sloped toward his head. He had to stoop now, to pass a cluster of stalactites. Beyond them his flashlight beam prodded to the inevitable point of intersection—where slanted ceiling met level floor. Leaphorn squatted under the lowering roof, moving forward. He advanced on hands and knees. Finally, he crawled.

The angle between floor and ceiling narrowed everywhere to nothing. Leaphorn let his forehead rest against the calcite, fighting off the first nudgings of panic. How much longer would the flashlight last? It was a subject he hadn't allowed himself to consider. He moved the tip of his nose through the film of gritty dust and was reassured. His reason told him this sandy stuff must have been carried in from the outside—from the world of light. But here in this cul-de-sac there was no air movement. He began crawling backward. He would find the moving air again and try to follow it.

But the air current was dying. At first Leaphorn thought he had simply been unable to find the area through which it moved. And then he realized that it must be nearing that time of day when this earthly breathing stops—the moment near the margin of daylight and dark when the heating/cooling process briefly reaches balance, when warm air no longer presses upward and cool air is not yet heavy enough to sink. Even in this slanting cavern, where narrowness of passageway multiplied the effect, there would be two periods—morning and evening—when the draft would be dead.

Leaphorn collected a pinch of the fine-grained sand between thumb and forefinger and sifted it out into the beam of his flashlight. It fell almost perpendicularly. Almost—but not quite. Leaphorn moved toward the source of air, repeating the process. And the fifth time he bent to replenish his supply of dust, he saw the footprint of the dog.

He squatted, looking at the print and digesting what it meant. It meant, first, that he was not doomed to die entombed in this cave. The dog had found a way in. Leaphorn could find a way out. It meant, second, that the cavity Leaphorn had been following down from high up the cliff must be connected to a cavern that opened on the canyon bottom. As the thought came, Leaphorn flicked off the flashlight. If the dog had been in this cave, it was probably the hiding place of Goldrims.

Even though he now used the flashlight only cautiously, following the dog's tracks was relatively easy. The animal had roamed through a labyrinth of rooms and corridors, but had quickly exhausted its curiosity.

At about 8 P.M. Leaphorn detected a dim reflection of light.

Exulting in the sight, he moved toward it slowly, stopping often to listen. He had a single advantage and he intended to guard it: Goldrims and Tull believed he was dead and out of the game. As long as they didn't know he was inside their sanctuary, he had surprise on his side. He became aware of sounds now. First there was a vague purring, which began suddenly and stopped just as abruptly about five minutes later. It sounded like a small, well-muffled internal-combustion engine. A little later Leaphorn heard a metallic clatter, and after that, when he had edged perhaps a hundred yards toward the source of light, a thumping noise. The light was general now. Still faint but enough so that Leaphorn—his pupils totally dilated by hours of absolute darkness—could forgo the flashlight entirely. He moved past one of the seemingly endless screens of stalagmites into another of the series of auditorium-sized cavities which water seepage had produced at this level. Just around the screen, Leaphorn stopped. The light here reflected and shimmered from the irregular ceiling far overhead. At the end of this room, he could see water. He edged toward it. An underground pool. Its surface was about three feet lower than the old calcite deposit which formed the cavern floor. He knelt beside it and dipped in a finger. It was cool, but not cold. He tasted it. Fresh, with none of the alkaline flavor he had expected. He looked down its surface, toward the source of light. And then he realized that this water must be part of Lake Powell—backing into the cave as the lake surface rose with spring runoff and draining out as the level fell with autumn and winter. He drank thirstily.

The dog tracks led Leaphorn away from the water into the next room. At its far end, Leaphorn saw, it, too, opened onto the lake surface. The light here was still indirect—seemingly reflecting out of the water—but it was brighter. There were sounds, blurred by echoes. Voices. Whose? Goldrims and Tull? Father Goldrims and Theodora Adams? And how had a doctor's daughter and a Franciscan priest become involved in this violent affair? He thought of the face of Father Tso as it had looked magnified through binoculars—the eyes intent on the elevated host, the expression rapt. And the face in the reflected glow of the flashlight at the canyon bottom—the man in the gold-rimmed glasses calmly discussing with Tull how to burn Leaphorn to death. Had his eyes tricked him in the flickering light? Could they be the same man?

The hunger cramps which had bothered him earlier were gone now. He hadn't eaten for thirty-three hours and his digestive system seemed to have adjusted to the oddity. He felt only a sort of lethargic weakness—the product, he guessed, of low blood sugar. An intermittent throbbing had joined the ache in his hip—probably the symptom of an infection beginning in the dog bite. That was something he could think about much later. Now the problem was to find a way out of here.

As he thought that, a beam of yellow light flashed across his face.

Before Leaphorn could react, the light was gone. He stood looking frantically for a place to hide. And then he realized that whoever was behind the light apparently hadn't noticed him. He could see the light only indirectly now, reflecting off the limestone far down the cavern. It swung and bobbed with the movement of the person who carried it. Leaphorn moved toward it as swiftly as he could without risking noise. The flat calcite floor deposit quickly gave way to rougher going—a mixture of stalagmite deposits jutting upward and outcrops of some sort of darker non-limestone extrusions which had resisted the dissolving water. The light disappeared, then its reflection appeared again between a high ridge of lime deposit and the cavern ceiling. Leaphorn climbed the ridge gingerly. He peered over the top. Below him, a thin man wearing a blue shirt and a red sweatband around his forehead was squatting beside a pile of cartons, gathering an armload of boxes and cans. The man rose and turned. He clutched his burden to his chest with his right arm, awkwardly retrieved an electric lantern with his left, and walked quickly from Leaphorn's view the same way he had come. The bobbing light of his lantern faded away. Leaphorn lay a moment, listening. Then he slid over the limestone barrier and climbed quietly down to the boxes.

They contained groceries—canned vegetables, canned meats, cartons of crackers and cookies, pork and beans, canned peaches. Sufficient, Leaphorn guessed, to feed a family for a month. He made a quick estimate of the missing cans and boxes. About enough gone to amount to thirty or forty man-days of eating. Either this cave had been occupied by one person a month or more, or by several persons for a shorter period. Near the cache of groceries was a row of five-gallon gasoline cans. Eight of them. Leaphorn checked. Five were full of gasoline and three were empty. Beyond them was a wooden crate. The word EXPLOSIVES was stenciled across the loosened lid. Leaphorn lifted it and looked inside. Dynamite sticks, neatly packed. Six of the twenty-four sticks were missing. He replaced the lid. Beside the dynamite case was a padlocked metal toolbox and two cardboard cartons. The smaller one contained a roll of blue insulated wire. The larger one originally had held a pair of Justin boots. Now it held what looked like the works of a large clock—a timing device of some sort. Leaphorn put it back and rearranged the paper padding as he had found it. He squatted on his heels. What might he do with dynamite and a timing device? He could think of absolutely nothing useful, beyond committing suicide. The detonators seemed to be kept somewhere else—a healthy habit developed by those who worked with explosives. Without the blasting caps the stuff could be fired by impact—but it would take a heavy blow. He left the dynamite and selected a box of crackers and an assortment of canned meats and vegetables from boxes where they seemed least likely to be missed. Then he hurried back into the darkness. He would hide, eat, and wait. With food and water, time was no longer an enemy. He would wait for night, when darkness would spread from the interior of the cave to its mouth. Then he could learn more about what lay between him and the exit.

Even during the long days of August, darkness came relatively early at the bottom of a canyon. By 9 P.M. it was dark enough. His bootsoles and heels were rubber and relatively noiseless, but he cut the sleeves from his shirt and wrapped the boots carefully to further muffle the sound of his footsteps. Then he began his careful prowling. A little before 11 P.M. he had done as much exploring as caution permitted. He had learned that his escape would certainly involve getting wet, and would probably involve getting shot.

He had found the cave mouth by edging his way down the

waterline, wading at times where the limestone formations forced him into the water. Just around one such outcropping, he had seen a wide arch of opalescent light. The night outside, dark as it was, was immensely brighter than the eyeless blackness of the cave. The cave mouth showed as an irregular, flattened arch of light. This bright slope was bisected by a horizontal line. Leaphorn studied this optical phenomenon a moment before he understood its cause. Most of the mouth of the cave was submerged in the lake. Only a few feet at the top were open to the air. Leaving the cave would involve swimming—simple enough. It would also involve swimming past two men. A butane lantern on a shelf of stone to the left of the cave entrance illuminated the men. One was Tull. In the dim light, he was sprawled against a bedroll, reading a magazine. The other man had his back to Leaphorn. He was kneeling, working intently at something. Leaphorn extracted his binoculars. Through them he saw the man was working on what seemed to be a radio transceiver, apparently adjusting something. His shoulders were hunched and his face hidden, but the form and clothing were familiar. Goldrims. Leaphorn stared at the man, pulled optically almost into touching distance by the lenses. Was it the priest? He felt his stomach tighten. Fear, or anger, or both. The man had tried to kill him three times. He stared at the man's back, watching his shoulders move as he worked. Then he shifted the binoculars to Tull, seeing the undamaged side of his face in profile. From this angle the deformity was not apparent. The face, softly lit by the yellow flare of the lantern, was gentle, engrossed in whatever he was reading. The lips suddenly turned up in a smile, and the face turned toward Father Goldrims and mouthed something. Leaphorn had seen the ruined face before in the flickering firelight. Now he saw it more clearly—the crushed cheekbone, the mouth pulled forever awry by the improperly healed jawbone, the misshapen eye socket. It was the sort of face that made those who saw it flinch.

Suddenly Tull's lips stopped moving. He swung his head slightly to the left, frowning, listening. Then Leaphorn heard the sound that had attracted Tull's attention. It was faint and made incoherent by echoes, but it was a human sound. Tull said something to Goldrims, his face angry. Goldrims glanced toward the source of the sound, his face in profile now to Leaphorn's binoculars. He shook his head, said something, and went back to work. Leaphorn lowered the binoculars and concentrated on listening. The sound was high-pitched, shrill, and excited. A female voice. Now he knew in what direction he would find Theodora Adams.

LEAPHORN MOVED CAREFULLY back into the labyrinth, circling to his right beyond the cache of supplies into another arm of the cavern. The calcite floors here were at several levels—dropping abruptly as much as four or five feet from one flat plane to another—suggesting that the cavern had flooded, drained, and reflooded repeatedly down through geological time. The darkness was virtually total again and Leaphorn felt his way cautiously, not risking the flashlight, less fearful of a fall than of giving away his only advantage. The distant sound of the voices pulled him on. There was a hint of light from ahead, elusive as the sound, which echoed and reflected, seeming no closer. Leaphorn stopped, as he had a dozen times, trying to locate the source exactly. As he stood, breath held, ears straining, he heard another sound.

It was a rubbing, scraping sound, coming from his right. At first it defied identification. He stared into the blackness. The sound came, and came again, and came again—rhythmically. It became louder, and clearer, and Leaphorn began to distinguish a pattern to it—a second of silence before the repetition. It was something alive dragging itself directly toward him. Leaphorn had a sudden hideous intuition. The dog had tumbled down the cliff. But he hadn't seen it hit the bottom. It was alive, crippled, dragging itself inexorably after Leaphorn's scent. For a second, reason reasserted itself in Leaphorn's logical mind. The dog couldn't have fallen three hundred feet down the face of that cliff and survived. But then the sound came again, closer now, only a few yards away from his feet, and Leaphorn was again in a nightmare world in which men became witches, and turned themselves into wolves; in which wolves didn't fall, but flew. He pointed the flashlight at the sound, like a gun, and pushed the button.

There was, for a moment, nothing but a blaze of blinding light. Then Leaphorn's dilated pupils adjusted and the shape illuminated in the flashlight beam became Father Benjamin Tso. The priest's eyes were squeezed shut against the light, his face jerked away from the beam. He was sitting on the calcite floor, his feet stretched in front of him, his arms behind him. His ankles were fastened with what appeared to be a strip of nylon.

Now Tso squinted up into the flashlight beam.

"All right," he said. "If you'll untie my ankles, I'll walk back."

Leaphorn said nothing.

"No harm trying," the priest said. He laughed. "Maybe I could have got away."

"Who in the hell are you?" Leaphorn asked. He could hardly get the words out.

The priest frowned into the light, his face puzzled. "What do you mean?" he asked. Then he frowned again, trying to see Leaphorn's face through the flashlight beam. "I'm Benjamin Tso," he said. "Father Benjamin Tso." He paused. "But aren't you . . . ?"

"I'm Leaphorn. The Navajo cop."

"Thank God," Father Tso said. "Thank God for that." He swung his head to the side. "The others are back there. They're all right. How did you . . . ?"

"Keep your voice down," Leaphorn said.

He snapped off the light and listened. In the cave now there was only a heavy, ear-ringing total silence.

"Can you untie my hands?" Father Tso whispered. "They've been numb for a long time."

Leaphorn switched on the flash again, holding his hand over the lens to release only the dimmest illumination. He studied the priest's face. It was a lot like the face of the man he had seen with Tull and the dog, the face of the man who had tried to burn him to death in the canyon.

Father Benjamin Tso glanced up at Leaphorn, and then away. Even in the dim light Leaphorn could see the face change. It became tired and older.

"I guess you've met my brother," he said.

"Is that it?" Leaphorn asked. "Yes, it must be. He looks something like you."

"A year older," Father Tso said. "We weren't raised together." He glanced up at Leaphorn. "He's in the Buffalo Society. My returning didn't help his plans."

"But what made you . . . how did you get here?" Leaphorn asked. "I mean, to your grandfather's hogan?"

"It was a long trip. I flew back from Rome, and then to Phoenix. And then I took a bus to Flagstaff and then to Kayenta, and then I caught a ride."

"And where's the Adams girl?"

"He came to the hogan and got us," Tso said. "My brother and that dog he has." Father Tso stopped. "That dog. He's around here and he'll find us. Are there other police with you? Have you arrested them?"

"The dog's dead. Just tell me what happened," Leaphorn said.

"My brother came to the hogan and brought us to this cave," Father Tso said. "He said we'd have to stay until some sort of operation was over. Then later . . ." He shrugged and looked apologetic. "I don't know much later. It's hard to keep track of time in here and I can't see my wrist watch. Anyway, later, my brother and a man called Tull and three other men brought a bunch of Boy Scouts and put them in with us. I don't understand it. What do you know about it?"

"Just what I heard on the radio," Leaphorn said. He knelt behind Tso and examined the bindings on his wrists. "Keep talking," Leaphorn said. "And keep it at a whisper." He fished out his pocket knife and sawed through the strips, a type of disposable handcuff developed for use by police in making mass arrests. The BIA police had bought some during the early stages of the American Indian Movement troubles, but they'd been junked because if the subject struggled, they tightened and cut off circulation. Tso's hands were ice cold and bloodless. It would be a while before he could use them.

"I just know what I heard too," Father Tso was saying. "And what the Scout leader told us. I guess we're involved in some sort of symbolic kidnapping."

Leaphorn had the strips cut from Tso's ankles now. Tso tried to massage them, but his numb hands dangled almost uselessly from his wrists.

"It takes a while for the circulation to come back," Leaphorn said. "When it does, it hurts. Can you tell me more?"

Tso began rubbing his hands briskly against his chest. "Every couple of hours or so Tull or my brother comes back and they have two questions they ask the Scout leader or one of the boys. It's to prove everyone is still alive or something. It seems they told the police they have to stay completely out of this part of the reservation. I think the deal is if they see any police they say they'll kill the hostages. Otherwise the police get to broadcast questions every couple of hours, and he—"

"Questions? What sort of questions?"

"Oh, one was where did the Scout leader meet his wife. And one was why he was late for a trip, and where was the telephone in his home. Trivial stuff that no one else could know." Father Tso grimaced suddenly and inspected his hands. "I see what you mean about hurting."

"Keep rubbing them. And keep talking. Do you know the timetable?" Leaphorn asked. "Did you hear anything about that?"

"They told the Scouts they'd probably be here about two or three days. Maybe less. Until they get the ransom."

"Do you know how many are involved? I've seen three in the cave. Are there more than that?"

"I've seen at least five," Father Tso said. "When my brother brought us back, first there was just a young man here they call Jackie. Just my brother and Jackie. Then when they brought the Boy Scouts there were three more of them. One with an awfully disfigured face, called Tull. He's still here, I think. But I haven't seen the other two again."

"This Jackie. How was he dressed?" Leaphorn asked.

"Jeans," Father Tso said. "Denim shirt. Red sweatband around his forehead."

"Yes, I've seen him," Leaphorn said. "Where are the other hostages? And how'd you get away?"

"They've got a sort of cage welded together out of reinforcing rods or something," Tso said. "Set back in a part of the cave way back there. That's where they put Theodora and me at first, and then they brought the Boy Scouts in. Then a couple of hours ago they took me out and moved me into another part of the cave." Tso pointed behind him. "A sort of big room back in that direction, and they put these things on my wrists and ankles and they sort of anchored me to a stalagmite." Tso laughed. "Tied a rope around it."

"How'd you get loose?"

"Well, they warned me that if I moved around too much with these nylon things on they'd tighten up and cut off my circulation, but I found that if you didn't mind a little of that, you could work the strip around so that the knot was where you could get at it."

Leaphorn remembered trying on the nylon cuffs when the department was considering them, and how quickly pulling against them caused them to cut into your wrists. He glanced at Tso, remeasuring him.

"The people who invented those things counted on people not wanting to hurt themselves," Leaphorn said.

"I guess so," Father Tso said. He was massaging his ankles now. "Anyway, these calcite deposits are too soft to cut anything. I thought maybe I could find some sort of outcropping—granite or something—where I could cut the nylon off."

"Is the feeling coming back?" Leaphorn asked. "Good. I don't think we want to waste any time if we can help it. I don't have a gun." He helped Tso to his feet and supported him. "When they come to the cage to get the questions answered, who comes? Just one of them?"

"The last time it was just the one with the red headband. The one they called Jackie."

"You okay now? Ready to move?"

Father Tso took a step, and then a smaller one, and sucked in his breath sharply. "Just give me a second to get used to it."

The breath hissed through gritted teeth. "What are we going to do?" he whispered.

"We're going to be there when they come back to the cage. If you can find a place for me to hide. If two come, we won't try anything right now. But if just one of them comes, then you step out and confront him. Make as much noise as you can to cover me coming, and I'll jump him."

"As I remember it, there's not much to hide behind," Tso said doubtfully. "Not close anyway."

They moved slowly through the dark, the priest limping gingerly, Leaphorn supporting part of his weight.

"There's one other thing," Tso said. "I don't think this Tull is sane. He thinks he dies and comes back alive again."

"I've heard about Tull," Leaphorn said.

"And my brother," Tso said. "I guess you'd have to say he's sort of crazy too."

Leaphorn said nothing. They moved silently toward the light, feeling their way. From ahead, suddenly, there came the sound of a woman's voice—distant, and as yet undecipherable.

"This is terrible for Theodora," Father Tso said. "Terrible."

"Yes," Leaphorn said. He was remembering Captain Largo's instructions. He flicked the flash on—getting direction—and quickly off.

"My brother," Tso said. "He stayed with my father, and my father was a drunk." Tso's whisper was barely audible. "I didn't ever live with them. All I know is what I've heard, but I heard it was bad. My father died of a beating in Gallup." The whisper stopped and Leaphorn began thinking of other things, of what his tactics would have to be.

"My brother was about fourteen when it happened," Father Tso said. "I heard my brother was there when they beat him, and that it was the police that did it."

"Maybe," Leaphorn said. "There're some bad cops." He flicked the light on again, and off.

"That's not what I'm talking about," Father Tso said. "I'm telling you because I don't think there'll be any hostages released." He paused. "They've gone too far for that," the voice whispered. "They're not sane. None of them. Poor Theodora."

They could hear the voice of Theodora Adams again, a matter more of tones echoing than of words. Leaphorn was suddenly aware that he was exhausted. His hip throbbed steadily now, his burn stung, his cut hand hurt. He felt sick and frightened and humiliated. And all this merged into anger.

"God damn it," he said. "You say you're a priest? What were you doing with a woman anyway?"

Tso limped along silently. Leaphorn instantly regretted the question.

"There are good priests and bad ones," Tso said. "You get into it because you tell yourself somebody needs help. . . ."

"Look," Leaphorn said. "It's none of my business. I'm sorry. I shouldn't have—"

"No," Father Tso said. "That's fair enough. First you kid yourself somebody needs you—which is easy to kid yourself about, because that's why you thought you had the vocation to start with. That's what the fathers tell you at St. Anthony's Mission, you know: Somebody needs you. And then it's all reversed: a woman comes along who needs help. And then she's an antidote for loneliness. And then she's most of everything you're giving up. And what if you're wrong? What if there's no God? If there's not, you're letting your life tick away for nothing. It gets complicated. So you get your faith back. . . ." He stopped, glanced at Leaphorn in the brief glow of the flash. "You do get it if you want it, you know. And so you try to get out of it. You run away." Father Tso stopped. Then he began again. "But by then, she really does need you. So what are you running away from?" Even whispered, the question was angry.

"So that's why you came—trying to get away from her?" Leaphorn asked.

"I don't know," Father Tso said. "The old man asked me to come. But mostly I was running, I guess."

"And you got tangled with your brother?"

"We're the Hero Twins." Father Tso made a sound a little like laughing. "Maybe we're both saving the People from the Monsters. Different approaches, but about equal success."

Now the voice of Theodora Adams was close enough so that they could understand an occasional word. The cavern narrowed again, and Leaphorn stood against the wall, one hand holding the priest's elbow, and stared toward reflected light. The light was harsh and its source was low—probably a lantern of some sort placed on the calcite floor. Here a hodgepodge of stalagmites rose in crooked lines from the level floor and curtains of stalactites hung down toward them. The light cast them in relief—black against the dim yellow.

"The cage is just back around that corner," Tso whispered. "That light's from a butane lamp sitting outside."

"Does the guard have to come past this way?"

"I don't know," Tso said. "It's confusing in here."

"Let's get closer, then," Leaphorn said softly. "But keep it absolutely quiet. He might be there already."

They edged through the darkness, keeping in the cover of a wall of stalagmites. Leaphorn could see part of the cage now, and the butane lantern, and the head and shoulders of Theodora Adams sitting in its corner. Close enough, he thought. Somewhere near here he would stage his ambush.

"I wonder why they took me out of there," Father Tso whispered.

Leaphorn didn't answer. He was thinking that maybe with Father Tso subtracted, the cage held the symbolic number—eleven children and three adults. Father Tso would have spoiled the symmetry of revenge. But there must be more reason than that.

In the darkness, time seemed to take on another dimension. After three exhausting days and nights virtually without sleep, Leaphorn was finding it took much of his concentration simply to stay awake. He shifted, moving his weight from his left side to his right. In this new position, he could see most of Theodora Adams. The lantern light gave her face a sculptured effect and left her eye sockets dark. He could see two other hostages of the Buffalo Society. A man who must be one of the Scout leaders lay on his side, his head cushioned on his folded coat, apparently asleep. He was a small man, perhaps forty-five years old, with dark hair and a delicate doll-like face. There was a dark smudge on his forehead, rubbed into a brown streak across his cheek. Dried blood from a head cut, Leaphorn guessed. The man's hands lay relaxed and limp against the floor. The other person was a boy, perhaps thirteen, who slept fitfully. Theodora Adams spoke to someone out of Leaphorn's vision.

"Is he feeling any better?"

And a precise, boyish voice said, "I think he's almost asleep."

After that, no one said anything. Leaphorn longed for a conversation to overhear. For anything to help him fight off the dizzying assault of sleep. He forced his mind to consider the furious activity this kidnapping must be creating. The rescue of this many children would have total, absolute priority. Every man, every resource, would be made available for finding them. The reservation would be aswarm with FBI agents, and every variety of state, federal, military, and Indian cop. Leaphorn caught himself slipping into a dream of the bedlam that must be going on now at Window Rock, and shook his head furiously. He *couldn't* allow himself to sleep. He forced his mind to retrace what must have been the sequence of this affair. Why this cave was so important was clear to him now. On the surface of the earth, there was no way an operation like this could remain undetected. But this cave was not only a hiding hole under the earth; it was one whose existence was hidden behind a century of time and the promises made to a holy man's ghost. Old Man Tso must have learned that the sacred cave was being used—and desecrated—when he came to take care of the medicine bundles left by Standing Medicine. That seemed now to be what was implied in the story Tso had told Listening Woman. And the Buffalo Society either knew he had found them, or had learned he used the cave. And that meant he could not be left alive. A dream of the murder of Hosteen Tso began merging with reality in Leaphorn's mind. He ground his chin deliberately against the stone, driving away sleep with pain.

And the police would never find this cave. They would ask the People. The People would know nothing. The cave would have been entered only by water—on which no tracks can be followed. From outside, the cave mouth would seem only one of a hundred thousand dark cliff overhangs into which the water lapped. They would ask Old Man McGinnis, who usually knew everything, and McGinnis would know nothing. Leaphorn fought back sleep by diverting his thoughts into another channel. The same "fade-away" tactics employed in the Santa Fe robbery were probably being used here. Those who seized and delivered the hostages would have run for cover. They would have gone safely away long before the crime was discovered. Only enough men would have been left here to handle the hostages and collect the ransom. Probably only three men. But how would *they* get away? Everyone had escaped, except three. Tull and Jackie and Goldrims. They would have set up a way to relay and rebroadcast the radio message that kept the police away. Easy enough to rig, Leaphorn guessed. It wouldn't take much—if the transmissions were kept brief—to confuse radio directional finders. But how did the Society plan to extricate the final three when the ransom arrived? How could they be given time to escape? No one except the hostages would have seen them. If the hostages were killed, there would be no witnesses. Still, Goldrims would need running time—an hour or two to get far enough away from here to become just another Navajo. How could he provide himself with that time? Leaphorn thought of the dynamite, and the timing device, and of John Tull, who believed himself to be immortal.

Leaphorn caught himself dozing again and shook his head angrily. If he hoped to leave this cave alive, he must stay awake until Goldrims, or Tull, or Jackie came alone to check on the hostages, or ask the ritual questions of one of the Scouts. He must be awake and alert for an opportunity at ambush, at overpowering the guard, at getting a gun and changing the odds. To accomplish this he had to stay awake. To go to sleep would be to wake up dead. Thinking that, Lieutenant Joe Leaphorn fell asleep.

Leaphorn's dream had nothing at all to do with the cave, or kidnapping, or Goldrims, or Hosteen Tso. It was involved with winter and with punishment, and was motivated by the cold of the stone beneath his side and the pain in his hip. Despite his exhaustion, this discomfort kept dragging him back toward consciousness, and finally to a voice which was saying:

"All right. Wake him up."

For a moment the words were nothing but an incomprehensible part of a chaotic dream. And then Leaphorn was awake.

"Let's not waste any time," the voice was saying, and it was the voice of Goldrims. "I need the one named Symons." A panicky second passed before Leaphorn realized that Goldrims was standing by the cage door and the words were not directed at him.

"You're Symons?" Goldrims asked. The voice was loud and the words echoed through the cavern. "Wake up. I need to know your birth date and what your wife gave you for your last birthday."

Leaphorn could hear Symons's voice, but not his answer.

"May third and what? May third and a sweater. Okay."

"Are you going to let us go?" It was Theodora Adams's voice, but she had moved out of the corner now and out of Leaphorn's vision.

"Sure," Goldrims said. "When we get what we're asking, you're free as a bird." The voice sounded amused.

"What have you done with Ben?" she asked.

Goldrims said nothing. Leaphorn could see his back and his right profile, silhouetted against the reflected lantern light. Far behind him, at the edge of the darkness, John Tull stood. The lantern light glistened on the shotgun Tull held casually by his side. The shadow converted his ruined face into a gargoyle shape. But Leaphorn could see Tull was grinning. He could also see there was no chance for an ambush.

"What have I done with Ben?" Goldrims asked. He moved abruptly to the cage's gate, and there was the click of the padlock opening. Goldrims disappeared inside. "What have I done with Ben?" he asked again. The voice was fierce now and there was the sudden violent sound of a blow struck. Near him in the darkness, Leaphorn heard a sharp intake of breath from where Father Tso was standing, and there was a muffled scream from the Adams woman.

"You bitch," Goldrims was saying. "You tell me what Whitey has done to Ben. It got him crawling on his belly to a white man's church, giving himself up to the white man's God, and then a white bitch comes along . . ." Goldrims's voice broke, and halted. And when it began again its words were paced, tense, controlled. "I know how it works," Goldrims said. "When I heard that this thing that claims to be my brother had become a priest, I got a book and read about it. They made him lay on his face, and promise to stay away from women. And then the first slut that comes after him, he breaks his promise."

Goldrims's voice halted. He reappeared in Leaphorn's view, opening the gate. Leaphorn could hear Theodora Adams crying, and a whimpering sound from one of the Boy Scouts. Tull was no longer grinning. His grotesque face was somber and watchful. Goldrims closed the gate behind him.

"Slut," he said. "You're the kind of woman who eats men."

And with that, Goldrims clicked the padlock shut and walked angrily across the cave floor, with Tull two steps behind him. The lantern Goldrims carried illuminated them only from the waist down—four legs scissoring, out of step and out of cadence. Leaphorn told Father Tso where to wait for a second chance at an ambush two hours later. And then he followed the now distant legs through the darkness. It was like tracking a strange uncoordinated beast through the night.

"NO, NO," GOLDRIMS WAS SAYING. "Look. It goes in like this."

They were squatted beside the radio transceiver, Tull and Goldrims, with the one they called Jackie sprawled on the bedroll, motionless.

"Like this?" Tull asked. He was doing something with the transmitter—changing the crystal or making some sort of antenna adjustment, Leaphorn guessed. From where he stood behind the stalagmites that formed the nearest cover, the acoustics of the cave carried the voices clearly through the stillness, but Leaphorn was too far away to hear everything. Tull said something else, unintelligible.

"All right, then," Goldrims said. "Run through it again." There was a pause. "Right," Goldrims said. "That's right. Put the speaker of the tape recorder about three inches from the mike. About like that."

"I've got it," Tull said. "No sweat. And right at 4 A.M. Right?"

"That's right—4 A.M. for the next one. If I'm not back by then. Just a second and we'll get this one broadcast." He studied his watch, apparently waiting for the proper second. Then he took the microphone, flicked a series of switches. "Whitey," he said. "Whitey, this is Buffalo Society. We have your answers and instructions."

The radio said: "Go ahead, Buffalo, ready to record."

"Your answers are May the third and a sweater," Goldrims

said. "And now we're ready to wrap this up. Here are your orders." Goldrims leaned toward the microphone and Leaphorn could hear only part of the instructions. There were references to map coordinates, a line drawn between them, one man in a helicopter, references to times, a flashed signal from the ground. Obviously instructions for the ransom drop, and like everything else about this operation, it seemed meticulously planned. No way to set a trap if the drop site wasn't known until the copter reached it. In all, the instructions took only a minute. And then the radio was off, and Goldrims was standing, facing directly toward Leaphorn, talking to Tull, going over it again. They walked away together, away from the pool of lantern light toward the water, still talking. Then the purring sound of a heavily muffled engine started. Not a generator, as he had thought, but almost certainly a muffled boat engine. The sound moved and faded toward the dim light of the cave mouth.

Leaphorn waited long enough to make absolutely sure that the man returning with the bobbing flashlight was John Tull. Then he moved quietly away from the stalagmites, back into the darkness. It would be at least an hour, he guessed, before the next questions were radioed in and the next answers extracted to prove the hostages still alive. Leaphorn intended to use that hour well. He had not seen the boat. He planned to make sure there was nothing else hidden in this darkness that he didn't know about.

The dynamite was gone. Leaphorn flicked the flashlight beam quickly across the cartons of supplies to make sure he hadn't simply forgotten where the wooden case had been. Even as he did, logic told him the dynamite, and the small boxes containing the timer and the electrical wire, would be missing. He had expected it. It fit into the pattern Leaphorn's mind was trying to make of this affair—of the relationship between Tull and Goldrims and between what seemed to be too many coincidences, and too many unanswered questions. He snapped off the flashlight and stood in the darkness, concentrating on arranging what he knew of Goldrims and the Buffalo Society, and of what was happening here, into some order. He tried to project, and understand, Goldrims's intentions. The man was extremely smart. And he was Navajo. He could easily vanish in the immense empty canyon country around Short Mountain, no matter how many people were hunting him. If he had another well-stocked hideaway like this, he could stay holed up for months. But finally he would run out of time. He would be the country's most wanted man. There seemed to be no real possibility of escape for Goldrims. That seemed out of character. A fatal loose end. Goldrims would leave no loose ends, Leaphorn thought. There must be something Leaphorn was overlooking.

The dynamite and the timer must have something to do with it. But Leaphorn couldn't see how blowing up the cave would solve Goldrims's problem. He glanced at his watch. In about forty-five minutes, the next set of questions would be broadcast and brought to the Boy Scouts for the time-buying answers. When that time came, Leaphorn had to be in position to jump whoever came with the tape recorder. In the meantime, he had to find the dynamite.

Leaphorn did find some of the dynamite. But first he discovered what had to be Hosteen Tso's tracks, undisturbed in the quiet dust for months. They were moccasin prints scuffed across the white floor. Mixed with them were boot tracks which Leaphorn had long since identified as Goldrims's. They led into what seemed to be a dead-end cavern. But the cavern turned, and dropped, and widened into a room with a ceiling which soared upward into a ragged hanging curtain of stalactites. Leaphorn examined it quickly with his flashlight. In several places the calcite surface was piled deep with ashes of old fires. Leaphorn took two steps toward the old hearths and stopped abruptly. The floor here was patterned with sand paintings. At least thirty of them, each a geometric pattern of the colors and shapes of the Holy People of the Navajos. Leaphorn studied them—recognizing Corn Beetle, the Sacred Fly, Talking God, and Black God, Coyote, and others. He could read some of the stories told in these pictures-formed-of-colored-sand. One of them he recognized as part of the Sun Father Chant, and another seemed to be a piece of the Mountain Way. Leaphorn came from a family rich in ceremonial people. Two of his uncles were singers, and a grandfather; a nephew was learning a curing ritual, and his maternal grandmother had been a Hand-Trembler famous in the Toadlena-Beautiful Mountain country. But some of these dry paintings were totally unfamiliar to him. These must be the great heritage Standing Medicine had left for the People—the Way to start the world again.

Leaphorn stood staring at them, and then past them at the black metal case that sat on the cave floor beyond them. His flashlight beam glittered from the glass face of dials and from shiny metal knobs. Leaphorn squatted beside it. A trademark on its side read HALLICRAFTERS. It was another radio transmitter. Wires ran from it, disappearing into the darkness. Connecting to an antenna, Leaphorn guessed. Taped securely to its top was a battery-powered tape recorder, and wired to both tape recorder and radio was an enameled metal box. Leaphorn was conscious now of a new sound, a sort of electric whirring which came from the box—another timer. The dial on its top showed its pointer had moved past seven of the fifty markings on its face. There was no way of telling whether each mark represented a minute or an hour. It was obviously adjustable. Behind the radio a paper sack sat on the floor—also linked to terminals on the timer box. Leaphorn opened the sack gingerly. In it were two dynamite sticks, held together around a blasting cap with black friction tape. Leaphorn rocked back on his heels, frowning. Why dynamite a radio? He studied the timer again. It seemed to be custom-made. Sequential, he guessed. First it would turn on the radio, and then the tape recorder, and when the recording was broadcast, it would detonate the dynamite.

Leaphorn extracted his pocket knife and carefully removed the screws that attached the dynamite wires to the timer. Then he cut the tape recorder free, sat on the floor, and pushed the play button.

"You were warned. But our people—"

The words boomed out into the cave. Leaphorn stabbed the off button down. The voice was that of Goldrims. But he couldn't risk playing it now. Sound carried too well in this cavern. He shoved the recorder under his shirt. He would play the tape later.

As it happened, Leaphorn had cut it close. He found Father Benjamin Tso waiting where he had left him, hidden among a cluster of stalagmites close to the cage door. He told the priest what he had learned, of Goldrims's leaving to pick up the ransom, and of the radio and the time bomb in the cave room where Father Tso had been left.

"I saw the radio," Father Tso said. "I didn't know what was in the sack." He paused. "But why would he want to blow me up?" The voice was incredulous. Leaphorn didn't attempt an answer. Far back in the darkness a tiny dot of light had appeared, bobbing with the walk of whoever carried it. Leaphorn prayed it was Jackie, and only Jackie. He motioned Father Tso back out of sight and climbed quickly onto a calcite shelf, from which he could watch and launch his ambush. He was still trying to control his breathing when the yellow light of a battery lantern joined the glow of the butane light at the cage.

"Time to talk again." The voice was Jackie's. "Got questions for two of these boys." He hooked his lantern on his belt, shifted the shotgun he was carrying to his left hand and fished a piece of paper from his shirt pocket.

Leaphorn moved swiftly. He had the walkie-talkie out of its case, holding it like a club as he came around the wall of stalagmites. Then he hesitated. Once he jumped down to the lower calcite floor, there was no cover. For thirty yards he would be in the open and clearly visible. It was much too far. Jackie would have him. He could spin around and shoot Leaphorn dead.

But Father Tso was there, walking toward Jackie.

"Hey," Jackie said. He swung the shotgun toward Tso. "Hey, how'd you get loose?"

"Put down the gun!" Father Tso shouted it, and the cavern echo-boomed: *"Gun . . . gun . . . gun . . . gun."* He walked toward Jackie. "Put it down."

"Hold it," Jackie said. "Hold it or I'll kill you." He took a step backward. "Come on," he shouted. "Jesus, you're as crazy as Tull."

"I'm as immortal as Tull," Father Tso shouted. He walked toward Jackie, hands outstretched, reaching for the shotgun.

Leaphorn was running now—knowing what would happen, knowing how Father Tso planned it to happen, knowing it was the only way it could work.

"God forgive—" Father Tso was shouting and that was all Leaphorn heard. Jackie fired from a crouch. The gunshot boomed like a bomb, surrounding Leaphorn with a blast of sound.

The impact knocked Father Tso backward. He fell on his side. Only after Father Tso lay still did Jackie hear through the booming echoes the sound of Leaphorn running, and spin with his catlike quickness so that the walkie-talkie struck not the back of his head, where Leaphorn had aimed it, but across his temple. Jackie seemed to die instantly, the shotgun spinning from his hand as he fell. Father Tso lived perhaps a minute. Leaphorn picked up the shotgun—it was a Remington automatic—and knelt beside Tso. Whatever the priest was saying, Leaphorn couldn't understand it. He put his ear close to Father Tso's face, but now the priest was saying nothing at all. Leaphorn could hear only the echoes of the gunshots dying away and over that the sound of Theodora Adams screaming.

There was no time to plan anything. Leaphorn moved as quickly as he could. He felt rapidly through Jackie's pockets, finding the padlock key but no additional ammunition for the shotgun. He glanced at the cage. A quick impression of a dozen frightened faces staring at him—and of Theodora Adams, sobbing in the corner.

"The other one's going to be coming and I'm going to take him," Leaphorn said. "Get everybody to sit back down. Don't give him any hint I'm out here." And with that, Leaphorn ran back into the darkness.

He stopped behind the stalagmites and stared in the direction from which Tull would come. Nothing but blackness. But Tull would surely come. The sound of the shot would have reached him at the cave entrance. And he would have heard the Adams woman screaming. If he came at a run, he should be arriving now. Leaphorn held the shotgun ready, looking down its barrel into the darkness. He swung it toward the glow of light, noticing with satisfaction that the bead sight was lined exactly in the V of the rear sight. He could hear Theodora Adams's sobbing—less hysterical now and more the sound of simple sorrow. For the first time, Leaphorn became conscious of the smell of burned gunpowder. As soon as Tull came well between him and the light—as soon as he could line up the sights on his silhouette—he would shoot for the center of the body. There'd be no warning shout. In this darkness, Tull was far too dangerous for that. Leaphorn would simply try to kill him. Time ticked silently away.

But where was Tull? Leaphorn was belatedly conscious that he had underestimated the man. Tull had not jumped to the obvious conclusion that Jackie had shot someone and come running to see about it. If Tull was coming at all, he was coming quietly, with his light turned off, stalking the lighted place to learn what had happened. Leaphorn lowered himself slightly behind the stony barrier, aware that Tull might be somewhere behind him—looking for Leaphorn's shape against the glow exactly as Leaphorn had looked for Tull's. But even as he crouched, even as he registered this increased respect for John Tull as an adversary, Leaphorn felt a fierce exultant certainty of the outcome. No matter how cautious Tull was, the odds had shifted now. Tull would see Jackie and Father Tso on the cave floor and the surviving hostages in the cage. That would account for everyone. He would have to come into the light to get the answers. And he would want to find out what had happened, how Jackie and Tso had died. With his weapon ready, with everyone accounted for, there'd be no reason for him to hold back.

"Hey." Tull's voice came from Leaphorn's right—well out of the periphery of the lantern light. "What happened?" The voice echoed, and died away, and silence resumed.

"They fought." It was the voice of the scout leader named Symons. "The priest attacked your man and I think they killed each other."

A good answer, Leaphorn thought. Smart.

"Where's Jackie's gun?" Tull shouted. "Where's the shotgun?"

"I don't know," Symons said. "I don't see it."

A bright light blinked on suddenly, its beam emerging from behind a screen of stalagmites far beyond the cage. It played over the bodies, searching.

Leaphorn felt a sick disappointment. Tull was even smarter than he'd guessed.

"You son-of-a-bitch," Tull shouted. "You've got the shotgun in there. Throw it out. If you don't, I'm going to start shooting people."

The light had blinked quickly off, but Leaphorn had him located now. A hint of reflected light, perhaps one hundred yards away. Leaphorn tried to line his sights on it, then lowered the gun. The odds of an effective hit at this range were terrible.

"We don't have the gun," Symons shouted.

In the dim light, Leaphorn could see Tull had already—without a word—raised his pistol.

It was still a high-odds shot, but there was no choice now. Leaphorn steadied the gun, trying to keep the dim form visible over the bead. He squeezed the trigger.

The muzzle flash was blinding. Leaphorn wanted desperately to know if he had hit Tull, but he could see only the whiteness burned on his retina and hear nothing but the reverberating thunder of the gunshot booming down the corridors of the cavern. Then there was the sound of another shot. Tull's pistol. Leaphorn crouched behind the stone barrier, waiting for sight and hearing to return. He became aware that the butane lantern was out. The darkness here now was total. Tull must have shot out the light. A quick-thinking man. Leaphorn stared into the darkness. What would Tull do? The gunman would know now that another person had somehow gotten into the cave. He might guess that the person was the Navajo policeman. He'd know the policeman had Jackie's shotgun and . . . how many rounds of ammunition? Leaphorn opened the magazine, poured three shells out into his hand, and carefully reloaded them. A round in the chamber and three in the magazine. Knowing this, what would Tull do? Not, Leaphorn thought, stand and fight in this blackness with a pistol against a shotgun. The darkness minimized the effect of the pistol's range and magnified the effect of the shotgun's scattered pattern. Tull would head for the entrance, for the light and the radio. He would call Goldrims for help. And would Goldrims come? Leaphorn thought about it. Goldrims had probably intended to radio to the copter as it passed and order it to land, order the pilot out, and then, if he could fly a copter, fly a few miles, abandon the aircraft, and begin a well-planned escape maneuver. If he couldn't fly a copter, he'd disable it and its radio, fix the pilot so he couldn't follow, and run. Why return to the cave? Leaphorn could think of no reason. Would he come back to help Tull in the cave? Leaphorn doubted it. Tull had been expendable at the Santa Fe robbery. Why wouldn't he be expendable now? The contest in this cave would be between John Tull and Joe Leaphorn. Leaphorn felt along the top of the rocky ledge for a flat place, put his flashlight on it, aimed it at the place where Tull had been, and flicked it on. He ducked three long steps to his right and then looked over the top. The flashlight beam shone through a blue haze of gunpowder smoke into a gray-white emptiness. Where Tull had been, there was nothing now. Leaphorn slipped back to the flashlight, flicked it off, aimed it at the place the hostages had been kept, and snapped it on again. The beam fell directly on the body of Father Benjamin Tso and illuminated Theodora Adams, kneeling inside the cage. She covered her eyes against the glare. Leaphorn turned off the flash, and felt his way through the blackness to the cage. He unlocked the padlock with the key he had taken from Jackie's pocket.

"Get the lantern off Jackie's body," he said. "Get everybody away from this place. Find a place to hide until I call for you." He didn't wait to answer any questions.

The speed with which Leaphorn followed John Tull toward the cave's mouth was reduced by a healthy respect for Tull. He skirted far to the left of the direct route, carrying the shotgun at ready. When he finally reached the area where light from the entrance turned the blackness into mere dimness, he found droplets of blood on the gray-white calcite floor. At another point, a smear of reddish brown discolored a limestone outcrop. Leaphorn guessed it was where Tull had put a bloody hand against the stone. Leaphorn hadn't missed. The shotgun blast had hit Tull, and hit him hard.

Leaphorn paused and digested this. In a sense, time was now on his side. A shotgun would make a multiple wound, hard to stop bleeding—and Tull seemed to be bleeding freely. As time passed, he would weaken. But was the crucial measurement of time here being made by Tull's pumping heart or by a clockwork mechanism attached to about twenty sticks of dynamite still unaccounted for? Leaphorn decided he couldn't wait. Somewhere in the darkness around him, Leaphorn was sure that missing timer—and perhaps other timers he had never seen—was counting away the seconds.

He found Tull where he thought he would find him—at the radio. The man had moved the butane lantern some fifty feet back into the cave from the place where Leaphorn had first seen him and Goldrims, and he'd turned on a battery lantern and adjusted its beam toward part of the cavern. The range of light thus extended substantially beyond the effective range of the shotgun. Leaphorn circled, trying to find an approach that offered some close-in cover. There wasn't one. The floor here was as dead level as a ballroom. From it ragged rows of stalagmites rose like a patchwork of volcanic islands from the surface of a still, white sea. Tull had moved the radio behind one such island and the lantern was beside it—giving Tull the advantage of deep shadow. From there, he could have a clear shot at anyone trying to get out of the cave mouth via the water. The lake protected one flank and the cave wall another. Approaching him meant walking into the lantern light and into the barrel of his pistol.

Leaphorn glanced at his watch, and considered. His hip now throbbed with a steady pain.

"Hey, Tull," he shouted. "Let's talk."

Perhaps five seconds passed.

"Fine," Tull said. "Talk."

"He's not coming back, you know," Leaphorn said. "He'll take the money and run. You get stuck."

"No," Tull said. "But I tell you what. You throw that shotgun out there where I can see it, and we'll just make you one more hostage. When we cut out of here, you're a free man. Otherwise, when my friend gets back, he's going to be behind you, and I'm going to move in from the front, and we're going to kill you."

And that was about the way it would work, if Goldrims did come back, Leaphorn thought. He would be fairly easy to handle by two men—even with the shotgun. But he didn't think Goldrims would be coming back.

"Let's quit kidding each other," Leaphorn said. "Your

friend is taking the ransom and running. And you're supposed to wait around for some more broadcasts, and then you'll run. And when you run, you're blowing this place up."

Tull said nothing.

"How bad did I hit you?"

"You missed," Tull said.

"You're lying. I hit you and you've been losing blood. And that's another reason you're not going to get out of here unless we make a deal. I can keep you in here, and you can keep me in here. It's a Mexican standoff, and we can't afford a standoff because your boss has a bomb set to go." Leaphorn paused, thinking about where he had found the bomb and the circumstances. "He didn't tell you about the bomb, did he?"

"Screw you," Tull said.

No, Leaphorn thought, he didn't tell you about the radio setup and the bomb in the room with the sacred paintings. Tull's tracks hadn't shown up there, and six sticks of dynamite had been missing when Leaphorn had first found the cache. Probably that bomb had been set up separately. This was a Buffalo Society operation, but part of it, Leaphorn was increasingly certain, might be a very private affair of Goldrims himself.

"I'm going to play a tape recording for you," Leaphorn said. He took the recorder from under his shirt and adjusted it. "Haven't heard it myself yet, so we can listen to it together. It was fastened to a Hallicrafters radio transceiver way back in a side room. There was this radio, with a timer set to turn it on to broadcasting, and let it warm up and then turn on this tape recorder. And after the tape ran, the timer was set to detonate some dynamite in a sack there. You ready for it?"

There was silence. Seconds ticked away.

"Okay," Tull said. "Let's hear it. If it exists."

Leaphorn pushed the on button. Goldrims's voice boomed out again.

". . . have seen policemen in the territory you agreed would be kept clear of police. You have broken your promise. The Buffalo Society never breaks a promise. Remember this in the future. Remember and learn. We promised that if police came into this corner of the Navajo Nation, the hostages would die.

They will now die, and we warriors of the Buffalo Society will die with them. You will find our bodies in our sacred cavern, the mouth of which opens into the San Juan River arm of Lake Powell less than a mile below the present lake-level mouth of the river, approximately twenty-three miles east by northeast of Short Mountain, and exactly at north latitude 36, 11, 17, and west longitude 110, 29, 3. To those of the Buffalo Society who seized these white hostages, know that we three warriors kept our honor and our promise. To the white man, come to this cave and recover the bodies of three of your adults and eleven of your young. They died to avenge the deaths of three of our adults and eleven children in the Olds Prairie Murders. With them will be bodies of three warriors of the Buffalo Society: Jackie Noni of the Potawatomi Nation, and John Tull, of the Seminole, and myself, whom the white men call Hoski, or James Tso, a warrior of the Navajo Nation. May our memories live in the glory of the Buffalo Society."

The clear, resonant voice of Goldrims stopped and there was only the faint hiss of the blank tape winding into the take-up reel.

Leaphorn pushed the off button and rewound the tape. He felt numb. His logic had told him that Goldrims might kill the hostages to eliminate witnesses, but now he realized that he hadn't really believed it. The impact of hearing Goldrims's pleasant, unemotional voice declare this mass murder/mass suicide was stunning. And in that split second, he also became aware that the name of Father Benjamin Tso was missing from the catalog of the dead. He confronted the implications of that gap in the roster. It meant that Goldrims had planned even better than Leaphorn had guessed.

"You want to hear it again?" Leaphorn shouted. "From the beginning this time."

Tull said nothing. Leaphorn pushed the on button. "You were warned," the tape began. "But our people have seen policemen in the territory . . ." When the recorder reached the list of bodies, Leaphorn stopped it. "I want you to notice," he shouted to Tull, "there's a name missing from this list. Notice it's the name of your buddy's brother. I want you to think about that."

Leaphorn thought of it himself. Bits of the puzzle fell into place. He knew now who had written the letter summoning Father Benjamin Tso to his grandfather's hogan. Goldrims had written it himself. He felt a chill admiration for the mind that had conceived such a plan. Hoski had realized he could not escape from the manhunt. It would be massive and inexorable. So he had devised a way to abort it. What the dynamite left of his brother, as Hoski had arranged it, would be found with the shattered radio and identified as Hoski's body. Everyone would thus be accounted for. There would be no one left to hunt. As he realized this, Leaphorn also realized that his own problem had been multiplied. Goldrims would have to respond to Tull's radioed call for help. He couldn't risk having Leaphorn, or anyone who had seen Father Tso, escape from the cave. Hoski would have to come back.

Leaphorn pushed the play button again, ran the tape, pushed stop, pushed rewind. He was awed by it. Perfect. Flawless. Impeccable. It left nothing to chance. The big score for James Tso would not just be the ransom. The big score would be a new life, free from surveillance, free from hiding. There would be no reason to question the identity of the body. Hoski had never been arrested or fingerprinted. And no one knew the priest was here. No one, that is, who would remain alive. And there was a family resemblance.

"Hey, Tull," Leaphorn yelled. "Have you counted the bodies? There's Jackie, and all those Boy Scouts, and the woman, and one of the Tso brothers, and you. You're there on the list of dead, Tull. But your friend Hoski is going to be alive and well. And wealthy, too."

Tull said nothing.

"Goddamn it, Tull," Leaphorn shouted. "Think! He's screwing you. He's screwing the Buffalo Society. Kelongy won't see a dollar of that ransom. Hoski's going to disappear with it."

Leaphorn listened and heard nothing but the echoes of his own voice dying in the cave. He hoped Tull was thinking. Hoski would disappear. And someday a man with another name and another identity would appear in Washington, and contact a woman named Rosemary Rita Oliveras. And somewhere, wherever he was hiding, a madman named Kelongy would wonder what went wrong with his crazy scheme and perhaps he would mourn his brilliant lieutenant. But there was no time to think of that now. Leaphorn glanced at his wrist watch. It was 2:47 A.M. In an hour and thirteen minutes it would be time to broadcast the answers that would keep the law at bay for another two hours. What had been Hoski's timing? He had called the helicopter to deliver the ransom at 4 A.M. Probably he would have picked up the money about two-thirty. When was the Hallicrafters set timed to broadcast its tape, and to detonate its bomb? Since Hoski would want to make sure that broadcast was recorded, he'd probably time it at one of the regular two-hour broadcasts. But how soon? Leaphorn tried to concentrate, to shut out the throbbing of his hip, the aching fatigue, the damp, mushroom smell of this watery part of the cave. It would be soon. Hoski would need very little running time. An hour or two of darkness would be enough to get well clear of the cave and its neighborhood. Because there'd be no search once that tape was aired. There would only be a great flocking of everybody to find this point on the map—the smoking mouth of a cave. There would be chaos. The hunted would have been found. Hoski/Goldrims, safely outside the circle of confusion, would simply walk away. Leaphorn was suddenly confident he understood the timing of Hoski's plan.

"Tull," Leaphorn shouted. "Can't you see the son-of-a-bitch set you up? Use your head."

"No," Tull said. "Not him. You made that tape up."

"It's his voice," Leaphorn shouted. "Can't you recognize his voice?"

Silence.

"He didn't tell you why he moved his brother away from the Boy Scouts, did he?" Leaphorn shouted. "He didn't tell you about this tape. He didn't tell you about the bomb."

"Hell, man," Tull said. "I helped him put them together. I've got one right here with me, by this radio set here. And when the time comes, it's going to blow you to hell."

"You and me together, Tull," Leaphorn said. And as he said it, he heard the muffled purring of an outboard motor.

"You weren't here when he made one of those bombs," Leaphorn said. "And he didn't tell you about it. Or about that tape. Or about broadcasting it over that spare radio. Come on, Tull. You were the sucker in Santa Fe. You think you're immortal, but don't you get tired of being the one who gets screwed?"

Tull said nothing. Over the echoes of his own words, Leaphorn could hear the purring motor.

"Think," he shouted. "Count the dynamite sticks. There were twenty-four in the box. He used some to seal the other end of the cave. And some in a bomb to wipe out the Scouts, and you probably have a couple there. So does it all add up to twenty-four?"

Silence. It wasn't going to work. The tone of the outboard motor had changed now. It was inside the cave.

"You said there was dynamite in a sack by that Hallicrafters," Tull said. "Is that what you said?" His voice sounded weak now, pained. "How many sticks did you say?"

"Two sticks," Leaphorn said.

"How many dynamite caps?"

"Just one," Leaphorn said. "I think just one. With a wire connected." The purring of the outboard stopped.

"I'll bet Hoski set the timers himself," Leaphorn said. "I'll bet he told you that bomb with you there will go off about six o'clock. You're going to make the four o'clock broadcast and then cut out and run for it. But he set the timer a couple of hours early."

"Hey, Jimmy," Tull yelled. "He's over here."

"What's he have?" Hoski yelled. "Just Jackie's shotgun? Is that all?" Hoski's voice came from the water's edge, still a long way off.

"God damn it, Tull," Leaphorn shouted. "Don't be stupid. He's screwing you again, I tell you. He's got you listed among the dead on that tape, so you gotta be dead when they get here."

"He just has the shotgun," Tull shouted. "Move around behind him."

"He set the timer up on that bomb you have," Leaphorn shouted. "Can't you understand he has to kill you too?"

"No," Tull said. "Jimmy's my friend." It was almost a scream.

"He left you at Santa Fe. He didn't tell you about that tape. He's got you listed with the dead. He set the timer . . ."

"Shut up," Tull said. "Shut up. You're wrong, damn you, and I can prove it." Tull's voice rose to a scream. "God damn you, I can prove you're wrong."

The tone, the hysteria, told Leaphorn more than the words. He knew, with a sick horror, exactly what Tull meant when he said he could prove it.

"He's talking crap," Goldrims was shouting, his voice much closer now. "He's lying to you, Tull. What the hell are you doing?"

Leaphorn was scrambling to his feet.

Tull's voice was saying: "I can just move this little hour hand up to . . ."

"Don't," Goldrims screamed, and Tull's voice was cut off by the sound of a pistol shot.

Leaphorn was running as fast as heart and legs and lungs would let him run, thinking that each yard of distance from the center of the blast increased his chances for survival. From behind him came the sound of Goldrims screaming Tull's name, and another shot.

And then the blast. It was bright, as if a thousand flash-bulbs lit the gray-white interior of the cavern. Then the shock wave hit Leaphorn and sent him tumbling and sliding over the calcite floor, slamming finally into something.

Leaphorn became aware that he could hear nothing and see nothing. Perhaps he had lost consciousness long enough for the echoes to die away. He noticed his nose was bleeding and felt below his face. There were only a few drops of wetness on the stony floor. Little time had passed.

He sat up gingerly. When the flash blindness subsided enough so that he could read his watch, it was 2:57. Leaphorn hurried. First he found his flashlight behind the rocks where he had left it, with the shotgun nearby. Next he found two boats—a small three-man affair with an outboard engine, and a flat-bottomed fiberglass model with a muffled inboard. In its bottom was a green nylon backpack and a heavy canvas bag. Leaphorn zipped the bag open. Inside were dozens of small plastic packages. Leaphorn fished one out, opened it and shone his flashlight onto tight bundles of twenty-dollar bills. He returned the pouch and carried the backpack and bag into the cave. Near the blackened area where James Tso and John Tull had died, he stopped, swung the heavy bag, and sent the ransom money sliding down the cave floor into the darkness.

By the time he had everyone in the boats it was after 3 A.M.

At ten minutes after three, both boats purred out of the cave mouth and into open water. The night seemed incredibly bright. It was windless. A half moon hung halfway down the western sky. Leaphorn quickly got his directions. It was probably eighty miles down the lake to the dam and the nearest telephone—at least four or five hours. Leaphorn's hip throbbed. To hell with that, he thought. There would surely be aerial surveillance. Let someone else do some work. He picked up the spare gasoline can, screwed off the cap, floated it on the lake surface, and—as it drifted away—blasted it with his shotgun. It erupted into flame and burned, a bright blue-white beacon reflecting from the water, lighting the cliff walls around them, lighting the dirty, exhausted faces of eleven Boy Scouts. Normally it wouldn't be noticed in this lonely country. But tonight it would be. Tonight anything would be noticed.

At three-forty-two he heard the plane. High at first, but circling. Leaphorn pointed his flashlight up. Blinked it off and on. The plane came low, buzzed the boat with landing lights on. It looked like an army reconnaissance craft.

Now Leaphorn was keeping his eye on the dark shape where cliff and water met—and the darkness that hid the cave mouth. The second hand of his watch swept past 4 A.M. Nothing happened. The hand swept down, and up, and down again. At 4:02 the blackness at the cliff base became a blinding flash of white light. Seconds passed. A tremendous muffled thump echoed across the water, followed by a rumbling. Slabs of rocks falling inside the cave. Too many rocks for the white men to remove to clear the path to Standing Medicine's sand paintings, Leaphorn thought. But not too many rocks to remove to salvage a canvas bag heavy with cash. A foot-high shock wave from the blast spread rapidly toward them across the mirrorlike surface of the lake. The reflected stars rippled. It reached the boat, rocked it abruptly, and moved down the lake.

They sat, waiting.

Leaphorn stared over the side, into the clear, dark water.

Somewhere down below would be the hiding place of the helicopter, and the grave of Haas. He imagined how it happened. Haas with a gun in his ribs hovering the craft over this same boat, the bank loot being lowered into it, the passengers climbing down. Had they shot him then, or left a bomb aboard to be triggered when the copter was a safer fifty yards away? Whatever method, it left a trail impossible to follow.

From down the lake came the sound of another helicopter, traveling low and fast toward them.

How many, like Haas, had died to make Goldrims's trail impossible to follow? Hosteen Tso and Anna Atcitty, certainly, and almost certainly Frederick Lynch. Leaphorn considered how it must have happened. Goldrims had been told of the secret cavern as the oldest son. He had stocked it as the base for this operation, and killed his grandfather to keep the secret safe. Then he must have returned to Washington. Why Washington? Kelongy must be there with the Buffalo Society's funds from the Santa Fe robbery. And when the time came for the kidnapping, Goldrims had returned to Safety System, Inc., and taken the dog he had coveted and corrupted and his ex-employer's car, and left Frederick Lynch in no condition to report the theft and in no place where he would ever be found again. That crime, Leaphorn guessed, would have been as much personal vendetta as motivated by actual need. As for Tull, he was simply something useful. And as for Benjamin Tso . . .

Theodora Adams interrupted his thoughts. "Why did Ben do that?" she asked, in a choked voice. "It was like he knew he would be killed. Did he do it to save me?"

Leaphorn opened his mouth and closed it. Ben did it to save himself, he thought. But he didn't say it. It wasn't something he could explain to her if she didn't already understand it.